Marriage Mayhem

A *novel by*

SAMUEL L. HAIR

Q-Boro Books
WWW.QBOROBOOKS.COM

An Urban Entertainment Company

Published by Q-Boro Books
Copyright © 2007 by Samuel L. Hair

ISBN-13: 978-1-933967-25-7
ISBN-10: 1-933967-25-0
LCCN: 2006937067

First Printing December 2007
Printed in the United States of America

10 9 8 7 6 5 4 3 2

*This is a work of fiction. It is not meant to depict, portray or represent any par-
ticular real persons. All the characters, incidents and dialogues are the products
of the author's imagination and are not to be construed as real. Any references or
similarities to actual events, entities, real people, living or dead, or to real locales
are intended to give the novel a sense of reality. Any similarity in other names,
characters, entities, places and incidents is entirely coincidental.*

Cover Copyright © 2006 by Q-BORO BOOKS, all rights reserved.
Cover layout/design by Candace K. Cottrell
Cover photo by JLove Images; models Jeniffer Morillo and Donald
Carmichael
Editors: Andrea Blackstone, Richard Klin, Candace K. Cottrell

Q-BORO BOOKS
Jamaica, Queens NY 11434
WWW.QBOROBOOKS.COM

Author's Note

Words can make life brighter or darker. Words can generate love, words can create peace, and words can also initiate a war. They can build people up or break them down. Words can spread a cloud of misery or forge a chain of unhappiness. Words can create an environment of good or evil. Love is a language that is unfailing in all ways. "Love never faileth." (1 Corinthians 13:8)

Language can build or destroy relationships, and love is a language everybody understands.

If you or your spouse is physically or emotionally abusive, mentally ill, sexually deviant, or addicted to any self-destructive substance or behavior, consult with a therapist before situations escalate.

This book demonstrates the *marriage mayhem* that ignited many incidents of verbal, physical, and emotional abuse.

Prologue

"**Y**ou mean to tell me that before I married you, you sold pussy up and down the streets of the same fuckin' city that we live in?"

"Yes, I did, Jermaine, and I'm not ashamed to admit it. I was addicted then, and all that is a part of my past."

"Damn!" Jermaine yelled, nodding in disgust. "That means I married a goddamn ho! Ain't no way on God's earth that I can convert a ho into a housewife. No way in hell."

"I was housewife before I was a ho, Jermaine, so it's not like I'm not capable of being a good mother and wife. I did what I had to do to support my habit; I fucked both men and women, I sucked a countless amount of dicks of all races, but the good thing about it was that I wasn't giving up much pussy. I've lost my kids on a couple occasions due to drugs and the life I was living, and I have been known to set muthafuckas up, so watch what you say and do to me. I do know a whole lot of gangbangers out here and they won't hesitate to kick your ass or take you out if I tell them to. Like I said, Jermaine, that was my past and if you can't accept the way I am today as opposed to the way I used to be, then fuck you and move on! Men come a dime a dozen, you know what I'm sayin'. Just like you picked me up the first time you saw me, other muthafuckas will too. I look good for my age, and I damn sure know how to please a man, so do what you wanna do if you can't accept my past, nigga!"

They had been married a little less than three months. Jermaine had introduced her to a middle-class lifestyle opposite to the street life that she was accustomed to.

Prior to meeting Jermaine, Karen's life consisted of continual failure, long streaks of bad luck, and being a reputed drug addict and prostitute. All of this took place due to the way she chose to live. Now, because she was Mrs. Jermaine Hopkins she thought her shit didn't stink and that because she had exceptional sex to offer that she could get away with doing or saying anything to anybody.

The fact that Jermaine was an outstanding husband and father to each of her kids did not prevent her daily bitching or disrespectful, foul mouth. She had crossed the line a week after they were married by pulling a knife on him, and had gone even further by calling his mother and daughter bitches and whores. What really pissed him off was when she refused him sex out of spite simply because she knew he craved it.

Arguing was right down Karen's alley. She debated all of his decisions, opinions, plans, and advice regardless of how sensible they were. When they'd first met, Karen didn't have a pot to piss in or a hole to throw it in, but now, as if she'd recently switched brains with Albert Einstein, there was not a thing in the world that she didn't know. Jermaine couldn't teach or coach her on anything.

"When I first met your sorry ass, you didn't own a car, didn't have a place of your own to live, and you didn't even have a goddamn plan! Now all of a sudden you know every damn thing!"

"Fuck you, Jermaine! You think you're big shit because you drive a BMW, wrote a book, own a few houses, and make lots of money driving trucks, but you ain't nothing but a piece of dog shit! All you do is floss around town in your fancy cars and talk about people who are less fortunate than you! What really pisses me off is that you're always trying to belittle me one way or another. If you knew how to talk to me maybe you could get anything you wanted out of me whenever you wanted it. I had tricks that treated me better than you. At least they talked to me nice and treated me special. There were times that I drove over a hundred miles just to give a man some head who had talked to me nice over the phone."

"The only reason they talked to you so nice is because they wanted a good, satisfying head job, but you were too stupid to recognize it. Hell, don't hate me for my accomplishments, Karen. If your thinking was right, you could accomplish whatever you set forth to do, and have nice things, but that's your problem, Karen. Your thinking pattern is all fucked up. All you want out of life is a goddamn welfare check and a place for you and your kids to sleep. Your own sister told me that you've been on crack, and a ho for as long as she can remember."

She struggled to maintain composure, but his words were about to set her off at any given moment.

"Jewell told me the reason you're always saying or thinking unusual things and carry on like an uncivilized nut is just because you're on some kind of psych meds." He paused to smirk. "She also told me that you have never, out of all the worthless men you've been with, had a good, responsible, successful man. She said that's the reason you don't know how to treat me. She told me that all the men of your past were either one of your tricks, a crackhead who called himself trying to make money, but y'all were too busy smoking up the product, or a wannabe thug!" He nodded in disgust.

"That a goddamn shame, Karen. It's unbelievable, but of course drugs cause people to do disgusting things. It's a shame that a woman would have losers in the presence of her children. What that really tells me, though, is that you have no self-respect, no respect for you kids, and your self-esteem is gutter level." He had wanted to say those things to her a long time ago.

Karen stared at him angrily but silently for a few moments, but then approached him, smiling.

"The bed that you bought and sleep in when you're home, I just want you to know that I've been fucking Tyrone, Lester, and big dick Danny in it while you're so goddamn busy making money driving trucks cross-country. At least I'm being honest about it." Then she smiled and added. "Ump, as big as their dicks are I'm surprised you couldn't tell when you called yourself fucking me last night." Then she walked away feeling somewhat compensated for the verbal beating he had given her.

"What! I'll kill you, bitch! You had another muthafucka in my house and in my bed while I was working! I'll kill you, Karen!" he yelled, and then stormed toward her.

The kids witnessed the entire incident, which unfortunately they had seen take place between their mother and a number of men.

Chapter 1

Jermaine cruised in a black Explorer en route to pick up his paycheck but was distracted by a short, light-complexioned woman pushing a baby stroller. Trailing behind her a few feet away was a little boy. Jermaine did a double take, then quickly made an illegal U-turn and pulled over to cheerfully approach her. It had been years since he had used his so-called rap on a woman, but out of loneliness and the desperate need of a mate he decided to go for what he knew. Being a cross-country truck driver did not actually provide him the time to be involved in a serious relationship, but he was anxious to change that.

"Hey, sweetheart. How are you today?" he asked, smiling, revealing his even pearly whites.

The little boy gave him an angry "leave my mama alone" look, but Jermaine ignored it and pressed forward.

"Fine, and you?" replied the woman. She had observed the look her five-year-old son had given Jermaine, but during that time in her life she was desperately in need of a man. A real man.

Her living arrangements and self-esteem were at their lowest peaks. *Maybe he can help me out of my situation. I'll bet he has a good job, his own place to live, and probably has money in the bank. Hell, some other woman has probably already got him sewed up. If it came down to it, shit, I would have no problem being the other woman. Let me see what he's about. I have nothing to lose and everything to gain,* she thought.

"I'm Karen, and you are?" she said, smiling. It wasn't often that she ran across decent men. *He just might be the ticket to me and the kids having a good life.*

"I'm Jermaine," Jermaine responded. Glancing at the little boy, seeing that he was getting angrier, Jermaine quickly diverted his attention to him.

"What's up, little man?" The kid frowned, then turned his head. "What do you want for Christmas, little man? How about I buy it for you?" Jermaine asked.

Instantly, Karen's eyes lit up, as well as the child's .

"His name is Stevie," said Karen, grabbing the boy by the arm. She could not afford to let her son mess up this possible winning ticket. "Stevie, say hi to Jermaine and tell him what you told me that you want for Christmas." She gave an embarrassing laugh. "I'm a single parent, and Christmas is probably going to be scarce this year," she tested.

A few days prior Karen had a long, serious talk with Stevie regarding her financial situation. She told him that she could not afford to buy him anything before Christmas, but when her welfare check came on the first she would pay Mr. Pete the rent money then she would spend what was left on him and his sister.

"I can only afford to buy you a scooter and a couple pair of pants for Christmas, Stevie. They cut my welfare check again, and I just can't afford to give y'all the Christmas I want to, but I promise you that if I have to work three jobs and hustle on the side, next year Christmas will be a real

Christmas for both of you. Hell, or maybe I'll get lucky and find y'all a daddy by then," Karen had told him.

"I want a dirt bike, a PlayStation, a whole bunch of games, some new clothes that's not from a thrift store, a basketball court, and a—"

"Is that right," Jermaine asked, pleased about suddenly having Stevie's approval. "Why don't we head to the toy store then?" he asked with a smile. Minutes later Karen and her two kids were inside the Explorer with him.

Wanting to further impress her, Jermaine made sure to show Karen the new big rig that he drove across country as a long-distance truck driver. She nodded in admiration. He then stopped at Bank of America to withdraw a few hundred dollars to shop with. Now he was set.

While driving they began discussing past relationships, plans, and present situations and issues. Jermaine discovered that Karen actually had four children, and each of their fathers were crackheads, alcoholics, drug addicts, and womanizers. Jasmine, Karen's oldest daughter, was doing very well for herself despite the negative upbringing she was exposed to. She managed a McDonald's, and also attended college, determined to obtain a degree in nursing, while her teenaged son Marvin lived with her sister Jewell.

Feeling at ease conversing with Jermaine, Karen revealed the fact of her being a cocaine addict, but she had made it clear that she had been clean and sober for twelve months straight. She also told Jermaine that she'd been to jail on a few occasions but for nothing serious.

Before Karen was sentenced to a live-in drug program, she was living with her twenty-one-year-old lover, Tyrone, inside his mother's house. Due to Tyrone having a humongous dick and being able to fuck all night long, his age hadn't been a factor to her at all.

"That was your past, sweetheart," Jermaine had said. "I'm

not concerned with what you've done in the past, to me it's about how you think and conduct yourself today. Most importantly, hopefully you've learned from your mistakes and realize that there's only one way through life and that's the straight way. Think about all the celebrities who were addicted to drugs: Mary J. Blige, James Brown, Bobby Brown, Robert Downey Jr., Natalie Cole, Smokey Robinson, Samuel L. Jackson, and the list goes on, you know. Hell, I even heard that ol' Bill Clinton was getting high in the White House and getting blow jobs. People that are followers, people that are easily influenced, people who do wrong things just to fit in, those people are weak and can lose focus just like that. Sometimes they'll even hit rock bottom before facing reality."

Because of her beauty, Jermaine found it very hard to believe the things she had revealed to him. He simply overlooked her forty years of stressful living and negative associations and involvements and made her feel at ease. After all, this could possibly be the beginning of something meaningful and he felt that he was off to a good start.

"Personally, I admire people that pull themselves out of negative situations and position themselves in positive, rewarding situations." Jermaine's words were like sweet melody to Karen's ears. He had said all the right things.

Jermaine had been a happy-go-lucky long-distance truck driver earning close to five thousand dollars a month. He was used to having control over his life, which allowed him to have the finer things in life, all but with women. The fact of him making good money, owning real estate, and driving fancy cars had never seemed to promote him in connecting with a decent, sensible woman. Both of his sisters constantly stayed on him about the type of women that he was always attracted to.

"A man with your intelligence, ambition, determination, and brains deserves to have the cream of the crop when it comes to women, but for some reason, Jermaine, you always end up with the bottom-of-the-barrel type; the ones that are on welfare who don't want a damn thing out of life but a county check, some dick, and a man to play daddy for all their kids."

Jermaine owned four vehicles: a new BMW, an Eddie Bauer version of an Explorer, a new convertible Mustang, and his pride and joy weekend cruiser was his 1937 Fleetline Chevrolet.

He was decently handsome and extremely intelligent, standing five foot nine, with smooth chocolate skin. He wore his hair in short, neat waves and a mostly kept a smile that reflected his happiness and good living.

As Jermaine pulled into the Toys "R" Us parking lot, Stevie was filled with excitement. Entering the store, Stevie glanced around, wishing that he could have everything that his mother was not able to afford.

"Mama, look, Mama!" Stevie said excitedly.

Noticing his exhilaration, Karen handed him his asthma inhaler. "Calm down, Stevie, before you have another asthma attack, boy." A couple pumps of the inhaler had calmed him a little, but not completely.

"Mama, Jermaine, look at those bikes and scooters over there!"

"Would you like a bike and scooter, Stevie?" Jermaine asked, moving to hold Karen's hand, trying to score some extra points.

"Yeah, that would be cool, but I want that and that and that too," replied Stevie, pointing his fingers to various toys.

"While you two look I'm going to the restroom," Jermaine said, then headed down the aisle alone.

Once Jermaine was out of sight, Karen anxiously approached Stevie.

"Call him 'Daddy,' boy! He wants you to call him 'Daddy,' I can feel it."

"But Mama, he's not my—"

"I said call him 'Daddy,' Stevie. Do you hear me? We both got the opportunity to have a good man in our life and I ain't about to let you blow it. Now you heard what I said, Stevie."

"Okay, Mama."

When Jermaine returned, Stevie was joyfully sitting on a bike, smiling.

"Daddy, can I have this one?" Karen played it off and looked at Stevie like she was actually surprised at him calling Jermaine "Daddy."

Jermaine was taken aback, but didn't want to risk losing Karen's interest. "Are you sure this is the one you want?" Jermaine was now completely confident that he'd won Stevie over.

"Yep, I'm sure."

"Then so be it, Stevie; it's yours." Seeing the smile on Stevie's face had actually made Jermaine feel good whether or not he scored any points with Karen. Just to know that he was providing presents for kids whose mother probably wasn't able to afford and their father wasn't supplying gave Jermaine a feeling of gratification. Besides, he had already begun fantasizing about himself, Karen, and the kids all in the same household. If spending a couple hundred dollars was going to fulfill his fantasy, then money wasn't a thing at all.

After gathering a few dolls and toys for Alexus, a bike, scooter, and a few other toys for Stevie, Jermaine—accompanied by his possible ready-made family—paid the cashier, and then happily exited the store. The purchases totaled a little over three hundred dollars. To Jermaine that was a small price for what he was hopefully about to receive.

Jermaine then reached into his wallet and handed Karen five hundred dollars. "Merry Christmas, baby. This isn't much for now, sweetheart, but I can assure you that the best is yet to come."

Greedily, Karen snatched the money from his hand. "Thank you, Jermaine," she said, smiling, as she leaned forward to kiss him on the cheek. Jermaine now felt like he'd made a major accomplishment. Karen continued. "I feel that our acquaintance is definitely a part of God's plan. I mean, it's like we're connecting on everything; neither of us drink alcohol or use drugs, we're both single and looking for a meaningful, peaceful relationship, we both enjoy reading and writing, and I really find it amazing that our favorite color is the same color. I mean, it's like the perfect connection. Thank God you made that U-turn, Jermaine. Thank God." She looked deep into his eyes then slid her hand into his as they strolled back to his truck.

"Yes, we absolutely need to thank God for connecting us, sweetheart. I actually feel that he has much more in store for us, but let's let time and our patience mold this and hopefully all will be good," said Jermaine, caressing her fingers. He desperately wanted another kiss, but didn't want her to think that he was being too pushy or aggressive. As if she was reading his mind, she put her arms around him and gave him a long, wet, kiss. Stevie had no objections now to Jermaine being intimate with his mother. Observing them kissing, he had simply covered his eyes and remained silent.

It was 9:30PM when Jermaine dropped Karen and the kids off at the one-room shack she was renting from a man she'd met at a cocaine anonymous meeting. Their night ended with a long, wet, kiss and a grind so fierce that it had set the both of them on fire.

Once inside Karen had excitedly told her landlord, Mr. Pete, about her day with Jermaine.

"I didn't know there were still men like him in this world, Mr. Pete," Karen said. "I mean, damn, he's an ultimate complete package. He drives one of those big rigs for a living, he's handsome, intelligent, ambitious, Stevie loves him, he's never been into gangs or drugs. I mean, what more can a woman ask for? He's a one-of-a-kind man, that's all I know. And would you believe that Stevie already calls him Daddy?"

"That doesn't surprise me at all, Karen. Hell, that boy will call any man Daddy about right now," replied Mr. Pete, sarcastically.

On a few occasions, after Karen's kids were asleep, Mr. Pete had quietly opened the door to Karen's bedroom and stood naked, massaging his penis in hopes to get an erection, but unfortunately he couldn't get it up.

"Karen, wake up," he would whisper. "I need some pussy and I'll bet you've got some good stuff between your legs. I can tell by the way you walk, girl." Being seventy-eight years old didn't decrease his sex drive. The only thing was that mentally he wanted it, but physically he couldn't get a hard-on. He had once been told that smoking so much crack in the past caused his penis to be a dead soldier.

"No, Mr. Pete, no. I told you when I moved in that this will be strictly business and no sex, so get that out of your mind." Glancing at his penis, she observed that it was short, wrinkled, and limp.

"Well, come play with it a little bit. Please? I'll deduct a hundred off next months rent, and if you give me a little head, I might even forget about the rent," he said, still massaging his penis.

"Get outta here, Mr. Pete! Now!" yelled Karen.

"Come on, Karen. I need some lovin'. Please, just give me a little bit and I'll be all right."

"I told you, no."

"Then fuck you, bitch! I don't want you using my goddamn telephone anymore, and don't use my fuckin' dishes to cook for you and your fatherless kids, either! Hell, all I wanted was a quick piece of pussy and everything would have been all right, but no, you've gotta cherish that pussy of yours like you're a fuckin' nun or somethin'! You wasn't cherishing it when you were giving it away to those no-good, dope-smoking, gangbangers! But now you wanna put a lock on the muthafucka! Bitch!" Then he would slam the door and go back to sleep.

"Fuck you, Mr. Pete!" Karen would yell. *I gotta move outta here before I stab this muthafucka.*

The night Jermaine had dropped Karen and the kids off at Mr. Pete's, unfortunately Mr. Pete was in the mood once again for sex and stood naked at Karen's bedroom door.

"I'm sick and tired of you hounding me for sex in the presence of my kids! Fuck you, Mr. Pete. You aren't nothing but a dirty old, horny dog that thinks somebody owe you some pussy because they live in your shabby, run-down apartment! Me and my kids are leaving here, fuck you!" she had screamed, then immediately called Jermaine.

At the time, Jermaine was bragging to his twenty-five-year-old daughter, Denise, and his son-in-law, Maurice, about Karen. Jermaine was temporally living with them due to major construction being done on his home.

"I finally found her," explained Jermaine, optimistically. "She's pretty, she's intelligent, she's computer literate, and the best thing about it is that she's available. Her son already calls me Daddy, can you believe that?"

"I'm happy for you, Daddy," Denise replied, pleased to see her father happy.

"When can we meet her?" Maurice asked.

At that moment the phone rang. It was Karen. As soon as she began explaining to Jermaine about what happened, Mr. Pete grabbed the other telephone and began yelling into the receiver. "Get off my fuckin' phone, bitch!"

Hearing Mr. Pete's yells, Jermaine promised to come to her and the kids' rescue.

"I'll be right there, baby," replied Jermaine, realizing this was another golden opportunity to chalk up more points.

"Thank you, Jermaine, I appreciate it. Me and the kids will be standing in the front yard."

Before rushing out the door, Jermaine quickly answered Maurice's question.

"Well, it looks like you guys are going to get the opportunity to meet her more sooner than later. Apparently, there's a problem going on with her and her landlord and she wants me to come get her. I'll be right back." Jermaine hurried out the door.

Once Jermaine had returned with Karen and her kids and introduced them to Denise and Maurice, Denise coincidentally remembered her from being a passenger on her bus. The last time Karen and the kids had rode on Denise's bus, Denise had given Alexus a piece of her doughnut to prevent her from crying.

"This is a small world, isn't it?" Denise said, smiling.

They had talked briefly on a few occasions during times Karen was a passenger on her bus. Knowing how lonely her father had been for female companionship, and not wanting him to be taken advantage of by any gold diggers, she said, "You've gotta watch some women, Daddy. Not all of them, but a whole lot of them are only out to take advantage of a good, working man. Sex is a small price for them to pay when they're getting what they want out of the deal. Believe me, Daddy, once they find out you own a home, got a few nice cars, and have lots of money in the bank, they'll be throwing sex at you like hard raindrops falling from the sky. They'll try to put babies on you that they know aren't yours. They'll lie and tell you they're pregnant just to get money out of you. They'll try to get you to take care of their kids, and some of them will even try to turn you against me. But you just always keep in mind that I'm your only biological child, Daddy."

Denise made it her business to screen any woman that he associated himself with or tried to be a part of his life. They shared a very open father-and-daughter relationship. Even though she was his daughter he would still sometimes ask her opinions on certain situations or issues pertaining to his life. Denise had no problem expressing her opinions to her father about things she felt were not right, and Jermaine confided in her and respectfully trusted her judgment.

Jermaine turned Nickelodeon on for the children to watch, including his grandson, Cordell, who was awake and happy to have company his age to play with, while the grown-ups sat talking at the dining room table. Karen had begun openly speaking about Mr. Pete's behavior and also about her unfortunate present living situation.

"Why didn't you call the police on him?" Denise asked, getting emotionally involved.

"Then where would me and my kids live?" Karen replied. Being jobless and receiving welfare check of $387 a month meant she did not have too many options. She definitely needed a miracle in her life and she strongly hoped that Jermaine was the miracle she'd been praying for.

"That pervert needs his ass beat," Maurice uttered in his Jamaican accent. Then he mumbled a few other words, which only he and Denise understood and then he stood and began pacing.

"Is it okay with you guys if Karen and the kids stay here for a night or so until I can figure out something?" asked Jermaine, hoping to maybe get a few more kisses or possibly even some sex.

"Sure, it's okay," said Denise. "Now you and those kids make yourself at home. My apartment may not be big or luxurious, but you're more than welcome to stay here."

"Are you sure that won't be a problem? Because I kind of planned to get a motel room for a few days until I figure out what I'm going to do. I hate to be a burden on someone, and—"

"Say no more, Karen. My house is your house for as long as you need it," said Denise, thinking that things would be fine with Jermaine around.

"Thank you, baby, and thank you too, Maurice. We really appreciate it," said Jermaine, trying hard to conceal his excitement.

During their discussion, which lasted another thirty minutes or so, Jermaine had briefly excused himself to go lay the kids in his grandson's spare bed. When he rejoined the other adults, Denise and Maurice gave Jermaine and Karen a hug and said good night.

It had been a long, tiresome day for both Jermaine and Karen. They talked for another hour or so, then they decided to try and get some sleep. Once in his bedroom, behind closed doors, Jermaine stripped to his boxers and then lay next to Karen. She had already taken off her pants and blouse. The fact that her breasts were extremely small did not prevent Jermaine from getting aroused. Her petite frame, her long brown hair, her smile, and her smooth yellow skin were enough for him.

In a matter of seconds, their tongues and lips fell in rhythm simultaneously, quickly heating the both of them, and then suddenly without warning Denise opened the door.

"Oops," she giggled, covering her eyes. "Sorry to intrude, Daddy and Karen, but I only wanted to welcome you and your kids into my home for as long as you need to stay."

"Thank you, Denise," Karen said, shamelessly. "I really appreciate that."

"Why don't you try knocking next time, Denise? After all, I am paying rent and this is my room," said Jermaine, in a joking manner.

"Why don't you try locking the door, Daddy?" replied Denise, smiling. She then locked and closed the door and then disappeared.

Immediately, Jermaine and Karen picked up where they had left off before the intrusion. While kissing wildly, Karen began stroking Jermaine's hardness and massaging his balls. She was actually used to bigger and better things, but she had no problem dealing with his medium size, considering the needed rewards that should come out of it.

Jermaine responded by playing with her clit and fingering her wet, hot pussy. Seconds later they were both naked, still kissing and rubbing each other in all the right places. Karen began licking and sucking Jermaine's penis. Her mouth was hot and experienced, producing so much pleasure that Jermaine's toes began to curl. She skillfully licked up and down, then slowly sucked the head while caressing his balls. Then suddenly she sped up her rhythm, sucking faster, then slowed it down a notch and concentrated on licking.

She gave him head for close to fifteen minutes before he came. Like a pro, she sucked him dry, causing him to go a little limp, but then she began licking again until he was fully erect again.

"I want it ride it now," said Karen, smiling.

She then climbed on top and straddled it and then gave him the ride of his life. Regardless of his penis not fitting hand in glove inside her slippery, wet pussy, it still felt good to him.

She rode it like a jockey about to cross the finishing line at the Kentucky Derby until she came once, then twice, and then a third time. They kissed again, and then the both of them fell asleep. From that night he was hooked like a fish.

During the course of the next three weeks Jermaine spent each day with Karen and her kids. He had requested local runs other than runs that would keep him gone anywhere from a week to three weeks for the sake of building a relationship with Karen. He rented a room for them at Motel 6, but on a couple of occasions they had spent the night at his daughter's.

Twice a week they took the kids to the movies, on weekends they picnicked in parks. Some days after work they shopped at the local mall, and they even went to Knott's Berry Farm and Six Flags Magic Mountain. Also, they had taken a day to meet one another's relatives. Karen was milking her cash cow for every drop it had to offer.

Life was going quite well for Jermaine. He strongly felt that he had finally found the right woman.

Karen definitely felt that Jermaine was Mr. Right as far as being a husband, a good father figure, and an excellent provider, but the one thing he lacked, which was what she simply couldn't overlook, was a big dick.

Karen had promised herself years earlier that when she did find Mr. Right he would have to possess the following things: a good-paying job, his own home, a couple nice cars, and he would absolutely have to be a positive father figure. *Damn. He's everything I ever desired in a man, but why couldn't his dick be about four inches longer and two inches thicker?* Karen thought.

One day after having sex they began making small talk. "Damn, baby, you sure know how to whip that pussy on a brotha. You've got your own unique way of riding a dick and giving head. I could swear you've got a degree in sex or something," emphasized Jermaine. "Actually, sweetheart, I have never had a woman who could come anywhere close to competing with you in the sex department."

"I'll take that as a compliment," replied Karen, smiling, but her thoughts were, *I've heard this shit umpteen million times. Hell, I used to fuck and suck for a living, so what do you expect?*

Jermaine and Karen had been together for almost two months the day Denise had entered their bedroom smiling. Seeing her father happy and content made her happy and very well pleased. Now she felt it was time to put a little icing on the cake.

"I've been doing some serious thinking lately about you two. I mean, you guys must be paying an arm and a leg weekly at Motel 6, right?" Jermaine started to reply, but Denise had already continued.

"Anyway, Maurice and I agreed to let you and your kids move in—that is, if you want to—for two-hundred and seventy-five dollars a month in addition to what my daddy is paying me now. That way you guys will have the opportunity to enhance and elevate your relationship being free of any financial stress and not have to expose the kids to crackheads and whores running in and out of the motel rooms," Denise said thoughtfully. She was not only a bus driver but a businesswoman as well. Actually, her aim was to try to make things decent for her father. She was the actual one who made lots of the final decisions and had the ultimate say-so about things around the house or certain situations. Maurice never had too much to say and would always respect her decisions.

"Thank you, Denise, thank you very much. I appreciate your offer, that is, if Jermaine doesn't mind," replied Karen in good spirits.

"That sounds fine and dandy, Denise, but I spoke with the contractor in charge of the construction on my house, and he said that it will be ready in a few more weeks. But what I will do is pay you a month's rent right now and hopefully by then we'll be gone," said Jermaine.

"Man, Daddy, you've been here for so long that I almost forgot you even have a home of your own," Denise replied sarcastically, and then added, "I was just trying to be helpful."

"That's my baby," Jermaine said, smiling.

Once Denise disappeared, Karen unzipped Jermaine's pants and began giving him some enthusiastic head. Minutes later she wanted it inside her.

"How do you want it, baby?" asked Jermaine, standing erect, as if he had what Karen really wanted.

"Deep and slow, baby. That's how I like it, deep and slow," Karen replied, fantasizing about Tyrone's huge penis.

Jermaine inserted himself and began penetrating as slow and as deep as he possibly could. The fact of the matter was that he simply did not have the right tool to satisfy her.

The entire time that Jermaine was penetrating her and giving her all that he had to give, she was fantasizing about

Tyrone's big, long, dick inside her. *Damn, I wish he had a dick like Tyrone's. I need a big dick deep in me, not a medium-sized one, and damn sure not a Vienna sausage. I need my pussy filled up with a big, long, fat dick, but fuck it, I guess I gotta deal with this. After all, he's capable of providing a decent, secure life for me and my kids, so if I have to fake it, then that's what's I gotta do. I'm gonna make him think he's killing the pussy.* Then she began moaning and almost crying like he was hurting her. Hearing those sounds made him feel like he was putting in work.

"Damn, Jermaine, you sure know how to fuck good. Ain't no way in hell I'm gonna let you get away from me, not after you just did what you did, so don't even think about it." She had to make him feel good by saying all the right things. Her words were strictly based on the security he could provide for her and her kids.

"Don't worry, sweetheart. I'll belong to you for a long, long, time. I've finally found what I been searching for in a woman." His words were sincere and humble.

Karen had been a nympho since the age of twelve. She fantasized often about big dicks whether she was inside a bathtub, lying in bed alone, driving, and she even went to the extent, when inside a supermarket, of going to the produce section just to hold a large cucumber. On a couple occasions she had picked up the largest cucumber she could find and took it to the restroom where she sat on it and rode it until she climaxed.

The following day, after Jermaine was done moving Karen and her kids' belongings into Denise's apartment, he headed for the East Coast on his big rig. He simply was not making the kind of money driving local that he was accustomed to from driving cross-country. Before leaving, he handed her keys to his Mustang and five hundred dollars. Of course, she gave him something to remember her by.

Chapter 2

Because Denise and Maurice worked nine-to-fives, Karen and her kids were home alone from 7AM to 3PM every day. Even though Jermaine called her umpteen million times a day on his cell phone, Karen still found time to talk to Tyrone.

Karen had lately fantasized about Tyrone's penis so much that she desperately needed a piece of him right away. She could not fight the feeling any longer. She picked up the telephone and dialed his mother's number, hoping that he answered instead of his mother, Bertha, who happened to be her girlfriend.

Karen was more optimistic about someday being married and becoming a faithful housewife now that she was with Jermaine, but fighting off the urges of having a huge penis inside her, she found unbearable. Tyrone was a high school dropout who smoked weed all day and drank Olde English 800, and was known for doing drive-by and walk-up shootings, which was how he earned the nickname KillaT.

He was also known for having a big, fat, long dick and knowing how to use it very well.

Karen was introduced to Tyrone one day while drinking with Bertha; Tyrone had been released from prison two days earlier. On this particular day Bertha and Karen were drinking gin and listening to oldies when they ran out of liquor. Even though Bertha was already drunk, she wanted more.

"Girl, we're all out of gin. Guess I gotta make a store run right quick," Bertha said, then stood and almost fell.

"I know that's right, girlfriend. You know us black women gotta have our gin. They say that gin makes you sin, and I'll tell you, girl, I feel like doing some sinning today to take out mind off all the bullshit that's going on in my life, you know."

"I know that's right," replied Bertha, and then added, "And don't worry about Tyrone, he wouldn't hurt a fly. Hell, from what his cousins tell me, he's still a virgin. Besides, ain't no babies coming in this house anyway, you know what I mean, girl? Hell, I still gotta lot of living to do and I ain't got time to be taking care of no damn grandbabies. If anything, I'm gonna get me a man up in here cause I need me some dick. And not just any ol' dick, a big, long dick."

"I heard that, girl. We don't get older we just get better, you know what I'm sayin'?"

"Hell yeah, I know what you sayin', 'cause I know I'm good in pleasing a man." Then she grabbed her purse and stumbled out the door.

It was a good thing she didn't have a car and the store was in walking distance. Bertha's daily thing was getting drunk until she passed out. Then she would sleep until the next day, and then start all over again.

After Bertha had left, Karen stood and began dancing

alone while sipping the last of her gin. The entire while she had been there, Tyrone had never taken his eyes off her. He had undressed her in his mind several times, sensing that she was a freak. Her body language told him that she was hot and her bedroom eyes told him that she wanted him.

Tyrone was dark-brown complexioned, stood about six foot two, and always wore his hair in braids. His pants always hung off his ass, representing the thug that he was. In his case, a broke thug. His friends had told him several times that older women knew how to lay it on a younger man mainly because of their experience and age.

"I'm telling you, Tyrone, nigga, if you get an older women with a good job, even if the bitch is on welfare, nigga, all you gotta do is fuck the hell out of her and lick her pussy every day and the bitch will love the hell out of you and do just about anything in the world for you. Man, you won't have to work or do nothing, nigga. The only thing you'll have to do is have a stiff dick waiting for her when she comes home and the world could be yours, nigga. And if the bitch don't have a job, then fuck her and lick her about three or four times a day, and the bitch will hand you her whole county check every goddamn month," one of the O.G.'s from the neighborhood had told him.

Now was his golden opportunity to check this out for himself.

Grooving to the music and looking at Tyrone, Karen thought, *Umph, a virgin, huh? I'll bet my life that if I whip this good pussy on him he'll probably stick to me like Krazy Glue. Hell, my pussy is so good it tickles me when I walk so I know it's the bomb.*

While Karen was smiling at her thoughts, Tyrone walked over to the stereo and put on a tune by R. Kelly entitled, "Feeling on your Booty." Then he approached her.

"May I have this dance, Ms. Lady?"

She was overwhelmed by his boldness and aggression. She had suddenly forgotten about both of their ages.

"You can't handle this, youngster, so why would you wanna tease yourself?" she replied flirtatiously, feeling twenty years younger.

Knowing he was being challenged because of his age, Tyrone boldly grabbed her hand and shoved it down his pants letting it rest on his weapon.

"Now what do you think?" he asked, smiling.

"Damn, is that all you or is this one of those blow-up dicks?" She was stunned but yet excited.

"This is the real deal, baby. No blow-up, no additives; all beef, baby." He then proudly whipped it out and stood there, letting it hang.

Karen stared at it a moment, then touched it, and then began rubbing it. It felt so good in her hand; so real, so meaty, so fat, and so long. It was unbelievably real to her. Being the freak that she was she wished that she could take it everywhere with her, everywhere. Her rubs had caused it to quickly harden and now it was as solid as penitentiary steel and stiff as a soldier. I *don't give a damn about his age*, Karen thought. I *need a piece of this right now, and I mean right-fucking-now before Bertha gets back. It's not everyday you run across a dick like this.*

Reading her mind, Tyrone hurriedly undressed her then quickly stripped out of his clothes.

"Damn," Karen said, ready to feel him deep inside her. "Do you know how to use this thing, or do I have to teach you?"

"No time for talking or lessons, shorty. My mama will be back in a few minutes, so let's just do the damn thing right quick, you know what I'm sayin'? If you think I need lessons, then I'll voluntarily be your full-time student, but for right now let's get busy. Girl, I just got out and I'm ready to kill some pussy, you know what I'm sayin'?"

He then quickly picked her up by her butt cheeks and walked her over to the nearest wall and inserted himself inside her while standing. Normally she liked her pussy wet and hot before intercourse but there was no time for foreplay. Tyrone rammed it in as far as he could then began fucking her hard and rough like a jackhammer tearing up cement. After two minutes of rough pounding he came and then pulled it out.

"It doesn't make sense for a man to have a dick this damn big and can only fuck for a minute."

"I got mines, shorty. Didn't you get yours?"

"Hell no! You know damn well I didn't get mines!" She was furious.

Then suddenly they heard the squeaky gate opening so they hurriedly got dressed.

"You owe me, Tyrone. You owe me big-time!"

"I got you, shorty, don't trip. As soon as my mama get drunk and fall to sleep, I got you."

Seconds later Bertha walked in.

"Let's get this party started, girl."

Bertha could hardly wait to take a drink and in less than an hour she had passed out on the couch. That gave Karen and Tyrone the green light to do their thing. Without hesitation he signaled her to his bedroom where they wasted no time getting undressed. This time Karen was the aggressor.

"Take me, Tyrone, and fuck me good. I'm gonna teach you how to fully satisfy a woman sexually, not just get yours and call it. Just follow my lead and you can't go wrong. You've got a gold mine between your legs and don't even know it."

From that day on Karen slept with Tyrone just about

every night of the week. Opportunely for her, because of her instability and living the street life, her kids were living with her sister, Jewell. That gave her the go-ahead to do as she pleased.

Hearing his voice through the telephone had instantly aroused Karen and had caused her to visualize his penis fully erect.

"Do you miss me?" she asked, rubbing her clitoris.

"Hell, yeah I miss you, shorty! Where in the fuck have you been?" He was angry at the fact of her leaving him without notice. Like many others, he was hooked on her sex and hadn't seen her in ages.

One morning while Bertha and Tyrone were asleep Karen had awakened and had come to the conclusion that she wanted her kids back and wanted to live a clean, sober, and normal life. With that in mind she had quickly gotten dressed then split, leaving neither Bertha nor Tyrone a note. I *gotta do what I gotta do*, she thought, walking out the door.

That same day she checked into a live-in rehabilitation program, but unluckily during that time there were no openings, so like many other women she was placed on a waiting list. Fortunately, she met a woman at a bus stop who directed her to a place that immediately accepted her and she was able to pull herself together.

"I miss you too, boo, and I think about you all the time. I did what I had to do to get back my kids, and now I feel a hell of a lot better. We'll catch up on what each other has been doing in due time, but my question to you for now is how soon can you get to Lancaster?"

"Lancaster? Where in the hell is that, shorty?"

"About an hour from you if you're driving and it's about a three hour ride on a bus, which I don't have that type of time for," explained Karen.

"Shorty, you know goddamn well I ain't got no car, no job, and no goddamn money to catch a fuckin' bus—"

"Leave right now and go to the check cashing-place on Broadway. That's the closest place to you that I know of that has a Western Union. There will be a hundred dollars there waiting for you but don't forget to carry your ID. Then I want you to catch the bus downtown and transfer to the metro link train that comes to Lancaster," she instructed, still rubbing her clit. This was very risky but she was willing to take that chance.

"Shorty, you know I ain't ever been out the hood, girl. What gangs they got out there? Crips or Bloods?"

"What difference does that make, Tyrone?"

"Shit, it makes a whole lotta difference to a nigga like me. I've already been shot seven times and I ain't got nine lives like a goddamn cat, you know what I'm sayin? A nigga like me just can't go wherever he wanna go, 'cause I got enemies that I don't even know."

"Listen Tyrone, you've gotta leave the hood sometimes without worrying about your enemies seeing you. All of this damn talking is getting me out of the mood, so if you want to see me as bad as you say you do, then show me." After a few moments of silence she finally broke it.

"Write down this number and call me as soon as you get to Lancaster."

"Okay, shorty, that's all good. I'm on my way, but my mama wanna talk to you." Not wanting to hear Bertha's mouth about her sexing her baby, Karen quickly hung up the phone. Although Bertha had allowed Karen to spend the night in Tyrone's room over and over again, when she was most sober, she expressed her disapproval.

She had borrowed two hundred dollars from Bertha and had promised to pay it back when she received her welfare check but didn't. She had no intentions of listening to Bertha's drunken bullshit until she was able to pay her.

She had recently spoken with Denise, who assured her that both she and Maurice were still working overtime and would not be home until later. She could not afford to get busted and mess up a good thing. She had to do this right.

Three and a half hours later Tyrone arrived at the residence. Karen wasted no time grabbing him by his pants and leading him to the bedroom. The kids were asleep on the sofa. Once inside the room she closed the door and unzipped his pants. She desperately wanted him, right then. They began kissing wildly while rubbing each other and then suddenly Tyrone wanted to talk, but at the moment, discussions were not a part of Karen's itinerary.

"We'll talk later, baby. Right now I need some of this," she said, easing him on the bed while caressing his erection. She climbed on top of him and eased the head inside. Then she eased a few more inches inside her until it hit the bottom of her pussy. There were still about five inches left that she couldn't handle, but by the time this was over she planned to have taken it all or have a pleasurable time trying.

She had taught him just the way she liked it. His movements fell right into her rhythm.

"Ooh, yes, ooh, mmmee," moaned Karen, enjoying the ride. She then sped up her rhythm. The phone rang several times but she ignored it.

"I miss you, shorty, and I—I—I—I—" She covered his mouth with her finger.

"Sheeeee. Now is not the time for words. Ram that dick inside me, then fuck me doggystyle."

"I love you, shorty, and I—I—I—I—" He wanted to express his emotions. He had never said that to anyone, not even to his own mother. The phone rang again but she ignored it.

"I sent for you so we can fuck, Tyrone. Shit, we can talk over the goddamn telephone, man! I've already got a man to love me and the only thing I need you for is to fuck me real good with this big-ass dick of yours," she explained, still riding, but he was screwing up her concentration with this bullshit.

"You haven't called me in months, shorty. Don't you understand goddammit! I fuckin' love you, girl?" His words did not mean anything to her at the time. She'd waited much too long for this and was not about to stop. Besides, she had just invested a hundred dollars and risked being caught by Denise, Maurice, or her kids. Finally, she caught one orgasm, then another, and then another, then another. But she wasn't finished yet.

"Now fuck me froggy style and quit all that goddamn talking!"

"But we need to talk, shorty, and I'm serious, baby." He was only trying to let her know that he was ready to settle down with her and raise a family. He had made up his mind to leave all the bullshit and his homeyshomeys alone and live a normal life.

Suddenly Alexus started crying.

"Fuck me, Tyrone, come on, man." The phone rang another ten times, then stopped.

"I wanna talk, shorty, and I wanna talk right goddamn now," insisted Tyrone.

Angrily, Karen jumped from the bed and got dressed, ignoring Alexus's cries.

"I keep telling you, Tyrone, we don't have anything in common but fucking, so get that love shit out of your mind! You know what, just leave and take your ass back to the hood where you belong!" Then she walked out of the room and picked up Alexus. Stevie had awakened, hearing his mother's voice.

As Tyrone stepped into the living room shirtless Stevie stared at him curiously.

"Who is this, Mama?" asked Stevie, inquisitively.

"This is someone who better get the hell out of here before I call the police," Karen yelled, still holding Alexus.

"Fuck the police! Now you wanna put the police in our business, huh? Ain't this about a bitch! You're the one who sent me money to come out here, so what the fuck are you talking about, shorty?" He then put on his shirt.

"Get out!" yelled Karen. She then sat Alexus down and stormed to the kitchen. Seconds later she returned holding a butcher knife in striking position. Little did Tyrone know, Karen was known for stabbing people. She had stabbed her sister, all three of her brothers, and several people who had stolen dope from her.

"Oh, so now you're gonna stab me, huh?"

She suddenly thought about the eight years she would do if she violated probation, which caused her to calm herself.

"Listen, baby, let's go outside and talk this thing over." She had to resolve this situation quickly and thoughtfully. She then set down the knife.

Once outside, she apologized for her behavior, then she told Tyrone about Jermaine.

"Listen, baby, I'm in a relationship with a truck driver who loves me and who cares about me and the kids' well-being. I just can't afford to fuck things up for myself, you know. I may not ever meet a man like him again, and—" She held her head down and shed a few tears.

"That's what I wanted to talk to you about, shorty." He gave her a hug. "I been doin' some thinkin', you know what I'm sayin', and I feel that you're the woman that I want to have my kids. I'm ready to settle down, get a job, and leave all the bullshit alone, shorty. You make me feel like somebody, you know what I'm sayin'?" His words were earnestly spoken. Lately he'd been having nightmares about being tortured by his enemies.

"A serious relationship with you is impossible, Tyrone. I'll fuck around with you to get my rocks off, but as far as us being in a down-to-earth relationship, it can never happen. Why do you think I called you? Well, since you don't know, I called you because my boyfriend isn't capable of satisfying me the way you do. He's an excellent provider and father figure, but he just doesn't have what it takes to fulfill my sexual needs. So I'm asking you, Tyrone, to go along with this. I can promise you that we can be together at least two to four times a week, but strictly for sex."

Not accepting what he was hearing, Tyrone gave her a mean, hard look then turned and walked away.

Jermaine had attempted several times to call Karen from his cell phone, but due to Tyrone's presence she had intentionally ignored the rings. Finally, she decided to answer.

"Hey, baby," said Jermaine, excited to hear her voice. "Girl, I thought you had abandoned me or something."

"Never that, honey. I took a little nap while the kids were asleep."

"You had me worried, baby. For a while I thought that you'd found another man to take my place. Please, sweetheart, at least answer the phone and let me know what you're doing, okay? Being out on this road sometimes causes a man to think the worst, especially when he can't get in touch with his woman and particularly when he has someone who's got it good like you."

"You can be assured, honey, that I'll never cheat on you

or leave you. There's not a man on this earth who can take my mind off you, Jermaine." One thing Karen prided herself on was convincing and persuading people into believing her lies.

"I hope not, sweetheart, because believe it or not, I think I'm falling in love with you."

I've gotta blow his head up and tell him what he wants to hear, Karen thought. "I've got that same feeling, you know. It's like love at first sight and in love overnight. This is totally unbelievable, like a dream come true."

"You know what, baby? We've been together for a few months now and already I'm thinking about marriage. Am I crazy or am I just in love?"

"You're not crazy by a long shot, baby, because I found myself visualizing the same exact thing. I gave lots of thought to what it would be like being Mrs. Jermaine Hopkins and believe me, the thought made me smile and feel good inside."

"My first mind, my mother, and my sisters told me to give it at least six months or so because by then we'll have had the chance to get to know more about one another's mood swings, likes and dislikes, and what causes one another pleasure or pain."

So this is the type of muthafucka that lets his family make decisions for him. I had a feeling he was a mama's boy. "Love at first sight and people getting married right away isn't unusual, Jermaine. I can feel that our love for one another is real. My aunt met my uncle on a Thursday morning and the next day he asked her to marry him. That Saturday they got married and that was thirty-five years ago and they're still married to this day," Karen said, wanting to keep him on the subject of marriage. This was a one-in-a-million chance of a lifetime and she did not want to blow it.

"Is that right? Well, they say that timing is everything,

and if a person doesn't take advantage of certain situations and opportunities at the time they occur, then more than likely they'll regret it later. I don't want you to slip away from me, Karen, and if marrying you will always keep you in my life, then so be it, we'll get married. Besides, I can't think of anything more pleasurable than coming home to you off the road. Sweetheart, I get hard just thinking about the things you do to me; I wanna marry you, Karen," stated Jermaine firmly.

"I strongly believe that's what God wants, Jermaine. God put us in each other's lives for a reason, and like you just said, if a person doesn't take advantage of a situation, especially when God is involved, they'll regret it for the rest of their life."

"Yep, you're right, baby," agreed Jermaine.

They talked a few more minutes, then broke the connection.

While driving through the state of Texas, Jermaine began thinking. *Damn, it's all good. I think I've got myself a winner. She's pretty, she's intelligent, she has damn good pussy, and on top of that she gives some bomb head. Damn, what more could a man ask for in a woman?*

While watching Jerry Springer, Karen's thoughts were, *Boy, I've got it going on. Hell, I've got myself a truck driver who makes damn good money, the kids like him, he's a good father figure, he owns three cars and a couple of homes, and with a little persuasion soon we'll be married and soon moving in with him. And on top of that, I can still have Mr. Ultimate Dick Tyrone whenever I want him. I hope Tyrone doesn't start acting stupid and fuck things up for me.*

Tyrone was drinking a forty-ounce of Olde English on his mother's porch. Each swallow caused him to get more and more frustrated, which triggered him to yell.

"Fuck that! That bitch is mines and I can't deal with an-otha nigga gettin' what's mines! How is she just gonna leave me for anotha nigga! I can't accept that, hell naw, I ain't havin' it! Fuck that!" Out of anger he threw the empty bottle in the street where it shattered and then lit another joint.

At nine-fifteen the following morning Tyrone was knock-ing on Denise's and Maurice's front door. He had talked his mother out of money to catch the metro rail and to buy him a couple joints and a forty ounce. He was strapped with a nine-millimeter and had just finished smoking a joint of chronic and drinking a forty ounce. Luckily, Denise and Maurice had already left for work, because Tyrone was high as a kite and angry as hell.

"Open this goddamn door, shorty!" Tyrone yelled, while pounding on the door with one hand and his nine-millimeter in the other. He was ready to bring on the drama. He had come to claim what he figured belonged to him.

Karen appeared a few seconds later in her robe and with an attitude.

"What are you doing here?" she asked, standing in the doorway.

"I come to take you back to my mama's house, shorty. You my girl, goddammit, and that's just the way it is, you know what I'm sayin'. I ain't 'bout to let no square-ass truck-driving nigga take you away from me." He then flashed his gun. "Where's that fool at, shorty! I need to have a man to man talk with him."

"What did I tell you, Tyrone? Why are you so goddamn hardheaded?" she replied in a calm voice, not wanting to awaken the kids or the neighbors. Then she continued.

"I told you over and over that the only thing we have in common is fucking; that's it and that's all. And if you keep on acting childish and stupid you're going to fuck that up."

"You don't even care about my goddamn feelings, shorty! I might be a gangsta, but I do have a feeling, you know. But it seems like to me that you only want me 'cause I got a big dick, but it's not going down like that because my emotions are involved now." He then paced back and forth with his finger on the trigger.

"First of all, Tyrone, put that fucking gun down. And secondly, I don't know why you're talking crazy when I've already told you what's going on. Now keep your damn voice down before you wake up the kids and the neighbors."

"I ain't tryin' to hear that bullshit you talkin', shorty. I'll shoot this muthafucka up if you don't come with me! Don't test me, please don't test me. And believe me, I don't give a fuck about the neighbors or a fuckin' landlord, goddammit I'm a gangsta! If you don't want me to get stupid around here, then wake up the kids, grab a few clothes, and let's go back to my mama's house," he demanded, pointing the gun at a vehicle parked in the stall.

"Put that damn gun up, Tyrone!"

"So how we gonna handle this? Are you comin' back to my mama's house, or do I gotta act a damn fool?"

"You make things so complicated when they can be so fuckin' simple. All right, I'll go to your mother's house but only for a night or so. I'm not about to fuck up the possibility of marrying a decent man for you." He then put away his gun.

"Where's that nigga anyway? Like I said, me and him gotta have a man-to-man talk, you know what I'm sayin'?"

"He's at work where he's supposed to be. Go wait for me in the parking lot next to the black convertible Mustang while I get the kids dressed and grab a few clothes." She had to give in to keep him calm. Bertha and a couple of his homeboys had told her that he was trigger-happy and lord knows that she didn't need any demonstrations at the moment.

Feeling he had somewhat gotten his way, Tyrone followed her instructions. She then quickly phoned Jermaine and lied to him, telling him that she was going to spend a couple of days with her sick Uncle Simon.

Chapter 3

During the ride to Los Angeles, Tyrone and Karen rode in complete silence while he wore a mean look and entertained malicious thoughts. Before Karen could get the kids out of the car, Tyrone had already stormed out of the car and into the house. Once inside, he made a quick phone call, then told his mother he had a run to make and would return shortly. He had totally ignored Karen without saying a single word to her.

Before going to prison, Tyrone had been involved in a home invasion, a carjacking, and several drive-by shootings. Crime had been a way of life for him since the age of eight, but due to three of his homeboys recently killed by rival gangs, Tyrone decided to lay low for a while until things cooled down. Once Karen had come into his life, he figured that if she and her kids were a part of his life that would somewhat motivate him to live right, do the right things, and put crime behind him. But now, unfortunately, someone was standing in the way of his plans. That someone was Karen's husband-to-be.

After leaving his mother's he went to meet with three of his homeboys and angrily ran down the scenario to them about what was happening and what he planned to do about it. Without any questions asked, they headed for Lancaster in a stolen car. Whenever one of the homeys needed help of some sort, whether he was in the wrong or right, the homeys had his back without question. That was how they did it in the hood.

They posted in front of Denise and Maurices's apartment, waiting impatiently for a male to approach the door. Tyrone didn't know what Jermaine looked like, but his plan was to approach, take action, and state his case afterward. His homeboys were down with him simply because he had assisted them on many criminal activities.

Maurice exited his Toyota and walked toward his apartment.

"There he is, let's get that fool!" instructed Tyrone, ready for action.

The thugs hurriedly stormed out of the car and rushed up to Maurice before he reached the stairwell that led to his apartment.

"What's up, fool?" Tyrone yelled, aiming his nine-millimeter at Maurice's head.

His homeboys quickly surrounded Maurice, and then suddenly, one of them hit Maurice in the head with the barrel of a gun.

"Yeah, nigga, you been fuckin' around with my girl! Nobody fucks with Killa T's girl, cuz. This is Front Hood Crip, nigga, and you in straight violation, cuz!" Tyrone shouted, still aiming at Maurice's head.

"What the fuck you talkin' about, man?" yelled Maurice in his Jamaican accent.

Maurice was totally dumbfounded to the thug's accusations. Maurice then said something accented that none of the thugs understood, but before he could finish Tyrone shot him twice in the chest, and then took off running to the car. A few neighbors heard the gunshots and responded by coming outside, but by then Tyrone and his crew had fled without being seen. Julio, a neighbor who lived downstairs, dialed 911 on his cell phone. Several neighbors stood over Maurice's motionless body as he lay unconscious in a pool of blood.

Denise was asleep when Charlene, another neighbor, stood pounding nonstop on her front door. Finally, she awoke and went to the door, albeit half asleep.

"What is it, Charlene? What's so important that—"

"Somebody just shot Maurice! He's lying on the ground bleeding like crazy," yelled Charlene, while crying hysterically.

"What!" Denise could not believe what she was hearing.

"Someone shot your husband and he's—" Charlene pointed to Maurice, and then rushed back down the stairs.

"No! No! No! Who did this? Why? My husband is a good man who works every day. He's a family man and he would never hurt anyone. Why?" cried Denise.

"He's gonna be all right," said Julio, kneeling over Maurice, attempting to talk to him. But Maurice still lay unconscious.

"Maurice is a good man, Denise. God is watching over him, don't worry. God will surely punish whoever did this," interjected the landlord, Patricia.

Minutes later Maurice was rushed in an ambulance to the emergency room at Antelope Valley Hospital with his wife at his side. Denise cried hysterically during the ride.

The medical staff wasted no time performing surgery on Maurice in hopes to save his life. Luckily, the bullets had landed a quarter of an inch from his heart and didn't do too much damage. Denise phoned several relatives from the waiting room, including her father, who was driving through New Mexico at the time, to enlighten them on what had happened.

When Tyrone made it back to his mother's house, Bertha was passed out on the sofa as a result of too much gin and King Cobra beer. Momentarily, Karen was fingering herself while being entertained by porno movies in Tyrone's bedroom. Her kids were lying next to her asleep.

"Daddy's home," Tyrone announced, walking inside the room as if nothing had happened. Then he began getting undressed.

"You're right on time, baby. I need you and I need you right now. Bring it to me, daddy. Bring it on home to mama," insisted Karen, getting more aroused and wet from the sight of his dick.

"We're gonna make love, shorty, but we gotta talk, you know what I'm sayin'. No ifs, ands, or buts, about it, you know what I'm sayin, we gotta talk." He then climbed on top of her and gave her what she'd been waiting for exactly how she wanted it. The kids remained asleep through all the sex cries, moans, groans, and movement, but Tyrone had suggested, when Karen initiated giving him head, to lay them on the living room floor.

After forty-five minutes or so of pleasurable sex, Karen was tired, worn-out, and sleepy, but Tyrone was fueled and ready to get something off his chest.

"Now it's time for me to tell you what's up, shorty," Tyrone said, now in a totally different mood. "First of all, I ain't gonna just sit back and accept you fuckin' around with anotha nigga, you know what I'm sayin'? I'm a gangsta, shorty, and gangstas just don't get down like that. I've got emotions invested in you, and like I told you before, I'm ready to settle down with you and the kids and leave all that criminal bullshit alone. You should respect that, you feel me? I ain't ever met a female that made me feel like this, shorty, and now that I got you in my presence, I ain't about to hand you over to any nigga, and that's real talk." His words were sincere, but they didn't mean anything at all to Karen.

What have I gotten myself into? she thought. *Give a thug a piece of pussy and a little head and the muthafucka falls in love. Who would think a thug knows how to love somebody? I didn't even think they had feelings. Hell, it seems like a bip-bam-thank-you-ma'am would be more their style.*

"Tyrone, listen. I—"

"I don't wanna hear about you and that other nigga!" Tyrone yelled, furiously. Then he stood and put on his boxers.

"I told you I'm marrying him, Tyrone, so why you tripping?" She tried to play it off, but she was frightened by his cruel look and body language. She had never seen him behave in such a manner.

"How in the hell can you say you're about to marry that nigga, but you're fuckin' and suckin' me? What's up with that picture, shorty?"

"Tyrone, I had no idea you were going to fall in love with me. That wasn't a part of the plan." She tried hard to reason with him, but he didn't have any understanding of what she was saying.

"But I did!" he yelled. "I fuckin' fell in love with you! I ain't ever loved a female in my goddamn life! All I ever did was fuck 'em and forget 'em, but with you it's different! Can't you see? Don't you feel me, shorty? I'm ready to quit gangbanging and leave all my homeys alone for you and that's a big turn for a nigga like me! How can you just say fuck me, for another nigga when I'm the one who had you first? I can't accept that, shorty, and I won't accept that!" He then seated himself at the edge of the bed. They sat in silence until he revealed to her what had taken place in Lancaster.

"You did what!" Karen yelled. "Jermaine is on the east coast working, so you couldn't have possibly shot him."

"I'm tellin' you, shorty, me, Capone, Ace Rat, and 8Ball went to Lancaster and I shot that nigga. That fool got a Jamaican accent, don't he?"

"No, he doesn't. Oh my God, Tyrone. You shot Maurice! He's Jermaine's daughter's husband. Oh my God."

"Well, shit, you shoulda fuckin' told me there was more than one nigga living in that apartment. Hell, it's too late now, so fuck it! What's done has been done and I can't take that back. Another one bites the dust, you know what I'm sayin'," responded Tyrone, showing no remorse for shooting the wrong person.

Karen couldn't figure out what to do. She knew that she couldn't snitch on Tyrone, because that would disclose her relationship with him and would probably put her in harm's way. After continually thinking about it, she then finally built the courage to phone Denise's residence, but there was no answer. Next she decided to dial Jermaine.

She looked at Tyrone. "Please be quiet and don't say anything to fuck this up. You've already fucked up enough."

At first Tyrone was sitting next to her, calmly listening to her conversation, but after the jealousy kicked in he could no longer remain composed.

"What's up, nigga! This is Killa T coming at you from Front Hood Compton Crips, nigga! Karen belongs to me, that's it, and that's all. If you got a problem with that, then come see me, nigga!"

"Tyrone, shh," said Karen, holding her finger across her lips. Jermaine had heard someone yelling, but luckily he did not hear what was said.

"Who was that?"

She had to think quickly. "That's my cousin and his friend trying to act like they're gangsters."

"Oh. Anyway, Maurice has been shot and I'm on my way back to California. He's in a coma at Antelope Valley Hospital."

"You're kidding me," responded Karen, playing dumb. "Why would anyone want to hurt Maurice?" she asked guiltily. She hadn't even thought to ask how Maurice was doing. "Well, anyway, my uncle hasn't gotten any better so I think I'd better spend another day or so with him. By that time you should be back and we can go to the hospital together." She glanced at Tyrone who was pacing back and forth, angry as hell, but going alone with her game. "When do think you'll be home?"

"Probably late tomorrow night. I think I'll drive back without sleeping."

"Whatever you decide to do just be careful, okay? I'll see you tomorrow night, okay, sweetheart?"

"I can't wait," he said, fantasizing about the way she rode him. Then thoughtfully, he added. "I hope your uncle's condition gets better more sooner than later."

"Me too, honey. Take care, drive safe, and I'll be waiting for you tomorrow night. Love you, bye-bye," said Karen, while massaging Tyrone's erection.

As soon as she hung up the receiver, Tyrone stood and then slapped the hell out of her.

"Bitch, don't you ever disrespect me like that! How in the fuck are you gonna tell another nigga that you love him when you know that I'm in love with you! You got me twisted, bitch! You got a lot of fuckin' nerves, shorty!"

She was so used to being hit by men that his slap didn't even faze her. She shook it off and remained cool.

"I had to do what I had to do, Tyrone," she explained.

"That's why I had to do what I had to do, Shorty!" After cursing her for another hour or so then telling her how much he loved her, he then climbed into bed and then flipped her on her back. Then he roughly forced his penis inside her, when normally he was gentle with it, and began plunging her brutally and deep, causing her to yell and cry as if someone was beating her, but actually she began liking it. Usually she instructed a man to fuck her easy and deep, but in this case—

"Fuck me, big daddy, fuck me," were her words.

Karen eased out of the room and sat at the dining room table, sipping the remains of the gin that Bertha had not finished. She then began thinking. *What a fine mess I've gotten myself into. I only wanted to fuck this nigga, that's all, but this stupid muthafucka has gotten himself pussy-whipped and has fallen in love with me. And now the nigga hit me. I could have gotten ugly up in here, but I gave him that one, because I was wrong for dissin' him. But hell, I had no other choice. I've got a crazy nigga on my hands that I don't give a fuck about so I've definitely gotta play my cards right to get out of this bullshit.*

Stevie had awakened and sensed something wrong with his mother.

"What's the matter, Mama?"

"Nothing, baby, now go on back to sleep. Mama is all right, okay?"

"I don't wanna sleep over here, Mama. I wanna go back to Denise's house," said Stevie, weeping. Then he added, "Mama, why do you and Tyrone be sleeping together and you said that you and Jermaine are about to get married?"

"Stevie, Tyrone is nothing more than a good friend, that's all." Her lies came as automatic as if they were premeditated.

Stevie was not as naive as Karen thought. He'd heard a

few of their conversations and had even seen them having sex. They assumed that he was asleep, but he was peeping from underneath the covers.

The following night, Karen gathered her kids, crept out of the house, and headed back to Lancaster. Thoughtfully, instead of going to the apartment, she made her way to the hospital to check on Maurice. Jermaine had been calling her cell, but Tyrone had taken her cell phone for a few hours, but Karen had a lock code on it so it couldn't be used or answered.

As she entered the room where Maurice was housed she spotted Jermaine, Denise, Cordell, and a few unfamiliar faces surrounding a bed. Seeing her, Jermaine approached her with open arms and gave her a kiss and a hug, and then he embraced Stevie and Alexus.

"I missed you guys so much," Jermaine said, looking at them as if they were already a family.

"I miss you too, Daddy," Stevie said, smiling.

Alexus blurted something in baby talk that only she understood, but more than likely she was repeating what Stevie had said.

At that moment Karen walked over to Denise and gave her a hug.

"Is he going to be all right?"

"The doctors said he'll be okay, but—"

"Then he'll be okay, baby," Jermaine said, interrupting, and then continued. "He's a very blessed man, baby. The bullet came very close to hitting his heart, but thank God, he's gonna make it."

Jermaine said that he was going to take the kids to the cafeteria then go outside to get a breath of fresh air.

Karen walked over and held Maurice's hand.

"You're going to be fine, Maurice. You're gonna be just

fine," she said to him, rubbing him arm and forehead. Then she began crying, thinking. *Why did Tyrone do this? He was really trying to kill Jermaine. Fuck! Why in the hell did I give a gang-banger some head and pussy? I got myself sprung on a piece of dick and this is what it resulted in.*

While staring at Maurice, Karen then realized just how dangerous Tyrone really was. She walked off with tears still trailing from her eyes.

Even though Maurice's eyes were barely opened and his condition was slowly improving, his mind still was not 100 percent sound. He recognized the people surrounding him and understood what was being talked about, but following the doctor's orders, he didn't respond to anything.

Two detectives had come to question him about the incident the day before, but doctors had advised them to delay their questioning for a few days, hoping that Maurice would be coherent and strong enough to respond sharply.

As Karen was exiting the room the same two detectives entered.

"I'm Detective Cross and this is Detective Baker. We need to ask Mr. Banner a couple of questions to get this investigation going." After the introduction, the detectives attempted to approach Maurice's bed.

"I'm sure you do have many questions, Detective, but my husband isn't in any condition to answer them at this time." Denise said, with an attitude. She was blocking their way from getting near her husband.

"Show some respect, Officer," Denise's mother said. "My son-in-law is in no condition to talk to you guys right now. Give him a few days or so, and if it's the Lord's will, he'll be better by then and can answer your questions." Denise's mother was very fond of Maurice and loved him like he was her own son. She was grateful that her daughter had married such a man.

Understanding what was being said, Maurice weakly spoke. "Gangbangers. They were gangbangers," he managed to say in a low voice.

Taking advantage of this opportunity. Detective Cross, who was the aggressive one, began asking questions while Detective Baker took notes.

"Why are you guys so fucking hardheaded? I told you that—" Denise spat before being cut off.

"If something happens to my son-in-law while being questioned by you guys, I'm gonna have a lawsuit so big on you personally and on the police department that both of you will regret ever being born," said Denise's mother, angrily.

"Mama, the doctors have already told these officers to wait until Maurice is better, but they just insist on being disrespectful assholes who don't give a damn about—"

"Mrs. Banner, we're only trying to get enough information to get started on finding out who did this. If you don't want the people punished that did this to your husband then basically I don't give a rat's ass. Now, if you will please allow us to ask only a few questions," said Detective Cross.

"Gangbangers," Maurice repeated in the same weak voice.

"Did you get a good look at them? What race were they? What were they wearing? Do you have any enemies? Are you affiliated with gang members?" All of those questions were asked at one time, which frustrated the hell out of Denise.

Karen reappeared in the room to hear the detectives, but fortunately Denise had put a stop to it before Maurice had responded to either of them.

"That's enough for now! Let my husband rest! How can you guys expect him to answer a series of questions when he's too damn weak to talk?" Denise fired.

"Okay, Mrs. Banner, we'll delay this for now, but in a couple days we'll be back. There are still lots of unanswered questions," said Detective Baker.

The detectives handed Denise business cards and then exited the room.

"The nerve of those idiots!" Karen said, angrily. "Can't they see that he's in no condition to answer questions?"

"I know damn well they can see that, but the thing about it is they don't give a damn," said Denise's mother.

Karen and Denise then went outside to have a cigarette. In the elevator they ran across Jermaine and the kids, who walked them back to the smoking area.

Once on the patio they began discussing what Maurice had said to the detectives.

"My husband is a working man who wouldn't harm a flea," Denise said. "I just can't figure out why any gangsters would want to shoot him. But I do know one thing; my brothers are coming out here and somebody's going to get fucked-up." The thought of what happened caused her to instantly want vengeance.

Denise's brothers had been locked up for murder since they were teenagers and had been recently released from prison. This kind of drama was right up their alley.

"This had to be a mistake," Karen said.

"A mistake?" Jermaine replied. "How in the hell can some gangbangers shoot someone twice in the chest and it be a mistake? Hell, they tried to kill him."

Jermaine then diverted his attention to Denise.

"Is Maurice into any illegal activities, Denise?"

"No, Daddy, no! Maurice isn't like that. The only thing Maurice does is work six days a week and tries to get all the overtime he can get. As a matter of fact, he doesn't even have any friends, nor does he hang out in the streets. Besides, Daddy, if he were into illegal stuff I wouldn't have ever married him. He's a good husband and father and everything he does he does it with me and Cordell." Denise had never known about Maurice's past.

"Maybe they thought he was someone else," Karen said, knowing that was the truth.

"Sooner or later the truth will come out. When it does, someone is going to have hell to pay whether or not they didn't kill him," Denise said.

They sat talking for a few more minutes and then made their way back to Maurice's room.

Maurice was released from the hospital three days later. His condition was a lot better, but he still was not considered to be 100 percent well.

Since things had somewhat gotten back to normal, Jermaine went back to work the following day, headed for the East Coast. The wedding date was set for Valentine's Day. When Denise suggested that the wedding be held in Las Vegas, she and Karen wasted no time going online searching for reasonable hotels on the strip, but found that during that time of the year the majority of the major hotels and wedding chapels were already booked for Valentine's Day. Apparently, hundreds of other people had already made the same plans for that same day. After hours of searching for a decent room on the strip, the only thing available was a motel room that was located in Downtown Las Vegas. Realizing that her options were running out, Denise used her credit card and booked it right away. The only family member Karen thought would probably attend her wedding was her daughter Jasmine. After phoning several family members informing them about the wedding, her instinct was right. Out of the numerous relatives she asked to come to her wedding, Jasmine was the only one willing. Denise thought it was sort of strange for Karen's relatives not to even consider being present at her wedding, but little did she know, Karen had a bad rapport with 99 percent of them. She had stabbed a few of them, cursed out just about all of them at one time or another, fought the majority of them, and had stolen from practically all of them during her addiction. None of them were fond of her, and it had been that way for many years. Her sister Jewell only tolerated her because of her kids; other than that she fed Karen with a long-handle spoon.

Denise booked three rooms on her credit card and also paid the fee for the wedding chapel. City Hall in Las Vegas was open 24-7, so getting a marriage license would not be a problem.

Denise felt happy and content knowing that Karen would soon be her stepmother and since she liked her so much and had a little juice at her job, she arranged for Karen to be placed in the next training class to drive city buses. Looking out for the best interest of her father, Denise figured two incomes were better than one. Hopefully, by the time Jermaine made it back home they could surprise him by telling him about her new job.

Karen completed the one-week classroom course and also the driver training course successfully, but once she found out that she had to pass a background investigation, she immediately backed out. She knew the company would not hire her for two reasons: She was currently on probation for child endangerment and assault with a deadly weapon, and she had been to prison twice and served time in the county jail on numerous occasions for prostitution, drug paraphernalia, and possession of cocaine. Instead of revealing her criminal history to her job, Jermaine, Denise, and Maurice, instead she told them she was on medication and was ordered by her doctor not to accept any job pertaining to driving.

Before Karen backed out of the job, Denise had introduced her to several of her coworkers as being her step-mother-to-be. Unluckily for Karen, three of them knew Karen from the past and had much to say.

"Your daddy is going to marry *her*? She was one of the biggest crackheads in Pasadena. Do you know that she stabbed two of her brothers and her sister too? It was all in the newspapers, girl," one of the employees had said.

"She whipped her kids with plastic pipes whenever she got mad at them for interfering with her crack smoking. She beat those kids something horrible, girl! Do you like her? How in the world did your father get involved with a woman like that? She's bad news, Denise," said another employee.

"She lived with me for a couple days," said an employee named Michael. "But the bitch was crazy as fuck. She thought just because she gave me head that I was going to let her and her kids permanently move with me and live rent free. I ain't gonna lie, her sex was the bomb, but she just wasn't the type you could take home to Mama. After I told her to leave she pulled a knife on me and I had to call the police on her to get her out of my house."

That was when Denise's suspicions began. She wasted no time calling Jermaine and bringing this to his attention. She could tell by his voice tone and then by his silence that he was hurt and disappointed. He was so confused that he didn't know whether or not to confront Karen about the accusations. After the connection was broken, Jermaine turned off his radio and rode in complete silence while driving through Pennsylvania. After an hour of contemplating what Denise had shared with him, he decided to make that call.

Jermaine confronted Karen with the things that were brought to his attention and she denied it all. She began crying and saying that people only spoke bad things about her because no one wanted to see her with anyone worthwhile or happy. She said that they'd rather see her on crack, selling her body, and living on the streets, and then they'd have something to talk about. She went on to say that lots of people hated her because she had successfully completed rehab.

Jermaine was highly sympathetic to her.

"Whatever you did in the past doesn't matter to me, baby. As long as you're doing the right thing today is all that counts to me. Regardless of what people say or what they think, we're still going to be together and we're still going to get married." He did his best to calm her, simply because he loved her without question.

Afterward, he called Denise.

"Whoever gave you that false, bullshit information, they just hating on Karen," explained Jermaine. "This world is filled with jealous people who try to stain your character by saying bad things about you. People have been talking about me since the third grade without me even giving them a reason to. People will say bad things about you before they say anything good about you. Keep that in mind, Denise."

"But Daddy, do you actually think that everyone's lying on her?" These people were reliable sources to Denise and she figured they had no reason to lie on Karen. She wished her father would quit being so goddamn naive.

"I said what I said, Denise, and I don't want to hear anymore about it." It appeared to him that his daughter's attitude toward Karen had suddenly changed.

"Well, I'm going to say this, Daddy, and then I'm finished with it: If I find out that she has something to do with what happened to Maurice, I swear on a stack of Bibles, Daddy, that I'll kill her or have her killed." Denise was serious as a heart attack.

Jermaine hung up in her face and began thinking. *Why are*

they hating on my baby? They've got my daughter believing all those damn lies! And besides, if God forgives people for their sins, then people should forgive and forget her and leave what's in the past buried. Some people just don't want to see you making it and happy, that's all it is.

Karen continued her daily rituals, which was sleep until noon, and then wake up and watch talk shows, Court TV, and then squeeze in a few porn movies while the kids were asleep. With Maurice being on sick leave, he spent his days exercising for a couple hours, then on the computer playing Las Vegas casino games, and for the remainder of the day he'd watch television.

Tyrone would sometimes call and hang up when someone other than Karen answered the phone. Karen had been actually trying hard to get him out of her system, but thoughts of his huge, pleasurable penis haunted her mind daily, which made it hard for her to completely dismiss him from her mind.

Denise and Maurice became more suspicious of Karen. Lately, Karen had been voluntarily answering the telephone an awful lot, and she would hold both short and long conversations, using a hushed tone. Finally, Denise, using her caller ID feature, immediately dialed Tyrone's number after being abruptly hung up on.

"Why do you keep calling my house and hanging up?" Denise asked with an attitude.

"Bitch, what the hell are you talkin' about?" He was not expecting her to call, so now he had to play it off.

"You just called my house, man, and I wish you would stop calling here."

"Fuck you, bitch!"

"Fuck you too, punk!"

Maurice then grabbed the telephone from Denise.

"Who the fuck is this?" Maurice yelled in his Jamaican accent.

"And fuck you too, muthafucka! You're supposed to be dead, nigga! I should've shot your ass in the fuckin' head, nigga," Tyrone said, without thinking about the damage his words had caused. Then he quickly hung up.

After telling Denise what the caller had said, they then went into their bedroom, closed the door, and had a discussion. They wondered first of all how the caller got their telephone number. Then, thinking back to all the times someone had called and hung up whenever they answered, but did not hang up when Karen answered, was questionable. Karen's words, *Maybe they thought it was someone else*, kept ringing in Denise's head. She then decided she needed to have an instant one-on-one with Karen.

The following day after work Denise and Karen had a brief talk. To Denise's surprise, she found out that Karen had a recent relationship with a cousin of hers named Bernard, who had been a crackhead for the past twenty-something years. She had also found out that Karen and Bernard had lived with her Aunt Mable for a week, then Mable had kicked them both out. Karen had met Bernard in the rehabilitation program and unfortunately had fallen for his charm, which he used on women each time he was sentenced to a rehab program. He had filled her with promises, lies, hopes, and fantasies that she believed simply because he was the son of a famous musician. The main thing about him was that he had a huge penis and knew how to work it. He had promised her that he was going to marry her and provide her and her kids with a mini-mansion, his-and-hers Beamers and Porsches, and a lifestyle that only the rich and famous could live. And like a damn fool she believed him all the way, until in time she discovered that he was nothing but a crackhead.

Denise knew that people will only tell you what they

want you to know, so, following her conversation with Karen, she called her Aunt Mable to see what she could find out.

"Girl, you'd better get that wicked bitch out of your house!" advised Aunt Mable. "She's trouble, Denise, nothing but trouble. Do you know that I caught that heffa and Bernard smoking crack in one of my rooms? And that's not all, girl; one day I opened their bedroom door and saw her pulling a bag of crack out of her baby's pussy! Can you believe that shit, girl? I tried to help them by letting them stay here until they could save enough money to get their own place, but they just couldn't leave that goddamn crack alone! Take my advice, girl, and get that scandalous bitch out of your house. And I don't know what your father sees in that woman, anyway. I think he's in for a nightmare."

"They're talking about getting married, Auntee."

"Well, he's in for marriage mayhem then, honey. Bernard told me that the girl used to turn tricks to support her crack habit up and down Sierra Highway, but hell, he's the biggest crackhead in the world, so he can't even talk."

During their conversation Denise had told Mable about the phone calls and also about what the caller had said to Maurice.

"I'll put my life on that bitch having something to do with it! She's bad company, Denise. She's been to prison a couple times and been to county jail an countless amount of times, so I wouldn't put anything past the ho. I did my homework on that bitch, Denise, and I'm glad that you're doing yours."

After the connection was broken, being the gossipier that Mable was, she immediately phoned every relative that she could think and told them about her conversation with Denise. They all had the same thing to say: *Why does Jermaine always get those low-budget welfare women? As smart as he is and as much as he has going for himself, he should have chosen someone that was at least on his level But I guess them women be having him pussy-whipped."*

Denise now had a total different outlook on Karen. Her disappointment and hatred toward Karen grew daily, especially after talking with Bernard, who had assured her that Karen was in fact an undercover crackhead and slut. Bernard had also told Denise that Karen was a smooth talker and could just about talk herself out of any fateful situation. Bernard's relationship had ended with Karen when she had him thrown in jail for assaulting her. Denise wasted no time calling her father. However, after he heard what she had to say, he figured it was all just a bunch of bullshit and didn't believe a damn word of it. The reality was that he didn't *want* to believe it.

Chapter 4

Another month had gone by and Jermaine's home renovation had not yet been completed. Living at Denise's apartment was beginning to get intolerable for Karen. Denise no longer respected Karen as her father's fiancée or as a human being. Most days when Denise came home from work she would not speak to Karen, but would always speak to the kids, because, after all, they were totally innocent and had nothing to do with their mother's actions or past. Karen sensed the change in Denise's and Maurice's attitudes, but tried her best to deal with it even though she found it very hard to do. Karen had always been an outspoken person who had also always been the type of person who didn't take any form of disrespect from anyone. Even though she was just a wee bit taller than four feet, she had the roar of a lion. She mentioned how she felt about the recent attitudes to Jermaine, but being the calm, peaceful man that he was, he would say things to try and pacify her.

"Soon we'll be out of there, sweetheart. Just hang in

there the best you can without being disrespectful and without doing anything to tick them off."

"I'm trying to, baby, but believe me, it's hard. Your daughter can be a real bitch when she wants to, and where I come from, bitches get dealt with. She looks at me sometimes like she hates me. She'll look right at me, and then turn up her nose without saying anything, and walk away. The only time she says anything to me is when the kids have broken something, or if one of them hit Cordell, or if they're making too much noise when they're playing. I don't know why she has a sudden change toward me," she lied. "But I don't like it and I can't take too much more of it. Anyway, my uncle called and he's not feeling any better at all. Once we move into the house I think I'll go and nurse him for a few days, since no one else in my family seems to give a damn about him," she lied. She had recently promised Tyrone some of her time. Besides she craved his penis and it was now time to once again satisfy her needs.

"Okay, baby, that's fine, as long as you keep in touch with me."

"Don't worry, I will. Drive safe, baby, and have a great trip. Keep your eyes on the road, but keep your mind on Jesus." She was now ready to get the hell out of Denise's apartment.

Setting aside being slapped and cursed out by Tyrone, and more so overlooking what he'd done to Maurice, Karen made her way to Los Angeles to scratch her itch.

Once the kids had fallen asleep, Tyrone had immediately initiated an argument with Karen. She had come for sex, but he wanted to be heard.

"I'm tired of this shit, shorty!" Tyrone yelled, pointing his finger in Karen's face.

"Tired of what, Tyrone? I'm living up to my promise even

after you've hit me, and after what you done to Maurice.
What more do you want? Besides, I didn't come all the way
from Lancaster to argue with you, I came to spend some
quality time with you. Calm down, baby, and let's get busy
while the kids are asleep," insisted Karen, ready for what
she'd been missing.

"There you go again with that bullshit, shorty! All you
want me for is my goddamn dick! I want you to be my
woman, not my fuckin' sex toy!"

"Tyrone, how many times do we have to go through this
shit? I'm marrying Jermaine. What part of that don't you
understand?"

"None of it! I had you first, and I ain't into sharin'!"

"Can we at least get our groove on before we start argu-
ing?" She eased up to him and began rubbing his penis.
She then led him to the bathroom, unzipped his pants, and
began slowly sucking him, wanting it to get rock hard.
Three minutes later he came in her mouth and went limp.
He then attempted to zip his pants, but she stopped him.

"Aw, hell no! Give me what I came for and nothin' less,"
Karen demanded, pulling down his pants. Then she began
sucking it again, trying to make it fully erect.

"We gotta talk, shorty, and I mean right goddamn now!"
He pushed her down and then pulled up his pants.

"Why did you push me, Tyrone? You promised me that
you would never put your hands on me, but you just
pushed me. Just because you know I'm hooked on the dick
don't start trippin' on me, nigga! If you ever put your hands
on me again, I swear I'll tell the police you shot Maurice,
and I'll press charges on your black ass for assault. I told
you that I'm fed up with niggas thinkin' that they can just
put hands on me whenever they feel like it!"

"What did you say?" He gave her a crazed look. "Bitch,

did you say you'll call police on me?" Then he cocked his fist back and socked her so hard that her head made visible prints on the wall. Then he began yelling while kicking her ass. "If you ever say some shit like that to me again, bitch, I'll fuckin' kill you!" He kicked her in the ass, and then walked out and slammed the door behind him.

Karen lay on the floor crying until she had finally gathered enough strength to pull herself up. Then she glanced into the mirror, and then suddenly had flashbacks of her exes beating on her. Her right eye was bloodshot and her left eye was half closed. Staring into the mirror, she suddenly regretted driving to LA chasing Tyrone's dick, and then she regretted ever being involved with him. *He's not going to get away with this, hell no! He'll pay for this one way or another, and I fuckin' mean it!*

Tyrone had gone to his room and put on a song by 2Pac, and then lit a joint.

After washing her face, then reexamining herself in the mirror, Karen finished what was left of the gin, and then sat on the floor against the wall entertaining thoughts of revenge. *"I'm gonna get this muthafucka. Fuck that!"*

At 3:30AM everyone was asleep except Karen. This was the time she'd been waiting for. Quickly, she grabbed her kids and hurried them to the car, and then went back inside the house and headed to the restroom, where she grabbed a razor blade. Then she went to Tyrone's room. She had to act quickly. He was lying across the bed in his boxers, which was perfect for Karen. Like nothing had ever happened between them, she pulled out his long penis and began rubbing it, licking it, and sucking it, until it was rock hard. He opened his eyes and then closed them while enjoying the pleasures of her tongue and lips.

"Suck it good, Shorty, yeah baby, that shit feels good.

Give big daddy what he deserves. Lick it up and down the vein, then lick the balls, baby," he said in a low tone, lying in complete ecstasy.

Suddenly, Karen slipped the razor out of her pocket and began furiously slashing his penis numerous times, and then she slashed his testicles a couple times. Blood spurted everywhere as he yelled in pain and cursed her, but fortunately for her he was momentarily crippled and could not move.

"I'm gonna kill you, bitch!" he yelled, continuously.

She had already run out of the house.

It was 4:30AM when Karen made it back to Denise's residence. The combined sounds of the door opening and Alexus's cries had caused both Denise and Maurice to awaken. Furious, Denise got up and approached Karen with an attitude.

"Don't you know that we're working people around here? Why are you coming into my house at four-thirty in the morning, Karen?" Denise was standing in her robe with her hands on her hips.

"I'm so sorry Denise, but after dropping off my uncle at the hospital, I—"

"Yeah, yeah, yeah, right," Denise said, sarcastically. "My Daddy might believe your bullshit, but I don't believe a goddamn word you say." The fact of Karen holding Alexus did not prevent Denise from getting in her face. Stevie sensed this was about to get ugly so he seated himself on the couch and remained silent.

"What are you talking about, Denise?"

"You know what I'm talking about, Karen! Your bullshit manipulating games are over! I talked to my Aunt Mable, I talked to Bernard, and I talked to a few people that know you from Pasadena, so I know all about you now, Karen, so save the bullshit. One thing I hate is a fake-ass person, and especially one who's manipulating my daddy."

"I don't have to listen to this shit, and I can care less who you've talked to," replied Karen, and then stormed toward the bedroom.

"Stevie, come help me pack our stuff so we can get the hell outta here."

"Just make sure you don't steal anything, because I know you're still on crack. Hell, that's probably what you've been doing tonight. You don't have any respect for yourself, for people who try to be nice to you, nor for your kids. That's a damn shame. Yeah, bitch, I've heard all about you," said Denise, following Karen to the bedroom.

As difficult as it was for her to hold her tongue, Karen ignored the derogatory remarks and continued packing. A few seconds later Maurice appeared, standing next to his wife, and began giving Karen an evil look.

Minutes later Karen and the kids stormed out of Denise's residence, carrying three backpacks full of her belongings. She decided to get a room at the Motel 6, but first she felt that she needed to enlighten Jermaine on what had taken place. Using her cell phone, she called him.

"I just got cursed out and put out by your disrespectful, rude-ass daughter. Me and the kids are on our way to the Motel 6 to get a room for the night," Karen explained.

"What?"

"Yeah, babe, I figured that sooner or later something was going to happen." She then began crying. "I tried, Jermaine. Lord knows I tried my best to get along with your daughter, but for some reason she just doesn't want us to be together. She hates me, Jermaine, and she showed it right in front of the kids."

"What happened, sweetheart?"

At that moment Jermaine was driving through Wisconsin.

"After nursing my uncle a few hours I called my brother, Jasper, to come relieve me so that I could come home and get some sleep because I was tired. Anyway, when I made it to your daughter's she began attacking me with an attitude and started talking crazy to me because it was four-thirty in the morning and Alexus was crying. Then she began telling me that her Aunt Mable and my ex, Bernard, had told her a whole lotta negative bullshit about me." Her cries and weeping grew even louder.

Jermaine was furious. "I'm sick and tired of my daughter trying to ruin our relationship! Don't worry, sweetheart, tomorrow I'll call the contractor and tell him that I urgently need to move back in my home right away. And meanwhile, I'll have a talk with that daughter of mines."

"She doesn't want us together, Jermaine, can't you see it?" She continued crying.

"Regardless of what she wants, what she suggests, or what opinions or input she has toward our relationship, we're going to be together, and we're still getting married on Valentine's Day. I'll be home in a few days, sweetheart, and until then, you and the kids get some rest and stay out of harm's way. I apologize for my daughter's behavior, but I can assure you that once we're in our home you'll feel comfortable, content, and you'll be happy."

Now that Karen and her kids had the privacy of their own room and were not being monitored, disrespected, or falsely accused by anyone, she felt a little better. Sensing that Tyrone would try to get revenge against her, Karen knew that Denise's apartment would not be a safe place for her and the kids, anyway. Actually, this was perfect timing.

It was 1:30PM when the loud, irritating sound of Alexus's cries awakened Karen. Suddenly realizing that she had some important business to take care of, Karen hurriedly changed Alexus's diaper, and then instructed Stevie to get dressed.

"Mama, when is Daddy coming back?" Stevie asked, while getting dressed. He asked that same question at least three times a day. Calling Jermaine Daddy now came automatic to Stevie.

"He should be here in a few days, Stevie. And he said that as soon as he gets back we're moving into his house."

"Will I have my own room, Mama?" asked Stevie, excitedly.

Alexus repeated the question using baby talk.

"I guess so, Stevie. Hell, the man has four bedrooms, so unless you want to sleep with me and him, you'll be sleeping in your own bedroom."

"Yes!" shouted Stevie.

"Yes!" Alexus repeated.

En route to the welfare office, Karen made up her mind that she was no longer going to be unfaithful, deceiving, or manipulative toward the man that loved and cared so much for her and her kids. She had been through a countless amount of men to get to this one so she had to make this work, regardless of the size of his penis. *I'll just buy myself a big dildo and be content with that*, Karen thought while driving.

When Jermaine made it back to town it was 2:45AM on a Wednesday morning. The kids were asleep and Karen had been impatiently waiting for him to walk through the door. She had a surprise for him, something that he would never forget, and something that he could think about while traveling down all those lonely interstates and highways. She had made the kids a spot on the floor to sleep, which left the king-size bed available for her and her fiancé.

I've got to lock this in. I've got to give him something that he can feel. It's not every day an opportunity like this comes my way. I'm going to fuck him and suck his dick so damn good that his toes will curl. I'm going to give him the red-light special. Sex was actually the only thing she had to offer.

They made love until the sun came up. She made Jermaine feel pleasures that no other woman had ever came close to making him feel. This was a definitely a feeling that he wanted to come home to, every day if possible. *Damn, am I glad she's going to be my wife,* thought Jermaine, lying back smiling, completely satisfied. *All I ever wanted was to come home to a woman who knows how to sexually satisfy me, a woman that respects me and appreciates me, a woman who loves me for me and not for what I've got, or for what I can do for them.*

Later that day, Jermaine and Karen went to spend some time with Jasmine, Karen's daughter. Karen wanted Jermaine to get more acquainted with Jasmine. On the same token she wanted to show Jermaine that Jasmine was totally opposite from Denise. Seeing that Jermaine was nothing like the men in her mother's past, Jasmine liked him instantly. Jermaine had told Jasmine about his job as a truck driver, his experience as a real estate investor and a loan officer, and also about a book he was presently working on and striving to have published. Jasmine was very impressed and also extremely happy for her mother. To Jasmine, Jermaine was someone positive who could be an optimistic influence in her mother's life as well as be an excellent father figure to her sister and brothers.

They sat talking for a couple of hours until Jermaine volunteered to treat everyone to dinner at the Sizzler.

Once they returned to Jasmine's apartment, Jermaine asked for permission to use the computer, and then decided to e-mail his daughter a letter. The letter read:

I hope you come off your high horse and come back down to earth and accept the reality of having a new stepmother. Regardless of the lies and bullshit that people have fed you and Maurice about Karen I'll always love her no matter what, so please accept that. Indeed, you are my daughter and I will never deny that, but now I'm about to get married and you're about to have a new stepmother so like I said, please acknowledge and accept that. I hope you have not changed your mind about going to my wedding in Las Vegas on Valentine's Day. I hope to see both you and Maurice there.

Sincerely, with unconditional love,
Your Father

Jasmine was used to her mother only having thug boyfriends who did not work or contribute to their well-being, but instead hang out on street corners and liquor stores smoking dope and drinking.

Jasmine and Jermaine exchanged phone numbers, embraced in a hug, and then afterward Karen and Jermaine left.

Jasmine appeared to be a respectful, ambitious young lady. Having a two-year-old daughter and an unemployed boyfriend whom she had been in love with since middle school did not prevent or distract her from striving toward success or from excelling in life. She was now in her second year of nursing school and had been manager of McDonald's for two years. Despite of her living in a low-income environment, she drove a brand-new Nissan Altima, dressed nicely every day, and kept a positive attitude about things. Jasmine had A-1 credit and was also very good at saving money.

In the past, both Marvin and Jasmine had been taken away from Karen by the courts because of her drug addiction, instability, and because of her repeated criminal convictions. Thank God that Karen's sister Jewell stepped up and went to court to get full custody of them, not wanting them to be raised in a foster home. Marvin had been diagnosed with brain damage, which was a result of falling off a rooftop at the age of seven. Doctors had no choice but to place a steel plate inside his head. He was slower in school than kids his age, and had to be placed in a slow-learning classroom. The state rewarded Karen a check for seven hundred and fifty dollars each month for Marvin, which was turned over to Jewel after being awarded full custody of him. After a few months of Marvin being in Jewell's custody, Karen, along with just about all of her family members, knew that Jewell and her husband were using Marvin's check for the benefit of their own kids and for themselves. While Jewell's kids dressed in name-brand, fashionable clothing, Marvin wore raggedy attire and worn-out shoes. Jewell's intentions in the beginning were good until influenced by her husband, who had never worked a day in his life.

While Jasmine lived with them, even though they received a welfare check for her, they treated her bad and talked to her very impolitely. Karen's kids did not get treated the same as their own.

Jasmine, being the clever young lady that she was, moved out of Jewell's house the day she turned eighteen. Her boyfriend Raymond's parents had accepted her with open arms. They were glad to see that a young lady, who was so intelligent, so determined and ambitious, have an interest in their son. They hoped that someday Jasmine's positive energy and determination rub off on their son. They sensed that one day she was going to make something of herself.

After getting the green light to move back into his home, Jermaine went and bought expensive new furniture for the entire house. He also purchased five state-of-the-art DVD players, two HP computers, two Fisher stereo systems, a 60-inch plasma screen television, three 27-inch televisions (one for each bedroom), an oak desk to beautify his home work area, and also a thirty-five-hundred-dollar bedroom set for the master bedroom. The other three bedrooms were already completely furnished.

The following day Jermaine purchased a thirty-five hundred dollar wedding ring for Karen and had also bought her a beautiful wedding dress that cost him a little over twelve hundred dollars. Karen had come up with the idea of renting a dress, but that's not what he wanted.

"Sweetheart, I want you to have this dress for the rest of your life. I want you to look at this dress once a year and tell me how you feel about our marriage," Jermaine had said to her.

Chapter 5

It did not surprise Jermaine or Karen that Denise and Maurice did not show up at their wedding. Other than the minister who married them, Jasmine, accompanied by her boyfriend Raymond, and Jermaine's sister Elaine, escorted by her boyfriend Matthew, were the only ones present at the wedding.

"As long as we have each other, babe, that's all that matters to me. Having you makes me feel like I own this whole world and everything that's in it. I love you so damn much, Karen, and I just wanna thank you for being my wife," Jermaine said sincerely, while holding her hand and looking into her eyes. She had never met a man so sincere.

She responded with a long, meaningful hug, followed by a significant kiss that triggered him to think, *Damn, she really loves me.*

Karen's appearance was absolutely stunning on that day. Jasmine was bewildered by her mother's beauty and so was Jermaine. Her beige wedding dress gripped her petite body so perfectly, revealing her rounded butt, while the split going down its sides revealed her thighs and smooth legs. Her hair lay neatly down her back and shoulders with Shirley Temple curls at the ends. Her huge smile reflected happiness and her walk indicated pride. This was the happiest day of her life.

Later that evening everyone decided to change into something more comfortable, and then hit the gambling floor. Unfortunately, five hours later, the newlyweds had come out on the losing end after inserting over five hundred dollars into the slot machines. Luckily, Jasmine won over a thousand dollars. Being the person that she was, she gave her mother and Jermaine three hundred dollars as a wedding present. By that time the newlyweds were tired and ready to call it a night, so off to their room they went. They were so happy and in high spirits about now being husband and wife that even a blind person could notice.

After a few drinks of Hennessy, the newlyweds topped the night off with some good, pleasurable, everything-goes sex. Then they fell asleep.

Instead of being at her father's wedding, Denise was getting ready to leave for the San Diego stadium to be entertained by numerous reggae groups. Being that Maurice was Jamaican, the thing he loved aside from his family was his music. When he and Denise had first met, Maurice was a drum player for a popular reggae group. He enjoyed dancing, playing drums, and just about all the exciting things that America has to offer, but one thing he did not like was being crossed, especially by someone who claimed to be his friend, or by someone he had helped in one way or another.

Up until the time that shit start hitting the fan at Denise's residence, things had been going quite well with Denise, Maurice, and Jermaine. But lately, especially after receiving that letter, Denise and Maurice felt that Jermaine was being influenced by Karen to sway away from them. Together, they had made the decision not to be a part of Jermaine's wedding.

"I know that's your father, Denise, but the way I feel about him right now, fuck him and Karen! How in the fuck is he gonna turn on us after all that we've been through! He can't even come talk to us like a real man; instead he e-mails you some stupid bullshit like we're the ones that's wrong! Why should I go to their wedding and pretend like everything's all right when I know it isn't! And I know that bitch had something to do with me being shot, but I just haven't put it all together yet," Maurice said.

"I know she did too, baby." Denise said. "And it's a damn shame that my daddy don't see through her deceit and bullshit. I'll never claim her as a stepmother! Never!"

"I know what's wrong with him, babe; the muthafucka is pussy-whipped. I thought he was smarter than that. How in the hell does he think he can turn a ho into a housewife? That bitch sucked his dick like a real pro and now he's hooked and blinded from reality."

"He'll find out about her in due time, though, and then he's gonna come crying back to us," said Denise.

"Why should she get a job when all she has to do is fuck and suck him when he comes off the road and live like the goddamn queen of the United States? She sleeps until noon every day, and then she wakes up and starts watching Jerry Springer, Maury, and Judge Joe Brown. What kind of fuckin' life is that?"

After that discussion, Denise and Maurice made their way to the reggae concert.

Tyrone was as hot as fish grease. Day after day, while under the influence of alcohol and PCP, Tyrone plotted to get revenge on Karen. The cuts were so deep on his penis that he had to have several stitches and a few surgeries.

"I'm a gangsta!" he shouted after coming home from the hospital.

"Ain't nobody gonna get away with doin' no shit like this to me! I'm gonna kill that bitch, I put that on my hood, I'm gonna kill that bitch!" he repeated as he rubbed ointment on his wounds.

After smoking a couple of joints and turning up a forty ounce of Olde English 800, Tyrone then made two quick phone calls to his homeboys. He could not put this off any longer.

"I'm fixin' to do the damn thang, you know what I'm sayin'. Yeah, I'm about to handle my fuckin' business!" He was talking to himself.

Tyrone, accompanied by two of his most ruthless homeboys, was packing an AK-47 assault rifle, a .44 magnum, and a fully loaded 9mm as they headed to Lancaster in a stolen vehicle. A 2Pac CD motivated them to commit violence and so did the chronic, the PCP, and the Olde English 800.

An hour and forty-five minutes later, Tyrone and his crew stood pounding on Denise's apartment door.

"Who is it?" asked Denise, wondering who in the hell was disrespecting her home by continually pounding.

"This is Killa T. I need to holla at you a minute." He held the gun behind his back keeping his finger on the trigger.

The sound of an unfamiliar voice caused Denise to alert Maurice, who hurriedly appeared at her side.

"Who the fuck is it?" Maurice yelled, in his accented voice.

"Killa T, nigga. Let me holla at you a minute, cuz!"

"That looks like the muthafucka that shot me!" Maurice

said, glancing through the peephole. Then quickly he ran to the bedroom and grabbed his pistol from underneath the mattress.

"I am the muthafucka that shot you, man! Listen, nigga, I didn't come out here to trip on y'all, I just wanna holla at y'all a minute! If you want war, nigga, we prepared for that too, but it ain't y'all I come for; I came for that bitch, Karen. And don't try nothing funny, cuz, 'cause you're in a no-win situation," yelled Tyrone.

Denise attempted to call the police, but Maurice quickly stopped her and then slowly opened the door. Maurice was now standing face-to-face with the man who had recently tried to kill him. Instinct told him that the gangsters did not come to harm him which caused him to hold his gun at his side.

"Check it out, cuz. I apologize from the heart for shooting you, you know what I'm sayin'? I made a mistake, homey, and I'm glad that you ain't six feet under. That's on my hood, homey. I thought you was that nigga who was fuckin' around with my girl. When she told me I had shot the wrong person, you know what I'm sayin', I regretted it, homey. Now I said what I had to say about that and hopefully you can forgive a nigga." Tyrone then initiated a handshake.

"You've got a lot of fuckin' nerves coming back over here, man!" yelled Maurice, angrily.

Seeing that Maurice was getting heated, Tyrone's homeboys revealed their weapons.

"Nigga, I told you that I didn't come here to trip on y'all, but nigga, if you want some drama, then fuck it, we can do the damn thang. I keep tellin' you, cuz, I came here for that bitch! Now let's put these guns away and talk like men, you know what I'm sayin'?"

After everyone had put away their guns and had somewhat composed themselves, Tyrone began boldly enlightening Denise and Maurice on his relationship with Karen. He made sure not to leave out the fact of Karen cutting up his penis.

After hearing this, Denise hated Karen even more. She could not wait to tell her naive-ass father.

"I knew it, I knew it, I fuckin' knew it!" Denise yelled. "That's why she made that comment at the hospital saying that 'Maybe they thought you were somebody else.' That bitch knew who had shot you all along."

Maurice stood, nodding his head, not knowing how to respond.

"When I catch that bitch I'm gonna fuck her up for what she did to me. She can run but she can't hide for long! Anyway, I feel for your father 'cause he's getting played like a muthafuckin' piano, but maybe after you holla at 'im about what I just told you, maybe he'll wake up and smell the coffee. Later, I'll holla," Tyrone said. Then he and his crew left.

When Denise told Jermaine about what Tyrone had revealed to her and Maurice, Jermaine did not believe one single word of it. Before Denise could actually finish telling her father what she'd discovered, he hung up in her face. Jermaine immediately brought up the accusations to Karen, but like always she denied everything. Afterward, she gave him a head job and a ride that was so good to him that everything his daughter had told him was erased from his mind.

The following weekend, Karen came up with the idea of having a party. Even though Jermaine was not the party type, he went along with it to grant his wife's wishes. Actually, the real reason Karen wanted to throw a party was to invite relatives and friends who talked about her when she was down and out, on drugs, and a low-rate prostitute, to see how she was living today. She wanted them to see how God had blessed her with a good husband who loved her and her kids, how she was fortunate to be living in a four-hundred-thousand-dollar home.

Denise had revealed to all of her family members what she had found out from Tyrone and unfortunately, when Jermaine had invited a few of them to the party, they all had made excuses for not being able to come. Even though the majority of Jermaine's family had not met Karen, based on what Denise had told them they disliked her and had no intentions of meeting her.

There were lots of people from Karen's past at the party. She had even gone to the extent of inviting a couple of her tricks and exes, but had introduced them to Jermaine as long-term family friends. Without question, he believed her.

DJ Groove was on the mic and the turntable keeping the party rocking. Hennessy, Remy Martin, gin and juice, pizza and buffalo wings were on the menu, all compliments of Jermaine.

Some people were dancing around the pool, while some were swimming. Jermaine smiled and nodded when seeing a couple have shameless sex in the pool. There were two couples inside the Jacuzzi and others were dancing on the patio, in the kitchen and living room, in the backyard, and even on the stairwell. Karen was dressed in a long peach dress that matched perfectly with her golden necklace and sparkling bracelets, which were both filled with diamonds. Her appearance was totally stunning. All eyes were on her, and the greater part of the conversations were about her. She paraded through her home sipping a glass of Hennessy, smiling and grinning and enjoying the attention she was receiving. Even though she had very bad credit, no money in the bank and nothing to show for her forty years of living, on that day she felt like a million bucks and a queen.

Jermaine was sporting a green short suit and had a pair of matching leather sandals on his feet. Even though he had never been much of a dresser, he still proudly owned a large walk-in closet filled with three-piece suits of all colors, jeans, Dockers, football and basketball jerseys, and he also had a collection of shoes for whatever the occasion might be.

The fact of Jermaine purchasing all the liquor for the party did not influence him to drink any. He was content sipping ice-cold water. He believed in keeping a sober mind at all times. He was a thinker and did not want his thoughts, plans, or decisions to be made while under the influence. Karen would sometimes tell him to loosen up a bit, but he would always respond, "Please, just let me be me. So far, I have been truly blessed and successful being who I am, thinking the way I do, and doing things the way I see fit, so please, sweetheart, don't knock my style, just roll with it and I can assure you that you will never regret our being together."

Jermaine socialized with everyone like he had known them for years. Every so often, while engaged in conversation, he would scan the room looking for his wife. He suddenly had the urge to kiss his wife and dance with her. Little did he know, she had disappeared with three of her old acquaintances. They had gone inside the restroom upstairs and were smoking crack. It had been a while since Karen had taken a hit, and when she was offered one, instead on saying no, her response was, "One hit won't hurt."

"Excuse me for a moment, Lewis. I'll be right back, okay? Hell, I've only been married a little over a week and already I'm missing my wife. I'm in love, man." Jermaine had no idea that Lewis was one of Karen's exes.

Watching Jermaine walk up the stairwell, Lewis thought, *I wonder if that nigga know that his new wife has sucked and fucked damn near every drug dealer and crackhead in Pasadena. Damn, I can still remember how good she can ride and suck a dick.* He smiled and grabbed his crotch while reminiscing.

Jermaine had asked each group of people had they seen his wife, but no one had seen her within the last forty-five minutes. Then he searched inside of every room both upstairs and downstairs, but still no signs of his wife. As he headed back toward the stairwell he heard voices; female voices. The voices were coming from inside one of the restrooms. Slowly, he neared the restroom door, listened for a moment, and then knocked gently.

"Sweetheart?" Jermaine called out. "Karen, are you in there?"

She was paranoid as hell. After taking one hit, she wanted another, then another, and then another until she was totally fucked-up.

"Is Karen in there?" Jermaine asked again.

"Huh?" replied Karen in a low whisper.

"All I want is a kiss and a dance, baby, that's all." Jermaine said sincerely, dumbfounded to what was really going on.

Karen's mind suddenly began playing tricks on her. *He's going to kill me,* she thought. *He knows I'm getting high. He's going to kick down the door and shoot me. Maybe these bitches set me up. I think I hear my probation officer talking. Aw goddamn, he's called my probation officer, the police, and he probably even got in touch with Tyrone. Aw shit, I'm about to die.*

Seeing that Karen was paranoid, incoherent, and stuck on stupid, one of her friends spoke up.

"We're just talking girl talk and about the good ol' days, Jermaine," said Valerie, who was the type of person that could smoke hundreds of dollars of crack and still appear to be normal.

"Okay, I'll leave you girls alone for now, but don't leave

me waiting too long, baby. I need a kiss, a dance, and a few quality moments with you."

"Okay, baby," said another friend, trying to imitate Karen's voice. Karen was so paranoid that she just stood there wide-eyed and still.

Jermaine then made his way back downstairs and continued mingling with the others.

After Karen and her friends had smoked the contents of a thirty-dollar bag of crack, even though Karen was already high as a kite, she wanted more. Neither of her friends had money enough to buy more crack, but Karen had full access to Jermaine's money.

She left her friends inside the restroom and then rushed to her bedroom. Then she hurriedly opened Jermaine's safe and pulled out six crisp one-hundred-dollar bills, along with his ATM card. Shortly after, she and her friends went on the patio to mingle for a few moments and minutes later, without being seen by Jermaine, they nonchalantly eased outside and then quickly climbed into Jermaine's Mustang and peeled out. Lewis witnessed the scenario and smiled. Instinct told him that they were on a get-high mission and would probably end up in Pasadena. His instincts were right.

Meanwhile, Detective Cross and Detective Baker were questioning Maurice. The detectives were glad that his wife was not present. One thing that pissed them both off was a big-mouth, sarcastic, woman who wore the drawers in a house where a man resided.

Momentarily, they were playing the good-cop bad-cop role on Maurice.

"You mean to tell me that you don't have any idea who shot you or why?" asked Detective Cross, who was playing the bad-cop role. He was standing face-to-face with Maurice.

"I told you, man, I don't know who the fuck shot me, okay, so why don't y'all do what y'all do best and go back to a doughnut stand and drink coffee?" replied Maurice in his Jamaican accent.

Detective Cross grabbed Maurice by his shirt collar and then slung him against a wall.

"Okay, asshole, I've had just about enough of your refugee bullshit! I know why the fuck you got shot! You're no different than any of those other illegal aliens that smuggle drugs to the U.S. from your fucked-up country! You guys bring your stinking asses over here thinking that you're gonna come over here and be the man! But let me tell you something, you lowlife piece of shit; I'll have your ass back on that fucking banana boat quicker than you can wink your fucking eye, so don't fuck with me!" yelled Detective Cross furiously.

Then the good cop spoke.

"Think hard, Mr. Banner. Have you been in an argument with anyone lately, or involved in a road rage incident, or banging someone else's woman?"

"Fuck you, man!" replied Maurice. Then he shouted a series of words in Jamaican patois. Even though the detectives did not understand him, they could tell by the tone of his voice and his facial expressions that he was talking shit.

"Come on, Baker, we've got bigger fish to fry. The next time we see this asshole he'll probably be in the fucking morgue. Let's get the hell out of here," instructed Detective Cross.

As the detectives walked away Maurice began yelling at them.

"Fuck you, man! Suck these refugee nuts, muthafucka! I can handle my own shit! You ain't nuthin' but a bitch with a badge, punk! We kill muthafucka's like you in my country!"

Luckily, again the detectives did not understand what Maurice was saying, but Detective Cross made sure that Maurice heard what he had to say.

"I'll tell you what, Mr. Asshole; if I hear anything about an individual or a group of Jamaicans kicking up some dust here in Lancaster, I'm gonna make it my business to come straight for you first since you didn't want to cooperate. And not only will I arrest you, but I will personally make sure that you instantly get shipped back to where you came from! That's not a threat, that's a fucking promise," clarified Detective Cross. The detectives then pulled off.

Maurice was infuriated by their remarks, attitudes, and accusations. He wished that he could have just had thirty seconds with that asshole detective simply to show him how a native Jamaican can get down on the battlefield.

An entire week had passed and Jermaine still not heard from Karen. Realizing how embarrassing this was, he was not going to tell his daughter or any of his family under any circumstances. He would keep this silent for as long as he possibly could.

Jermaine had taken Stevie and Alexus to Jewell's house and had then called his job to request a leave of absence. His aim was to find his wife by all means necessary. He was not concerned or angry about the money and ATM card she had stolen, nor was he irritated by her sneaking away from the party without letting him know. All he wanted was to have his wife back.

Jermaine received his first tip one day as he was about to leave his home. Then the telephone rang; he had practically broken his leg running to answer it.

"Is this Karen's husband?" asked the female caller.

"Yes it is," Jermaine replied. "Who is this?"

"This is Mary, Jermaine. I know where your wife is, do

you? I was inside the bathroom with her at the party that day. If you didn't know, we were getting high smoking crack. I kind of blame myself because I should have never brought the shit out there knowing how weak Karen is, but I didn't hold a gun to her head and make her take a hit," explained Mary.

After a lengthy conversation with Mary, Jermaine climbed in his car and headed to Pasadena. He considered what he'd just heard from Mary, and then thought back to what his daughter had heard about Karen. He planned to immediately admit his wife into a rehabilitation program and stick by her side until she completed it.

Mary had assured Jermaine that she would lead him to Karen, but there was a catch to it: her price was five hundred dollars up-front. Karen had boasted to her friends and family just about each time she talked with them about how much money Jermaine made, about his expensive cars and home, about his success, and about how good of a man he was. With that in mind Mary knew that five hundred dollars was like five cents to a man like him. Besides, Karen had cut her in the face with a box cutter a few years earlier over a hit of crack and this was her chance to get somewhat get even. Each time Mary looked in the mirror at that ugly scar across her used-to-be-pretty face, she secretly hated Karen and wanted to kill her. A year after the incident they reunited as friends over a bottle of wine, a bag of crack, and sex. Ever since then they been cool with one another and had pretended to put the incident behind them.

Jermaine met Mary at a park in Pasadena. Mary then climbed into the car and began telling all that she knew, trying to secure the pay. She told him that after they had spent and smoked up the six hundred dollars Karen stole out the safe, and all she could get from the ATM machine, Karen then pawned the Mustang to a crack dealer. Mary then pointed to her scar, then she went on to tell Jermaine that Karen had been exchanging sex for crack with dealers or whoever offered her a hit. Hearing this negativity about his wife stunned Jermaine, but the bottom line was that he still loved her and wanted her back in his life regardless of what she had done.

After turning a few corners, Mary spotted Karen in an alley, sitting among several drug users smoking crack.

"There she is right there!" Mary said. "Pay me, and I'm gonna hop out."

As Jermaine peeled Mary off five one-hundred-dollar-bills, he never took his eyes off Karen. Momentarily, she was sitting on a grocery cart, looking around paranoid with a box-cutter in her hand. As soon as Mary got out of the car, Jermaine sped toward his wife. Noticing the Beamer and the face of her husband, Karen stood and began running down the alley. Jermaine parked and then jumped out and began running after her, but being the native Pasadena woman that Karen was, she knew what fences to jump, what backyards to hide in, and basically how to ditch him. The addicts that Karen was sitting with did not want to get involved so they continued smoking their crack. As far as they were concerned, Jermaine could have been a parole officer, an undercover police officer, a trick she had beat out of some money, or someone she owed money to.

Chasing after her unsuccessfully, Jermaine abruptly thought of another plan. He turned around and headed back toward the addicts that Karen had been sitting with. Then he approached them and identified himself, and then offered a one-hundred-dollar reward to whoever brought his wife to him. Hearing this, four of the crackheads sprung up from their seats and accepted the mission. Jermaine had parked around the corner.

Knowing that Karen had a box cutter and would not hesitate using it, the crackheads thought it would be best to stay as a group and try overpowering her when they saw her. Unfortunately, an hour and a half later when they found her in a vacant house taking a hit, they attempted to grab her, but two of them got sliced with the box cutter. The other two ran away and headed to where Jermaine was parked to tell him what had happened, and where she was. Even though they were unsuccessful in bringing his wife to him, they still had the nerve to ask him for money. Jermaine reached into his pocket and gave them ten dollars each for their effort.

After two days of driving up and down the streets of Pasadena searching for his wife and asking questions to drug addicts, Jermaine had finally decided to go home. His plan was to rest for a few hours, take a hot long bath, eat, and then return to Pasadena to continue his search. *Damn, I hope she calls me*, he thought.

Once home, he went to his mailbox and took out the mail. Looking over the mail, Jermaine stared at a letter that was addressed to Karen from the probation department. Curiously, he opened it and began reading it. To his surprise, Karen was currently on probation for child endangerment and facing a possible violation if she did not call or report to her probation officer within the next twenty-four hours. He then called the probation officer and made arrangements to meet with her later that day.

Mrs. Carter, Karen's probation officer, was a very attractive, classy, light-complexioned African American woman who appeared to be in her mid-forties. She invited Jermaine into her office and then openly began discussing Karen's probation conditions and current case with him.

"This is how she looked when she was arrested," said Mrs. Carter, showing the picture to Jermaine.

Jermaine could not believe what he was looking at.

Karen resembled the living, walking dead and represented exactly how a person looks who cares more about a hit of crack then they do about their appearance. Her teeth were yellow, her face was totally pale and lifeless, and her hair was uncombed and matched perfectly with the raggedy attire she was wearing. She was tore up from the floor up.

"Karen was in very bad shape before she was arrested," said P.O. Carter. Mrs. Carter then added, "I told her that she could have starred in any horror movie the way she looked. The streets and crack had taken its toll on her, but thank God she was saved by being arrested."

Jermaine sat speechless, staring at the picture.

Out of curiosity, Mrs. Carter asked a question.

"Has she been taking her medication?"

"Medication?"

"She didn't tell you that she was on medication prescribed by her psychiatrists? Karen has been an outpatient mental health case for the past eleven years. Her medication somewhat keeps her mentally balanced. Without it, she's crazy as hell, but if she takes it the way she is supposed to, her demeanor is calm and collected. Taking her medication is the only way that Karen is able to function in the real world," explained P.O. Carter.

"Is that right?" Jermaine asked, shaking his head, stunned by the news he was hearing. Then suddenly he began thinking back to days that Karen acted like a true bitch one minute and the next minute she was sweet as sugar and had no recollection of what she had previously said or done.

"For Karen to be on the streets, on crack, and not taking her medication, that means double trouble, sir. She was diagnosed by three doctors as being a bi-polar schizophrenic, meaning that she has a double personality like Dr. Jekyll and Mr. Hyde. In addition to that, Karen has a history of violence and assaults. I hate to be the deliverer of bad news, but I feel obligated to tell you these things because you're married to her and she's my client. If I were you, I would find her before she ends up dead, or before she does something that will get her life in prison," advised the probation officer.

During his ride back to Pasadena, Jermaine began praying out loud: *Please bring my wife back to me, Dear Heavenly Father. Forgive her as you have forgiven others for their sins. Set her back on the right track, Dear Father. Watch over her and protect her. Take control of her mind, body, and spirit, in the name of Jesus, Dear Heavenly Father. Please Father, I beg you to lead me to my wife and see to it that she comes home with me. In the name of Jesus, Father, let your will be done, and lead my wife back to me today.*

Meanwhile in Pasadena, Karen was a nervous wreck, sitting on the floor in a crack house. Like always, she pulled out her knife after taking a hit and began getting suspicious of everyone around her.

"Nobody move, nobody get hurt," yelled Karen, holding the knife in striking position.

The people that Karen was among had known her for years and were used to her tripping this way whenever she was high. They knew that as long as no one bothered her she would not harm them, but if she felt intimidated or threatened, then it could mean trouble.

Karen had a habit of searching people for weapons who entered a crack house, thinking that they were sent to kill her. Knowing that was how she tripped when she was high, incomers voluntarily let her search them to get it over with so that they could hurry up and get high.

During Jermaine's hunt for Karen, he had finally run across an addict who had recently seen Karen at a known neighborhood crack house. "Man, I'm telling you, I know where she's at, but I ain't goin' inside that damn house anymore. Too many people have gotten killed in that house already, and I ain't about to be another statistic. But I'm tellin' you, man, I just left her about an hour ago, homey. Matter-of-fact, she was standing by the door when I left, holding a long butcher knife, and she was paranoid as hell. That's how she trip when she's getting high, you know what I'm saying. And she ain't the type that'll take a hit and then walk the streets, so I know that she's still inside," said the raggedy man.

The addict told Jermaine that for the price of twenty dollars he would lead him to her.

Jermaine had no choice but to trust the man.

He showed Jermaine where the house was and hopped out of the car, disappearing in a flash. After forty-five minutes of impatient waiting, Karen still had not come out. Then finally he built up courage enough get out of the car and knock on the door.

"Who is it?" asked Karen, holding a long butcher knife at her side.

The others were caught up doing their thing and paid no attention to the knocks

"It's Dino. Open up," lied Jermaine, saying the first name that came to mind.

Karen slowly opened the door and saw her husband standing there bug-eyed like a fish. She instantly dropped the knife, and then embraced him with a hug. They stood crying together.

"I'm sorry, baby. I'm so sorry," cried Karen.

"It's okay, baby. Everything is gonna be all right, okay. I love you so damn much, Karen, that it hurts me. Love hurts, baby, but you know what; no matter how much it hurts I'm gonna keep on loving you till the day I leave this earth. Now let's go home." Hugging her, he led her to the car.

Karen broke out in tears during the ride home and openly confessed to relapsing during the party, confessed to exchanging her expensive wedding ring for crack, and had even admitted to having sex with different men in exchange for crack. After hearing her confessions, Jermaine felt saddened and disillusioned, but somehow managed to put it all aside and be thankful for having his wife back in his presence.

Once they'd made it home, Jermaine ran his wife a nice, hot tub of water and then began preparing some soul food for their evening dinner. While sitting inside the tub Karen began thinking, *Damn, this man still loves me after all that I told him. He's damn sure not the average man. He's heaven-sent, and I really appreciate him. I've got to straighten out my life and start doing the right thing before I lose him. He's the best thing that has ever happened to me and my kids. I shouldn't have taken that hit, but thank God that's over now. I'll treat him to some good head and ride his dick like a bull rider rides a bull. That's a start.*

A few hours later while sitting at the dinner table, Jermaine noticed how fast and sloppy Karen ate, as if she had not eaten in months.

"Slow down, sweetheart. The food isn't going to run away."

Karen slowed down just a bit but still gobbled the food more quickly than Jermaine had ever seen.

After dinner, Jermaine thought that a serious conversation with her was extremely necessary, but he figured that first he would take a nice, hot, shower.

I hope and pray that everything works out between Karen and me, because I can't and will not tolerate any more nonsense or bullshit from her. I love her dearly but I'm not used to that type of lifestyle and I don't plan to get used to it. All I wanted was to have a soul mate that would love me, respect me, and appreciate me for who I am and for what I do. And as desperately as I want some sex from her, there's no way in hell that I could think about it after what she told me. I'm horny as hell, but I can't let my little head overrule my big head. I've got to take her to a clinic to have her checked out before we have sex. I've got to protect myself, thought Jermaine, while showering.

When Jermaine entered his bedroom, Karen was lying across the bed naked, playing with her clitoris, while watching a porno movie.

"Bring it to me, baby," demanded Karen, but Jermaine's mind was far from sex.

"I don't think sex is a good idea tonight, sweetheart. The logical thing to do based on what you've been doing is to first take you to a clinic to make sure you're okay. Besides, we still need to talk." Jermaine then sat at the edge of the bed. Karen continued fingering herself.

"I need you, baby, and I need you right now. Don't worry, I'm clean. If I had a disease I would know it," she replied, rubbing her clit, never taking her eyes off the movie.

"No sex until I take you to have you checked out," clarified Jermaine. The finality of his words annoyed her.

"I don't have a goddamn disease, Jermaine! Goddammit, if I had one I would know!" she replied, raising her voice.

"I don't sense an attitude, do I, Karen?" He could not believe that she copped an attitude because he wouldn't have sex with her.

"Fuck it then, I'll get myself off." She then closed her eyes and imagined Tyrone's huge penis while twirling her pearl tongue piercing in a circular motion. In less than a minute she came. Minutes later she fell asleep.

Dammit, I still didn't get a chance to talk to her. What the hell; I know she's tired from running the streets. I'll talk to her in the morning, thought Jermaine. He then climbed into bed, said a prayer, and then fell asleep.

Jermaine awakened at 5:00AM the following morning. After showering, he then went downstairs and began cooking breakfast. During the course of cooking he seated himself at his computer and attempted to work on his manuscript, but impulsive thoughts of Karen's recent words and activities kept attacking his mind. *I can't hold it any longer. I've got to get this off my chest, right now*, he thought. Then he made his way back upstairs.

He walked around to her bedside and stared at her a few moments. Two weeks of smoking crack and street life had deconstructed her whole damn face. Her jaws were sucked in, her eye sockets didn't look the same, she was already thin but had dropped at least ten more pounds. He shook his head as he looked down at her. *Damn, Karen, why in the hell did you mess yourself up like this? You were so beautiful and innocent looking, but now—*

"Karen, wake up," said Jermaine, but Karen did not respond. She lay there, snoring with her mouth wide open and slobber leaking down its sides.

"Wake up, Karen, we've gotta talk," Jermaine said again, but this he shook her.

"What? Leave me alone. I wanna sleep, baby. I'm tired," replied Karen, without ever looking at him.

Realizing how important having a talk with her was, Jermaine attempted again to awaken her.

"Wake up, Karen." He raised his voice a few notches. "We need to talk right this minute; not in a couple of hours, not tomorrow, not next year, but right now."

Sensing the firmness in his voice, she opened her eyes and gave him a hard look.

"What is more important than my fuckin' rest, Jermaine?"

"Hey, don't get an attitude, okay? I told you last night that we need to talk."

"I know what you said last night, Jermaine, but why in the hell did you have to disrupt my sleep to have a fuckin' conversation? That's disrespectful; that's very fuckin' selfish and disrespectful."

"Excuse me? Did you say that waking you up was disrespectful? Karen, you're unbelievable sometimes, you know. First of all, you disrespected yourself, me, and the kids when you took that hit of crack. Secondly, you completely disrespected me by fucking and sucking other men. Thirdly, and the list goes on, you have no defense whatsoever in the matter of this bullshit, so if I were you I would be grateful and thankful that my mate cared enough for me and had enough love for me to rescue me from the streets."

"What is it, Jermaine? Go ahead and take the stage," replied Karen, propping a pillow underneath her head.

Jermaine sat at the edge of the bed and looked at her.

"First of all, the only way I'm accepting you back is that you go to rehab, a clinic, and to see your probation officer. Do you have a problem with these requests?"

"No, Jermaine, I don't have a problem with them."

"Good. Most importantly, Karen, I want you to know that I'm very disappointed with you, but I do forgive you because I have not been an angel my whole life and God has forgiven me."

"I tried to show you my appreciation last night, Jermaine, but you—"

"Giving me a head job or riding the hell out of my dick is not a way of displaying appreciation, Karen. Sex is merely for pleasure; not for showing thanks or gratitude," Jermaine explained.

"Whatever, Jermaine. Can I go back to sleep now?"

"I don't think so. We've got lots of business to take care

of today so get up and get yourself ready. Breakfast will be done by the time you get downstairs."

Their first stop was at the probation department. A few moments after they seated themselves in the lobby, Mrs. Carter appeared.

"Well, hello, Mrs. Missing in Action," greeted P.O. Carter. Then she led them to her booth and continued talking.

"You don't know how blessed you really are to have a husband who cares so much about you. If it wasn't for him, I would lock you up right now without even hearing your sad story, Karen. I thought that you were on the right track, but once again you had me fooled and manipulated."

"I'm sorry for relapsing, Mrs. Carter. Believe me, I regret it and I know it was a stupid thing to do after all the positive things I have going on in my life. It was a combination of the party, the friends I grew up with that I hadn't seen in years, and the alcohol, that caused me to lose my focus and self-control, which led to my relapse. Once I had taken that first hit, that was it," explained Karen.

"You're always making excuses for your failures, Karen. Ever since I've known you, you have made excuses for being late to your appointments or for not showing up, for relapsing, for not having a job, for being broke, for not having transportation, for having your kids taken away from you, for violent acts that you've committed on people, and basically for just about everything. You cannot go through life making excuses for your failures. I know that your system is full of crack, therefore I am not going to ask you to test, but what I am going to instruct you to do is to enroll, today, into a six-month live-in drug rehabilitation program. Your other option is prison. Actually, you don't have an option, but because of your husband and his concern for you and your kids, I'm giving you the easy way out. Don't fuck up anymore, Karen. This is your last chance from me," said the P.O. firmly, staring hard at Karen.

Their next stop was the clinic. It was a good thing that Jermaine followed his first mind by not having sex with Karen. Her blood sample revealed that she was positive for syphilis and gonorrhea, and she also had crabs. It was a good thing she came when she did. After the results were given, Jermaine pulled the doctor to the side and asked him a question.

"Doc, I feel ashamed to ask you this question, but it's something I really need to know. Is it possible for a man to catch a disease by receiving oral sex from a woman?"

"That's a very good question, sir. If more people asked that same question, there would be a tremendous decrease of sexually transmitted diseases. The answer to your question is yes, simply because women carry more germs inside their mouths than they do inside of their vaginas. Think about it; a rotten tooth, an abscess or bad breath, each contribute to germs and bacteria, which will sooner or later trigger a form of a disease or infection."

"Thanks, Doc."

"No problem. Remember, no question is a stupid question," said the doctor.

Damn, thought Jermaine, walking back toward Karen. *Hell, I can't even get some head from her.*

Then he approached her.

"You see, you could have given me a damn disease, Karen. I'm glad I didn't let my little head outthink my big one."

"Yeah, you do have a little one," Karen mumbled, but not loud enough for him to hear.

"What did you say?"

"Nothing."

Karen was not shocked at all when hearing the test results.

"Shit happens when you're in the street, that's all I have to say," replied Karen. She remained emotionless and unashamed.

Their next stop was to see the kids at Jewell's house. Figuring that Jewell's husband Bobby would have something negative to say, Karen really did not want to go there, but she had to see her kids before leaving for the drug rehab.

After she walked inside, Bobby stared at her with those huge red eyes and shook his head in disgust. Then he took a long gulp of beer and continued silently staring at her. His look spelled hatred.

Karen actually never looked his way nor spoke to him.

Jewell didn't have too much to say to her sister either, simply because she was fed up with Karen's unnecessary shit. Each time Karen relapsed or went to jail Jewell would get stuck with her kids.

Jermaine and Karen sat with the kids a couple of hours and then dismissed themselves to continue taking care of their unfinished business.

Jermaine then took Karen to see her psychiatrist and to get a refill of medication.

Afterward, Karen led Jermaine back to Pasadena to find the crack dealer that she had pawned his Mustang to. She knew exactly where to find him. The crack dealer told Jermaine that he had fronted Karen four hundred dollars in crack in exchange for two weeks' use of the vehicle.

"Y'all ain't gonna beat me out of my time, aw hell naw. Somebody's gotta come up with some serious cheese or I'm keepin' till I get paid in full. That's it and that's all, homey," said the drug dealer.

"Why you tryin' to—"

"Be quiet, Karen, and let me handle this," said Jermaine, interrupting her. He could tell by the tone of her voice that she was about to say something disrespectful that may possibly get him in some shit. He then peeled off eight one-hundred-dollar-bills and handed them to the dealer.

"That's what I'm talkin' about," replied the dealer, handing Jermaine the keys. The man then walked away.

Jermaine then instructed Karen to follow him in the Beamer. He wanted to make sure his Mustang ran the same.

While following Jermaine back to Lancaster, Karen began thinking, *Damn, he really does love me. I better stay on the right track and treat this man with love and respect before someone else gets him. There are plenty of women out there that would love him, respect him, and appreciate him for who he is and for his position in life, especially when he doesn't mind taking care of their kids. I better check myself before I wreck myself.*

Their next stop was a live-in drug program located in Palmdale, California. The reason that Karen had knowledge of the program was because a judge had sentenced her to a year there a year and a half earlier. She completed the program, but after a few days on the streets and being influenced by her crackhead boyfriend she started smoking again.

The program was privately owned and operated by two heavyset African American lesbians named Gina and Pat. When Karen was there previously the State of California owned the place, but seven months earlier the place was up for grabs and fortunately Gina and Pat not only had the money to buy it, but also met the requirements to operate it. The reason Karen had suggested that particular program was because the staff liked her and helped her and even lied for her to get her out of a few jams. She knew that they would show her love, or simply turn their heads if she happened to get herself in any adverse situation.

After Karen and Jermaine completed the paperwork, Gina and Pat began laying down their rules and regulations in a rigid and direct manner.

"During your first thirty days you will not leave the program under any circumstances," said Pat, decisively, giving Karen a solid look. Then she continued.

"There is absolutely zero tolerance here for drugs, alcohol, or any form of sexual activity. There is no horseplaying or fighting! You cannot receive any visits, under no circumstances, until your thirty days are up. Do your chores and assignments as instructed! Lights out at ten PM and everyone here must be out of bed by seven AM. Once working, that is after your thirty days are up, your rent must be paid on time or late charges will incur. Failure to comply with these rules and regulations will result in an automatic termination of program, and your probation officer will be immediately notified."

Karen sensed that she was not going to get along with Pat or Gina, but she was willing to try her best.

"Okay, sir, you can go now," Gina said to Jermaine.

Jermaine then sat down the two duffel bags filled with Karen's belongings at her side, and then kissed her goodbye.

"Jermaine, you can't imagine how much I really love you," Karen said, as he walked away.

"You're just like the rest of them," interrupted Gina. "None of y'all don't even know how to love yourselves, so how in the hell can you love someone else?"

"Excuse me?"

"You heard what I said, I didn't stutter. I can already tell that I'm gonna have problems with you. You must have one of those short-people complexes or something. I don't know why most short people have big mouths. And sir, I told you that you can go. Come back in thirty days, that is, if she doesn't get any write-ups that could keep her inside thirty additional days," Gina said, holding her hands on her hips.

"I love you too, sweetheart," Jermaine responded before exiting the building.

Pat then escorted Karen to her room.

During his ride home Jermaine entertained the thought of finding a local truck driving job. He figured that might be a major factor in getting his marriage back on the right track. He partially blamed himself for Karen's relapse due to his absence.

The following day Jermaine applied and was hired driving for Albertsons supermarket. Because of his experience and good driving record they started him with $18.50 an hour, which was a little less than he was making driving cross-country, but it was enough to pay his bills and was also enough for him to drop at least a thousand in his savings account each paycheck. He was scheduled to begin work in three days. By then Albertsons would have received the results from his background and drug test.

Chapter 6

While sitting on his mother's porch under the influence of alcohol and PCP, Tyrone was contemplating on how to kill Karen for what she had done to him. He refused to put her out of his mind until he dealt with her. He and his homeboys drove to Lancaster twice a week hoping to see Karen, but had not run across her.

"That bitch can run, homey, but she can't hide forever!" Tyrone said to his homeboys.

Boldly, a couple times he had even gone back to Denise's apartment to ask if they had seen her.

"We haven't seen her," Denise said to him.

"Hey man, no disrespect to you or your crew, but I appreciate if you don't come here anymore. I understand how you feel about what Karen did to you, but on the other hand I feel that you are disrespecting me and my house by coming here. After all, man, you did shoot me. I just can't forget about it the way you think I should," explained Maurice.

"I feel you, homey," Tyrone replied. "But one thing I ain't into is kissin' ass, you know what I'm sayin'. I do things gangsta style, cuz, regardless of how the results might turn out, you know what I'm sayin'. Just thank God you living', nigga. Put that shit behind you, cuz, that's all I'm sayin', nigga. But if you see that bitch, holla at me. I gotta keep it gangsta, cuz. I don't care what time of day or night it is, just holla at me. Here's my cell number. Like I said the last time I was here, homey; I apologize for shooting you, and I don't mean any disrespect to your crib or family. I'm just out to get that bitch, cuz."

Tyrone and his crew then walked away.

Denise or Maurice did not feel good about accepting Tyrone's number, but what the hell; they also wanted revenge on Karen. They felt that Karen had betrayed and deceived them and wanted to see something drastic happen to her.

Tyrone continuously shouted from his mother's porch.

"I'm gonna kill that bitch, cuz! She fucked me up for life, and I guarantee you that bitch gonna get what's comin' to her, in a real way!" Tyrone yelled, feeling a streak of pain in his penis.

"I'm gonna kill that bitch, cuz!"

His penis was so sore that he hadn't had sex since Karen sliced it. The doctors had told him that it would probably take close to six months for his wounds to completely heal. They recommended no sex or masturbation. Killing Karen was definitely on Tyrone's mind.

Just as Karen had anticipated, she did not get along with Gina, Pat, or any of the women in the program. Because Karen only stood four foot two, she felt that people always tried to take advantage of her. Regardless of her height, her favorite saying was, "Dynamite comes in small packages!"

After Jermaine had departed the rehab program that day, Gina entered Karen's room.

"I know you've been out in the streets and haven't been

keeping up your hygiene, so first and foremost, I want you to take a shower. And make sure you wash your ass thoroughly," Gina instructed.

Trying to keep the peace and comply, Karen did what she was asked to do.

Gina followed her to the shower, and then stood there watching Karen undress and shower. Gina instantly got wet between her legs watching Karen lather herself up. Her imagination began running wild as she visualized herself making love to Karen.

"Can I have some privacy, Gina?" Karen asked, noticing the look in Gina's eyes.

"When I'm ready for you to have some privacy, you'll have it. Until then, you little tramp-bitch, this is my world and don't you forget it," replied Gina, matter-of-factly.

"I feel uncomfortable. I'm strictly dickly, you know. And even if I wasn't, I would never fuck around with a fat, ugly bitch like you."

"Let me tell you something, you little sawed-off piece of shit; I can make your life a living hell while you're here, or I can make it contented, so you really don't want to get on my bad side." Gina then walked away.

The following morning after breakfast, Pat instructed Karen to clean up the kitchen, the bathroom, rake the leaves in the backyard, and afterward work with the cooks to begin preparing the evening meal for the residents in the program. Karen was furious. She felt that this was a payback for rejecting Gina. The worse part about it was that she had forgotten to take her medication, which meant that she was momentarily mentally off-balance.

"What kind of shit is this? Is this a form of initiation, payback, or what?" Karen yelled, directing her question toward Gina and Pat.

"Listen," Pat said. "You do what we instruct you to do while you're here!"

"Unh-unh, y'all got me twisted! Both of y'all over-weighted, mongoose-looking lesbian bitches can kiss my yellow ass! I'm outta here," Karen yelled. Then she stormed to her room and began packing her belongings.

Minutes later, Karen stormed out of the rehab center, toting her bags. Being in the middle of the desert, the nearest telephone booth was close to two miles away, but driven by anger, Karen made it there. Aggravated by the long, hot walk, and by what had taken place at the rehab center, Karen dialed Jermaine's cell number.

"I've left the program, baby."

"You did what?"

"I refuse to put up with a bunch of bitches hating on me and disrespecting me!"

"What are you talking about, Karen?"

"Just come and get me, okay? I'm hot, frustrated, and feeling dehydrated, and I haven't taken my medication, so please hurry before I fall out," Karen said.

Luckily Jermaine's shift did not start until four PM. That gave him three hours.

Karen then phoned her probation officer to inform her of what had taken place at the rehabilitation center. She definitely had to cover her ass. Trying to be of assistance, Mrs. Carter gave Karen telephone numbers to a couple more programs.

"Karen, I know how bad that mouth of yours is, and I know how defensive and feisty you can be at times. Keeping that in mind, I'm about to call and find out exactly what took place. Don't hang yourself, Karen, you're already walking on thin ice," replied Mrs. Carter.

"I'm not lying, Mrs. Carter, and I wish that people would stop judging me by my past."

"Until you prove to me that you are a 100 percent changed person, I've got to call it like I see it and call it like your record reflects."

"Whatever," Karen answered, and then hung up.

When Jermaine arrived, Karen had already called both of the rehabs and made a decision to check into the rehab in Lancaster. The name of the program was The Straight Way.

After filling out the necessary paperwork and agreeing to the rules and regulations, Karen then went to her assigned room and got settled. So far so good. She sensed no arrogance or superiority in the staff members she had met so far, and the residents she'd met seemed to be cool and down-to-earth. After taking a nice, hot shower, and putting away her belongings, Karen decided to go to the auditorium and listen to a speaker who used to be an addict. He was speaking on his trials and tribulations; how his life was today as opposed to how it was when he was in his addiction.

Practically all the residents attended and were giving the speaker their undivided attention. Already, Karen liked this place.

"I was lost and turned out, my people," said the speaker. "I was living for a high and nothing more. Everything I did and planned to do was aimed toward getting a hit. In the beginning stages of my addiction it bothered me to associate myself with street people, gang members, and drug dealers, but after awhile I had gotten use to it. I didn't care who I was with, how they looked, or where we got high at. I smoked crack inside of service station restrooms, behind trash cans, in vacant houses, walking down the streets, in dangerous alleys, in cars whether they were parked or moving, and I even took a hit once inside my grandparents' house, who were both Christians. I've had sex with two-dollar whores, with fifty-dollar whores, and with women that only wanted a can of beer for some sex. At that time in my life none of that type of stuff bothered me not one bit. I've stole from my parents and relatives, and from the people who really loved and cared about my well-being. But I didn't care what I did or who got hurt behind my actions as long as I got me a hit. I have disappointed so many people who believed in me, but today, thanks to God and my awakening and my acceptance to repent, I have been clean and sober for six and a half years now. God woke me up one Sunday morning and led me to a church and then straight to the altar. Ever since that day I have been a changed man. Today I appreciate my life and I give all the thanks and glory to God."

The speech reminded Karen of herself. She related to everything the speaker had said. Afterward, she suddenly wanted to study her Bible, but first she decided to go take her medication.

Chapter 7

A few months later, while shopping inside a 99-cent store, Denise spotted Karen going down one of the aisles. She hurriedly grabbed her cell and phoned her husband. Karen had not seen her. That day was actually Karen's graduation from the rehabilitation program.

"Baby," Denise said. "That bitch is right here in the ninety-nine-cent store on Valley Central Way."

"Is that right?" replied Maurice. "I think we should leave that bullshit alone, and put it behind us, babe. She'll get what's comin' to her one way or another."

"Why you trippin', baby? We told Tyrone that we would call him when we seen her, and she's right goddamn here, so I'm about to call him."

"Leave it alone, babe. We don't need any trouble. Those damn detectives are lying dead to nail me with anything, so it wouldn't be a good idea to wake up the dead. Leave it buried, babe."

"You're trippin', Maurice."

"Whatever, Denise, just do like I said and leave it alone."

Denise suddenly thought about how Karen had caused animosity between her and her father, then she thought about Maurice being shot, and then she thought about what her Aunt Mable had told her. With all this in mind Denise left the shopping cart in the center of the aisle and left the store. Once inside her car she phoned Tyrone.

"Is this Tyrone?" Denise asked.

"Yeah, who is this?"

"This is Denise in Lancaster."

"Oh, what's up, baby girl?"

"I just wanted to let you know that I just saw Karen in a ninety-nine-cent store out here."

"No shit! Stick to that bitch like glue until I get out there! Follow her and find out where she lives. I'm on my way, baby girl."

"Now listen, Tyrone, I'm not trying to be a co-conspirator to a killing, you know. All I want you to do is teach the bitch a lesson," Denise clarified.

"Yeah, I'm gonna teach the bitch a lesson all right. It's all good, baby girl, don't worry 'bout nothin'," Tyrone said sarcastically, and then hung up.

Denise threw on her shades and sat low in her driver's seat. This was her one chance to get revenge on Karen from what she had done to her husband, and from poisoning her relationship with her father. Before Karen had come into Jermaine's life, Denise and her father used to have daily, open discussions just about any and everything. They cheered together watching Lakers games on television, they went to movies and to lunch occasionally, they rented movies from Blockbuster and watched them until they both fell asleep, and sometimes her father would even ride her bus while she was working. They used to spend lots of quality time together, but not since Karen had been in the picture. Denise was not normally the type of woman who entertained evil thoughts, but this was something different; this pertained to her husband and father. By no means could this be overlooked. It was now time to deal with this heffa.

Karen exited the store carrying a couple of bags, and then proudly proceeded to the bus stop. Then she grabbed her cell and called Jermaine.

"I love you so much, Jermaine. Words cannot explain how much I really love you. I appreciate your love and concern about me, and I also appreciate you staying in my corner and not giving up on me. God blessed me with you, and I promise to never do anything again to jeopardize our marriage and friendship." Her words were from the bottom of her heart.

"My vows were to love you through thick and thin, through sickness or good health, and for rich or poor. What you had was a sickness, sweetheart, and it just would not have been right for me to leave you while you were sick. I take my vows seriously, and like I said in the beginning, I'll love you until the day I die." His words were very intense.

Karen's next call was to her sister.

"Hey, girl," Karen said, in good spirits.

"Hey, Karen, how you doing?" asked Jewell, dryly. Jewell was basically tired of hearing the same old song from Karen each time she relapsed or went to jail. Even though she received a check every month for each kid, it simply was not worth the stress and inconvenience she had to tolerate. She was simply fed up with keeping Karen's kids and more so was her husband.

"You know I graduate today, girl. I feel so good today that I feel like screaming, but instead I'm just rejoicing and praising the lord. God is good, girl, and I am truly blessed. I've been going to church every Tuesday night, Thursday night, and Saturday night, and I've been reading my Bible every single day. Girl, I'm just feel amazingly blessed. Are you coming to my graduation?" Karen asked, hoping that her sister would come and bring the kids.

"Girl, these kids got me so tied up doing this and doing that, to be honest with you I don't think I'll be able to make it. Between your three and my four, my hands are tied twenty-four-seven," Jewell replied.

Even if she didn't have her hands full with the kids, she still wouldn't have gone. She was just simply tired of hearing the same old shit each time Karen got released from jail or graduated from rehab.

"Don't worry about it, sis, I understand. Anyway, Jermaine and I are coming over after my graduation to pick up the kids and take them home. If it's not a problem, please have their clothes ready, okay? Take care and I'll talk to you later." The connection was then broken.

Other than the residents and staff at the rehabilitation center, Jermaine was going to be the only one present on Karen's behalf. Her family members were simply tired of giving her support one way or another and being let down in the long run.

Denise ignored the continual calls from her husband and soon turned her phone off. Karen had just stepped onto the bus.

Denise then started her engine and began trailing the bus by a few car lengths. About twenty minutes later, Karen finally exited the bus and proceeded toward the rehabilitation center. Denise was very careful not to get too close. She had gotten too far to blow her cover.

Moments later, Karen was walking inside of the rehab center. Seeing exactly what house Karen went inside, Denise sped up to it, wrote down the address, and then sped off. On her way back to the 99-cent store to continue shopping, Denise gave Tyrone a quick call, giving him the address and also the directions to Karen's whereabouts.

"Let me know when you've handled your business," Denise said to Tyrone.

"Don't trip, baby girl, I'll let you know," Tyrone replied, en route to Lancaster.

Tyrone sped in and out of traffic, reaching speeds of a hundred miles an hour in hopes to catch up with Karen, but unfortunately the Regal suddenly cut off. He was out of gas.

"What the fuck, man?" shouted one of his homeboys from the backseat.

"The nigga probably out of gas," said his homeboy sitting in the passenger's seat.

"Fuck y'all niggas," Tyrone yelled, hoping that the car rolled to the shoulder, but it had abruptly stopped in the middle of ongoing traffic. People began honking and flipping them off.

"Look at the gas needle. I can't believe this nigga got us to go on a mission and didn't have any fuckin' gas. The fuckin' needle is behind empty, cuz.

"Who got a few dollars?" Tyrone asked.

"Nigga, don't tell me you ain't got no gas or no money."

"That's what I'm tellin' you, nigga. Now, my question was, do any of you niggas got a few dollars?"

"Man, my girl gonna break me off when she get her welfare check, but right now I'm tapped out," replied G Money.

"I don't see why people call you G Money and your ass is always broke. That kind of name belongs to a baller, not to broke-ass nigga," Tyrone said.

"Fuck you, nigga. My day is coming. The first is almost here, so don't trip."

"I ain't made no sales yet, and I had just re-copped, you know what I'm sayin'? A nigga short for the moment, homey, but it'll be greater later," answered Lil' Bo-low.

"I ain't got no money either, cuz. Hell, you're the one that came to get me to go on a mission, if anything, nigga, you should be paying me, but I ain't trippin'," responded Charlie C.

"I don't believe this shit!" Tyrone yelled. "Four niggas ain't even got one funky-ass dollar between them. That's a goddamn shame."

"Blame yourself, nigga. Don't be trippin' on us," said Charlie C.

They soon bailed out of the car and pushed it to the shoulder and left it, and then began walking to the next exit. Tyrone then called one of his homeboys named Papa to pick them up and take them to Lancaster. An hour later, Papa showed up.

"Damn man, I hope I don't miss that bitch! But fuck it, as long as I've got an address, I'm straight," Tyrone said as they pulled off.

Jermaine had purchased Karen a beautiful lavender dress with matching low pumps. He had also paid for her to get a manicure, pedicure, and a bad hairstyle. She looked totally stunning, somewhat like she looked the day of her wedding. She stood proudly, smiling onstage, accepting her award of completion along with a six-month clean and sober chip. She was required to make a speech expressing how the program had assisted her in her thinking, personality change, religion, and was also obligated to discuss her plans for the future. All eyes were on her as she began speaking.

"First of all, I would like to thank God. And secondly, I

want to thank my husband for never giving up on me. His love and support was unbelievably real. Actually, I thought I had lost him when I left home and took to the streets, but thank God we're reunited. I also want to thank the residents and staff for their encouragement, concern, and guidance. Today my thinking is totally different than it was when I was in the world surrounded by sin and cracked out. Crack had completely stripped me of all my qualities and morals. Today, God is the director of my heart and mind and my family is my reason to remain clean and sober. When I was out there I didn't care about if I lived another day, or how I looked, or what people thought of me; the only thing I cared about was how I was going to get my next hit. I thank God that I can see clearly now, and I thank God that the devil has no power or control over my mind."

Jermaine approached her onstage and wiped the flow of tears from her eyes, and then kissed her. Several staff members and residents surrounded her and embraced her with hugs, wishing her well.

"I am so proud of you baby," Jermaine sincerely expressed as he lovingly fed Karen forkfuls of cake that were served at the graduate's reception. Fifteen minutes later, Karen and Jermaine said good-bye, and then left.

Jermaine was very impressed by his wife's speech and appearance, but he hoped and prayed that her interior was just as pure and beautiful as her exterior was. One of his father's favorite sayings was, "A pretty woman without a good head on her shoulders or a good heart, is just like a Rolls-Royce without an engine; it's only good for its looks and nothing more."

Jermaine prayed that would not be the case with his wife.

Before picking up the kids Jermaine treated his wife to dinner at Red Lobster. While eating they talked, laughed, and made future plans to begin taking vacations once a year, and to begin spending more quality time together as a family.

Denise sat quietly thinking on her sofa, waiting for Tyrone's call. *He should have called me by now. I wonder if he already beat her up. I hope he doesn't kill her because that would involve me in a murder. Hurry up and call me, Tyrone.*

Maurice's mind was preoccupied watching Court TV, but he strongly sensed that his wife was up to something because normally she was not this quiet. Each time he asked her was she okay, she responded, "Everything is fine, babe." He could not pinpoint what was bothering her but he definitely knew that something was.

Due to Maurice being on disability, he spent his days watching television, babysitting his son, and occasionally taking walks, trying to rebuild his strength and energy. Being the workingman he had been for years, this type of lifestyle was very hard for him to accept, but during that time he had no other choice. His plans were hopefully to be back working the following month, but his doctor had told him that he would not be completely healed for at least another two to three months.

When Tyrone and his crew reached Lancaster, he anxiously called Denise for directions to Karen's last whereabouts.

"I'm down the street from your apartment, baby girl. How do I get to that bitch's address?" Tyrone asked.

His adrenaline was flowing fast, which triggered his mind to picture exactly how he was going to do this. The joint of PCP and forty ounce of Olde English played a major role in his thoughts as well.

"What took you so long?" Denise asked, playing it off like she was talking to one of her friends.

She did not want Maurice to hear her conversation, nor did she want him to know what was about to go down. She figured she'd wait a few days after the ass-kicking, and then tell him about it. By that time things would have cooled down. Then she went to her bedroom and closed the door, but little did she know Maurice was standing on the other side eavesdropping.

"We had a car problem, you know what I'm sayin', but it's all good right now. How do I get to where you saw her? I gotta handle my business quick, fast, and in a hurry, so I can get on back to the city, you know what I'm sayin'."

"I hear you, but just don't forget to call me and tell me about it," Denise said, smiling. Her day had finally come to get her revenge.

"Don't trip, baby girl, I got you."

After she had given Tyrone the directions, Maurice burst into the room and began yelling in his Jamaican accent.

"I knew you were up to something! I told you to leave that bullshit alone! You're fuckin' hardheaded! You're gonna fuck around and get yourself involved in some serious shit, Denise!" He was furious.

"Calm down, babe, calm down. All Tyrone is going to do is beat the bitch up a little, that's all. So quit—"

"Gangsters don't fight; they shoot and kill people! Did it look like he was trying to beat me up, or kill me? That nigga and his crew didn't come all the way out here to beat up nobody! I thought you had better sense than that, Denise! If something happens to Karen, and that detective finds out that you were somehow conspired, your ass is going straight to prison!" yelled Maurice.

Denise stood wide-eyed thinking about what her husband had said. *He's right. Gangsters don't fight, but they'll kill you in a New York minute. Maybe I should call Tyrone and give him some wrong directions. I don't want to go to prison, and I really don't want to see anything drastic happen to my father's wife. All I wanted to do was just teach her a lesson. Damn, what have I gotten myself into?*

Before the car even stopped in front of the address, Tyrone had already opened the door and hopped out. Then he swiftly approached the front door and began pounding. Seconds later a female counselor appeared.

"May I help you?" asked the heavy set Caucasian woman. She instantly wondered why this hoodlum was pounding on the door.

"Tell Karen to come outside, I need to holla at her!" Tyrone demanded, with a mean look.

"I'm sorry, sir, but Karen no longer resides here."

"You a goddamn lie, bitch!" Tyrone yelled, and then pulled out his gun. "I'll blow this muthafucka up, bitch! Now tell Karen to come outside or else we're comin' in!" He then signaled for his crew.

"Sir, I've already told you that—" Tyrone pushed her to the floor and hurriedly went inside. His crew followed his lead.

The woman remained on the floor panic-stricken while watching the gangsters trot from room to room looking for Karen. She wanted to ease away and dial 911, but seeing the assault weapons quickly changed her mind.

After searching the entire house and still not finding Karen, Tyrone then approached a different female counselor.

"She was here earlier, where in the fuck is she now?" Before the woman could answer, Tyrone slapped the hell out of her and then pushed her to the floor.

A thin Hispanic woman spoke up.

"Karen graduated from the program at noon today, and left with her husband. Neither of us have any idea where she is now. Please don't harm us, sir."

"Ain't that a bitch!" yelled Tyrone, furiously. "You mean

to tell me that she's been living here all this fuckin' time and just all of a sudden moved out today?"

"That's what I was trying to tell you," replied the heavyset woman, still lying on the floor.

The residents and staff were all in a state of shock. They did not know if they were about to die or what.

"Let's get the fuck out of here!" Tyrone said to his crew.

The gangsters then hurriedly ran out the door, and then hopped inside the car and burned rubber.

While making their way back to L.A., Tyrone called Denise and cursed her.

"You stupid bitch, you got me and my homeboys all the way out there for nothin'! You owe me gas money, bitch, or I'm fucking you up, too!"

"Kiss my big, black ass! I gave you the fuckin' address to where she was. Hell, don't blame me because you were too late getting out here. If it weren't for that raggedy car you drive, maybe you would have made it on time," said Denise, with an attitude.

"You betta check yourself, bitch. You can't just talk to me any kind of way."

"Fuck you, nigga. You might scare Karen, but you don't scare me," said Denise, and then hung up before he could say another word.

"I should go fuck her up right now. Big mouth, bitch," said Tyrone. Then he took a long swig of Olde English 800.

The director of the program had called the police after Tyrone and his crew left. Karen had not left anyone a phone number to contact her, which made it impossible for the police or staff members to notify her of possible upcoming danger.

When Stevie and Alexus saw their mother and Jermaine walk through the door, they both sprang up from the floor with joy and ran to their mother's arms. Marvin, Karen's oldest son, gave his mother a mean look, and without speaking he walked past her and went outside. He still had lots of animosity and bitterness toward his mother from her prior relapse and also from when he was placed in a foster home due to her continual drug abuse.

When Marvin was between the age of seven and nine years old Karen beat him with sticks and threw objects at him whenever he got into mischief. He could never forget being tortured by his own mother. Instead of putting him on time-out, Karen would lock him inside a closet after she had severely beaten the daylights out of him. He tried hard to put aside the memories of being tormented by his mother, but the nightmares and disturbing thoughts haunted him almost daily. With Marvin having so much hatred toward his mother, Jewell and Bobby were more than sure that he would at least live with them until he was eighteen. Marvin's mind was completely poisoned by the derogatory things that Jewell and Bobby said about Karen almost on a daily basis. Aside from that, he had witnessed his mother smoke crack on numerous occasions, give strangers who had offered her crack head jobs, and had even saw her on the whore stroll one day while with Jewell and Bobby. He simply wanted to exclude himself from her so-called family thing.

Even though Jewell received a welfare check for Stevie and Alexus, and a check for Marvin, being the kind of man Jermaine was, he still made it a point to give Jewell six hundred dollars each month for the kids' well-being. When Jewell first began receiving checks for Karen's kids, Bobby had persuaded her to purchase a van, since they did not have a vehicle. Actually, they had never owned a vehicle until then.

"Mommy, Mommy," Stevie shouted, running into his mother's open arms.

"Mommy, mommy," Alexus shouted, but instead of running into her mother's arms she ran to Jermaine.

Feeling remorse and suddenly regretting being in and out of her kids' life, Karen began to cry.

Bobby was seated on a worn-down sofa, sipping a tall can of Budweiser. He had spoken to Jermaine, but not to Karen. Jewell did not appear to be happy to see her sister at all. She was glad that Karen was taking her kids back home, but the thought of not receiving those checks anymore irritated her. After all, the checks that she was receiving had paid for her minivan, and would cover her rent and bills each month. The convenience of that allowed her to use her own welfare check as she pleased.

"I can say now that God has made me understand that poisoning my mind and body with drugs is not the way. I love my kids more than anything in the world aside from God, and I will never do anything again that will take me out of their presence," Karen said out loud, wanting Jewell and Bobby to believe that she was a changed person. They had heard that same old song way too many times, so neither of them paid her any attention.

"Praise the Lord, hallelujah, and thank you God. Thank you for my kids and husband, thank you for—"

"Shut the fuck up! Don't you see I'm trying to watch the damn game! Every time you get your ass out of jail or rehab you come here with that same old shit!"

"I feel bad spirits in here, I gotta get outta here quick before those spirits rub off on me," said Karen, making her way to the door.

"Well, get your tramp-ass out of here then!" yelled Bobby. "Ain't nobody told you to come here in the first goddamn place. Fuckin' crackhead bitch." Bobby then took another long swig of beer.

Jermaine remained silent and grabbed the kid's belongings. He then said good-bye and left.

Karen was excited to be back at home with her kids and husband. It had been a long, rough ride for her, but now it seemed like she appreciated life and her freedom more than before.

With Stevie and Alexus trailing at her side, Karen paraded through her home wearing a big smile. This was a feeling that she never wanted to go away. *This is my home*, she thought. *And I will never do anything again to jeopardize what I have. I appreciate my husband and kids. This is a life I never want to leave.*

Stevie was overwhelmed with joy to once again be able to play games on his own PlayStation, to be able sleep in his own bed, and to be able to go to the fridge whenever he wanted.

A few hours later Stevie had fallen asleep playing *Grand Theft Auto*. The controllers were still in his hand.

When Karen had attempted to lay Alexus in her own bed, she had cried and screamed so much that she had no choice but her let her sleep with her and Jermaine. More than likely, she was terrified of the fact of her mother leaving her again.

Once Alexus had fallen asleep, Karen eased next to Jermaine and began slowly massaging his penis and wildly kissing him. His body responded with a super-hard erection as his tongue and lips fell into rhythm with hers. Suddenly, she put her head underneath the covers and began sucking and licking and slurping him so good that his entire body shivered with pleasure. Before he climaxed, she stopped.

"I want it inside me, baby," Karen whispered, and quickly

thought, *I want a baby by him. That way he'll be a part of my life forever regardless of what happens in the long run between us. If he ever decides to leave me, then he'll just have to pay me alimony. Yeah, a baby by him will secure me and the kids forever.* Already, the devil had entered Karen's mind and caused her to think wickedly.

She climbed on top of Jermaine's penis and gave him the ride of his life. The both of them had so much energy to burn, that they had orgasm after orgasm and still continued. They had made love for close to two hours without stopping.

Karen was a little let down because Jermaine could not last longer, but the fact of having his semen inside of her gratified her.

Minutes later, as he was falling asleep, Karen started massaging his penis, and then sucking and licking it, trying to get it hard, but it was no use. It was a dead soldier.

At that moment, she got up and went to the closet and pulled out her favorite big, fat, long black dildo, and then put on an X-rated DVD. She then began satisfying herself. She simply could not go to sleep without having another orgasm.

The following morning, Jermaine awakened Karen at 8:00AM, but for some reason she got agitated.

"Are you crazy?" Karen asked. Normally she would not get up until a little after noontime.

Jermaine had spoken with a friend of his, who was the manager of Target, regarding getting Karen a job.

"I didn't mean to irritate you, but a friend of mines said that he'll give you a job if you fill out an application," Jermaine said, standing over her. "The job is yours. Basically the only thing you need to do is apply."

"A job!" she yelled. "It's eight o'clock in the goddamn morning, and you're talking about a job? I'm tired and sleepy, Jermaine, so please leave me alone for right now." She rolled over and attempted to go back asleep.

"You do want to work, don't you?" Jermaine asked, curiously.

"Not this time of goddamn morning." Now she was really getting irritated.

"I think you'd better take your meds, sweetheart. Then maybe you'll have a different view about what I'm saying."

"Why do I have to work? Hell, you make enough money to pay all the bills and the house note, why in the hell do I have to work? Quit sweating me about a damn job, Jermaine! Please don't piss me off," she replied, and then sprang up angrily. "And let's get another thing straight; I don't need you telling me when to take my fuckin' medication!"

Seeing that she was getting annoyed, Jermaine walked out of the room and had a seat at his desk and began thinking. His intentions were only to get her in the routine of waking up early and in the habit of doing something constructive that would assist on keeping bad temptations or evil thoughts out of her mind. He also wanted to get her in the practice of going to church. *The last thing I need is a woman who confesses to believe in God with her mouth, but her words and actions prove different. And I sure as hell don't need anyone who doesn't want to help with the bills around here*, Jermaine thought.

A few minutes later, Karen appeared at Jermaine's desk.

"Anyway, who said I wanted a job, Jermaine?" Her hands were on her hips.

"Every civilized, sensible human being should want to work, Karen," Jermaine stated. Then thoughtfully he asked her a question.

"You don't exclude yourself from that category, do you?"

"It's too early in the morning for this shit," she replied, then attempted to walk away.

"So you're telling me that you don't want to work?" His eyebrows rose.

"I didn't say that."

"Well, what exactly are you saying, then?" His look was stern and serious.

"Okay, okay. I'll go to the damn job. Fuck it," she responded. Then she walked away mumbling and cursing.

Working was not actually part of Karen's plan. First of all, she was not used to waking up early in the morning, and secondly, her plan was simply to do nothing more than provide him with superb sex.

After being interviewed by the manager, Karen was then given an application to fill out, and then afterward she was instructed to go take a drug test. Thanks to Jermaine, she now had a job, even though the results of her test would take three days for Target to receive. The manager scheduled her to begin work the following day.

After a couple of weeks passed, Karen felt pretty good about the fact of working. She was placed in the electronics department and her hours were from 9:00AM to 5:00PM Wednesday thru Sunday.

Jewell had agreed to pick up Stevie from school and Alexus during Karen's working hours for the small price of one hundred dollars a week.

Jermaine now felt somewhat at ease knowing that his wife was doing something constructive for the majority part of the day. Now that things were somewhat back to normal he could focus more on acquiring foreclosure properties and finishing writing his book.

His agent had recently informed him that his book had been accepted by one of the major publishing houses, and surprisingly a few days later he received a letter of acceptance and also a contract. Reading the acceptance letter, he was overwhelmed with joy and excitement. His dream of having a book published had finally come true. First he called his mother, then he called his sisters, and then he placed a call to his agent.

"Hi, Stephanie! Thank you for helping me make my dream come true," Jermaine said, fervently.

"You did it, Jermaine, not me. All I did was submit it to the right publisher," Stephanie replied.

"I could not have done it without you, Stephanie, and I thank God for bringing us together."

Jermaine was in the third grade when writing his first book. Even then he used to visualize his book on shelves all over the world. His dream was to one day write a book that would be distributed around the whole world and would possibly make him famous. His father used to say to him at an early age: "A quitter never wins and a winner never quits. What the mind of a man can conceive and believe it can achieve through a positive mental attitude. Don't just reach for a hill or a mountaintop, Jermaine; reach for the sky in all that you do. Associate yourself with positive, successful people and their way of thinking and getting good results will someday rub off on you. Always believe in yourself."

Chapter 8

During the next few weeks, heated arguments between Jermaine and Karen began happening on a daily basis. Karen had gone to the extent of breaking or damaging expensive items and furnishings of his. Some days she would go nuts for no apparent reason, and when he questioned her about whether she had taken her medication that would irritate her even more.

One day when Jermaine came home from work he discovered that the DVD player in their bedroom was broken. Stevie told him that Alexus had broken it. Immediately, Jermaine addressed Karen.

"Can't you teach Alexus to keep her hands off things she's not supposed to touch?"

He had recently witnessed Alexus pushing buttons on his amplifier, DVD players, his printer, his plasma screen television, his computer, and a few other things. He loved Alexus dearly, but was not going to tolerate belongings which he worked so hard for to continuously get broken.

"You better not say a goddamn thing to my kids about

your materialistic-ass shit! Kids are going to be kids, and if you can't accept that, then you shouldn't have married me!"

"You're only saying that because you didn't buy any of this so-called materialistic shit! When I met you, you were pushing a goddamn baby stroller down the street, Karen! You didn't have a fuckin' pot to piss in!" Jermaine yelled angrily.

The thing that really upset him was that Karen did not believe in disciplining Stevie or Alexus in fear that they would get taken away from her by children services. Being on probation for child endangerment, she really had to be careful how she treated her kids. They had already been taken away from her a couple times in the past and she did not want that to happen again. Basically, she let them do whatever they wanted to do.

Jermaine had always been the laid-back, easygoing type of guy who did not like to fuss or fight. Karen, on the other hand, had been used to that type of lifestyle since her early teens.

Early one Sunday morning, Jermaine and Karen were arguing because Karen had not checked the oil and water in his Mustang. She had a habit of driving fast, tailgating other vehicles, and strongly applying her brakes at the last minute. The worst thing about it was that she was in denial and never would admit her faults. Before she and the kids pulled off, Jermaine ran out the front door and hurriedly approached his Mustang. Instinct told him to check all the fluids.

"Unbelievable!" he yelled. "There's not a drop of water in the radiator, it's two quarts low on oil, the transmission fluid is low, and to top it off the goddamn brake cylinder is dry! Are you trying to blow up my goddamn engine?"

"Fuck you, Jermaine! All you care about is what you

spent money on! You're a very selfish muthafucka, do you know that? You don't give a damn about nobody but yourself!"

"Like I said over and over; you only say things like that because your money didn't pay for a damn thing. You have demonstrated that you don't give a damn about people's belongings or feelings, and I'm sick and goddamn tired of it!"

"Well, that's just too fuckin' bad, Jermaine. As a matter of fact, we're married now and that means the cars, the house, and everything inside of the house doesn't belong to just you anymore; it's mine, the kids, and yours. Don't get that twisted. I really wish you would quit tripping on materialistic shit!"

"Ain't that a bitch?"

"Fuck you!" Karen yelled.

"Double fuck you, you minimum-wage bitch!" Jermaine yelled, furiously. He was overheated and out of control, feeling totally disrespected. This was actually the first time he had cursed in the presence of the kids.

Karen sat angrily a few moments thinking, and then suddenly she stepped out of the car and composed herself, and then dropped the bomb on him.

"The bed that you bought and sleep in when you're home, I just want you to know that I've been fucking Tyrone, Lester, and big dick Danny in it while you're so goddamn busy making money. Umph, as big and long as their dicks are, I'm surprised you couldn't tell when you called yourself fucking me last night." She now felt that she'd gotten even for the verbal beating he had given her.

Before responding, Jermaine stood in a daze. The kids remained seated inside the car.

"Hand over my keys, Karen," demanded Jermaine, but she refused to do so.

"Fuck you! I told you already that this isn't your fucking car, it's ours. What's the matter, Mr. Big Stuff, did I break down your little ego? Are your feelings hurt because I told you I've been fucking men with big dicks?" She was in his face, smiling.

"Give me my fucking keys, Karen." He was getting angrier.

"Fuck you!" She stood there, still smiling, holding her hands on her hips.

She then attempted to get back inside the car, but Jermaine quickly snatched the keys from her. Karen reached underneath the driver's seat and pulled out a long butcher knife and approached him. She held the point of the knife at his neck.

"Don't fuck with me, Jermaine! I'll kill you, muthafucka! Fuck you, fuck your ugly mama, and fuck your fat, pigeon-toed daughter, and your stupid, conceited sisters! I hate your whole fuckin' family, fuck all of them!"

Karen had never met Jermaine's mother, but had spoken with her over the phone a few times. One thing that irritated the hell out of Karen was when Jermaine confided in his mother about certain issues, or plans, or marital situations he was having. One day Karen went into a frenzy when Jermaine had called his mother and asked her how to make a banana pudding and how to cook lasagna. Karen strongly felt that Jermaine should not ask or confide in his mother for anything.

Observing what was now happening, Stevie jumped out of the car and ran to his mother. Alexus remained sitting, wide-eyed.

"No, Mama! Put that knife down, Mama, put it down!" yelled Stevie, trying to wrestle the knife from his mother's hand. Finally he retrieved it and then took off running.

Karen then turned around and punched Jermaine in the face, then attempted to grab his testicles, but fortunately

Jermaine grabbed ahold of her and pushed her away. He could have easily picked her up and body slammed her, but he was not the type of man who hurt women.

Karen then pulled herself up and hurriedly grabbed Alexus out of the car, and then took off jogging toward Stevie, who knelt, crying, about thirty yards away. Karen then grabbed Stevie by the arm and began walking toward the main street.

Jermaine had mixed emotions. He thought about calling the police to have Karen arrested, but quickly dismissed that thought. *Maybe she hasn't taken her medication. If I have her arrested then she's going back to jail for violating her probation and an assault charge. The kids will go to a foster home, and—. This is fuckin' mayhem. What have I gotten myself into? She pulled a fuckin' knife on me, hit me, told me that she'd kill me, and then tried to grab my damn balls. And on top of that she's been fuckin' another man in my bed. I should have socked the shit out of her, but then I would go to jail. I have too much to lose to be locked up. Please, Lord, I beg you for strength and guidance to deal with this.*

Needing someone sensible to talk to, Jermaine called his mother. Afterward, he put his pride on a shelf and called his daughter. He told them both what had taken place.

"I'm going to let you make your own decision, son. Do what you think is best for you and your future," his mother told him.

"I told you that she was no good, Daddy, but you wouldn't listen. With her knowing you won't hit her, she's going to do it again if you take her back. You should have called the police on her. If she didn't think enough to realize that any crime she commits could result in the department of children services taking her kids away, then why should you care?" Denise said.

Karen led the kids to some shade in front of a church about fifteen miles from Jermaine's home. As Stevie and Alexus played tag, Karen sat thinking. *Damn, I've really fucked up now. I regret everything I said and done to him, but I know it's probably too late for regrets. I should have taken my fuckin' medication, then I wouldn't have acted like that.* Then suddenly she fell to her knees and began praying. "Lord Jesus, please forgive me for my actions and for what I said to my husband. I only said those things out of anger because I hadn't taken my medication. Please forgive me, Lord. I do love and appreciate Jermaine, and I know that you blessed me with him, Lord. Please set my marriage back on the right track and forgive me for my sins. Cleanse my mind, Lord, and bless me with more wisdom and understanding. I ask these things in Jesus' name. Amen."

A couple hours had gone by before Karen pulled herself together and began walking back home.

Once she arrived at the house, because Jermaine had taken the keys from her, she knocked on the door. Sensing that Jermaine was still angry and disappointed with her, Karen asked Stevie to respond.

"Who is it?" Jermaine asked from the restroom just inside the front door, where he stood, nursing his wounds.

"It's me," answered Stevie.

Alexus mimicked him like always. "It's me."

Seconds later Jermaine appeared at the door and let them inside.

"Daddy, Daddy," screamed Alexus, excited to see the man she thought was her real father. When Stevie saw the look on Jermaine's face, he headed to his room, sensing an argument. Karen attempted to kiss Jermaine, but he calmly pulled back.

"I'm sorry, baby," Karen said. "I didn't mean any of that

stuff I said, and I do regret pulling a knife on you. I hadn't taken my medication, and I guess I just turned into an instant devil." Then she had a seat at the dining room table and began crying. Without saying a word or even looking at her, Jermaine returned to the restroom and continued nursing his reddened eye.

As if nothing had happened between them, Karen followed him to the restroom and closed the door behind her. Then she approached him and unzipped his pants and then pulled out his penis and began sucking it. At first, Jermaine was not in the mood, but after a few slurps, licks, and sucks which triggered a super erection, he was all into it. It was all good.

Later that night after the kids had fallen asleep, Karen lay next to Jermaine naked and continued to try to make up for earlier physical and verbal abuse she had dished out. Sex still was not quite on Jermaine's mind, but Karen was simply irresistible when it came to sex. She began licking his testicles while stroking his penis. Then she started sucking it slowly and wetly licking it up and down its shaft. It felt so good to him that he suddenly forgotten about the vulgar words, the knife in his neck, and being kicked and slapped earlier. She took his cum in her mouth, and then rode him to sleep.

The following day things were back to normal between Jermaine and Karen, but Karen's words continuously tore Jermaine's mind apart. *The bed that you bought and sleep in, I just want you to know that I've fucked Tyrone, Lester, and big dick Danny in it* . . . He just could not seem to block those words out of his mind.

Jermaine decided to give Jewell and Bobby a visit, hoping that they could enlighten him a little more about his wife and his feelings about certain issues. With Jewell being

Karen's sister, Jermaine felt that if anyone could shed some light on Karen's behavior, Jewell could.

As usual, Bobby was seated, sipping a twenty-four ounce can of Bud. Momentarily, Jewell was changing her baby's diaper. After seating himself, Jermaine then began articulating what happened.

"I couldn't believe it, Jewell. She poked the tip of a butcher knife in my neck, then socked me a couple times in the face, and then kicked me in the ass. Then for no reason at all, she started calling my mother and daughter bitches and whores. Did she act this way toward all of her past boyfriends and husband, or is it because she figured I'm not going to hit her back?"

"It's not you, Jermaine, it's her," Jewell assured him.

"Man, that bitch is just crazy as a muthafucka, that's all," injected Bobby, after taking a long swallow of Bud.

"I mean, she was carrying on like a jungle woman or something. After all I do for her and her kids I don't deserve that kind of treatment," Jermaine explained animatedly.

"Ain't nuttin' jungle 'bout the bitch, she just ghetto as a muthafucka. Man, you gotta understand that she ain't neva' had a good nigga like you. The only kind of niggas she's ever had was ghetto fabulous muthafuckas, that's why she's the way she is. That bitch ain't neva' had an educated nigga with a good job that offered to take care of her and her crumb snatchers," Bobby explained. Then he took another long gulp of beer and continued. "Man, I'm tellin' you, she's been through more niggas in two years than the average woman goes through in a lifetime. I'll bet that her pussy is tore the fuck up and is probably wide as the muthafuckin' sky," said Bobby, then burst into laughter.

Jewell then spoke up. "The thing is that my sister just isn't used to a man like you, Jermaine. No man has ever bought her kids a damn thing but you. You buy those kids name-brand clothes and shoes, and you're always buying them whatever they ask you for. You've got to understand that she has had bad luck with men since junior high school. Stevie and Jasmine's daddies are crackheads from way back, Alexus's daddy is a wannabe gangbanger, but the nigga can't stop smoking that crack, and Marvin's daddy, hell, Karen gave him some pussy the first night, moved him in the next day, and a month later she found out that he'd been fucking everything with a pussy in the projects where she lived. After she got on that shit she started selling pussy and dealing with any man that had some dope or a few dollars. So now you should have a clear view of the type of men my sister has been with for the past twenty-something years."

"The bitch ain't no good, anyhow," yelled Bobby. He took a long gulp to finish what was inside the can, and then began talking again. "What woman in her right mind would leave her kids at home alone at two o'clock in the fuckin' morning to go buy some goddamn crack? What kinda woman would leave her kids with her sister for months and months at a time while she run the streets selling pussy and smoking dope? What kinda woman in her right mind would keep introducing her kids to different men and tell them to call him Daddy? I'll tell you what kinda woman would do that, man: a woman that doesn't give a fuck about nuttin'! I hate to say it, man, but how in the hell can that bitch love you and she don't even care about herself or her own kids?" Bobby then went to the fridge and grabbed another beer.

"Karen doesn't appreciate you, Jermaine. She's used to street niggas. That's it and that's all."

" 'Cause the bitch is retarded, that's why! She needs a fuckin' mental tune-up, that's what she needs!" yelled Bobby, then seated himself.

With an open mind, Jermaine sat listening to the people who had known Karen for practically all of her life. They expressed things about her that he really did not care to hear, but needed to hear for his own good.

"Man, you better make sure that bitch take her medication too, because if she doesn't, man, you're gonna catch hell. That heffa gets violent, loud, and ignorant as a muthafucka when she don't take those fuckin' psych meds. She's been to prison two times for assault and once for attempted murder. Apparently, nigga, you ain't done your homework. Your ass got sprung on her pussy and head, and then married the bitch," Bobby said, then busted into laughter again.

Having heard enough negativity about Karen, Jermaine excused himself and left for work. When he walked out, Bobby was still laughing.

On numerous occasions Jermaine had witnessed Karen driving his Mustang fast and recklessly. He was the type of driver that never appeared to be in a hurry. One of the mottos he lived by was "Whatever a person doesn't take care of, will sooner or later let them down."

One day after seeing her turn a corner doing about thirty miles an hour, he thought, *Damn. I've got to get her out of my Mustang before she tears it up. I'll buy her a bucket tomorrow. That way she can screw up her own car rather than mess up mine.*

The following day, two good things happened for Karen while she was working. The first good thing occurred during her lunch break. Jermaine approached her and a few coworkers standing in front of Target and handed her a set of keys.

"Here baby, these fit the ignition to your Honda Accord," he said, smiling. Then he grabbed her hand and led her to the car. Like Romeo and Juliet, they hugged and kissed all the way to the car. Her coworkers looked at one another in complete jealousy.

"I wish my man would buy me a damn car. Hell, I have to ride the bus to work every day," said one coworker.

"I wish I had a man," voiced another coworker.

"Hell, she should appreciate her husband and quit hitting on Rodger. One day while I was showing her where I wanted a new product shelved, hell, she couldn't keep her eyes off Rodger's dick imprint. I mean, it's obvious the man is packing beef, but the way Karen stared at it was shameless and made me turn my head, girl," said Karen's department manager.

"Yeah, you ain't lying, because she's damn sure been paging him to electronics an awful lot lately," said another worker.

"Rodger? You mean old tired-looking Rodger?" asked Shaquita.

"Yeah, I mean old tired-ass Rodger," replied Dot. "I know damn well all of y'all have seen his big dick print in those tight-ass pants he be wearing all the time. Hell, it looks like the man has a damn anaconda between his legs, how can you miss it? I'll bet that every woman who works here have seen that big, long snake between his legs."

"Hell, I see it just about every day, but it doesn't excite me. Rumor has it that he can't do a damn thing with it but piss. Mary told me that the damn thing don't even get hard, girl."

They busted in laughter a few moments until another asked a question out of curiousity.

"What could Karen possibly want with Rodger? Hell, he couldn't have any money working here at Target with us," stated Meagan, and then exhaled her cigarette smoke.

"It's not always money, girl. Haven't you ever saw those movies where the woman is filthy rich, but ain't got a dick in her life. Or that woman whose always home alone because her husband is constantly away on business. Hell, I even heard of a case where a husband couldn't satisfy his wife so they both agreed to drive to the ghetto and pay a black man with a big dick to satisfy her. I'm telling you, girl, it's some weird people out there," explained Dot.

"But that's not the case with Karen. Hell, she had a good man that takes care of kids that aren't even his, he makes damn good money, and from what she tells me he has money invested in real estate, and he wrote a book. The only thing I can think of is that she's a freak for big dicks," said Shaquita.

"Just because she tells you that she's happy and content doesn't mean she really is. People will tell you what they want you to know. If she were happy and satisfied with her husband then why in the hell would she be staring at Rodger's dick? Besides, you guys are missing the whole point! Just because her husband is this and that, does not mean he's fucking her right! Women like to be fucked, licked, and caressed slowly and gently, and—"

"Calm down, Dot, before you get wet between the legs," another worker said.

It had been years since Dot had a piece of dick. She had to suddenly excuse herself to go to the restroom. Talking about sex caused her to get soaking wet, but she did not want the others to know.

The one thing Dot had been right about was Karen's attraction to Rodger. Rodger was sixty-four years old, tall and slender, and dark brown complexioned. Even though it was 2004, Rodger still chose to dress as he did in his forties and fifties, wearing tight clothes and outdated shoes. Most of the Target employees made fun of him whenever they would see him, but not Karen. She smiled whenever she saw him. Regardless of Rodger's appearance, he possessed something she liked: a long, fat dick.

An hour prior to Jermaine showing up, Karen had put aside her job responsibilities to go look for Rodger. After searching with no success, she decided to page him over the intercom to her department. Dot had also heard the page and decided to be nosy. Nonchalantly, Dot stood on the next aisle pretending to be stocking product, but was actually waiting for Rodger to show. When Rodger finally showed, unfortunately Dot could not clearly hear their conversation, but heard enough to spread to employees and managers throughout the store.

"Did someone page me to electronics?" asked Rodger. Like every day, he had on those skintight pants.

"Yes, I paged you, Rodger," Karen replied, smiling. She tried to give him eye contact, but could not keep her eyes off that huge, long imprint in his pants. She suddenly wished she could put her hand inside his pocket to get a quick feel. *Boy, would I like to ride that*, she thought.

"How may I help you, Karen?"

"Actually, I just wanted some advice from you, Rodger. With you being a senior employee and all I felt that you would have more knowledge than other employees here about certain things. I hope you don't mind me taking a little of your time," Karen said, smiling, while throwing occasional glances at his crotch.

"Not at all, Karen. It's my pleasure to be of assistance to people."

"There are a few things inside the employee handbook that I don't quite understand and if you don't mind, I'd like for you to clarify some of those things after work. It seems like all the department managers and store managers are always too busy to clarify things to me, so if you don't mind, I'd like you to."

"That would be my pleasure. Anything I can do to help a

fellow employee makes my day," replied Rodger, with a big Target smile.

He then gave her his home address and agreed to go over the entire employee handbook with her at 6:30PM, fully aware of her intentions.

Chapter 9

Denise was mad as hell at Karen for taking advantage of her father. During her anger she continuously tried calling Tyrone, but unfortunately he kept hanging up in her face. He was still upset at her for having him make a blank trip. Denise then began calling family members informing them on what had taken place, but each of them had told her to let her father resolve his own issues. They had also advised her to not try and come between her father and his wife. Knowing that her father was the calm type and nonviolent, Denise felt that she had to step up and do something. This had now gotten personal.

A few hours later, Tyrone finally decided to call Denise back.

"What's your problem?" Tyrone asked, with an attitude.

"Have you forgotten about what that bitch did to you or something? The reason I ask is because I haven't heard from you. Talk to me, what's up?" asked Denise.

Maurice was at work and her son was asleep. She had nothing better to do than to plot revenge.

"Bitch, you had me and my homeys come all the way out there for some bullshit! Why in the fuck you keep callin' me? You must think I'm some kinda goddamn toy or something!" Tyrone took a long swig of Olde English 800.

"I wish you would stop calling me a bitch. Your bitch is the one who sliced your dick and played you like a piano."

"What?" He could not believe she was talking to him like this.

"You heard me." Her aim was to get him angry enough to come back to Lancaster.

"I know you didn't say what I think you said."

"Yeah, I said it, now what?" Denise was getting bolder.

"You betta check yourself!"

"Anyway, how is that wound of yours?" she asked sarcastically.

"What the fuck do you want? I ain't got time for this bullshit! Have you seen Karen or you just need a conversation?"

"No I haven't seen her, but I'll know where to find her within a day or so."

"Well holla at me when you got somethin' solid, and don't call me with no more bullshit," Tyrone said, and then hung up.

She had not been to her father's house since he'd gotten it remodeled, but today she planned on paying him a lengthy visit. After all, she was Daddy's little girl, regardless of his wife, his mother, or any other woman that thought she could come before her.

Later that day Denise treated her father to lunch at Sizzler. To her surprise, she gained much more than she had anticipated. With Jermaine not having any more blood relatives within a couple hundred miles, he gave her a spare set of keys to all of his cars and also to his home, and also gave her the combination to his safe. He was preparing himself for if something was ever to happen. Based on what he found out from Karen's relatives and from people that had known her for years, he felt that she was definitely capable of physically harming him, especially if she had not taken her psych meds.

After lunch, Denise followed Jermaine home. Everything was going as planned.

When entering her father's home, she could not believe the renovations he'd made.

"Daddy, your house is beautiful and so immaculate. Where did you get all this good taste?"

"I guess I got it from my mama," he replied, smiling.

"I guess so. I never knew that a man could have such good taste in decorating a home. Now when it comes to cars, I know guys have better taste than women, but furnishing and decorating a house is another story."

"I like nice things, and like things to coordinate."

Once she stepped inside Jermaine's front door, the new marble floor immediately caught her eye. Inside the living room there was a beige sectional sofa that had recliners at each end. To the right of the sofa there was a hundred-gallon aquarium filled with exotic saltwater fish. On the wall there were pictures of tigers in the jungle and African art.. Also, there was a five-shelf glass stand where he had placed numerous African art pieces that matched perfectly with the pictures. Making her way to the dining room, Denise noticed another beautiful picture of an African American family sitting at the table blessing the food at breakfast time.

"Ooh, Daddy, I love that picture. How much did it cost?"

"I think it ran me about four hundred."

"Four hundred dollars for a picture?"

"Sometimes when you really want something you don't

care how much it costs. I call it treating yourself," Jermaine replied, smiling.

"I guess," said Denise.

Jermaine then showed her the two rooms that had been added on during the time he had moved in with her. He had converted one of the rooms into a family room. The other room that he referred to as his game room had a pool table, an air hockey game, and a chess table, a 42-inch plasma television on the wall, and had even had a wet bar built.

"You are something else, Daddy."

"You only live once, baby, and you've got to do it right."

After seeing his backyard and upstairs, Denise gave her father a kiss, and then left.

She wasted no time stopping at the nearest phone booth to call Tyrone.

"Don't be bullshittin', Denise. The homeys are already mad at you for making a blank trip out there the last time," Tyrone said.

"Man, I ain't got time for this. I'm telling you that she lives with my father. If you don't believe me, then fuck it, stay your black ass in LA. And one other thing: under no circumstances do you harm my father. He doesn't have anything to do with what Karen did to you and he has nothing to do with any of her bullshit. As a matter of fact, I think he's on the verge of divorcing her."

"Don't trip, baby girl, I ain't got no beef with your daddy. It's all good. I'm on my way."

Tyrone then immediately called a couple of his homeboys to go on a mission with him. Like always, they were down for anything and ready to bring on the drama.

Meanwhile, Karen was sitting next to Rodger on his living room sofa. When she had gotten off work she could not wait to pay him a visit. *Make my day, Rodger, make my day,* Karen thought.

"I really enjoy working at Target, but it's my future that I'm concerned about," Karen said, while sipping coffee.

"Well, let me tell you, Karen, if you're looking for a company that's going to give you a whole lot of money and benefits, then you're employed by the wrong place. I've been a Target employee for a little over six years now and as far as raises or benefits I have seen no changes. Of course, there's been talk about it like at any other company, but that's about it," Rodger explained.

Karen's mind was elsewhere as he spoke. Her eyes were on the long, fat bulge between his legs. Rodger continued talking about his experience at Target. Realizing she did not have much time to work with, Karen decided to make a move. She sat her coffee cup on the table, and then leaned over and boldly began kissing Rodger, while slowly rubbing his bulge. He started to pull out his dentures to better respond to her kisses, but quickly dismissed the thought. There had been numerous female employees who had spotted Rodger's penis print. Some had asked him out to lunch, some had asked him to come over to do maintenance around their apartments or homes, and others had asked him to sit with them during breaks. Rodger was overwhelmed by the advances and attention he was getting, but the thing was, he could never get it up. His penis was a dead soldier.

Seeing that his penis was not responding to her kisses and caressing, Karen then unzipped his pants and whipped it out. Rodger smiled and sat calmly, letting her do her thing even though he knew it was pointless.

"Damn, it's so big and long. It feels good in my hand, but I bet it will feel even better inside me," Karen said, while stroking it.

"Yeah, that's what they tell me," said Rodger, proudly. Her touch felt good to him, but it would have felt even better if he would get hard.

"Why won't it get hard? Most men respond to my touch with an instant erection."

"Well, it must be you, because I don't have a problem getting hard for any other woman, so it must be you," Rodger lied. He knew that his penis was useless as far as sex was concerned, but he enjoyed women caressing it and playing with it in hopes that they would begin sucking it.

Karen stripped out of her clothes, then she positioned Rodger at the edge of the couch, and then she got on her knees and began licking his fat, long, snake and sucking it nice and slowly. Rodger felt like he was in heaven. He took off his bifocals and relaxed, smiling, enjoying the pleasures of her lips and tongue.

"Damn, that feels good. This is the best head job I've ever had in my life."

Karen was not in the mood for flattery. She wanted to ride it. She sucked, licked, slurped, and did everything possible to get it hard, but the damn thing would not budge. She then tried turning on some music, dirty dancing for him, but that did not work either.

"Damn, Rodger, your dick won't respond to anything I do."

"Then maybe you should try something new."

"Let me see if I can get the head in, then slide down on it and ease it in."

"Oh, I like the way you talk," replied Rodger, smiling and grinning.

She then climbed on top and attempted to put it inside her hoping that her hot, juicy, wet pussy would cause it to stiffen, but still it was no use. The damn thing just would not respond.

"Damn Rodger, what's going on?" She was tired, frustrated, getting angry, and now ready to go home and watch a porn movie to get herself off.

"It's you, baby. Let's start over, maybe it'll be different this time," Rodger suggested, smiling.

Karen had already begun getting dressed. Rodger remained on the sofa, wanting her to suck it and play with it some more.

"I've got to get you some Viagra," Karen said, picking up her purse.

"If you think that will work, then go ahead and buy some. What I really think you should do is try it again," Rodger suggested, smiling, stroking his penis.

"Thanks for inviting me over. You have a good day and I'll see you tomorrow at work. Oh, and please don't go running your mouth to the people at work about our business. If you be a good boy, tomorrow I'll bring you a couple pills of Viagra. It doesn't make sense for a man to have a dick that damn big and the damn thing won't even get hard." Then she walked out and closed the door behind her.

Rodger sat back, smiling stroking his penis, and then suddenly remembered the video camera was still going. He got up and took the disk out of the camera and then put it inside his computer and began watching it.

So far, Rodger had videotaped over twenty-five Target employees, naked and in action trying to get him hard. Even though his penis had never gotten hard during any of those events, he enjoyed watching the movies for his personal entertainment. Thinking about the different techniques women used on him kept a smile on his face while working.

When Karen finally made it home, she walked inside to an infuriated husband.

"Why are you so late getting home?" Jermaine asked, knowing that she had gotten off work almost two hours ago. He had gotten off early and had already picked up the kids.

"I had to take care of some business," Karen lied.

"Mommy, Mommy," shouted Stevie and Alexus, running toward their mother. She tried to block Jermaine out and give the kids her attention, but Jermaine was not quite finished with her.

"I bought you a cell phone to keep in contact with me, Karen. If you had business to take care of then why didn't you let me know?"

"I thought I was a grown-ass woman. And why is it that you're trying to keep tabs on me? If you don't trust me, you shouldn't have ever married me," she said with an attitude.

"If I knew half the things that I know now, believe me, I wouldn't have ever said 'I do'."

"Oh well."

"And look at this house, it's a mess! The damn toilet is stopped up, because Alexus dropped something inside it, my keyboard doesn't work because she spilled milk inside it, the vertical blinds are bent and have black scribbling all over them, there's Kool-Aid and milk stains all over my new sofa, and my goddamn plasma television has ketchup and scratches on the screen! Will you please discipline and control your kids?" Jermaine was extremely heated.

"I've had about enough of your shit, Jermaine! All you do every day is fuckin' complain about my kids and I'm tired of it! Kids are going to be kids!" she yelled.

"I realize that kids are going to be kids, but there is such a thing as disciplining them and teaching them right from wrong. I ask you not to let them eat or drink inside the living room, but you insist on letting them. I ask you to pop

Alexus on the hand when she's messing with my belongings, but you don't do a damn thing but say, 'Stop, Alexus,
I'm gonna whip you,' but you never spank her. All you do is
threaten her."

Jermaine then suddenly diverted his attention to Stevie.

"Stevie, take out the trash and go clean up your room!"

Stevie started crying. Karen felt she needed to speak up.

"I don't feel that Stevie should have to take out the
trash! You take it out, Jermaine!"

"What?" He could not believe that she had said that.

"You heard me, goddammit, I said you should take out
the trash, not Stevie. Quit trying to make my son work all
the time." She had always been overprotective of Stevie.

A few days earlier Jermaine had told Stevie to smash the
cans that were scattered about on the patio, but Stevie
had run to his mother crying. Like always, she defended
him.

"You're going to make a sissy out of that boy ! A little
work isn't going to hurt him! All I'm doing is getting him
use to responsibility, and get him in the habit of working,"
explained Jermaine.

Jermaine's parents had started him working around the
house at the age of seven. He washed dishes, cut and
edged the lawn, took out the trash daily, kept his room
clean, raked leaves, and even vacuumed the entire house
willingly and dutifully. His earlier plans were to raise Stevie
and Alexus with the same morals, principals, and discipline that he was raised with, but from the looks of things
Karen was not going to let that happen.

"Don't call my son a sissy!" Karen replied, giving Jermaine a hard look.

"I didn't call him a sissy; I said that you're going to make
him a sissy."

"Fuck you, Jermaine, your daddy's a sissy, and your mama is a bitch!" She stood there with her hands on her hips.

"What?"

"You heard what I said, bitch!"

Jermaine left her standing there and walked into his office and began thinking. *What the hell have I married? Bobby was right, she is crazy. The things she says are uncalled for. I don't deserve this. All I tried to do is love her and her kids, and this is the thanks I get?*

After a few minutes of hard thinking, Jermaine walked into the bedroom and stood in the doorway. Karen had sent Stevie and Alexus to their room to watch cartoons. She was lying naked under the sheets watching porn, playing with herself, thinking about Tyrone and Rodger's penis.

"I think we made a terrible mistake of getting married, Karen. I think that we should have dated for at least a year, then we would have known one another better. We actually did not give ourselves the chance to get to know one another."

"I don't want to hear that bullshit, Jermaine. You're just mad because things can't always go your way." Her focus remained on the porn.

"I want you out of my house, and I have made the decision to get a restraining order against you. I feel that you are a liability to me. I also feel that you will never respect me or never appreciate me," Jermaine said honestly.

"That's because you're a scary-ass punk bitch, Jermaine. You're nothing but a bitch in a man's body." She continued fingering herself and being entertained by the X-rated movies.

"That's it, I'm calling the police," Jermaine said, then walked toward the telephone.

Karen suddenly jumped out of bed and attacked him and

then grabbed the phone before he could reach it. She socked him in the head, then kicked him in the butt, and then punched him continuously in the face. Then she picked up the cordless phone and threw it at him, striking him in the head. Being that Jermaine was raised against hitting women, he did not hit her back.

Karen then proceeded to snatch out all the phone cords from the wall and then ran to the bedroom. Jermaine stormed out of the house and called the police on his cell phone. Stevie and Alexus stood crying, witnessing the entire episode.

When the police arrived Jermaine explained to them what had taken place. He emphasized to the police of having her arrested and had also stated that he wanted to press charges on her for assault.

"I didn't hit him or throw anything at him. He's lying. Ask my son if you don't believe me."

Two of the six policemen who were present took Stevie into a bedroom and questioned him. In the past, when Stevie had witnesses his mother commit acts of violence on one of her exes, she had always told him that if he told the truth that he would be taken away from her by the Department of Children Services and placed in a foster home. To avoid that from happening Stevie lied each time he was questioned by the police.

When the two policemen returned, first they huddled with their partners and discussed what Stevie had said to them, and then the senior officer spoke.

"I'm sorry, sir, but the little boy said that his mother never hit you, kicked you, nor did she throw anything at you." The officer figured that Stevie was lying to protect his mother, but there was nothing he could do.

"That's his mother, Officer," Jermaine said. "She told him

to lie. He knows that if he tells the truth that he and his sister could possibly get placed in a foster home. Before you guys came Karen told him to lie, or else."

"We can't just put a mother and her kids out on the streets, sir. And we have no evidence or witnesses to arrest her, so actually there's nothing we can do," said the senior officer.

"This is unbelievable," Jermaine yelled angrily. "If she called the police and said that I hit her, you guys would haul me off to jail quicker than eye wink!"

"Calm yourself, sir," advised one of the officers.

"I don't believe this!" Jermaine yelled again.

Before leaving, the senior officer pulled Jermaine outside and suggested that he spend the night elsewhere until things cooled down a little.

"You mean that you're telling me to leave my own house and I'm the fuckin' victim?"

"We're not telling you to leave, sir, we're asking you to consider it."

Not wanting to be in the presence of Karen or a stepson who had lied to protect her regardless of all the things he'd done for him, Jermaine went to his daughter's house and spent the night.

Tyrone and his crew had finally made it to Lancaster. Following the directions Denise had given to him, he made it to Karen's location at 11:30PM. From all of the home invasions they had pulled off in the past they knew exactly how they were going to do this. They parked a couple houses away from the Jermaine's house, then threw on their black masks and then hurriedly bailed out of the vehicle. At first, they were going to knock and play like they were looking for someone who didn't exist, but Tyrone preferred the sneak attack. Tyrone crept alongside of the house and into the backyard, then quickly broke a window using the gun handle. One of his homeboys was posted at the front door in case Karen tried to run out and the other two were at his side. Seconds later they were inside.

"Pull out the telephone lines," whispered Tyrone.

Tyrone then crept upstairs, silently checking each room until he found Karen. She was asleep and snoring like a bear in hibernation. Without hesitation, Tyrone took aim and fired three times. One bullet to the head and the other two hit her lower torso. The gangsters then swiftly fled the scene.

Even though Tyrone had handled that business, he still felt that he had some unfinished business to take care of. He then called Denise's cell.

"What's wrong with you calling me this time of night? What is it?"

Luckily she was driving and on her way home from the doughnut shop.

"It's all good, baby girl, mission accomplished. Sorry to bother you so late, but I just wanna to give you a little sumphin' sumphin' for helping a nigga out, you know what I'm sayin'. Where can we meet right quick?" Tyrone said.

"So you're paying me for my info, huh? Okay, that's cool. Where are you?" Denise asked, with dollar signs on her mind.

After giving Denise his whereabouts, Tyrone waited impatiently for her to arrive.

Minutes later Denise pulled in back of the vehicle Tyrone had described to her and sat, already making plans for the money she was about to receive. Tyrone jumped out of the car and trotted to her vehicle, then aimed his 9mm at her and shot her twice in the head.

"Leave no witnesses, homey. Leave no muthafuckin' witnesses, you know what I'm sayin'," Tyrone told his comrades.

The gangsters then made their way back to Los Angeles.

Missing his wife's touch and not being able to sleep, Jermaine tossed and turned in his grandson's bed and then suddenly awakened. He had a throbbing erection and only knew of one woman that he could possibly insert it into. There had been so many days and nights inside of his truck that he settled for masturbating, but not this time. His pleasure womb was only minutes away.

He planned to first apologize for calling the police. After that he would begin kissing her, then lay her on her back, and give her a good slow, licking.

Assuming that his daughter and her family were asleep and not wanting to awaken them, Jermaine eased out of the apartment and then made his way home.

When he pulled into his driveway, he heard Alexus's loud cries and also heard Stevie screaming. He quickly ran inside, sensing that something was terribly wrong. The kids were yelling even louder now.

"Stevie, Alexus, Karen," Jermaine yelled, while checking the rooms downstairs.

"Daddy, Daddy, come here! It's Mommy," cried Stevie.

Jermaine then shot up the stairs to find Karen lying in bed soaking in a pool of blood.

"Oh my God," Jermaine shouted, staring at his wife. He quickly checked for a heartbeat but there wasn't one.

He then picked up Alexus and hugged Stevie while calling the police.

"Mommy, Mommy," cried Alexus, pointing at her mother.

"I heard three loud noises, Daddy, but I was scared to come out of my room. Then I heard somebody running down the stairs and I really got scared then," said Stevie.

"Did you see anybody?"

"No. I was scared and—"

Minutes later the police arrived.

A passerby driving a blue Mazda had pulled over when observing Denise's vehicle parked alongside the road with the lights on. Seeing that she was unconscious and noticing blood leaking from two holes in her head, the man grabbed his cell and dialed 911.

Chapter 10

Detectives Baker and Cross found themselves having a extremely busy morning. They received a call that a possible homicide had taken place not too far from where they were located. When discovering the victim was the loud-mouth wife of the Jamaican who had been shot months earlier, the detectives were totally astounded.

"Well I'll be damned," Detective Baker said. "First the husband gets banged and now his wife. I think that Jamaican has gotten himself into some deep drug-related Mafia-type shit, that's what I think."

"Or his bigmouth wife got him into some shit. Don't forget she has a pretty bad, disrespectful mouth on her," said Detective Cross, thinking back to the day at the hospital.

"Yeah, you're right, but two shots to the head over some words? Something just doesn't add up."

"That Jamaican definitely knows something. He's the key to solving this shit."

"Hell, maybe he tried to kill her himself. I see it like this: Jamaicans are very dominant over their women, right? He demands her to do something, she mouths off to him, he waits until she leaves, and then kills her out here to make it seems like someone else did it. I'll bet my job that he's at home pretending to be asleep with no one to confirm that," said Detective Baker.

"You've got a point there, Baker. Hopefully, she'll pull through, and we can get to the bottom of this."

"Yeah, hopefully. Let's head on over to the other crime scene."

When the detectives made it to Jermaine's residence, police officers were there taking notes, but Jermaine had followed the ambulance to the hospital. The kids were with him. He had called Jewell to tell her what happened and had asked her to meet him at the hospital.

As Jermaine paced up and down the hallways of the emergency room, hoping to hear some good news from one of the doctors, suddenly five nurses were swiftly wheeling a patient by him who resembled his daughter. Jermaine proceeded to catch the nurses to get a better look at the patient.

"Wait a minute, that's my daughter! What happened to my daughter?"

"She's been shot a couple times in the head, sir," replied the head nurse while pushing the bed.

"What?" yelled Jermaine, not believing that his wife and daughter had been shot on the same night.

Denise was transported to an operating room a couple doors down from Karen, but unfortunately she died a few seconds later.

Maurice rushed into the hospital in his pajamas only to hear the heartbreaking news of his wife's death. He was destroyed by the news, but his mind suddenly diverted back to his wife talking to Tyrone over the phone. Instinct told him that no one other than Tyrone was behind this.

"I'm going to kill the muthafucka! I'll fuckin' kill 'im!" yelled Maurice, angrily, pacing the hallway.

"Kill who?" asked Jermaine. "Do you know who killed my baby? Why would anyone want to kill her?"

Maurice hesitated answering. He thought it would be best to leave Jermaine in the blind for now. He would handle this his way. He would show those muthafuckas what a real Jamaican was capable of.

"I'm not sure, Jermaine, but I think I know who had something to do with it. It may have been those same muthafuckas that shot me," replied Maurice.

"Well you need to inform the police and—. Wait a minute; why would someone shoot you, then turn around and kill my baby? Are you involved in some kind of illegal shit or something?"

"No, Jermaine, I'm not, but if it's who I think it is, then that wife of yours can lead us to the shooter. I'll explain more to you when I've done my homework. Trust me on this one and let me handle this my way. Don't say anything to the cops, okay, because they will be questioning both of us."

"I hope you know what you're doing, and I do want whoever that's behind this brought to justice," said Jermaine.

As Jermaine and Maurice were standing in the hallway mourning over Denise's death, Detectives Cross and Baker spotted them and rapidly approached them.

"Mr. Banner, Mr. Hopkins, you both have my condolences. I realize how difficult it must be for you to talk to us at this time, but if there's anything either of you could tell us that will give us a lead, please let us know," Detective Baker said.

Detective Cross was staring at Maurice, thinking about how much of a smart-ass he had been months earlier.

"Let's say we go to the cafeteria and talk over a cup of coffee," suggested Detective Baker.

"Sure," replied Jermaine. "Anything to be of assistance, Detective, but I can't stay too long. I told the doctor that I'll wait right here to find out what's going on with my wife."

"We'll take care of that, Mr. Hopkins. I'll let the doctors know that you're both in the cafeteria with us."

Maurice felt totally different about talking to the police.

"I don't feel like answering any goddamn questions. You guys are just like those fuckin' detectives on television. The next thing you know me or my father-in-law will be suspects."

"I see that your attitude and respect toward law enforcement hasn't changed since our last encounter, Mr. Banner."

For some reason, Detective Cross disliked Maurice and now his abhorrence toward the Jamaican grew even more.

"Calm down, Maurice, calm down. I know that she was your wife, but after all she was my daughter. So let's contribute what we can to help these detectives in order to get some closure on this matter," suggested Jermaine.

"This asshole thinks he's one of those Steven Seagal, Wesley Snipes–type guys that's used to taking the law into his own hands," Detective Cross stated, as he neared Maurice.

"If any crimes are soon committed by anyone that resembles a Jamaican, I'm coming straight for you, Banner. I'll personally see to it that before you get shipped back on a banana boat that you serve the maximum sentence here first in the U.S. And that's a fuckin' promise!"

"Easy, partner," said Detective Baker.

Maurice gave Detective Cross an evil look and then mumbled something that the detective could not understand. He and Jermaine then followed the detectives to the cafeteria.

After conducting a slight interrogation, the detectives had ruled both Maurice and Jermaine out as suspects.

"Are you finished now? Listen detectives, only white folks kill their wives and kids, black people aren't into that kind of crazy shit." Maurice then stood and walked away.

"I'm warning you, Banner, don't do anything stupid."

Jermaine shot out of the cafeteria and hurried back to ICU.

Detectives Cross and Baker remained seated, planning their next move.

The highly trained medical staff at Antelope Valley Hospital worked overtime and diligently to save Karen's life and luckily their hours of effort paid off. Karen was in critical condition, but the doctors had assured Jermaine that she was going to live. Denise's funeral was a week later.

Chapter 11

After coming to the United States, Maurice had promised himself that he was no longer going to sell drugs, or do any harm to anyone. Being a citizen of the U.S. was both a blessing and a privilege to him, and under no circumstances would he do anything to jeopardize that.

In Jamaica, Maurice worked directly for a kingpin named Ronnie Black. If someone owed Ronnie Black money, regardless of the amount, Maurice would be sent to take care of it by all means necessary. If Ronnie Black wanted someone dead, Maurice handled it without question. Ronnie Black had given Maurice the rank of a lieutenant and had promoted him to be in charge of his army.

Because of Maurice's loyalty to Ronnie Black, when Maurice informed him that he wanted to get out of the game and go to the U.S. and start a new, straight life, Ronnie supported his desires. Not only did Ronnie Black arrange for Maurice a new identity and passport, but he had also given him two hundred and fifty thousand dollars cash to set himself up in something nice. Ronnie Black had also offered to supply Maurice with a couple kilos a month and a few of his men, but Maurice turned down his offer and told him that he was ready to get married, have kids, and be a family man.

"I'm finished with that life, man," Maurice told Ronnie Black.

"You say that, but I don't think so, man. A man doesn't just walk away from having things his way, to a life that he knows nothing about. Here, you have your choice of bitches sucking you and fucking you, you have all the power you need here, and you have more money than you can spend here! Not in America! I respect your wishes, my man, but when the white man rejects you for a lousy fuckin' job because of your dreadlocks, or any other fuckin' race reject you because of where you're from and who you are, you'll see what the fuck I'm talkin' about, man!" replied Ronnie Black.

Everyone in Jamaica feared Ronnie Black, even the police. Ronnie had lieutenants, sergeants, and even captains and chiefs on his payroll. He made it well worth their time to take care of any business that Maurice couldn't. He was a reputable, notorious, wicked Jamaican who had no emotions and would kill quicker than the wink of an eye.

Once Maurice made it to the U.S., even though he had plenty of money, life just was not what he had anticipated. After purchasing a new Cadillac and a luxurious apartment in Inglewood, California, Maurice then began seeking employment, but there still a slight problem to the employers about his appearance: the dreadlocks. He was stereotyped and rejected by everyone that interviewed him. He knew the problem was his hair, but under no circumstances, especially for any fucking job, was he going to cut them off.

After two months of being refused employment, Maurice had decided to go back into the drug game.

There was an area in Los Angeles that was referred to as Little Jamaica. An associate of Maurice's named Slick Rick had schooled him on Little Jamaica and had shown him where it was. Numerous Jamaicans had migrated there, some with the intentions of living a better life, but the majority with the intentions to sell drugs and get rich quick.

When Maurice made his first appearance in Little Jamaica, he had run across three wicked men who had worked under his command in Ronnie Black's army. Maurice wasted no time recruiting those men. He knew of their past and more so of their capabilities and loyalty to their leader.

The beginning of Maurice's drug-dealing operation went well and was very profitable. Customers began coming from afar to buy his drugs, simply because his quantity and quality was the best thing around to win the favor of the addicts, and to steal his competitors' clientele.

Within a couple months, Maurice's operation had gotten so large that he was forced to hire more security. He had soon accumulated an armory of artillery and men who would not hesitate killing anyone. It was in their nature. The local drug dealers did not approve of someone who wasn't from their neighborhood selling drugs on their turf, but they did not dare bother or confront anyone associated with Maurice's operation.

Two addicts who had tried to beat Maurice out of some drugs were found dead. Witnesses said that both addicts had died after taking a hit of crack that had been personally given to them by Maurice. Rumor had it that Maurice had a particular batch of cocaine that was mixed with rat poison and cyanide that he kept for addicts who tried to cross him.

After a five-year reign of being "the man," Maurice finally decided to retire. Fortunately, he had gotten out of the game clean without ever being arrested or without ever being a suspect by the police on the murders he was associated with. He quit while he was ahead.

He relocated to Reseda, California, where he rented a one bedroom apartment and settled for an under-the-table job working for a moving company. He had even sold all of his expensive vehicles and purchased a non-flashy, older model Grand-Am.

A few weeks later, Maurice was on his way home from work one day and was distracted by a pretty young lady. She was standing at a bus stop looking as striking as ever. He hung a quick U-turn and doubled back to the bus stop.

In the beginning, Denise was not attracted to him at all. One thing she did find cute about him was his accent. Maurice's persistence and determination soon paid off. Denise moved in with him in three weeks. Four months later she announced to him her pregnancy, and on that day they got married.

At that point they had developed a deep, strong, unbreakable love for one another and had promised to never let anyone or anything interfere with or damage that love.

Meanwhile, back at headquarters, Detectives Cross and Baker were meticulously going over Denise's cell phone records. Actually that was the only piece of evidence they had. Since there were no fingerprints found in Jermaine's home, that case was going to be much more difficult to even get a lead on.

"Maybe this is our lucky break, Baker," Detective Cross said, staring at the phone call received at 12:15AM the morning of Denise's death.

Examining the records, Detective Cross noticed that calls had been made to and from Denise's cell to that particular 323 area code telephone number.

"Let's say we make a call and begin our process of elimination, Cross," suggested Detective Baker.

"I'll bet my fuckin' badge, Baker, that this was probably a call from someone she was banging. That asshole husband of hers probably wasn't piping her right and caused her go elsewhere for satisfaction. Most times, loudmouth, muscular men have small dicks and can't satisfy their women, you know. They may be good with their tongues, but a woman wants to be piped down every now and then. That makes them feel like a real woman, you know." He spoke as if he were an expert on women.

"Yep, it's possibly a booty call."

Detective Cross then dialed the number.

"What's up, this is Killa T?" answered Tyrone. He was sipping a forty-ounce and smoking a blunt.

"This is Detective Cross of the Lancaster police department. If you don't mind, sir, I'd like to ask you a few questions regarding a call you placed a little after midnight on the night of September sixth."

"What the fuck you talkin' about, fool?" Tyrone replied, wishing he had not answered the phone.

Tyrone suddenly hung up, and then threw the phone down and stomped on it.

"Goddammit!" Detective Cross yelled. "Let's call the phone company and see who that phone is registered to. I should have done that before calling, but that's all right, we'll get that fucker!"

"Yep, we'll get 'im, Cross. I feel that we're on to something."

The detectives then called the telephone company, but unfortunately they discovered that the phone had been reported stolen almost a year earlier.

"Another fuckin' dead end!" said a frustrated Detective Cross.

Karen was still in a coma and things were not looking as good as they were days ago. According to the doctors, Karen only had a fifty-fifty chance of living.

So far, the only family member who had visited her was her daughter, Jasmine. Jewell actually wanted to go visit her sister, but hearing Bobby's derogatory statements toward Karen had changed her mind. She knew that Bobby would get angry if she made any attempts or voiced any thoughts about going to the hospital and that would cause them to begin arguing.

"The bitch got what she deserved!" Bobby had yelled. "She was only taking up space in this world, anyway. The bitch has been a ho ever since I've known her. Every man she meets she tells her kids to call them Daddy! What kinda shit is that? I hope that bitch rots in hell!"

Whenever Bobby got enraged and begin speaking on Karen, Jewell most times agreed with him, but this time she did not have too much to say. Even though her sister had done her wrong on many occasions, she still did not wish bad luck on her. After all, that was her only sister.

Bobby's hatred toward Karen had first developed when she gave four of his friends a head job and would not give him one. He had brought a few of his homeboys to her apartment, who had given her over a hundred dollars of crack in exchange for sex. Bobby figured that since he did her the honor of seeing that she was supplied with dope, that he should get some head too. Karen felt that Bobby might someday tell Jewell about it, so she simply passed on him. Bobby was furious.

Weeks later, Karen told Jewell that Bobby had asked her for a head job. Jewell did not believe her. Instead, Jewell got angry with Karen and did not speak to her for a few months.

Another thing that really pissed off Bobby was Karen's

choice to be on the streets getting high and selling her body instead of being a mother or a provider for her kids.

Like a faithful and concerned husband, Jermaine had taken a leave of absence and stayed at the hospital with his wife on a daily basis. At this point he was not concerned about who did it or why. His only interest was his wife's well-being. He had even requested that the nurses place a bed for him alongside of Karen's, but unfortunately the hospital denied him that convenience.

Jermaine prayed several times a day for his wife to be healed and to overcome this tragedy. He promised himself and promised God that regardless of what she had done in the past, and regardless of what her friends and relatives thought about her, that he would continue to love her unconditionally and continue to be a humble, loving, considerate man. He promised not to argue with her so much and he promised to treat her like a queen until the day he left the earth.

Chapter 12

Tyrone's words, "Front Hood Crip," and "Killa T" kept ringing in Maurice's mind. When Detective Baker had phoned Maurice and asked him whether or not the 323 area code telephone number meant anything to him, even though his answer was no, he was confident that the number belonged to Tyrone. Once he matched the telephone number with a number on his caller ID, he was then assured that Tyrone had killed his wife.

Thinking back to when Tyrone had shot him, and then had the nerve afterward to knock on his door, fueled Maurice even more to go after him. He would not rest until Tyrone was six feet under.

Maurice had recently sent for three ruthless killers that were straight from the heart of Kingston, Jamaica. They were the type of guys that killed for recreation.

"Where's the boy?" asked Mike B, who had a reputation in Kingston for killing anyone who looked at him wrong. His eyes would instantly scare the hell out of anyone.

"The boy in some gang," Maurice replied. "I remember

the boy yelled something like 'Front Hood Crip' and 'Killa T,' but I know the boy is nothing but a coward piece of shit!"

"Killa T, huh?" said Robbie, snickering. "I show the boy who the real killer is." Robbie was reputed in Kingston for slashing throats. He had earned his rep at the age of eleven after slashing an undercover police officer's throat with a machete.

"I kill up the boy's whole fucking gang," inputted Boom, who was on Jamaica's top ten most-wanted list for murder.

"The boy is a skinny piece of shit!" yelled Maurice.

"What about the girl in the hospital, man? If she was fucking the boy, she has to know where the boy lives," Mike B said.

"The bitch is probably still in a coma, man," Maurice answered.

"One way to find out," said Robbie.

The Jamaican mob wasted no time making their way to the hospital.

Once there, they swiftly strolled through the hospital, not caring about the attention they were attracting. When making it to Karen's room, they noticed that she was still in a coma. Jermaine was sitting beside her, reading scripture to her even though she could not hear him.

"The bitch got all these fuckin' wires and monitors hooked up! Why they trying to save her life, and she's the cause of your daughter being dead?" said Mike B, staring at Karen.

Robbie gazed at Jermaine and then swiftly approached him. Maurice hurriedly stood between the two.

"Why are you reading the Bible to this bad girl, man? Let the bitch die!"

"Excuse me, but this is my wife," replied Jermaine, standing.

"Sit down, boy!" yelled Robbie. "Say one more thing, boy, and I'll slash your fuckin' throat!"

Jermaine then had a seat and silenced himself and listened.

"This has nothing to do with you, Jermaine, so please stay out of it. I just don't know how you got mixed up with that bitch. Believe it or not, she's the reason that my wife, your daughter, is dead. Think about it. I ain't the type of man that can just lie down and do nothing, so please don't knock me for the way I'm handling this," Maurice said.

"What about that detective, Maurice? You know that detective's going come looking for you if some shit goes down."

"Fuck the police, man," yelled Mike B. "No police wanna fuck with me, believe that!"

"Right now, I can't worry about that fuckin' detective, Jermaine. He's got a job to do, and so do I."

"Fuck that!" yelled Robbie. "Let's pull the plug on the bitch! Why should this cum-drinking bitch live, and my homeboy's wife had to die!" Robbie then approached the monitors and angrily yanked the life-support plug.

"No, no! Regardless of what she's done, she's still my wife!" Jermaine quickly plugged up the life support, then rushed out to alert the nurses.

Suddenly, six guards stormed into the room ready to strike with their batons and demanded the Jamaicans leave.

"You gunless rent-a-cops wanna rumble, huh?" yelled Boom, approaching the guard closest to him.

Boom then grabbed the guard's testicles and squeezed them until the man fell helplessly to the floor, and then stomped the man several times, while Robbie and Maurice instantly attacked the other five guards.

Within seconds all six guards were laid out on the floor.

Almost the entire floor of nurses and doctors had witnessed the disastrous episode, but seeing the wildness and aggression of the Jamaicans caused them to not want to put themselves in harm's way. Once the Jamaicans finally fled the scene, six nurses rushed to see about Karen while another one called the police. Fortunately, Karen's heart was still pumping.

Hearing the call over the radio, even though it was not a homicide call, Detective Baker and Detective Cross appeared on the ward and initiated an investigation. Detective Cross had instantly sensed that Maurice was behind it.

"I knew that fuckin' asshole would try something!" said Detective Cross. He then turned his attention to Jermaine, who was leaning over his wife. "Where is he, Hopkins?"

"Hell, I don't know, Detective." Even if Jermaine knew of Maurice's whereabouts, he still would not snitch on him simply because he was protecting his daughter's honor.

"You're lying!" yelled Detective Cross. "You're fuckin' lying! Those dreadlock-wearing muthafuckas might put fear in other people's hearts, but they damn sure don't put any fear in mine! I'll nail that fuckin' asshole if it's the last thing I do!"

Maurice and his crew had headed straight for Los Angeles. Due to Maurice missing his son, their first stop was at Denise's mother Renee's house.

When Maurice had taken a leave of absence from his job and had asked Renee to keep his son for a little while, Renee sensed that he was going to do something toward avenging her daughter's death. Standing face-to-face with these cruel-looking Jamaicans confirmed her instincts.

"Where's my son?" Maurice asked. His crew had already seated themselves.

After getting the okay from Maurice, Boom then pulled

out a cigar-sized joint and fired it up. Trying to show some hospitality, Renee offered them some Hennessy. They gladly accepted.

"He's in my bedroom, asleep," replied Renee. "He's been crying like hell for you and Denise ever since you dropped him off." Renee then held down her head and began sobbing.

Maurice went to the bedroom and kneeled over his son and kissed him.

"I'll get that punk who took your mother away from us. I promise you, son, I'll get 'im," said Maurice. He then picked up his son and gave him a long hug.

Minutes later Denise's half-brothers, Blaze and Red, walked into the house. Blaze was twenty-one years old, and Red was nineteen. Both of them were members of a Blood gang, and they both had reputations in their hood for fighting people who were twice their size and kicking their asses. They were also well-known for killing enemies.

Maurice's brothers-in-law both greeted him with a hug and a handshake upon him exiting the bedroom. Then they stepped outside and had a talk.

After revealing what gang Tyrone was from to Blaze and Red, they automatically wanted to assist in avenging their sister's death. To Maurice's surprise, Denise's half-brothers' gang had been rivals with Tyrone's gang since way back in the days. This was another opportunity to take out a few of their rivals. Now all they had to do was to find Tyrone.

Without his mother seeing him, Blaze went to his bedroom and grabbed the two AK-47's from underneath his mattress and then rushed out the front door and stashed them inside of Maurice's car.

The Rasta men were impressed by the youngster's bravery and readiness.

"You guys remind me of myself in my younger years," said Mike B to the youngsters, after taking a long pull from the joint.

"Let me hit that, blood. A nigga gotta get ready, you know what I'm sayin'," said Red.

Maurice then led the crew to the garage where they began making reprisal plans.

It was 4:30PM when Maurice and his crew touched down in Tyrone's neighborhood. After questioning a couple crackheads, for ten dollars one of them had directed Maurice to Tyrone's house. The addict also told Maurice that every day Tyrone and his homeboys hung out on his mother's porch smoking PCP and drinking beer, while making crack sales.

Sticking to the plan, upon spotting Tyrone, Mike, Boom, and Robbie jumped out of the car and strolled nonchalantly toward Tyrone's house. They approached the porch and asked Tyrone where they could score some weed. As usual during that time of day, Tyrone and his homeboys were on the porch getting high.

"Let me smoke those muthafuckas!" demanded Blaze, while eyeing the person who had killed his sister. He attempted to get out the car.

"Yeah, Maurice, let us do this. She was our sister, man, so let us handle this shit," said Red, grabbing one of the AKs.

Maurice thought about his wife, then his mind abruptly flashed to the day Tyrone shot him. That moment the three ruthless Jamaicans pulled out their guns and shot Tyrone and his homeboys, and simultaneously Blaze, Maurice, and Red bailed out of the car and ran toward the house firing their AKs. The fact of Tyrone already being dead did not mean anything to Maurice. He still fired a countless amount of rounds at the man who had killed his wife.

There were several neighbors and passersby who had witnessed the scenario, but only one of them had the courage to identify the criminals on network news.

"Three of them had long dreadlocks, one of them had a short, neat haircut, and the other two dark-skinned boys with the red bandannas tied around their heads looked to be teenagers," said Mr. Roper, the reputed nosiest man in the neighborhood.

An ordinary day to Mr. Roper meant driving through the neighborhood checking things out. Mr. Roper knew who sold the drugs, who smoked dope, he knew who the whores were, he knew who the neighborhood thieves were, and basically he knew everyone's business in the neighborhood. He made it a point to collect all the gossip he could and he did not have a problem snitching on anyone.

Even though this incident was out of Detectives Cross and Baker's jurisdiction, after making a few calls and then getting permission from the captain to go to Los Angeles, the detectives hurriedly made their way to the city. They insisted on following this case and putting together every piece necessary until things were completely resolved, even if that meant flying to Jamaica. This case had become personal to the both of them.

The detectives were going over a few loose ends until they observed Mr. Roper being interviewed by *Eyewitness News*, voicing what he had witnessed.

"I think we need to have a talk with that witness. If we show him this picture of Banner and he positively identifies him, then we've got him by the balls," said Detective Cross.

"Yeah, you're right, Cross, but that won't help us solve

the murder and attempted murder that took place in our own jurisdiction. Besides, with us being out of our jurisdiction now, we do not have the authority to really even question this witness. We'll have to go down the proper channels to get that authorization."

"That fucking Banner is behind this, Baker! This has something to do with his wife's death and I know it does. Banner and his flock took those gangbangers out because he knew that they had something to do with killing his wife. I know I'm right, Baker, I can feel it."

"First, let's talk with the investigating officers, and then we'll have a talk with the witness," suggested Detective Baker. Luckily, Detective Cross had retrieved a picture of Maurice from the immigration department months earlier.

The homicide detectives in Los Angeles Southwest Division that were handling the case were very cooperative with Cross and Baker. Baker discovered through Tyrone's mother that the 323 area code telephone number belonged to Tyrone in the past, but not presently. The detectives also discovered that Karen had spent numerous nights in Tyrone's bed during her marriage. The most significant information the detectives had gotten from Tyrone's mother was that during a heated argument, Karen had sliced Tyrone's penis in several places. His mother also told the detectives that ever since that particular incident she had heard Tyrone on many occasions say that he was going to kill Karen.

Pieces of the puzzle were now beginning to come together for the detectives. With Mr. Roper's statement and positively identifying Maurice as one of the shooters, the detectives now had a case against Maurice, since Tyrone was no longer in the picture.

"Well, Baker, at least we no longer have to search for suspects. But what really puzzles me is how does Denise Banner fit in to all this," said Detective Cross.

"C'mon, I thought you were smarter than that. The way I see it is that Tyrone attempted to kill Karen and Denise, but he didn't kill Karen. We know the reason Tyrone wanted to kill Karen, right? So obviously, Denise somehow knew that Tyrone planned to kill Karen, and Tyrone didn't want leave any loose ends, so he tried to kill her too." Detective Baker was confident in his theory.

"You're right, Baker, you're absolutely right. The only person who can confirm our speculation is that asshole Banner. We've gotta nail him before he has the opportunity to leave the country. I've got to live up to what I promised that asshole," said Detective Cross.

Detective Baker had always been the wise one and Detective Cross had always been the hothead who often didn't use his brain or common sense.

The following morning, while at a motel watching *Eyewitness News*, Maurice saw Mr. Roper's account of the killings. Realizing that there was more than likely a warrant out for his arrest, Maurice went to Bank of America to drain his account, then picked up his son from his mother-in-law's, and caught the next flight out of LAX to Jamaica. His comrades had left the night of the murders.

Chapter 13

After two weeks of being at his wife's bedside hoping, wishing, and praying for her recovery, Jermaine's prayers were finally answered early one morning while reading scripture to her from the Book of Romans. Karen had opened her eyes.

"Nurse, nurse!" Jermaine yelled, excitedly. "She opened her eyes!"

Jermaine had yelled so loud that everyone on the entire ward heard him. Nurses and doctors stormed into Karen's room as if she was having a cardiac arrest.

"Sweetheart, baby, I love you so much," Jermaine cried to his wife. Tears were pouring from his eyes like a rainy day in Georgia. He began rubbing her arm and forehead, and then he kissed her several times on her face. She mumbled something incomprehensible, but as Jermaine looked into her eyes he sensed that she was trying to tell him that she loved him too. He stepped aside and let the nurses and doctors perform their necessary tasks.

* * *

A week later Karen was released from the hospital. Her recovery was going quite well. Jermaine felt like the happiest man in the world—that was, until their first argument, which had taken place less than a month after she had come home.

Jermaine had come home from work and observed scribbles on his living room sofa that were made with a black and red marker. With the sofa being a light tan color, the scribbles were extremely noticeable.

"Karen!" Jermaine called, clearly irritated. "Look at these scribbles on my damn sofa!"

As usual, while Karen was asleep, Alexus had been terrorizing things around the house.

"What are you raising hell about, Jermaine?" Karen asked, standing, wiping sleep from her eyes. She normally slept until afternoon.

"That," Jermaine said, pointing at the scribbles.

"Alexus probably did it," replied Karen.

"It's quite obvious Alexus did it, but maybe if you had been awake or had her in the room with you this wouldn't have happened!"

"She's only two years old, Jermaine. Kids are going to be kids, I've told you that over and over."

"This is bullshit!" yelled Jermaine, and then stormed to his bedroom.

Minutes later he found something else Alexus had gotten into.

"Karen!" yelled Jermaine again. Karen was now inside the restroom.

"What is it now, Jermaine?"

"Come here and you'll see!"

Every week Jermaine purchased DVDs from Wal-Mart, pawnshops, or wherever they were on sale. So far he had collected of a little over a thousand movies. He kept them neatly stacked on a bookshelf and took much pride in his collection.

"Look at this!" Jermaine was pointing at several DVDs that were out of their case and had been painted with red fingernail polish.

"Alexus must have done it while I was asleep," replied Karen. She was tired of him complaining about her kids.

"This is ridiculous! The more I try to build up, my shit keeps getting damaged or torn up! You've got to get a handle on her, Karen. I can't take too much more of this shit!"

"You just fuss, fuss, fuss, about all your materialistic shit! Hell, you shouldn't have never married a woman with kids if you were gonna fuss about every little thing they do."

"My materialistic shit cost me money, Karen! You haven't paid for a goddamn thing in this house!" Jermaine was infuriated.

"Fuck you, Jermaine! Kiss my yellow ass!" Karen replied, and then walked away.

During the next few weeks, Jermaine and Karen argued almost every day. If it wasn't one thing it was another. Their relationship just was not going the way he'd hoped. They had not had sex since she had come home from the hospital and each time he asked her she simply refused him, which caused him to get even angrier.

"Why do you refuse me sex, Karen?"

"I don't feel like it, so quit asking me."

"I just don't understand why you refuse the man who takes care of you and your kids, when not too long ago you were fucking and sucking men in the streets for some goddamn crack. That just doesn't make any sense to me."

"I did it because I wanted to, fucker!" she snapped. "I did what I had to do to support my habit. Besides, why are you throwing that up in my face?"

"Because sometimes I just don't understand you, Karen."

"Well, let me tell you something that you might understand. The reason I was fucking Tyrone was because I like to ride big dicks, not little ones like yours. You have never satisfied me sexually and I've tried hard to deal with that, until I just couldn't take it anymore. Each time we finished having sex, I still had to play with myself to get off. I don't mean to stain your little ego, but I figured it was time to let that out." She then shamelessly walked away, smiling.

Jermaine stood there stunned, thinking. *Why does she always say things to hurt me? I've tried to show her and her kids nothing but love, but this is the thanks I get. I need to start thinking of a plan for this ungrateful-ass slut, because I know this marriage isn't gonna last much longer.* He then stormed out of the house.

Karen knew she had pissed him off and she felt a sense of victory. She smiled, and then seated herself at her new oak desk, and then logged on to a singles chat room using the new computer Jermaine had recently purchased for her.

Since Karen's younger years she had a habit of saying whatever she wanted to say to people whether or not it hurt their feelings. Of course, there were guys who simply did not tolerate her mouth and would kick her ass when she mouthed off.

Each of her kids' fathers had beat her like she was a man and had hospitalized her on several occasions, but that still did not stop her from mouthing off. Alexus's father had knocked out four of her teeth, which caused her to wear dentures, and Stevie's father had kicked her in the vagina after she had Alexus, and that prevented her from having any more children.

Knowing that Jermaine was not the type of man who hit women, Karen used that to her advantage and soon began saying all sorts of disrespectful, rude things to him. Then she would erase the memories of her disrespect from his mind by giving him some superb, pleasurable sex at bedtime. His mind was so screwed up he did not know whether to divorce her or keep her.

Later that night, after things had cooled down, Jermaine stepped inside his bedroom and as usual, Karen was laying naked watching porno movies, playing with her clit.

"Come here, baby," Karen said in a whisper.

"You think that you can say whatever you want to say to me and then give me sex to ease my mind!" he replied, staring at the woman he had married. She sensed his anger by the tone of his voice. "You've crossed the line this time, Karen. You've crossed the fuckin' line."

"I only said those things to make you mad, Jermaine," she said, continuing to play with her clit. "Come here, baby, and let me ease your mind a little."

"I'm tired of you disrespecting me! Sex can't cure the damage that you've done to me, Karen."

He then took off his shoes and clothes and went to the shower. After masturbating, Karen stepped into the shower with him and then knelt down, and began sucking and licking his penis.

"I love you so much," Jermaine said, after releasing in her mouth. She had sucked him completely dry.

"I love you too, Jermaine," she replied, looking at him sincerely.

Once in bed she sucked him again until it was hard and then sat on his erection and rode him to sleep.

The fact of things not being peaches and cream in Jermaine's marriage did not affect his success in real estate or the publishing of his book. Instead of using negative energy to argue with his wife, he locked himself inside his home office when he came home from work and either worked on his second book or searched the Internet for foreclosure properties in the Los Angeles and Riverside areas.

His aggressiveness, persistence, and patience had begun to pay off. He had recently acquired two single-family homes and was in the process of borrowing two hundred thousand dollars from his equity to purchase an apartment complex that appraised for a little over five hundred thousand dollars. In addition, the publishing company offered Jermaine a twenty-thousand-dollar advance on a three-book deal, and royalties thereafter, for which he anxiously awaited his contract.

Jermaine began corresponding via e-mail with the president of the publishing company, whose name was Barbara Thompson. Through e-mails and searching websites, Jermaine discovered that Barbara was a stunning, middle-aged Belizean who had started her own publishing company years earlier, and who also had twelve books published. Jermaine would often visit Barbara's website to admire her beauty while composing e-mails to her.

One day as Jermaine sat reading an e-mail from Barbara, to his surprise she had asked him out of the blue whether he could just write sex well, or was he actually capable of performing sex exactly the way he had written it in his book. That question was right up Jermaine's alley. One thing he enjoyed was writing and talking about sex. From that day on the e-mails began getting kinky, freaky, and arousing to the both of them. Jermaine had gotten to the point where he rushed home from work each day just to read Barbara's e-mails. Barbara had gotten to the point where she would think of certain parts of his book on her way to work and would play with herself while doing so.

He knew that he was wrong in communicating with Barbara, but he figured, what could it hurt?

One day Jermaine left his home to make a quick trip to Home Depot, but he had forgotten to close his e-mail. Karen, being the nosy person that she was, began reading them; all of them. Before Jermaine made it back home Karen e-mailed Barbara a nasty, disrespectful note.

It read:

> *Listen, bitch, lay off my husband before I catch the next thing leaving for New York and come blow out your fuckin' brains! Apparently Jermaine hasn't told you about me. I'm his wife. I might be in L.A., bitch, but I ain't too far to reach out and touch you! I've read your e-mails and I've seen your ugly ass on your website, but, bitch, you ain't all that. I'll use what you sent to my husband to destroy you, bitch, so back the fuck off.*
>
> Sincerely,
> *Jermaine's wife*

Karen greeted Jermaine at the door when he returned.

"So, you and your publisher have a little something going on, huh?"

He played dumb. "What are you talking about, Karen?" *Damn, I forgot to close my fuckin' e-mail!* He ignored her and continued walking toward his office.

"So tell me something, Jermaine," Karen said, standing with hands on hips. "Are you fucking her? If you are, just tell me, so I won't be looking stupid."

"Use your damn brains, Karen. How in the hell could I be fucking her and she's over three thousand miles away?"

"Well, anyway, for your information, player, I e-mailed the bitch and gave her a piece of my mind. I'll bet that the slut doesn't e-mail you anymore." Then she walked away.

"I hope you didn't threaten her or write some crazy shit."

His first thought was the possibility of Barbara canceling his contract. His second thought was to slap the taste out of Karen's mouth. His mind quickly began racing.

Once Karen cooled down, Jermaine decided to e-mail Barbara to apologize for what his wife had written, but just that fast, Barbara had changed her e-mail address.

"Damn!" shouted Jermaine, continually pounding on his desk. "How in the hell did I forget to close my e-mail?" He felt like kicking himself in the ass.

Karen had heard the pounding and appeared at his office door.

"What's the matter, Jermaine? Are you angry because I rained on your parade? I don't know why you told her all those damn lies, because you damn sure can't fuck the way you can write it. Hell, you haven't made me cum since we've been together."

"Fuck you!" Jermaine yelled, irritably.

"No, fuck you, Jermaine. You see, the problem is that you can't fuck me because you can't satisfy me. I can care less about how much money you make, about how many cars you got, about this fuckin' house, or about a damn book being published. You see, if a man can't satisfy me in bed then all that other bullshit is irrelevant."

"If your pussy wasn't as big as the Pacific Ocean then maybe a normal man with a normal sized dick could satisfy you. Don't forget, you used to be a nickel and dime ho that fucked men of all races with huge dicks pounding in and out of your pussy on a daily basis. Or have you forgotten that? But I blame it on myself for trying to turn a whore into a housewife. I just wish I would have known more about you before I married you," said Jermaine.

Angrily, Karen grabbed the cordless telephone at Jermaine and struck him in the eye. Then she grabbed his flat screen monitor and PC and slammed them both on the floor. Jermaine held his hand over his left eye and picked up the phone and dialed 911.

"Come get this bitch before I kill her!" Jermaine yelled into the phone. "I wanna press charges! I want her locked up! Send someone out here, right now!"

Momentarily, Stevie and Alexus were watching cartoons but they could not help but hear the screams and yells. Stevie cracked the door enough for him to peep without being seen.

"Stevie, put on your shoes and coat and get Alexus dressed. We've got to get the hell out of here because this bitch-ass nigga called the police!" Karen yelled.

When the police had arrived Karen and her kids were already gone.

After a few hours had passed, Karen finally put her pride on a shelf and called Jermaine. Actually, because none of her family members would allow her to live with them, she had no choice but to try and make peace with Jermaine. It was hot, she and the kids were tired from walking, and she desperately needed a shower, so she made that call. She needed to feel him out, see whether he was still angry or not. Jermaine apologized to her, as if her were wrong, and accepted her and her kids back into his household. Then he phoned the police department to inform them that he wanted to drop his complaint.

Later that night, Karen sexed Jermaine so damn good that the memories from earlier had been once again erased from his mind.

The following day he took her and her kids to the mall on a shopping spree.

Due to the e-mail Karen had sent to Barbara, Jermaine had not heard anything at all from the publishing company. His agent had also attempted several times to contact Barbara and had left several messages, but Barbara simply would not return them. The fact of his book not being published due to his wife's actions bothered Jermaine, but he prayed each day for time to heal the damages and threats that were made by her to his publisher.

Karen raised hell about one thing or another every day around the house. The fact of her having been on her deathbed was not a wake up call, and the disrespect, name-calling, and physical abuse continued. As a matter of fact, she had gotten worse. Every suggestion or opinion that Jermaine voiced, Karen disagreed with him. Each time he made plans she always wanted to do something different. They just could not see to see eye to eye on anything and deep inside that really bothered Jermaine.

Another heated argument occurred one day when Jermaine asked Stevie to rake up some leaves that were scattered all over the backyard. Like always, Karen interfered.

"Why don't you rake them, Jermaine? Why are you always picking on Stevie and trying to make him work?" asked Karen, with an attitude.

"It's not that I'm picking on him, Karen. All I'm trying to do is teach him responsibility at an early age, that's all," stated Jermaine.

"Responsibility, my ass! You hate Stevie, and you know you hate him!" Karen yelled.

"If I hate him, then why in the hell did I make sure he had a Christmas? Why do I buy him all the latest shoes and clothes if I hate him so much? And why do I buy him expensive video games each week, and give him my hard-earned money if I hate him so much?"

"That's only a front, and you know it. You hate my kids and I know you hate my kids."

"You're brain is all fucked-up, Karen. How in the hell could I hate your kids, and love you?"

"Man, you don't love me. You just can't find anyone else to suck your dick and fuck you as good as I can. You don't love me; you only want me for sex."

"If I didn't love you, I would have left you when you pulled that knife on me not even a month after I married you."

"What-the-fuck-ever! I wouldn't have given a fuck if you did. What you fail to realize, Jermaine, is that just like you came along, another sucka will come along too," Karen stated, and then turned and walked away.

Because Karen did not work anymore, she had lots of free time to do basically whatever she wanted. Being unemployed was typical for her, but being broke and having to ask Jermaine for money became a problem to her.

Karen came up with the idea of becoming a call girl one day while online. *Hell, I need my own money. I'm tired of depending on my tight-ass husband. Every time he gives me money or does something for me or my kids I have to hear his shit and I'm tired of it. Hell, as good as my sex is I should be able to make at least two or three hundred dollars a day.* She smiled at the thought.

Eager to act out her thoughts, Karen dropped off the kids at Jewell's and then went back home and changed into a tight skirt that revealed her nice rounded butt and smooth legs. She then appraised herself a few moments in the mirror. Satisfied with her appearance, she then grabbed the keys to Jermaine's Beamer and split. *I've got to go where the money is*, she thought while driving. *Beverly Hills, Hollywood, Orange County, here I come. I'll tell Jermaine I'm job hunting.*

Her first stop was at a restaurant in Beverly Hills. A waitress seated her at a table that sat in the center of the restaurant where she could get all the attention she wanted. Within minutes men began making passes at her and offering to buy her drinks. Three of the men were doctors, three of them were lawyers, and the other two were contractors. Karen conversed openly with them, especially on the subject of sex. Her conversation toward sex was so persuasive and tempting that each of the wealthy men had offered her a few hundred dollars for a quick piece, but she was on a totally different page than that for the moment. She was after something more worthwhile with greater rewards. She exchanged telephone numbers with each of them but for the moment that was it. *I'm gonna get all I can out of these muthafuckas. They want good sex; I want an apartment, a weekly allowance, a couple of credit cards, and a nice car. This is America; nothing is free or cheap*, she thought.

So far, Richard, a Caucasian doctor, was the only applicant that Karen was really interested in. He had also been the only one willing to fulfill Karen's expensive requests right away. After a forty-five-minute conversation, Richard offered to rent Karen an apartment or a suite at the Holiday Inn and to pay her rent in advance for the first three months. He also offered to provide her with a substantial weekly allowance and to purchase her a decent car. That sounded fine and dandy to Karen, but she felt that she had to clarify that because she was a call girl, that she would not be devoted to only him or be obligated to meet any of his demands other than sex. He agreed.

"I'll take care of you, as long as you take care of me. I'll provide you with money, a nice car, a wardrobe, whatever you need, as long as you take care of me, and as long as you put me first," explained Richard.

"I'm gonna hold you to your word, so please don't make any promises you can't keep," said Karen, smiling.

"That's not my style, Karen, but before we get seriously into this, do you mind giving me a sample of what you say that's so good, and that will keep any man coming back? I've run across lots of women that say they have the best sex in the world, but ninety-nine percent of them were total disappointments," said Richard.

"I've definitely got some come-back pussy, baby, and a

sample for you is no problem at all," replied Karen. "I'm desperate to see what you're working with anyway."

After Richard had given the waitress an extremely generous tip, he and Karen left the restaurant holding hands. She then followed him to Holiday Inn where he rented a suite.

Karen whipped sex so good on the doctor that he purchased her a Nextel cell phone and added her to his plan, gave her five hundred dollars cash, and paid the rent on the suite for the next two months.

"You are so amazing, Karen. No woman has ever made me feel the way you just did. I need you every single day of the week."

"That sounds good, honey, but I'm out to make my money, and I explained that to you. I hope you don't begin getting too obsessed with me and get jealous if you come over and a client is here."

"Have you been listening to me? You don't need another man, Karen. I'll take care of all your needs and desires."

"Sorry, baby, but we've already discussed that."

"Well, I guess some of you is better than none of you," replied the doctor, smiling.

"That's a good way to look at it, honey."

She then took his limp penis in her mouth and sucked it until it was fully erect, then rode the hell out of it. His penis was very small, but this was business.

After they departed a few hours later, Richard begin to continually call Karen's cell, but seeing his name appear on the caller ID screen she ignored the call. *Damn*, she thought. *He's falling in love already. If the rest of them get hooked as quickly as he did I'll be set for life.* She smiled at that thought.

When Karen made it home that evening Jermaine was furious.

"Where have you been?"

"I'm a grown-ass woman, Jermaine. You're not my mama or my daddy, and I really don't feel that I have to answer to you each time I walk through this door," she replied, and then walked away.

"Who gave you permission to take my Beamer and to use my credit card!" he asked angrily, following behind her.

"I don't need permission. Have you forgotten that I'm your wife? What's yours is mine." She faced him, smiling.

"If you were the type of wife that makes me feel like what's mine is yours, then it would be different, but you're not. You are a disrespectful, ungrateful, sneaky, street-slick, unappreciative woman that thinks she's got it made. That's what you are. The next time you take my damn credit card without asking, I'm gonna have your ass arrested."

"My ex-husband tried the same thing, but the police looked at him like he was stupid when he told them we were married and living together. So go right ahead and make yourself look stupid if you like," she replied, smiling, and then walked away again.

Then suddenly her cell phone began vibrating. She glanced at her caller ID and saw that it was Bernie, one of the contractors she had met earlier.

She had made it clear to each trick that her price was two hundred dollars per visit, and not to call unless they were ready for business at that moment.

Karen ran to the restroom to take the call. The contractor was seeking right-away action. Once she was finished with the call, she approached Jermaine. By that time he had calmed himself.

"By the way, I found a job today."

"Is that right? Doing what?"

"I'm an on-call computer-tech trainee."

"Computer-tech trainee, huh? How much does it pay, and where's it located?"

"My salary varies depending on how many calls I make, and the job is in L.A. That was the only place I could find a decent paying job. As a matter of fact, I just received a call from my trainer to go on my first job. Isn't that something?" she replied, smiling.

"Why didn't you consult with me before making the decision to drive to my car to L.A. everyday?"

"You don't consult with me before you make decisions, so why should I?"

"Number one is because you're driving my car, and number two is because I don't trust your judgment on certain things."

"Well, I won't be driving your car much longer, you can bet on that, and as far as you not trusting my judgment, oh-muthafuckin-well," she replied, and then walked out of the house.

After a month of being in business Karen was amazed by the amount of money she had earned. She had earned close to two grand her first week of business, and the rewards from her second week reached twenty-five hundred.

Business for Karen was booming, but the married life was beginning to stress her out more and more by the day. It was basically interfering with her business.

Getting married was just something Karen had done during her times of struggle and not having a steady place for her and the kids to live, but now since she had it so good she regretted ever marrying Jermaine. It was real simple: she just did not love him.

Now that her call-girl business had shown profits, she didn't have to depend on him anymore. She had begun to seriously entertain thoughts of moving on without him. Her goal was now to make fifty to sixty thousand dollars her first year, and then retire and open some type of legitimate business.

One day, while Karen was inside her suite counting her earnings there was a soft knock on the door. Richard had phoned her earlier and told her that he was leaving his wife and wanted to discuss plans for their future together.

"Richard, I've told you over and over that I'm not ready for another relationship," Karen had said to him.

"But why? I can give you the world, baby. I can assure you and your kids a good life, Karen, and then you won't have to do what you're doing to make money. I want you to belong to me and only me. I don't want to share you anymore. My mind is made up, and I've already initiated a divorce. I'll see you when I get off," said Richard, determined to convert Karen into a housewife. He was not used to being rejected and would not accept no for an answer.

Leaving the shoebox full of money on the bed, Karen approached the door.

"Richard?" she called out.

"Nope, sorry, this isn't Richard, it's David."

Damn, it's that kinky real estate man, thought Karen, and then opened the door.

"Why didn't you call before coming, David? I've asked you not to come by without calling first." She let him inside and then closed the door.

"Thank God you're not busy with a client," David said, and then sat his carryall bag on the sofa.

"I have an appointment with an exclusive client in an hour and a half, so we'd better make this quick, David."

"I thought slow and deep was your motto," replied David, smiling.

"Yep, you're right, but that's only when I don't have another engagement lined up."

David was a wealthy African American real estate broker who paid Karen four hundred dollars a sex session. The fact of him being married did not prevent him from having sex with whores four to five times a week. He had revealed to Karen during their first encounter that his wife was from the old school and did not give blow jobs, which caused him to go elsewhere.

"Lots of my clients tell me that," Karen sympathized. "And I really think it's a damn shame that some women just aren't capable of keeping their man inside their own bed. If a woman has a good man, she has to satisfy him in all aspects of sex in order to keep him from fucking around."

David would always insist on doing kinky things before or during sex. He would bring X-rated videos, handcuffs, vibrators, ropes, and took pleasure in wearing different costumes. That particular day, while Karen disappeared into the kitchen to fix them a drink, David had quickly changed into a Superman suit, put on his mask, and then turned on an X-rated video. There was a huge hole cut in the crotch area of his suit, which allowed his long, thick penis to hang freely. After watching a few seconds of his favorite movie, he was fully erect. Like Tyrone, David had a horse dick that Karen took much pleasure in riding.

When Karen returned with the drinks, she glanced at David and smiled.

"Just the way I like it," she said.

She then handed him his drink, and then began stroking his erection. Then they toasted to pleasurable moments.

"So tell me, baby, what do you have in store for this today?" asked David, standing with a proud erection.

"I'm going to suck it, lick it, slurp it, and then I'm going to ride the hell out of it," said Karen, smiling.

"Damn, girl, I love it when you talk dirty to me."

Realizing he hadn't paid her yet, Karen held out her hand.

"Business first, and then pleasure, my big-dick friend."

"You got me so damn excited, I almost forgot." She continued stroking his erection as he walked over to his pants to grab his wallet.

He then peeled off four crisp one-hundred-dollar bills and handed them to her, smiling. Karen accepted the money and then put it amongst the other money inside the shoebox. She then slid the box underneath the bed.

Wasting no time, Karen fell to her knees and began giving her client a slow head job and massaging his balls while doing so. Instead of watching Karen's lips and tongue, David focused on the X-rated movie that was showing a scene of a long-dicked black man inserting himself inside a white woman's rectum. Seeing the painful expressions on the woman's face excited David and triggered him to grab Karen and position her, doggy-style.

"Wait one minute, stay right there and don't move," David said, and then went to his carryall bag, pulled out some Vaseline and rubbed it over his penis, and then made his way back to Karen. Then without notice or asking, he rammed his dick inside of her rectum.

"Ooowwee! Ooowwee, no! Take it out, David!" Karen yelled, but he ignored her and dug even deeper. He had a tight hold on her, preventing her from moving.

"Stop, David, you're hurting me! Take it out!"

"Shut up, bitch!" yelled David. Then he began pounding in and out.

Karen finally eased out of his hold enough to cause his penis to slip out, but that only made him angrier. She then attempted to run to the door, but he went after her and grabbed her and began punching her like she was a man. Her weakness allowed him to regain control over her and soon he had reinserted himself back inside her rectum and continued pounding. Blood began heavily discharging from Karen's rectum, but that still did not stop David's hammering. He finally came fifteen minutes later. Seeing that Karen was weak and helpless, David hurriedly changed back into his business suit and tie, and then grabbed the box of money from underneath the bed along with his car-ryall bag and then split.

Even though Karen was too weak to respond to David's violence, she had observed everything that he done. She lay helplessly on the floor visualizing what had taken place. She thought about alternatives, but she had none. She thought about contacting the police, but quickly dismissed that thought, realizing that she had committed the crime of prostitution. Then she thought about stealing more money from Jermaine's bank account to hire a hit-man to kill David, but the only problem was that she had no idea where to locate him.

Moments later she finally came to the conclusion that she was completely defenseless, and had to accept the loss and chalk it up to the game. She would use this experience as a lesson to be learned.

She pulled herself up and went to the restroom. While looking in a mirror at her bruises and feeling the pain in her rectum, Karen realized that she needed to think of a quick lie to tell Jermaine and the kids. *I'll check myself into the hospital and tell everyone I got beat up and raped in the butt*, she thought.

It took her almost two hours to make it to the hospital. After being examined by the nurses and doctors in the emergency room, tests reflected that the crime of rape and assault had been committed on Karen, so the police were immediately notified. To strengthen her lie, Karen had one of the nurses call Jermaine, Jewell, and Jasmine to inform them that she was in the hospital, and also to tell them what had taken place.

Neither Jermaine, Jewell, or Jasmine believed Karen's lie.

The following day Karen was released from the hospital. Once she'd made it home, Jermaine did not show her any love or affection. He sensed that she was full of shit and was playing him one way or another.

Chapter 14

A few days after Karen left the hospital her attitude toward Jermaine had gotten even worse. Life for him became more and more depressing, stressful, and shameful by the day. The fact of him taking off work to look after her did not mean anything to her. Regardless of his kindness, concern, and sincerity, Karen still showed no appreciation whatsoever. She continued to disrespect him, to curse him, and to call him and his family members awful names for no apparent reason. He had gotten so mad one day that he finally blew his cool. He could not and will not tolerate anymore of her bullshit.

"I don't have to take this shit! Fuck that!" he shouted, while driving his big rig. "She's an ungrateful bitch, and nothing's gonna change that! I've been patient and tried everything possible to make this marriage work, but it's im-fuckin'-possible! I'm tired of her going against every suggestion, decision, or advice that I give! I'm tired of her calling my mother and daughter bitches and whores, and I'm tired of her talking to me any kind of way. I'm tired of her getting defensive when I say something to her kids about eating in my living room, about messing with buttons on my TVs, about fuckin' with my PC or my laptop, or about writing or scribbling on my damn walls! I'm tired of you, Karen! I'm the one who provides a roof over your head and make sure you drive a nice car! I'm the one who made sure your kids had a Christmas! I'm the one who buys your cigarettes, gives you gas money, and buys Pampers and milk for Alexus! I'm the one who buys your tampons when you're bleeding! Is this the muthafuckin' thanks I get? And now you think I'm stupid enough to believe that goddamn lie about someone raping you and beating you up! Bitch, I'm not stupid! Fuck that, I deserve to be treated better than this! I'm getting a fuckin' divorce then I'll find me someone who appreciates me! Yeah, that's exactly what I'm gonna do."

Jermaine stormed into his home like a madman after work. He bypassed the kids without speaking and headed straight for the bedroom. Karen was laying down, watching Jerry Springer.

"We've gotta talk!" he said, and then closed the door.

"Can't you see I'm watching TV?" she replied, never looking at him.

He then approached the television and snatched the plug out of the wall.

"I said we've gotta talk!"

"Are you on your fuckin' period again because you're sure acting like a bitch!" She then got up and attempted to plug the television back up.

"This is my fuckin' TV, my fuckin' electric bill, and my fuckin' bed you're laying in!"

"So fucking what! Who gives a flying fuck! That's your fucking problem; you're always talking about what's yours, and about what you've bought! Since you make so much fuckin' money you need to pay a damn doctor to make your dick bigger, then maybe I'll wanna fuck you more often. I know you're just mad because I won't give you pussy or suck your little dick head when you want me to, but oh-fuckin'-well."

"I want a divorce, Karen, and I'm gonna initiate it ASAP!" Jermaine said, giving her a serious look.

"People in hell want ice water too. I don't give a fuck about your wants; I'm not signing any goddamn divorce papers! And if you happen to find a way to divorce me without me signing, I'm going to fuck you royally, Jermaine, and that's a promise! If you keep talking I'll call the fuckin' police right now and tell them you raped me! I'll have your black ass locked up quicker than lightning strikes, muthafucka! Don't fuck with me, Jermaine, I'm warning you! When I finish with you, you won't have a damn thing, but expensive monthly payments!" she replied, standing in his face.

"Yeah, right. Have you forgotten that I came into your life and saved your sorry ass? I took you and your kids in, gave you a fuckin' car to drive, made sure your kids had presents on Christmas, found you a fuckin' job, and the list goes on, bitch!"

"Your mama is a bitch, your dead daddy was a bitch, and your ugly-ass daughter was a bitch!"

"What?"

"You heard what I said, muthafucka. I didn't stutter!"

He balled his fist and stood in silence for a moment. "I told you about talking about my people!" He wanted to knock out her teeth, but quickly thought about the assault charges he would face, which would automatically send him to jail. "That's why I'm divorcing you! You could never be the right woman for me. You don't appreciate a damn thing I've done for you and your kids, and you're just not capable of being sincere. I don't know why I married a damn schizophrenic anyhow."

She spit in his face, then pushed him, and then tried to get a grip on his balls, but his movements were too quick for her.

"I've been waiting on you to put your hands on me again so I could have you arrested! Your ass is gone now," he said, then reached for the telephone, but she reacted quicker and snatched the cord out of the wall. Then she rushed him, throwing a series of punches, landing a couple of good ones to his eye and nose. Again she reached for his penis or balls, and this time she had a firm grip.

"Aw shit! I'm fuckin you up now!" yelled Jermaine. He was now forced to push her, hoping she would release her grip. Thank God it worked. He then stormed out of the house and dialed 911 on his cell.

Karen went on a rapid rampage. She stormed into his office and picked up his computer, scanner, fax machine, and flat screen monitor, and slammed them all on the floor. Then she ran from room to room and scratched each of his televisions with a fork. Afterward, she rushed to the garage and grabbed a bucket of paint and a can of gasoline and then poured it over his Beamer and Escalade.

Thinking about the consequences she'd have to face if sent to jail, Karen ran back inside and grabbed Alexus and Stevie, and then climbed into the Mustang and split the scene.

Sergeant Miller was the first officer on the scene. Observing the damage and vandalism done to Jermaine's home and belongings, Sergeant Miller instantly initiated a police report. Jermaine revealed to the sergeant that Karen had been to prison for assault and battery and was currently on probation for child endangerment. He then told the sergeant how he had met Karen, and went on to tell him about the things that he had been through since marrying her.

"I feel for you, Mr. Hopkins," said the sergeant. "And I can assure you that you've done the right thing by not hitting her. Most men would've reacted by beating the hell out of her, but thank God you kept your cool and called us."

"It was hard, sarge, but I'm not trying to go to jail, you know?"

"I know what you mean, Mr. Hopkins."

After advising Jermaine to get a restraining order, Sergeant Miller then put out an APB on Karen and on Jermaine's vehicle.

The following day, Jermaine sat in court all day until he received a restraining order against Karen. Once the judge granted the restraining order, Jermaine then made his way to the probation department to enlighten Karen's probation officer on what had taken place. After talking with her for close to an hour, he then initiated a divorce. It was a good thing that they had no kids or property together and had been married for such a short while.

Later that day, Jermaine hired a couple of Mexicans to assist him in moving all of Karen and her kids' belongings out of his home.

It had been six long months of mayhem since they day they'd said "I do."

Chapter 15

Karen had parked Jermaine's car at his job then she and the kids had caught an express bus to Los Angeles. She realized that the police would be looking for her and she did not want to be too easy of a target driving Jermaine's car. A deputy sheriff spotted the Mustang minutes after she had abandoned it. Jermaine was notified right away.

Realizing that she was in trouble with her husband, and in deep trouble with the police and her probation officer, Karen decided to leave Lancaster for good, and relocate back to the city where she was born and raised, and to the city that her life of drug usage and crime had begun: Pasadena, California.

She dropped her kids at her aunt's house, and then hit the streets of Pasadena on foot seeing what she could get in to. Having the "I don't give a fuck anymore" attitude led her to the nearest crack house.

Once inside, the addicts that had not seen her in a while gave her hugs and told her that she was looking well, but they refused to share their crack with her. She desperately needed a hit.

"This is all I got," one addict said to her.

"I ain't gonna be the one responsible for you relapsing, so I ain't giving you a damn thing," another addict said to her.

"I had to take a penitentiary chance to get this, and I ain't giving nobody shit!" said another addict.

"This shit ain't free, Karen. You gotta do what you do best if you wanna get high, girl. Go out there and get paid, girl, hell, you know the game," suggested Peaches, a reputed prostitute and crack addict.

Karen then left and decided to give a couple dealers a visit that she knew for a fact would exchange a head job for a twenty dollar piece of crack.

As long as my kids are taken care of, I'm straight, thought Karen. *I know I'm going to jail soon, so fuck it; I may as well have all the fun I can before I go. I fucked up again with my husband, and I can't blame anyone but myself. He's a good man, and he does deserve someone better than me. I wonder if he still loves me. I wonder if he'll take care of the kids if I get locked up. I wonder if he'll send me money. I wonder if he's really going to divorce me, or will he come looking for me again like he did when I relapsed the last time? I wonder if—*

Her determination to earn some crack soon became a reality after giving three crack dealers head jobs. Neither of them wanted to fuck her, but they were very much pleased from the pleasures of her tongue and lips. They referred to her from back in the days as "the head master." Some of her old tricks and small-time hustlers referred to as "eat-'em-up."

Now with a few rocks in her possession Karen began thinking.

I'm gonna sell some, and smoke some. I can't fuck up all my profits and go out backwards because ain't nobody gonna look out for me,

but me. I admit that I fucked up a good thing and I do regret it, but I
ain't a punk or an ass-kisser and I got tired of kissing Jermaine's ass.
Fuck it; I gotta do what I gotta do.

Karen recruited two addicts who were known prostitutes
to assist her with her operation. She fed them crack to
spread the word about the new dope spot, and once they
returned she fed them more crack to lick her pussy while
she laid back smoking, enjoying the bliss of their tongues
and soft touch. Karen was known to be a control freak, especially with women, whenever she had drugs for sale.

They set up shop in an abandoned house in one of the
many ghetto areas in Pasadena. Because the spot was not
known, the first few days of business was slow, which
caused Karen to begin dipping into her product. Each time
she took a hit, she gave her workers a hit.

When customers began coming, Karen had pinched off
the product so much that it was to a point that it was not
salable or acceptable to anyone.

Karen's hopes had failed days after the grand opening.
She was completely out of business and had to rethink
things.

Her recruits were laughing at her and talking about her a
couple days later.

"How can an alcoholic manage a liquor store?" asked
one of Karen's recruits.

"I knew she was going to go out backwards. She was trying to act like she was all that because she had a little dope
sack," inputted the other recruit.

Broke, disgusted, with no options to choose from Karen
felt she had no other choice but to do a repeat with the
dealers. *I gotta do what I gotta do,* she told herself.

Her attempts went unsuccessful; neither of the dealers
wanted blow jobs at the time. Seeing they were not interested in her offer, she tried reasoning with them to front

her a dope sack, but because of her bad reputation and because she had not been around for a while, they refused her. She begged and pleaded, and made promises, but they still denied her. "Fuck it!" she yelled."I'll make my own goddamn money and buy my own fuckin' dope."

That attitude led her straight to the whore stroll.

Once she hit the whore stroll she had no problem being picked up.

A couple weeks later the street life began taking its toll on Karen. She had gotten to the point that the only thing she thought about was a hit of crack. She did not care about her appearance, her unbrushed teeth, nor did she care about wearing the same clothes and panties each day. When her period came she used toilet tissue and napkins from McDonald's in place of tampons. She was tore up from the floor up, but because of her reputation of giving extreme sexual pleasures, both men and women picked her up on a daily basis. That lasted a few weeks until she was arrested by the Pasadena police for smoking crack on a bus stop. Her arrest resulted in an automatic probation violation and additional charges of assault on Jermaine, possession of paraphernalia, and possession of a controlled substance.

Chapter 16

Jermaine received a call from Jewell the following day during his work hours. She told him that Karen had been arrested, and was also facing a probation violation.

"Maybe now she'll realize just how good she had it," Jewell had said.

"Maybe, maybe not," replied Jermaine.

"Yeah, you're right, Jermaine. My sister has been hardheaded and used to doing things her way since I can remember. Hopefully, she'll turn her life around this time."

"I hope she does, Jewell. For the sake of her kids, I hope she does."

"Speaking of her kids, my aunt dropped them off earlier this morning and both of them asked about you more than they asked about their own mother. I didn't tell them she was in jail, I just told them that she was on a vacation and would be home in a few months. As smart as Stevie is, I kinda figure he senses she's locked up."

"Yeah, Stevie is pretty smart for his age and he's probably figured it out. Let me speak to them."

Due to Karen's massive arrest record and convictions, she was sentenced to two years in state prison. With good behavior she would be out in thirteen months.

Being incarcerated was nothing new to Karen. This was actually her eleventh time in jail.

For the first two months of her incarceration Karen was housed at the Los Angeles County Jail women's facility called Sybil Brand.

During her stay in the county jail, Karen slept practically the entire day while other inmates played cards, wrote letters to their loved ones, watched television, talked about past relationships, and, of course, engaged in unashamed lesbian acts.

During the inmate processing procedure Karen informed a jail nurse that she was currently on Zoloft and Prozac, which are psych meds.

"You'll be evaluated by our psychiatrist and put on a list like hundreds of others who claim to be taking medication. You have two choices of housing: I can either house you on the mental ward with the rest of the nuts, or I can stick you in general population," stated the nurse.

General population consisted of a huge dormitory with sixty cells; thirty cells were on each side and the cells were designed for two inmates. Karen was housed with a Mexican woman whose name was Maria.

This was Maria's fourth trip to prison, mainly due to her heroin addiction. She and Karen were the only inmates who did not come out of their cells at dayroom time. As Karen slept the day away, Maria laid on the cement floor in unbearable pain, sweating and scratching, kicking heroine.

After a week of being cellmates, Karen and Maria finally had their first conversation.

"What's your name?" Maria asked.

"Karen. What's yours?"

"What are you in for?"

"Being fucking stupid. Yep, I'm locked up for being fucking stupid," replied Karen. Then suddenly she began crying.

"Actually, I think I'm the stupid one," said Maria, rubbing on Karen's shoulder, trying to comfort her.

As time passed Karen and Maria became more and more familiar with one another. They talked about the good times, and the bad times. They talked about their exes, their kids, and even talked about the way their parents had raised them. As they began to get more comfortable with one another, they shared their deepest secrets.

When they were first incarcerated the both of them looked like they had suffered from malnutrition. They were both skinny, had sunken, skeleton faces, and had no breasts at all, only a long nipple.

After a couple months their faces had begun to regain structure, and their shapes had begun to fill in and transformed back to normal. Being incarcerated had actually saved the both of them.

One night as Karen stood looking into the stainless steel mirror on the wall, brushing her long, pretty hair, Maria silently watched. Karen felt her watching her, but continued brushing her hair and thinking about the life she used to have. Then suddenly Maria eased up to her and began massaging her shoulders. The touch was so soothing that Karen did not resist; instead, she gave a positive response.

They began kissing wildly and fingering one another like they'd been waiting for this moment for several years. Seconds later they were naked.

Maria was the aggressor and Karen breathlessly and willingly followed her lead.

After easing Karen to her bunk, Maria continued caressing her and began slowly and skillfully licking all around her wet, hairy pussy. It felt so good to Karen that she could not hold back her moans. No man had ever made her feel like this before. Out of all the sexual encounters she had with other women, none of them compared with Maria. This was actually her first time in life experiencing multiple orgasms during oral sex.

After climaxing, Karen returned the pleasure to Maria and began kissing her, licking her, and sucking her pussy nice and slow.

"Lick the clit, baby, yes, now lick the inside of it, yes, now suck the clit, suck it harder, um, yes baby, yes, I'm cumming, ooh, ooh, oooh, yes," moaned Maria, in complete ecstasy.

Lovemaking became a daily and almost hourly routine for Karen and Maria. Unlike the inmates who did their thing in the midst of others, Karen and Maria always shared their intimacy inside their cell.

One day while Maria was asleep, Karen sneakily wrote Jermaine a letter:

> Jermaine, I am so sorry for the embarrassment and pain that I have cost you. I love you so much, and I will always be in love with you. I have said and done some pretty damaging things to you for the short period we've been married, and I do regret them all. I hope that you can find it in your heart to forgive me and give me another chance. After all, I am your wife. Will you please write me sometimes, or have you found someone else to occupy your time and take care of your needs and wants? If you have I'll kill the bitch! You belong to me, Jermaine, and that's just the way it is. I know it's a shame that I didn't realize what I had until now, but this is the high price I had to pay to bring me to my senses. I consider us as being nothing more than temporarily separated. Hey, can you please send me a couple hundred dollars in good faith? I'll be catching the chain to the prison soon, and I don't want to have to ask

anyone here for anything. What ever you borrow in a place like this, you'll have to pay back double, or suffer the severe consequences. I've already stepped into enough shit as it is, and Lord knows I don't need any trouble. One more thing before I close this letter; you have been a wonderful, supportive, husband, and an outstanding father to my kids. I really appreciate you, and I'm looking forward to a brighter, happier, and a more pleasant and peaceful future with you and my kids. You are my life and there's no me without you.

PS Regardless of us being divorced, I'll never stop loving you.

Your wife, Karen

Maria suddenly awakened and observed Karen writing a letter.

"Who are you writing, honey?" Maria asked, now standing over Karen.

"My husband. I felt that I owed him an explanation for my actions and stupidity," replied Karen, addressing the letter.

Maria studied the address, and then meticulously stored it in her memory. There was a thing or two that she had to bring to Karen's husband's attention; all in due time.

Then abruptly, Maria began caressing Karen's shoulders and then knelt over and began kissing her wetly and passionately. Seconds later they were in the bunk making love once again. It had gotten so good to them that they did not respond to chow release.

Once their lovemaking session had ended, Maria initiated a conversation.

"Listen, baby, I'm here for you, but you must realize that now is now, and yesterday and last month is gone. We can't pick up spilt milk. I sympathize with you for the things you went through with your husband, but now that you're here you have to chalk him up as part of your past. I'm the one that's been taking care of your needs and wants and desires. I hope you recognize that. I'm the one who buys your cigarettes, sweets, stamps, and envelopes, and I'm also the one who make it possible for you to make calls when you need them. Your husband has not sent you not one copper penny since you've been here, and actually I don't think he will," stated Maria, while caressing Karen's buttocks and thighs.

Karen thought for a few seconds and then eased away.

"Regardless of your thoughts, Jermaine is a good man and I'm more than sure that he still loves me. I'm confident that in due time he'll send me whatever I ask him for."

"You sure have lots of certainty for a man that hasn't sent you a damn thing since you've been incarcerated."

"Like I said, he's a good man and I know that he'll come through. It was my stupidity, my ignorance, and my big mouth that's causing him to ignore me while I'm here, but like I said, he's not the type of man that holds grudges and I know that he'll soon come through for me. Hell, I can't blame him for any of this; I've got to blame myself." Then she began crying.

"It's okay, honey, it's okay," assured Maria, caressing her lover.

"I was a super bitch toward him and it wasn't even necessary. I cheated on him, I talked disrespectful to him just about every day, I physically fought him, and I even pulled a knife on him. He's been there for me and the kids since day one, but I had to fuck up. He's the best man I've ever had, and . . ."

"Okay, honey, you've said enough. I feel you baby, I really feel you," Maria said, while kissing and caressing Karen.

A few hours later the gates opened for dayroom time. Karen and Maria had finally decided to go out and mingle with the other inmates. They played a few games of spades as partners, winning five games straight before finally losing. Afterward, they sat among other inmates watching *The Jerry Springer Show*. The topic was about gays who had recently come out of the closet. They were being confronted by spouses, relatives, and long-term friends.

Suddenly a black inmate approached Karen and stood silently staring at her with a mean look. The woman was accompanied by two manly looking females. Karen and Maria ignored them and continued watching television.

Suddenly, the woman spoke, directing her words at Karen.

"Bitch, don't I know you from somewhere?" asked the inmate, staring hard and thoughtfully.

"Do you have a problem with my girl, bitch?" responded Maria, springing up from her seat, aggressively.

Inmates quickly diverted their attention from *The Jerry Springer Show* to the jailhouse drama. Karen was now standing face-to-face with the angry woman. She had not taken her medication since being incarcerated, meaning that she was like a ticking time bomb, just waiting to go off for any reason. The fact of Karen being four-two and the woman standing at least five feet nine did not put any fear in Karen's heart.

"You better stay out of my business and take your bean-eatin' ass back to Mexico, bitch!" responded the angry woman, directing her words to Maria.

Out of the blue Karen rushed the woman with a series of connecting punches. Maria joined in and took swings at the woman's associates, but by her being double-teamed she instantly got her ass kicked. Karen took charge and began dancing around like Muhammad Ali connecting severe punches to each of the unknown women as if she'd been training for this.

Suddenly the guards stormed in, spraying pepper-spray

and swinging their batons, taking complete control of the situation. All of the involved inmates were cuffed and escorted to the hole.

"I'm gonna kill you, bitch!" screamed the woman who had initiated the episode.

"You've been fucking my husband, and you fucked up my marriage! Watch your back, bitch! If it means losing my release date, I swear, I'm gonna fuck you up!"

"Bring it on, bitch, I'll be waiting for you!" responded Karen. She then blew Maria a kiss and gave her thumbs-up.

The hole consisted of a row of cells designed for two inmates, but each cell was only occupied by one inmate. If the hole began to fill with inmates then arrangements would be made according to the seriousness of the case to house two inmates in one cell.

A few minutes after the inmates who were involved in the brawl were placed in the hole, the black woman who initiated things started directing threats toward Karen and Maria.

"Just wait until y'all bitches go back to GP! Y'all gonna get fucked up, and that's a promise!" Her name was Sassy, and she was housed in cell twelve.

"Shut the fuck up you stupid, black bitch!" yelled Maria, from cell eight.

"Wait a goddamn minute," shouted a voice from cell six. "Bitch, you're out of line calling one of my sisters a black bitch! You're trying to start some racial shit up in this muthafucka!"

"Whatever," replied Maria.

"Be cool, Maria, calm down, baby," advised Karen, from cell two.

"I ain't scared of those bitches! Whatever they want to do, they can bring it on. And like I said, fuck you, you ugly black, manly-looking bitch. I ain't biting my tongue for none of you hoes. East L.A. in the muthafuckin' house, bitches! That's right, East L.A. in the muthafuckin' house!" yelled Maria, boldly.

"You illegal bean-eating wannabe Americanized, bitch! I'm from Compton, and I got crew from all over the muthafuckin' globe, ho! When we get through with you, you're gonna wish you were back in Mexico standing on a corner selling peanuts and oranges!" screamed Sassy.

It was considered to be disrespect when another race called you out of your name. It was okay for someone your own race to call you a name, but not someone that was another race. Maria had just crossed that line and Karen was fully aware of it. They both knew that it was a matter of time before they would be forced to deal with the consequences.

After the trustees had delivered chow, Sassy began mouthing off, which instantly set off a instant verbal riot.

"Yeah, bitch, it's goin' down! Talk your shit now! You've fucked with the wrong bitch, Julietta! I've got more juice than Minute-Maid up in this muthafucka, and soon you're gonna find out, bitch!" threatened Sassy.

"Bitch, you don't scare me! You're only talking shit because you're inside that damn cell. You're nothing but a fucking cell soldier, bitch!" yelled Maria.

"Chill out, Maria, chill out!" Karen yelled, not wanting her lover to bury herself into deeper shit.

"Black, ugly, gorilla-looking bitch," shouted Maria, and then laid across her bunk.

"I ain't finished with you yet! I'm gonna take out all my frustrations, all my past bad luck, and my being locked up on you! You'll think twice before fucking around with someone else's husband, bitch!"

"First of all, I'm not your bitch, bitch, and secondly, who in the fuck is your husband?" asked Karen, with an attitude, standing at the cell gate.

"Warren Brown, you know 'im, bitch!"

"You mean Warren that works at the shipyard, and drive a dark blue raggedy Cadillac?"

"Yeah, I'm talking about Warren who works at the shipyard and drive a blue Cadillac. I knew that was you. Are you going to deny fucking 'im and sucking 'im?"

"Let me tell you something, girl; your husband was, and still is the biggest trick in Antelope Valley. Every ho in Palmdale, Lancaster, Rosemond, and Acton knows your trick husband. He has a dick the size of a baby's finger, and always trying to pay somebody to suck it. Don't be mad at me, girlfriend; hell, he was just another trick to me. I did what I had to do to get my money on, and your husband just happened to cross my path. What I wanna know is how can you blame me for fucking up your marriage when Warren was fucking every ho on the stroll?"

"Because I caught you with him, that's why!"

"If you caught me with him, why didn't you confront me then?"

"Because my mind was so fucked-up at that time, and I was so hurt that all I could do was run away crying. I couldn't believe that he would turn to a ho for sex when I was giving him all that he wanted. I should've killed both of y'all muthafuckas, that's what I should've done! Back to the situation at hand, bitch, I'm still fuckin' you and your bitch up," Sassy assured.

"Like I said earlier, bring it on, no fear," said Karen.

Immediately afterward, the black inmates began passing notes, plotting not only against Maria, but against the entire Mexican population as well. They knew that if they made a move on Maria that her race was going to defend her without question.

The blacks in the hole outnumbered the Mexicans two-to-one, and outnumbered them in GP almost three-to-one.

The white race only populated a small percentage and did not pose a threat to anyone at all.

Two weeks later, Karen and the inmates that were involved in the scrap were released back into general population. Word had spread from the hole about Maria's racial remarks toward Sassy, and now Sassy planned to deal with it.

Sassy wasted no time prompting the black inmates on how and when it was going down. The fact of her release date nearing did not make a difference to her. After being locked up for close to five years, a few extra months would not hurt her. She could accept an ass-whipping if that's what it came to, but she refused to tolerate any form of disrespect, especially from another race.

The chow hall was packed for the Sunday morning breakfast, but Sassy and 98 percent of the black inmates' minds were far from eating at the moment.

After throwing a hard look at Maria, Sassy then whistled loudly, and then suddenly the blacks begin attacking the Mexican inmates, catching them completely caught off guard. Several black inmates used jail-made sharpened metal objects to assault their victims, while others attacked with forks and stainless-steel cups. The riot was total chaos and too much for the seven assigned guards to handle.

Sassy instantly rushed Maria, and stabbed her several times in the neck, chest, and in her lower body. Even though Maria was lying helplessly on the floor, Sassy continued stomping her and spitting on her.

"You fucked with the wrong bitch, Julietta! I don't give a fuck about a release date! Nobody disrespects me, nobody, bitch!"

Karen wanted to help Maria, but knew that since this had transformed into a racial thing and that if she joined forces with the other race, she could possibly end up dead. She also knew that by not participating in a racial riot would result in her being disciplined by her race, but that was the decision she chose.

Minutes later several guards stormed in wearing riot gear, swinging batons, and spraying pepper spray at the aggressors, soon having the situation under control.

The majority of the blacks were taken to the hole, while a large percentage of the Hispanics were taken to the infirmary, including Maria.

Luckily for Karen, because she did not have any bruises or blood on her, and had been standing alone in a corner when the guards stormed in, she did not get escorted to the hole.

Karen spent the rest of her days alone in her cell with mixed emotions. She was in love with both Jermaine and Maria but neither of them were in her presence. At night she longed for Maria's touch, but she settled for the orgasms caused by her memories of Tyrone and Maria. Those memories were the only thing that gave her comfort.

A few weeks later Karen caught the chain to Chowchilla State Prison for Women located in Central Valley, California. The bus ride to prison was long and boring for Karen. She sat silently staring out the window, entertaining thoughts of Maria, Jermaine, her two youngest kids, her past, and her future. There were several loud, wild women talking openly and unashamedly about things that occur in everyday street life. Karen did not feel like listening to any of it but had no choice.

The inmate Karen was handcuffed to suddenly began making small talk.

"What are you in for?" asked the woman.

"Doing some stupid shit that I regret the hell out of," Karen replied, staring out the window.

"I know what you're talking about, girlfriend. The shit I'm

in here for was unnecessary as hell, and believe me, I regret it like hell too. By the way, I'm Michelle, but everybody calls me Chelle." She offered a handshake.

"I'm Karen. Sorry we had to meet under such unfortunate circumstances."

Karen discovered that Chelle had four children, who were all living in different foster homes due to her lifestyle. Chelle had been caught attempting to cash bad checks at a bank and this was her fifth prison term. She was raised in Los Angeles and had been on drugs since the age of nineteen. Her arrest recorded consisted of prostitution, fraud, possession of a controlled substance, and robbery. By her appearance you would never believe that she was capable of indulging in any form of wrongdoing, but never judge a book by its cover.

Karen felt at ease talking to Chelle. They clicked from the beginning and related to one another very well.

After thirty minutes of conversing and sharing deep secrets, Chelle suddenly felt the necessity to clarify something with Karen.

"I'm strictly dickly, okay? I don't fuck around with women."

"What made you say that?" asked Karen, puzzled.

"I'm just letting you know before you get any crazy thoughts."

"I'm cool with that. I told you I'm a married woman with kids," replied Karen, not wanting to acknowledge her divorce.

"From what I've seen, there's lots of married women who go both ways, you know what I mean, and I ain't down with that kind of shit."

Being from the hood and having lots of street knowledge and wits, Chelle was just the kind of associate that Karen needed in prison.

After four and a half boring hours, the bus finally made it

to Chowchilla. The females were ordered off in twos and were then instructed to walk in a straight line to the inmate reception center. Once inside a male guard gestured for them to halt.

"My name is Lieutenant Jordan!" he yelled, darting his eyes from inmate to inmate.

"Most of you have met me before, and for those of you who haven't, I can be like your best friend, or I can be you worst nightmare! I'm your mama, your daddy, and your God up in here. Do you understand?"

A few inmates nodded, but none of them responded verbally.

"I said, do y'all understand who's in charge around here!" yelled Lieutenant Jordan.

"Yes, sir!" shouted the inmates in unison.

"That's better! Y'all better recognize!" he yelled, and then began walking slowly, giving each inmate a hard look.

Lieutenant Jordan had been head of operations under the warden's supervision for the past fourteen years at Chowchilla.

During Lieutenant Jordan's reign he had gotten forty-nine inmates pregnant and had sex with over 95 percent of the population. Most inmates gave him sex at his request, and he raped the few who did not want to cooperate, then threw them in the hole for a few weeks.

The lieutenant was a six feet two, muscular, dark-complexioned black man with a clean-shaved head. His eyes were small and beady, and his voice was loud and powerful. Whenever the Lieutenant spoke everyone listened, including the corrupt warden.

After the Lieutenant Jordan speech, three female guards and three male guards began separating the inmates, placing ten in each cell.

Minutes later, another guard began calling the inmates

by last name to step out and take prison IDs. Afterward, they were examined by a doctor.

After that procedure, the inmates were instructed to take showers, which was Lieutenant Jordan's preferred moment.

After showering, they were escorted through the yard and on to their assigned dorms or cells.

Chapter 17

Jermaine's time and energy was now spent on making real estate deals and writing. He was now employed by RE/MAX as an agent. Being the intelligent, motivated and persuasive man that he was, Jermaine sold five houses in his first two months with RE/MAX.

Because Jewell and Bobby always bitched about not having money to provide for Karen's kids, Jermaine made it a point to deposit one thousand dollars on the first of each month for them into an account. The money was supposed to be split among Karen's kids, but because of Bobby's greed, that never happened. Even though Jewell received a check for Marvin each month, Jermaine did not exclude him.

Each weekend, Jermaine made it his business to pick up Stevie and Alexus to spend some quality time with them. They picnicked at parks, rented go-carts and dirt bikes to ride in the desert, went to the movies often, and had even gone to Disneyland on a couple occasions.

Regardless of him and Karen being divorced, Jermaine

still felt obligated to spend time with the kids. It was not their fault that they were caught in the middle of this unfortunate situation. They were totally innocent and had nothing to do with what happened between Karen and himself.

Jermaine began receiving letters from Karen like clockwork. They wrote sex letters to one another; Jermaine masturbated to her letters, while she masturbated, fantasizing about Tyrone's penis and Maria's lips and tongue licking her all over. She tried hard to get off reading Jermaine's letters, but found it impossible to do.

In their letters they made plans to get remarried and live a brighter and more peaceful family-oriented life; a future filled with happiness, togetherness, love, understanding, and sincerity. They admitted their faults and agreed to work on their flaws. They agreed to produce more love toward one another and to listen to what the other had to say. Karen had also promised to practice on her self-control; in the past she had abused Jermaine verbally so much that it was amazing that he had not left her sooner. Karen's lack of self-control had gotten her into so much shit that it was a miracle that she was still living.

Suddenly the letters stopped. Why? he asked himself. Initially Jermaine thought it was a simple delay in prison mail, until one day he finally received a letter from someone in jail, but that someone was not Karen. The letter was from her lover, Maria. The letter read:

From: Maria (Karen's Lover)
To: Jermaine
    I hope this letter finds you in a fucked-up situation and with a new bitch. I've heard all about you. I know that you're a selfish piece of shit who thinks that because you drive a Beamer and got a couple other cars, have a book published, and you're

into real estate that you're all that. But one thing that you lack, Mr. Big Stuff, is knowing how to treat a woman and keep her pleased and completely satisfied. Your loss, my gain. Karen has told me all about you. She now belongs to me, so buzz the fuck off. Since you claim to be so goddamn smart we thought that you would get the message when she stopped writing and calling you, but I guess you're not so smart after all.

Anyway, we're getting married as soon as we get out. The pleasure is all ours. Learn from your mistakes, Jermaine. You may have money, nice cars, degrees, and lots of other materialistic bullshit, but I got your woman, so get over it.

Sincerely, Maria
Your wife's lover

Jermaine was furious after reading the letter.

"Well, I'll be damn!" he yelled. "She's gone back to her old ways. How could she turn to another woman? The letters she wrote me were nothing but a bunch of bullshit words she wrote on paper to pass her time by. I can't believe this."

The letter had hit him like a knockout punch. He could not figure out whether to move on with his life, or to continue writing her in hopes that she would soon think like a normal human being.

Jermaine had never been a drinker, but after reading that letter he suddenly wanted to get drunk.

I can't deal with this. I think I need a drink. Something real strong, he thought, and then made his way out the front door and on to the liquor store.

Jermaine was so confused and stressed-out behind Karen that he almost had two accidents on his way to the store. He simply could not understand why Karen had sent him letters of regret, and letters stating that she had learned her lesson and that she wanted to reunite with him and the kids once she was released. His mind was baffled and out of sync, but for some reason he still loved his wife.

"Give me a fifth of Jack Daniel's," Jermaine said to the clerk, and then placed a one-liter bottle of Coca Cola on the counter. Never in his life had he drank Jack Daniel's, but he had heard from a coworker that Jack was the ultimate drink to assist you in dealing with your problems.

"Is that all for you, sir?" asked the clerk.

"No, it's not. I need my wife back, can you help me out?"

"That's between you and your wife, sir," replied the clerk, smiling.

"If you can't help me, then don't ask me about my needs," said Jermaine, giving the clerk a hard, serious look. He then paid the man and left.

He was not himself at all. Normally, Jermaine had a keen sense of humor and at the same time he was always very courteous and polite to anyone he'd meet. His mind kept changing channels going from Maria's letter, to letters Karen had recently sent him, to his wedding day, and then back to Maria's letter. He could not think straight, and the whiskey did not make things any better.

He sat on his sofa staring at the walls and ceiling while sipping Jack Daniel's. He was depressed and miserable.

He approached his stereo system and was about to listen to Al Green, but changed his mind.

"I don't want to hear no damn music, and I don't want to watch no goddamn TV, either. I need to hear myself think!" he said out loud. His voice began to get even louder.

"I need my wife back! How could she! Goddammit, how could she do this to me!" Jack Daniel's was responsible for his sudden anger.

"I gave her a good life!"

He began pacing the floor.

"I loved her despite all the bad things she said and done

to me! I gave her and her kids everything she needed, everything! I showed her time after time how much I loved her, how could do this to me! I don't deserve this; Lord knows I don't deserve this!"

After drinking half the bottle of Jack Daniel's, then vomiting, Jermaine cried his way to sleep.

A couple hours later he had a sexual dream about Karen.

"I wanna ride it," Karen had said to him, then climbed on top and mounted herself and began giving it with a serious look. A minute later he came, and then awakened and realized it was all a dream.

The following morning instead of going to work, Jermaine headed to the prison to visit his wife.

The ride to Chowchilla would normally take two and a half hours from Lancaster, but he made it there in an hour and a half. He was energized by thoughts of seeing Karen. He figured that his presence would change her mind and possibly win her back. He still loved her and nothing or no one, as far as he was concerned, could change that.

Maria had gotten transferred to Chowchilla a month earlier. By her being a veteran to the prison system she knew that for the exchange of items such as coffee, cigarettes, stamps, cosmetics, or sweets that she could get just about anything she wanted. Her aim was to be housed with Karen, and once she touched down in the reception center, her goal was obtained. She was reputable throughout the California prisons even though she was a dope fiend and a whore on the streets.

Maria paid a hundred bucks in items for the transaction to happen. She figured that was a small price to pay for what she was getting. Besides, her father, who was a wealthy businessman, graciously supported her each time she got locked up. Each time Maria was released from prison her father provided her with an apartment, a nice car, and a substantial bank account. He figured that was the least he could do for his only child.

On a couple occasions, her father had given her a job managing one of his restaurants, but unfortunately within a few weeks, Maria always went back to using heroin. Her thing was sex, drugs, alcohol, and women.

It was Jermaine's pleasure to stand in line and patiently wait to see Karen. He had craved this moment for so long that time was not a factor.

Actually, deep down inside, Jermaine did not love Karen the way he had in the beginning, but he was so hooked on her sex that he was willing to set aside all that she had done and said to him, just to have her back in his bed. He yearned for her sex daily, and would do or say anything to assure that she came home to him when she was released.

There were correctional officers observing each visitor and inmate at gunpoint. Like any other prison there were always those who visited or had visitors come for bad intentions. Recently, several visitors had gotten busted attempting to smuggle all sorts of drugs into the prison.

A month earlier a female visitor had been caught attempting to leave drugs inside of the restroom wastebasket, but thanks to one of the loyal snitches the guards were given a heads-up, and time enough to place hidden cameras in both restrooms. The visitor was arrested, booked, and sentenced to ten years.

Jermaine was the next visitor in line.

"Isle four, seat twelve," shouted the guard to Jermaine.

"Thank you, sir," replied Jermaine, and then proceeded to his area. For some reason he felt like he was in high school about to go on his first date. He felt a little nervous, but at the same time he was excited.

After seating himself his mind suddenly diverted back to the day he had met Karen. Her pretty smile, her long hair and petite shape; those were the main factors that made him say, "I DO."

Karen suddenly appeared, disrupting his thoughts. Her complexion had been restored back to its original smooth yellow color, and her hair was in a long ponytail with bangs neatly hanging in her face. He could see that she had gained about ten pounds, all in the right places. He smiled thinking, *It's all good.*

Her demeanor was calm and composed and she displayed no emotions whatsoever. She was actually ready to leave before she even sat down.

"Hi, sweetheart," Jermaine said excitedly, through the phone. Then he smiled like he had just won a million bucks.

"Hello, Jermaine." Her reply was plain and apathetic.

"I love you so much, that—"

"I love you too, Jermaine, but I'm sorry to say that I was never in love with you. Besides, you've demonstrated that you're in love with yourself, your cars, your money, and the accomplishments you've made in life. The only thing you ever loved about me, Jermaine, was my sex. That's it and that's all," she replied firmly, maintaining a controlled attitude. Maria had been making sure that she took her meds three times a day, as prescribed by the doctor.

"How could you possibly say something like that, Karen? I have proven my love for you and your kids since the first day we met, so how can you possibly say something like that? I have been providing for you since—"

"That's where you got things twisted, Jermaine. You may have provided for me and my kids, but actually, and please don't take this the wrong way, but you have not ever satisfied me sexually. I felt bad having to fake it each time we fucked, but I had to do what I had to do in order to keep the peace. And while we're on the subject of sex, I have a con-

fession or two to make: because of your non-ability to satisfy me sexually, I've cheated on you on a few more occasions," she said, staring him shamelessly in the eyes.

"You did what?" He stood angrily, giving her a hard look.

She remained cool, while he stood speechless and of-
fended.

"You see, Jermaine, it's not about what you can buy me
or my kids, and it's not about living in one of your fuckin'
so-called dream homes; it's about sexual satisfaction to
me, and I've told you that before. Each time we fucked, and
that's all we were doing because we damn sure wasn't making love, I desired more length and width of dick and to fulfill the needs of my pussy, but you couldn't produce that.
And each time you called yourself eating me out, you didn't
even know what the fuck you were doing. So yeah, I did
what I had to do to get that ultimate feeling that people
look for when having sex. I'm talking about that same feeling that you got when I sucked or rode your dick. You enjoyed my pleasures, didn't you, Jermaine? It's so fucked-up
having a husband that can't satisfy you. I mean, as much as
I wanted to be faithful to you, it was just impossible." Her
mouth had always been her defensive weapon, especially
when it came to breaking men down.

"You mean to tell me that not only were you fucking
other men, but you were faking like you were enjoying having sex with me?"

"Sorry to bust your bubble, Jermaine, but yes, I was faking the entire time we were married and yes, I have been
fucking other men during our marriage. You have never
made me cum, and I just feel like now is the time to come
clean with you. Oh, before I forget, I apologize for the letter
Maria wrote you, but I guess that she felt it was necessary
that you know about us."

He felt like snatching her through the glass, then he felt like pulling out his hair, and then he felt like kicking himself in the ass for marrying this inconsiderate bitch.

"You mean that bullshit about you and her licking pussies and getting married is true?"

"Call it what you wanna call it, Jermaine, but the definition of it is making love, something that you're not capable of doing." She smirked.

"Have you been taking your medication? I think you're crazy as hell and need to see the prison psych. How in the hell are you going to explain some shit like that to your kids? After reading your letters I thought that wanted to change, but I can now that your mind is all fucked-up, Karen."

"I think you're just angry because I'm in love with another woman and not you."

"I don't give a flying fuck if you're sucking pussies, bumping pussies, or sticking a fucking broomstick up each other's pussy; my only concerns now, since I see what page you're on, are your kids! You're a hopeless nutcase, Karen, and the bad thing about it is that you don't even know it. I remember all those times that you watched Christian programs on TV and walked around the house shouting 'Praise the Lord, God is good,' but Lord knows that you were full of shit when you were saying it! You read one scripture a week and sinned ten times a day! You pray to God with the same foul mouth that you curse people with. If I recall, God made Adam and Eve, not Eve and Evelyn. You shouldn't be playing with God like that, Karen, because you're headed straight for hell. Bad luck is going to pour down on you like a hard rain, just watch and see!" He wanted to continue, but his high blood pressure caused his head to start hurting.

"Fuck you, Jermaine; you're just angry like I said. Why are

you talking about me sinning and watching church programs? Hell, you don't even know the Bible or any scriptures."

"The devil can recite scripture! I know the Ten Com-
mandments; I pray and talk to God every day. I know that
Proverbs twenty-one, twenty-three states that 'Who so
keepeth his mouth and his tongue keepeth his soul from
troubles.' I know that Proverbs twenty-three, nine states
that 'Speak not in the ears of a fool; for he will despise the
wisdom of thy words.' I know that Proverbs twenty-six,
eleven states that 'As a dog runneth to his vomit, a fool
runneth to his folly.' Have you ever heard the saying, God
helps those who help themselves?"

"I'm confident that God blessed me with Maria." She was
as serious as an earthquake. Maria had convinced her that
God blessed them with each other for a reason.

"You're sick. You are fucking sick," Jermaine replied, shaking his head in disgust.

The phones suddenly went dead. Visiting time was now
over.

After placing their phones back on the hook they then
hurriedly disappeared out of one another's sight, avoiding
any form of eye contact.

Fuck it. Life goes on, thought Jermaine, walking away. *Her
kids are going to suffer from her ignorance, stupidity, and ungodly
acts. Lord knows that I tried.*

Chapter 18

The following day while working, Jennifer, a stunning Caucasian agent who on several occasions had been trying to give Jermaine some action, approached his desk. She stood about five foot seven and had long, pretty, red hair and a pair of sea-blue eyes. Her 34D's stood proudly and matched perfectly with her intellect and smile.

Jennifer had never dated or slept with a black man in her thirty years of living, but by watching black men on X-rated videos, she was curious to be with one. She enjoyed watching BET and movies starring Samuel L. Jackson, Denzel Washington, Will Smith, Ice Cube, and Chris Tucker, but Wesley Snipes was her favorite. She got wet whenever watching Wesley make love to a Caucasian woman in one of his movies.

"Hi. Great day, isn't it?" said Jennifer, trying to make conversation with Jermaine.

His response was plain and tired. "I don't see what's so great about it. Hello, Jennifer," Jermaine replied, maintaining a serious look.

He was momentarily preparing paperwork to close a lucrative deal. His commission would be a little over twenty grand.

"What are you working on, Jermaine?" Jennifer kneeled over him, purposely rubbing her breasts against him. Her aim was to get a piece of this handsome black man. She had two friends who married black men and their mottos were: "Once you go black, you'll never go back."

"I'm trying to seal the Hollis deal," replied Jermaine, while concentrating on his work.

"Anything I can assist you with?"

"Not really, but thanks for asking."

I *wonder if he's gay*, she quickly thought. *He's not wearing a ring and there aren't any family pictures on his desk, so I assume he's not married. Let me do a little prying and find out what's really going on with Mr. Mystery.*

"Did she piss you off this morning?" Jennifer asked boldly.

"Who?" She finally had his attention.

"Your wife, your girlfriend, or whoever it is that has you coming to work every day looking depressed and unhappy.

Jennifer had caught him completely off guard. He tried not to bring his personal problems to work, but apparently he was not doing a good job of it.

Since visiting Karen his mind had been screwed up and unstable. He tried hard to put her behind him, but for some reason he could not stop thinking about her.

"I'll tell you what, Jennifer, I'm kind of going through some issues right now and I do need someone to talk to. How about a conversation over lunch?"

"Sounds good to me." She was now in super high spirits.

"Is noon okay?"

"Excellent," she replied with a Colgate smile.

"Then noon it is." He then continued working.

Momentarily, his mind was not on sex or building a new

relationship, he just needed someone to talk to. She felt a sense of victory and walked away, smiling and thinking, *Yes!*

HomeTown Buffet was crowed as usual during lunch hours. For five dollars and ninety-nine cents, HomeTown Buffet offered everything from steak, fish, fried and baked chicken, roast, Mexican food, a complete salad bar, and all sorts of cake and ice cream. Most people took advantage of the term *all you can eat.* Of course, there were the greedy ones who'd gotten so full that they couldn't eat anymore, but insisted on stuffing their purses, backpacks, and overnight bags with food.

After fixing a plate of mashed potatoes and gravy, two pieces of fish and a buttered roll, Jermaine led the way to a corner table. Jennifer ate light, having only a salad. She worked diligently to maintain the prize body that she was blessed with.

"So, tell me Jermaine, what is it that's been keeping you in a depressed mood lately?" She wasted no time pursuing the information she wanted. Her aim was to find out all she could about him. Already, she was fantasizing about having sex with a big, black penis, and if it was good she would more than likely consider marrying him. Then she would say to her friends, "How do you like me now?"

"Well," Jermaine replied, pushing aside his plate. "I'm in a mess of a marriage." He then looked away and dropped his head.

"So you're married, huh?"

"Well, no. My ex-wife is in prison. I visited her yesterday for the first time since her incarceration and she told me that she was marrying another woman when she's released." He then revealed everything that had taken place during his entire marriage.

Two hours had gone by, but neither of them seemed to

care about getting back to work. Now understanding what kept a somber look on Jermaine's face, Jennifer sympathized with him. *She has to be dumb, blind, and stupid to treat a man like him with no love and respect. Some people just don't know a good thing when they've got it, but I do. He's brokenhearted and in low spirits, but I'm confident that I can change that. All he needs is a little TLC and someone to listen to him.*

His emotions had completely taken over to a point that he almost cried. Jennifer stood and held his hand, and then embraced him with a long, warm hug.

"You have to put her behind you and move forward with your life, Jermaine. Life is too short to be unhappy, and you deserve to be happy. Actually, Jermaine, she doesn't deserve you. A man like you deserves to be treated good and given much attention. Things happen for a reason."

She had suddenly transformed from a real estate agent to a marriage counselor. Her smile and body language coordinated just right with the pronunciation of her words, which were actually flattering to Jermaine. He had never imagined dating outside his race, but suddenly he was attracted to Jennifer's concern for him and also her intellect. He wondered what it would be like to date a professional, successful Caucasian woman.

"Would you like to see my home and watch a couple movies together?" All of a sudden he felt a lot better.

"I'd love that, but what about work?" replied Jennifer, smiling.

"I'll pick up where I left off tomorrow, if that's okay with you."

"Sounds like a winner to me."

She excitedly followed him home. She started to call her two friends but decided to wait and call them later in hopes to tell them some good news.

"Your home is totally immaculate and marvelous, Jermaine. Did you do the decorating yourself, or did your insignificant other do all of this?" she asked, admiring his home. Then she seated herself.

"Actually, I bought, chose, and positioned everything inside my home," responded Jermaine.

"Impressive. Very impressive. I didn't think men had such good taste. Your aquarium and your fish are so unique and attractive."

"Thanks. I love aquariums so much that I actually have them in just about every room in the house. Would you like to see upstairs?"

"I'd love to." Her pussy tingled, sensing that he was about to take her to his bedroom and do her.

Sex was far from Jermaine's mind, but Jennifer's temperature was close to being overheated. She desperately wanted this black man to lay her down and fuck her, exactly like they did it on the pornos, but unfortunately, once Jermaine had finished showing her the upstairs, he led her back downstairs.

She was disappointed at the fact that Jermaine had not yet made a move toward her, but what the hell, they had all night. *Maybe he wants to take his time with me*, thought Jennifer. *But I don't want him to take his time. I want him to fuck me right now.*

"What kind of movies do you like?" Jermaine asked.

She wanted to say, porn starring black men with big dicks, but decided against it.

"Wesley Snipes is my favorite. He has a way of being passionate with women, you know. Also, he has the ability to take control of any situation, and I mean any situation." She was hoping he'd get the message, but he didn't. *I wonder are all black men this patient when it comes to sex*, she thought.

"I think I can accommodate you with a Wesley Snipes

movie," he responded, making his way to his movie library. "Would you like something to drink?"

Now he's talking, thought Jennifer. *Get me drunk and fuck my brains out, you handsome black stud.*

"Yes, sure. Perhaps that would set off the evening. What are my choices?" *Long and fat, fast and hard, slow and easy. My choices are all the above.* She was excited as ever.

"Well, I'm actually not much of a drinker, Jennifer, but lately my mind has been so screwed up that drinking has been my way out, you know. I have some Jack Daniel's if that's not too strong for you."

"Jack will be fine," she replied, smiling, thinking, *Yep, this is gonna be the ultimate fuck of the century. I can't wait until he puts it in.* Her pussy was getting wetter by the second.

While he fixed drinks, she toyed around with her clit.

Jermaine was the perfect gentleman to Jennifer. His only flaw was that his mind was far from sex. It was on Karen.

The movie did not interest him at all; neither did the conversation between he and Jennifer. Jennifer sensed that something was bothering him, because suddenly he had that same depressed look again.

While sipping his drink and trying to keep his mind on the situation at hand, thoughts of Karen's damaging words and threats kept haunting Jermaine's mind. *"I wish you were dead! I've been fucking other men in the bed! I'll lie to the police and say that you raped and they'll lock you up and throw away the key! Fuck you, Jermaine! You're not a man, you're a bitch! I'll have someone kill you! I hate you, your mama, and your ugly daughter!"*

"Are you all right?" asked Jennifer, sitting down her drink. She then began rubbing his leg. Once her hand neared his penis she left it there. She was almost at home plate.

"Yeah, I'm okay. I apologize for daydreaming, but I can't seem to stop thinking about some of my ex-wife's unkind words and threats." He dropped his head in his hands and began sobbing.

Jennifer continued caressing him in hopes that he would get aroused enough to fuck her right then and there, but after seeing that it wasn't working, she aggressively made a move. First, she unzipped his pants and pulled out his penis and began massaging, and then she knelt over and began sucking it. While giving him head, she unbuttoned her blouse, revealing her big, attractive tits. Her nipples were long and the areolas were the size of a silver-dollar coin, but they did not appeal to Jermaine at all. His mind was still on Karen's words. Jennifer tried hard to relieve his mind but it just was not working. *His dick head feels so good in my mouth, so different, so black, so——. I'm about to give my pussy a total fuckin' party tonight. Yes!*

"You have to put her behind you, baby," Jennifer whispered, while sucking and licking his penis trying to get it rock-hard. His penis may have not been big enough for Karen, but compared to the Caucasian penises she'd experienced, it was a decent, acceptable size.

"You would think that I would have dumped her after visiting her, but it's like she has a strong hold on my mind that just won't loosen up." His words were so saddened he almost cried, regardless of Jennifer's pleasures.

"Let me see if I can help get your mind off her," she suggested, then began sucking it even faster until she had a nice rhythm going. Her aim was to get it hard enough so that she could straddle it and ride it, but unfortunately, his penis remained limp.

"What's wrong with you? Doesn't this feel good to you?" she asked, continuing to suck and lick.

"Please excuse me, Jennifer, but my mind just isn't on sex. I'm sorry, but——" Even though he was embarrassed, he was sincere.

"This is un-fuckin'-believable! You're right, Jermaine, you are sorry! And not only are you sorry, but you're a disgrace to all black men as well! I'm outta here," she said angrily, while buttoning her blouse. Then she stormed out the door and slammed it behind her.

Jermaine relaxed on the sofa, sipping the rest of his drink, thinking. *What's wrong with me? That was so damn embarrassing. I don't know if I could ever face her again. I can't believe that my dick wouldn't respond to a fine, redhead white girl like her.* A few drinks later he began talking out loud.

"I should kick myself in the ass! She was sucking the hell out of me and I couldn't even get hard! Goddammit, Karen, it's all your fault! First you fuck up my life and now you're fuckin' with my manhood!"

Afterward, he decided to watch his favorite porno movie and masturbate, hoping to release some steam and then fall asleep, but the damn thing would not get hard.

"Goddammit, Karen! Look what you've done to me!" he yelled.

After watching several X-rated movies and still not able to get hard, he finished his drink and then finally fell asleep.

The following morning while showering, Jermaine came to the conclusion that he was going to do his best to put Karen behind him and move forward with his life. Knowing that Karen's words and actions were spoken and carried out because of her anger, Jermaine felt that she would soon come down to earth and begin writing him and calling him like she did in the beginning of her incarceration. He prayed for that to happen more sooner than later.

When he arrived at work he noticed that his coworkers were looking at him strangely and snickering. *What's up with these idiots?* he thought. *Jennifer must have told them about last night. Damn!*

On his desk were a few letters typed in large, bold print. One of the letters read: VIAGRA WORKS! Another letter read: YOU'RE UN-FUCKIN'-BELIEVABLE!

He figured that Jennifer typed that one because last night he had heard her say those same exact words.

Another letter read: IT'S NOT PROPERLY WORKING, SO WHY NOT HAVE IT SURGICALLY REMOVED AND REPLACE IT WITH A PUSSY!

The last letter he read was different then the others. It read: I KNOW HOW YOU FEEL, JERMAINE. WE ARE TWO OF A KIND. MY PENIS ONLY GETS EXCITED WHEN BEING WITH ANOTHER MAN. I HEARD ABOUT WHAT YOU ARE GOING THROUGH WITH YOUR WIFE AND I DO SYMPATHIZE WITH YOU. HOPEFULLY THIS HORRIBLE TRAGEDY WILL SHOW YOU EXACTLY HOW WOMEN REALLY ARE. THEY'LL TURN ON YOU QUICKER THAN THE WINK OF AN EYE, BUT I NEVER WILL. I'M SEARCH-ING FOR A SOUL MATE, AND I AM VERY ATTRACTIVE TO YOU. CALL ME ANYTIME, CHAD.

661-555-1221

PS I'M FREE FOR DINNER TONIGHT.

Jermaine quickly glanced over his shoulder and noticed that Chad, one of his coworkers, was smiling at him, and even winked at him.

Jermaine stood and faced all of his coworkers and gave them the finger.

"Fuck all of you!" he yelled, then angrily stormed into his supervisor's office and announced his resignation.

The following day Jermaine was interviewed by a broker who owned a Century 21 real estate branch in Thou-sand Oaks, California, and was hired on the spot. While sorting papers and getting his desk in order, a beautiful Mexican woman approached him and introduced herself.

"Hi. I'm Sylvia."

He stared at her a few moments before answering.

Sylvia was a plain type of woman; no makeup, no jewelry, or no flashy clothes.

"I'm Jermaine, it's a pleasure meeting you, Sylvia." He wanted to say more, but was at a lost for words.

"I've been employed here for six years and if there's anything you need help with, please don't hesitate asking me."

He glanced at her finger and saw no wedding ring, which boosted his spirits and confidence ten notches higher.

"You will definitely be the first person I ask if I have any inquiries," replied Jermaine, smiling, and then out of the blue, he got bold and asked a question. *I've got nothing to lose and everything to gain*, he thought.

"Sylvia, would I be out of line if I asked you to have lunch with me today? That is, if your husband won't mind?" He did a little prying.

"You don't waste any time, do you? Normally, I don't do lunch with strangers, but since you're new here and seem like a pretty nice guy, lunch will be fine. I don't think lunch will harm to our work relationship," she responded, actually happy to be noticed by someone.

"It could possibly enhance it," Jermaine replied, giving her the best smile that he could.

She then returned to her desk and continued working.

As Jermaine went over some leads on foreclosure properties that his boss had given him, an African American male coworker approached him.

"What's up, my brother? I'm Reggie," said the man, offering a handshake.

"I'm Jermaine, nice to meet you, Reggie." Jermaine accepted the handshake.

"I seen you shooting a few lines at the mystery woman and just wanted to congratulate you on that. Sylvia hasn't smiled like that in the six years that I've been working with her. I don't know what you said to her, brother, but whatever it was, keep on keeping on. It might open a door for you, you know I mean?"

"Hopefully it will, Reg."

"Man, you're like me," Reggie said, and then pulled a chair next to Jermaine. "Sisters just insisted on disrespecting a brother, and not showing any type of appreciation or consideration whatsoever, so I started dating other races. And believe me, man, I'm lovin' it. When a brother is with a white woman or a Mexican woman, man, that really pisses sisters off; they turn up their noses and look at you like you got shit all over you, but I just smile at 'em and keep on stepping."

"I hear you, man, you're right," replied Jermaine.

Jermaine and Sylvia lunched at a Mexican restaurant called Baja Grill. While eating, they conversed on the real estate market, their parents and siblings, their likes and dislikes, and also their past relationships. Realizing that Sylvia was the shy, quiet type, Jermaine took pleasure in leading in conversation. They were enjoying the date, but before they knew it, it was time to go back to work.

Trying to be sincere, Jermaine had revealed his situation about Karen to Sylvia. Jermaine felt that he was ready to initiate another relationship. Sylvia was actually just as attracted to him as he was to her, but she did not show it.

She was very sympathetic to his issues and she was very much attracted to him, but decided to take things slow. She did not want to stumble across any trouble, especially with the evil, mean, black woman that Jermaine had described to her.

During the course of the next month Jermaine and Sylvia began spending time together, but neither of them had talked about sex. They did not want that to be the foundation of their relationship or possible marriage.

Jermaine's father used to always tell him, "Son, good things are worth waiting for. Any woman who gives it up on the first night isn't the type of woman you'd want to make your wife."

Jermaine was assured that Sylvia was worth waiting on, and her feelings were mutual. They were both in search of a lifetime commitment, not a one-night stand, or not just someone to get their rocks off with.

Being seen with a Mexican woman did not bother Jermaine at all. As a matter of fact, he held his head up proudly. Sylvia treated him like a king, respected him, and produced concern and love. What he really admired about her was that she carried herself like a virtuous, shy woman.

Sylvia had come from a decent family that instilled morals and principals inside her. Her parents exercised dignity, integrity, and the importance of family value. Her father had once owned a small cab company in Guadalajara, but opportunely, after struggling and sacrificing to save money, he sold his business in order to move his family to the United States so they could get an education and a shot at a decent life.

When Mr. Siordia, Sylvia's father, had first met Jermaine, he instantly did not like him simply because he was black. Because of his dislike toward Jermaine, Mrs. Siordia's feelings were mutual.

"I want you to marry a doctor or a lawyer, a mayor, or a politician, Sylvia. You deserve someone of that class and not anything less," her father had said to her.

"Father, even a doctor, a lawyer, a mayor, or a politician can be unfaithful or evil. The bigger the title, the more the cheat. I'm not looking for someone with a big title, Father, I just want someone who will love me for me, be faithful to me, respect me, treat me good, and someone who will appreciate my love. That's what I want in a husband, Father. I could care less if he's a garbageman, a mechanic, a plumber, or a security guard; as long as he treats me good and shows me that he loves me and cares for me, that will be enough for me. Jermaine really loves me, Father, and I haven't told him yet, but I love him too. You and Mother have taught us not to be prejudiced, Father, so please remember that in accepting Jermaine."

"Prejudice is not an issue here. What I'm concerned about is your disease. Have you told him that you have cancer, or are you hiding it from him?"

"I think it'd be best if I don't tell him right now. Revealing my disease could possibly change things, and I just don't think it's time yet."

"If he loves you, Sylvia, then your disease or condition would not be a factor in your relationship. Love is unconditional. It always has been and it always will be. When I married your mother, my vows were to love her for better or worse, through good times and bad times, and most importantly, through sickness and good health. Like I said, if he loves you like you say he does, and I truly believe that he does love you, then your disease should not be an issue," explained Mr. Siordia.

She embraced her father and began crying.

"I just don't want to lose him, Father," she sobbed.

"It's your life, Sylvia. I have no right to suggest you do things that are against your will, and I've always wanted what's best for you. Maybe I'm being a little over-protective, or selfish, or maybe just afraid of losing you to another man, but I have to learn to respect and accept any decisions you make in your life. I keep forgetting that you're a grown woman and not a baby anymore. You're an intelligent, responsible woman who's capable of making sensible decisions, but aside from all that, to me, you will always be

Daddy's little girl." Tears ran from his eyes as he hugged his daughter.

"You're right, Father. I will always be Daddy's little girl. Thank you for understanding, Father. I love you so much."

As time passed, Mr. and Mrs. Siordia had been observing how special and exceptional Jermaine was treating their daughter, which caused them to grow fonder of him. Besides, they both knew that there was nothing that they could say or do to change Sylvia's mind toward Jermaine. She was happily in love.

Sylvia had not had sex with anyone since her last relationship, which was two years earlier. The last boyfriend she had, whose name was Eduardo, had cheated on her with her cousin and also with her two best friends. She discovered that Eduardo had been sleeping with them all for almost two years and unfortunately, everyone knew except her. With Eduardo being her first, her heart was completely shattered to pieces.

Jermaine felt like this was something he should have done a long time ago. He felt that being with Sylvia was the right move for him. He told his mother and sisters about her, and they could tell by the excitement and enthusiasm in his voice that he really cared for her and would treat her very well.

"At least she's not one of those ghetto women that Jermaine is normally attracted to," his oldest sister had said

"I'm happy for him," said his other sister. "She's nice, intelligent, and has positive things going on in her life."

Working out of the same office became a problem for Sylvia and Jermaine, mainly due to everyone being in their business. Each day when Jermaine arrived at the office, Reggie approached him, smiling.

"Did you hit it yet, man?"

"You're getting kind of personal aren't you, Reg?"

"Just tell me if you hit it, man, that's all I wanna know. I've got a hundred-dollar bet with Larry, Shane, Marcia, and even the boss, saying that you've hit it, so I need to know so I can collect my cash, man."

"Reggie, do you actually think that I'd let you know something that personal?"

"Hell yeah, you my boy, ain't you?"

"Yeah, I'm your boy, Reg, but she's my girl, and I wouldn't say or do anything to hurt her."

"Damn, you fall in love to quick, man. That shit could be dangerous, you know. Check yourself, before you wreck yourself, man."

"Believe me, Reg, I know what I'm doing."

"Yeah, right. I'll bet that you knew what you were doing when you married that nightmare too, huh?"

"Chill, man, take it easy, Reg. Man, I really think you need to go buy yourself a can of business."

"Whatever."

One day during lunch Reggie, once again, began voicing his opinion toward black women.

"Man, I'm telling you that a high percentage of black women be trippin', and I don't understand it. This one heffa name Pam kicked me dead in the ass with a pointy-toed shoe, and then busted the windows out of my Beamer. Like a damn fool, I took her back, and a week later the heffa stabbed me. That's when it was time for me to say goodbye, you know what I mean? But being the pussy-whipped man I was, I accepted the heffa back again, man, and a week later I found out that she had fucked up my credit by using my identity to forge some damn loan documents to pur-chase all kinds of shit. Man, she had rented cars, maxed out my credit cards, and had even charged over three thou-

sand dollars worth of shit from Victoria's Secret. Yeah, she
was just one of the many unappreciative women I took care
of. After her, I dated another sista named Rochelle, right?
Man, this woman didn't have any shame about embarrassing herself in public. She would wait until she was in the
presence of a crowd of people and talk loud and ghetto to
me, you know? The bad thing about it was that she didn't
care who heard her, and didn't give a damn about what she
was saying. She was straight ghetto, man."

Listening to Reggie, Jermaine could have sworn that he
had ultimately described Karen, but he did not care to
comment at the moment.

Mornings when Sylvia arrived at work, a few nosy
coworkers would approach her and began making small
talk in hopes to get some information about her and Jermaine so they could gossip.

"How is he in bed?" asked Marcia.

"Does he have a big dick?" Sandra boldly asked.

"Have you exchanged juices yet?" asked Cheryl.

"How is life with a black man?" Lisa asked Sylvia that
same question just about every day.

"Why are you guys so into my business? If and when Jermaine and I ever get intimate, believe me, you inquisitive
hounds will never know," replied Sylvia, directing her response to all of them.

While sitting at the dinner table later that evening,
Sylvia made a suggestion.

"Sweetheart, I think that us working in the same office
will one way or another effect our relationship. I honestly
recommend that, for the sake of our relationship, we
should strongly consider working apart from one another."

"Yeah, babe, we're on the same page. I was thinking the
same thing. Reggie is all over me every day like white on

rice asking me all kind of questions about us, and to tell you the truth, I'm tired of it. Tomorrow, I'll call a few other local Realtors to see if they have any openings and if so, exactly what they have to offer. As long as I'm not too far away from you, I can deal with it, but you know how I get those sudden urges for your kisses."

"You're so silly, but I love you so much for your understanding, your consideration, your love, and your—"

"Stop flattering me, babe."

"I'm only telling the truth."

"Where have you been all my life?"

"Within your reach, and waiting patiently for you."

While kissing and hugging, their bodies began overheating. Before things escalated, Sylvia pulled back and looked Jermaine in the eyes.

"I think I'd better stop before we end up doing something that we promised we wouldn't do until we're married."

"I think you're right, sweetheart." He then kissed her forehead and walked her to her car.

The next day after being interviewed and tested by the Antelope Valley branch of Coldwell Banker, Jermaine was immediately hired.

Eight long months had slowly crept by, and then one day while watching a movie, Jermaine proposed to Sylvia. He could not hold back any longer.

He paused the movie, and then got on his knees, giving Sylvia a serious, intense look. Then he took her hand.

"Sweetheart, I thank God for you. Being with you these last few months has really confirmed my love for you, and I cannot go another day without asking you to be my wife. Sylvia, will you marry me?"

"I thought you'd never ask. Of course I'll marry you, Jermaine. What took you so long to ask? I love you so much, and I promise you that I will always love you, respect you, and be there for you no matter what."

"I love you too, Sylvia, and my promise to you is to always love you, respect you, cherish you, and do my best to keep you happy and content. Through sickness or good health, for rich or poor, through our good times or bad times, I promise to love you. "

Two weeks later they got married.

Sitting proudly on the front row was Mr. and Mrs. Siordia along with all of Sylvia's brothers and sisters. Jermaine's mother, his sisters, his nephew, and a few cousins were also present occupying the second row and the third row. Reggie and a few coworkers were also there. Members of the congregation and people that had known Sylvia's family since coming to the United States happily occupied the remainder of seats.

It had been Mr. Siordia's idea for them to be married at church. Neither Sylvia nor Jermaine had protested. As a matter of fact, they thought it was a great suggestion. Jermaine and Sylvia appeared to be the happiest newlyweds in the whole wide world after saying "I do".

The following day, Sylvia wasted no time moving into Jermaine's home. She had waited long enough and now she was ready to make love to her new husband.

A couple months later, she became cheerfully pregnant.

Chapter 19

While growing up, Jasmine had never been too fond of her mother, mainly because of the things that she was exposed to and the way her mother treated her. Bad memories would haunt her mind probably forever.

Now being an intelligent, self-motivated young lady, it was not hard for her to distinguish what was real from what was actually bullshit. She remembered seeing her mother smoke crack on many occasions, and then her mother would always yell at her about one thing or another, and would even beat her for no apparent reason. Also, she remembered her mother bringing strange men into the apartment, and minutes later hearing the headboard bang against the wall and loud sex cries.

She could never forget the time that her brother and her had to live in a foster home until her Aunt Jewell had come to her rescue.

She often thought about all the violent fights and vulgar language her mother used toward men who she had moved into her apartment. She remembered being hit with an iron that was thrown at her by her mother. She remembered being slapped by her mother on many instances. Those memories had scarred Jasmine's mind so badly that it was nearly impossible for her to forget about them.

While shopping at Wal-Mart one day, Jermaine ran across Jasmine.

"Hey, Jazzy, how are you doing?" It had been a while since they had last seen one another.

"I'm fine, and you?" She was delighted to see him. He was the only man that she had approved of her mother being with. Actually, she felt that he was too good of a man for her mother, and also felt that her mother would some-how lose him due to her bad mouth and actions.

"I'm good. How is the baby and Raymond doing?"

"They're fine, thanks for asking. When was the last time you heard from my mother?"

"Well, the last time I saw your mother she told me that she's marrying a woman she met in prison when she's re-leased, and that was almost a year ago."

"Umph, I wouldn't put it past her, Jermaine. My mother's mind has been screwed up for as long as I can remember. She has always been a liar and a good talker. She tries hard to convince people into believing her and most times it works, but being around her for all those years, I can see right through her bullshit. I know that I really shouldn't be saying derogatory things about my mother, but she's given me every reason to," explained Jasmine, beginning to cry. "She's always been a good-for-nothing mother, and a first-class slut!" Jasmine had always felt comfortable talking to Jermaine. He was like a positive male figure she never had. She then continued pouring out her emotions.

"Did you know that she had sex with my father's cousin named Gary? Gary has pictures of her holding her pussy open, smiling and grinning. When I saw those pictures they blew my mind, Jermaine. And not only that, I was told that she gave my boyfriend's best friend a blow job for a piece of crack, and he was only seventeen years old. I knew when I first met you that you were not her cup of tea, and I figured that sooner or later she would reveal her true identity and that you would have hell on your hands. Jermaine, you are actually the best man my mother has ever had. You're the only man who cared anything about Stevie and Alexus. All those other worthless assholes, including my father, were nothing but street trash. Now she's about to marry a woman, huh? I wonder has she been taking her psych meds."

"Jasmine, Lord knows that I was patient with your mother. I had prayed hard for her to someday let go of her ignorance, her filthy mouth, her being disrespectful to me, and turn away from her evil old ways. I tried everything possible to deal with her. I'm a firm believer that things happen for a reason, and finally I've gotten over her and found myself someone who loves and appreciates me. Your mother's problem was that she didn't know how to love anyone else, because she didn't know how to love herself. I thank God that I'm all right now. No more stress, no more arguing every day, no more headaches or being stabbed by someone who supposedly loves you, and no more being verbally abused on a daily basis." His look was solemn.

"I'm happy for you, Jermaine. You deserve to be happy. I wish you and your significant other the best of luck, peace, and happiness. My mother has to be the stupidest woman in this world for acting so ignorant, inconsiderate, and unappreciative toward you." She then hugged him.

"If you ever need anything, Jasmine, and I don't care what it may be; don't be ashamed or afraid to ask me. I'll always be there for you, regardless of what happened between your mother and me."

"Thanks, Jermaine, I really appreciate that. Have a nice day," she replied, and then continued her shopping.

Lately, Jasmine's relationship with Raymond had not been going well at all. Due to the fact of them being together since junior high school and having a son, Jasmine tried hard to make her relationship work, but her efforts proved to be worthless and insignificant.

Raymond was a good example of a lazy, irresponsible, insecure man, who had gotten used to Jasmine taking care of him. He had never had a job and had never attempted to find one. His idea of an ordinary day consisted of smoking weed, drinking beer, and hanging with his homeys, shooting the shit.

When Jasmine came home from a long day of school and work, Raymond instantly demanded her to cook, then pressured her into giving him sex.

Raymond's insecurities had caused him one day to hide in the backseat of Jasmine's car while she was inside one of her male classmate's mother's house studying for an upcoming exam. Raymond had automatically assumed that Jasmine and her study partner were having sex.

After a few hours of studying, Jamal, her study partner, walked Jasmine to her car. No intimate gestures were made and no words of a possible relationship were exchanged, but out of the blue Raymond opened the back door and leaped out like a lion and began beating the college boy like he stole something from him.

"Raymond, stop it!" Jasmine yelled.

"Who's this? What's going on?" Jamal yelled, attempting to shield Raymond's punches, but failing.

"Nigga, I'll kill you!" Raymond yelled, while socking Jamal in the face and head.

"Stop it, Raymond, I said stop it!" Jasmine was crying and yelling simultaneously.

"Shut up, bitch, because you're next. I know you've been fucking this nigga! You can't tell me that you ain't been fucking him! You've been talking to the nigga on the phone damn near every fuckin' day, and now you at this nigga's house? Bitch, please! What kind of fool do you think I am? I might not go to college like y'all muthafuckas, but I ain't stupid, bitch! Get your ass in the car and let's get the fuck outta here! You'll get yours when we get home!" said Raymond, giving her en evil look.

Jamal laid helplessly on the sidewalk with a busted nose, a knocked out tooth, two black eyes, and a couple knots on his forehead.

Jasmine was embarrassed, upset, and indignant by Raymond's unnecessary actions and assumptions. He had never gone to the extent of ever hitting her, but instinct told her that this situation bought up the possibility.

When they made it back to the apartment, Raymond rushed over to her computer and picked it up and slammed it on the floor. Then he grabbed her 17-inch flat-screen monitor and slammed it to the floor. Jasmine stood helplessly watching. She did not want to say anything that would make him even angrier.

Raymond then grabbed a bottle of bleach off the kitchen counter and poured it over her furniture, and then went to the bedroom and bleached all of her clothes. Feeling that all his frustrations were not completely compensated, Raymond then grabbed a butcher knife and stormed outside to her car and, like a madman, sliced all four of her tires.

Jasmine figured he had gone a little too far now.

"Why are you acting like a damn fool, Raymond? Jamal and I were only studying for an exam, and nothing more. There is nothing going on between us, but classwork and studying! Maybe if you were in college or naturally smart I could confide in you, but unfortunately you chose the streets as your way of life," said Jasmine, and then he cut her off.

"Bitch, you're a goddamn lie! What kinda fool do you take me for? Y'all muthafucka's were studying, all right; studying different fuck positions, that's what y'all was studying!"

"Fuck you, asshole! You've crossed the line now. You know what Raymond, you're not an asset in any form to me, you're a fucking liability. I've been paying your way through life ever since my first job. I've bought your clothes, pay your cell phone bills, put gas in the fucking car that I bought your sorry ass, and I've been feeding you and providing a roof over your worthless head, and this is the thanks I get? Fuck you, Raymond; I'm finished with you! I've had enough! You're history, and I want you out of my fucking apartment and out of my life right fucking now!" Jasmine was furious. It took a lot for her to get angry, but Raymond had gone overboard.

"Aw, you're just trying to get rid of me so you can move your college boy in here, but it ain't happenin', bitch! Hell no, I don't think so."

"I could care less about what you think, Raymond. Time has proven that your thinking is so fuckin' ghetto and distorted, that I really don't give a damn what you think anymore. I want you out of here, and I want you out right now! Not tomorrow, not the next day, not next year, but right fucking now!" She stood with her hands on her hips with a serious look.

"I ain't goin' nowhere, so you might as well take your ass to bed and sleep it off, bitch! I'm the man of this muthafuckin' house, now take your ass to sleep while you're still ahead," insisted Raymond.

Raymond then grabbed a can of beer and then made himself comfortable on the sofa and began playing a game on his PlayStation.

Frustrated, Jasmine sat at the edge of her bed, thinking. Realizing that she could not physically put Raymond out of her apartment, and not really wanting to get the police involved, she made the decision to call her Uncle Bobby and her Aunt Jewell for assistance. She told them everything that had taken place.

Minutes later Bobby and Jewell were knocking on Jasmine's door. Hearing the expected knock, Jasmine exited the room and responded. Raymond was so caught up playing the game that he did not hear the knock, but had observed Bobby and Jewell's presence.

Bobby aggressively approached Raymond.

"What's your problem, man?" Bobby was standing face-to-face with him and had a mean, serious look.

"I ain't got no problem, nigga," replied Raymond, standing when seeing Bobby's approach.

Even though Raymond and Bobby were so much alike, they disliked one another with a passion.

"My niece tells me that she want you out of here, so kick rocks, nigga," said Bobby.

"Man, why y'all muthafuckas up in somebody else's business? This shit is between me and my girl, so I don't know why y'all even here."

Bobby popped his knuckles, and then balled his fists.

"I'm here because my niece called on me, nigga, and I plan to handle my business by getting your punk ass outta here."

"You don't wanna step to me, nigga. If I were you I would turn around and let me and my girl handle our own shit," replied Raymond, balling his fist, positioning himself for a fight.

"Why don't you just leave, Raymond? Jasmine doesn't want you anymore, so why don't you take it like a man and just leave?"

Jasmine stood silently with her arms folded.

"Fuck y'all, this is my—"

Bobby attempted to throw a punch to Raymond's head, but his age and the three cans of beer he recently drank prevented him from connecting.

Raymond blocked Bobby's punch, and threw a series of connecting punches that floored Bobby immediately. Raymond then leaped on top of Bobby and began choking him.

"What's up, nigga? I told you, homey, you don't wanna step to this! I could kill your punk ass right now if I wanted to," Raymond yelled, keeping a firm chokehold around Bobby's neck.

"Stop choking my uncle, Raymond!" yelled Jasmine.

Defending her husband, Jewell grabbed a flower vase and tried to hit Raymond's head, but she was not quick enough, either.

While holding a firm choke hold on Bobby, Raymond then begin socking him in the head.

"I don't know why you call these weak, ancient, muthafuckas to come put me out!" Raymond yelled, while socking Bobby.

"Let 'im get up, and y'all go it again, Raymond," Jewell suggested.

"This nigga can't hang with me. Fuck it, I'll let him up, and we can do this shit again."

Raymond then eased his hold and then stood and took a few steps back.

It had taken Bobby a while to get up being that he was practically out of breath, but he managed to stand firmly and square up with Raymond.

Raymond then took a wild swing that did not connect, which gave Bobby opportunity to land a couple of severe punches to Raymond's jaw and eye. Bobby's confidence level suddenly skyrocketed.

Semi-blinded by the hit to the eye, Raymond had no choice but to leap toward Bobby and grab him. They wrestled around the living room, knocking down the entertainment center, which caused the television to fall, breaking the aquarium, which cause the fish to come out and flop around on the floor, and also knocking down the lamp and several pictures that were on the wall.

Bobby then quickly put a choke hold on Raymond.

"What's up now, nigga?" Bobby yelled, having control of the situation.

Due to the choke hold, Raymond could not respond.

While keeping a firm choke hold on Raymond's neck, Bobby dragged him out the front door, then socked him in the head a few times, and then pushed him to the ground.

"I told you that my niece called on me, nigga, and I'm here to handle my muthafuckin' business," Bobby yelled, feeling victorious.

Bobby and Jewell had decided to spend that night with Jasmine, ensuring that she would not encounter any problems with Raymond.

The following day, Jasmine had secretly phoned Raymond, apologized to him, and then asked him to come back home.

Chapter 20

Marvin had begun to look for love and acceptance from the wrong type of people, which soon led him to indulge in criminal activities. Growing up without a father or a positive role model had affected Marvin to a point where at times he punched windows with his bare hand, cursed his teachers, and started fights with other students for no apparent reason. That was his way of releasing anger.

Because Jewell and Bobby took him in, Bobby had taken him under his wing and taught him street survival tactics. Being from South Central Los Angeles, Bobby knew the streets well and knew how to deal with street people. Under the leadership and guidance of Bobby, Marvin began lifting weights at the age of ten and by the time he became a teenager he was muscular, strong, and built like the Incredible Hulk. The average kid his age did not stand a chance of beating him in a fight.

Marvin earned his reputation as a tenth grader after simultaneously beating the hell out of three twelfth graders.

Because of his mean look and muscular build, students, teachers, and faculty members feared him.

Marvin looked up to Jermaine and admired him, until Bobby's jealousy of Jermaine influenced him differently.

"That nigga ain't your real father, man!" Bobby had said to Marvin. "Fuck that nigga! Just because he give you a few hundred dollars every now and then doesn't mean that he give a fuck about you! Don't get that twisted, nigga! If I were you, I would just use him like a tool, to get what I need! If you need a pair of shoes, or a suit and limo for the prom, if you wanna take your girl out and need some money, or if you need a car, then holler at that nigga, you know what I'm sayin'? Think of him as a free money source, that way you won't get things twisted, my little nigga!" explained Bobby.

Marvin had always listened to and obeyed his Uncle Bobby in fear of being rejected by him, or being called harsh names like a punk bitch, a scary, weak, or a stupid muthafucka. Bobby had no shame in calling anyone bad names. Bobby suggested that Marvin hang around him to prepare himself for the streets.

When Bobby first met Jermaine, he envied him instantly, especially after Jermaine revealed all of the positive things that were going on in his life. After finding out that Bobby was a mechanic and also washed cars for people who lived in the neighborhood, Jermaine had asked him how much he would charge to wash his Beamer and his other two vehicles. Bobby had told him that he didn't feel like working at the moment.

A normal day for Bobby consisted of having a bunch of homeboys over drinking beer, listening to loud rap music, smoking weed, lifting weights, and talking about street occurrences.

Marvin had never been enthused about being a gang

member, but because he lived in a neighborhood where Bloods ruled, he associated himself with them.

There were times when he thought about the seven-hundred-and-fifty-dollar disability check that Jewell and Bobby received each month for him, which would really tear him apart. He was aware that they used his check to pay their bills and to purchase clothes and gifts for their own kids, and it was time that he spoke up and said something about it. There was so much anger built inside him for so many different reasons that he was about to burst.

He boldly approached Bobby one day.

"Uncle Bobby," Marvin said. "I need four hundred dollars so I can go to driving school, and so I can buy me some school clothes."

Bobby was washing a neighbor's car.

"You need what? Nigga, you better go get your ass a job at McDonald's or Jack in the Box flipping burgers or sumphin'! Ain't nobody got no money like that to be giving you! You think money grow on trees or sumphin', nigga?" said Bobby, continuing to wash the car.

Marvin then angrily neared him.

"Uncle Bobby, check this out, you and Auntie never give me more than twenty dollars when my check comes, and I ain't been saying anything about it, but now I need four hundred dollars to go to driving school and to buy me some decent clothes."

Angrily, Bobby threw down his towel and kicked over the bucket of water, and then stood eye to eye with Marvin.

"Nigga, what part of what I said don't you understand? And for your information, punk, the money we get for you goes toward your living here, so shut the fuck up! We're the ones who have been taking care of your punk ass ever since we got you out of that damn foster home, and we deserve every muthafuckin' penny we get for you, nigga! Your fuckin' daddy ain't seen you since you were a goddamn baby, and that silly-ass mama of yours can't stop hittin' the pipe and sellin' pussy, so we're stuck with you. You should be grateful that somebody cares about you enough to let you live with them. We're the ones that's been housing you, and we're the ones who—" Marvin interrupted him.

"I need some of my money, Uncle Bobby. You can leave everybody else out of this because they don't have a thing to do with this. This is between me, you, and Auntie. Look at me; these raggedy, outdated clothes, these cheap, Payless tennis shoes, and this dirty T-shirt that hasn't been washed in three days. I look like a damn bum, Uncle Bobby! I'm tired of y'all fuckin' me over, Uncle Bobby! On top of that you and Auntie don't give me, Stevie, or Alexus, a damn penny of the money that Jermaine puts in an account for us! Y'all gonna have bad luck, Uncle Bobby, because y'all doin' us wrong, man! Y'all gonna be cursed, just watch and see!" Marvin said, keeping his fists balled.

The more he talked and thought about how he was being treated, the angrier he grew, but Bobby was getting even angrier.

"Nigga, you ain't been hearing a goddamn thing I been sayin', huh? I said—" Before Bobby could finish, Marvin socked him in the eye, then in the head, and then socked him hard in the mouth causing his dentures to fall out and break. The punches had come like lightning. Bobby's knees instantly buckled and he fell helplessly to the concrete as if Mike Tyson had hit him.

The speed bags that Bobby had insisted on Marvin practicing on had increased the speed of his hands so much that the average person would not see them coming.

Realizing he had knocked his uncle out cold, Marvin took off running through the apartment building until he reached the main street. Then he began walking with no particular destination. With not too many places to go, Marvin decided to sit at a local park and gather his thoughts. Minutes later, a few thugs he sometimes associated with at school and in the apartments seated themselves next to him.

After telling them what had taken place, they suggested that he join their gang. Subsequently, he was initiated by seven of them who were the so-called toughest. He was now officially a part of the ruthless Blood gang.

After the initiation they celebrated by drinking forty ounces of Olde English, smoking blunts, and listening to 2Pac on the boombox. This was actually Marvin's first time-consuming alcohol or smoking weed.

There were two common things about the boys in the hood: Neither of them entertained positive thoughts, and all of them indulged in criminal acts one way or another.

Two days after Marvin's initiation he was handed a bag of crack and was instructed by a co–gang member to sit on some apartment steps and make sales.

"Just sit there and sip on a forty and smoke a joint or sumphin', homey. Crackheads will bring you money all day and all night long, Blood. Just hit me on my cell when you need to re-cop," his homeboy had told him.

The gang had provided Marvin with a cell phone, a pair of tennis shoes of his choice, two new pairs of khaki pants, and five white T-shirts. In addition to that, they gave him a hundred dollars for pocket change.

Examining himself, Marvin felt good about his appearance and about being accepted. He now had the appearance of a youngster that was making money and having his way in the ghetto.

Within a month's time Marvin purchased a Cutlass, even though he did not have a license to drive. He had not returned to school since knocking out his Uncle Bobby. His days were now spent selling crack, smoking weed, drinking beer, stealing cars, and having sex with women of all ages.

His first sexual encounter had occurred one day when a crackhead woman offered him a head job in exchange for a small piece of crack. He had heard Uncle Bobby talk about how good a head job felt, and had also heard a few of his homeboys talk about head, but Tangy, a well-known Lancaster crackhead, gave him a treat that he could never forget. Since that first encounter, Marvin looked for Tangy every single day of the week. He was now addicted to head.

Within a six-month period Marvin had gotten three separate young ladies pregnant. Two of them were eleventh graders and the other was a tenth grader.

Marvin now had it all as a teenager. He was handsome, drove a nice car that had 22-inch rims and nice paint job, he sported jewelry around his neck, wrists, and on his fingers, and always had his pockets filled with money. Girls were automatically attracted to him. He had the choice of having sex with nice, clean young ladies, or being licked and sucked by crackhead women. Life was good to him.

The burning desire to know his father remained inside of Marvin regardless of his elevation in the dope game. Even though he felt like he was on top of his game, he would give it all up just to see and be with his father.

Chapter 21

One day while at PetSmart, as Jewell was purchasing some feeder fish for her Oscars, she observed Jermaine and Sylvia checking out some exotic birds. Being the nosy type, Jewell approached them.

"Hey, Jermaine, what's up?" asked Jewell, shooting a quick glance at Sylvia. Then she diverted her attention back to Jermaine.

"How are you, Jewell?"

"I'm fine. Same ol', same ol', you know," she replied, and then looked at Sylvia again.

"Excuse me for being so rude by not introducing you ladies. Jewell, this is my wife, Sylvia, and Sylvia, this is my friend and ex-sister-in-law, Jewell." They shook hands and exchanged smiles.

"So, you got married again, huh?"

"Yep. I wish I would have met Sylvia years ago, then I wouldn't have had to put up with your sister," Jermaine said, sarcastically but seriously.

"You did the right thing by finding you someone else. My

sister is crazy and bad mannered and she's not about to change for anyone. You were actually the best thing that happened to her and she couldn't even see it."

"I tried, Jewell. Lord knows that I tried. I had overextended my patience and tolerance hoping that she would change, but unfortunately it never happened. I just hope and pray that the kids will be all right, you know. It's a shame that they have to suffer behind their mother's choices and ignorance."

"Well, it's like this Jermaine; she made her bed hard, so she's the one who has to sleep in it, that's the way I see it. My sister's mind and her way of thinking have been fucked up since before she was a teenager. If it's not one thing, it's another with her. She a drama queen and a crackhead who enjoys being with worthless men."

"Don't leave out women," injected Jermaine, smiling. "Didn't she tell you that she's about to marry another woman?"

"I wouldn't put it past her, Jermaine. She'll try anything once, and if she likes it, then she'll roll with it. Now that you mentioned it, I can recall a couple times that she got out of jail and lived with women she'd met while incarcerated. I'll tell you, man, she's confused as hell. Anyway, have you seen Marvin lately?"

"Nope. Not since the last time I saw him at your place. Why? Is he missing in action or something?"

"Well, he jumped on Bobby a while back, and then call himself running away. I heard through the grapevine that he's somewhere out here selling dope, got three girls pregnant, and has joined a goddamn gang. I swear, Jermaine, that boy is gonna end up exactly where his mama is."

"You mean to tell me that Marvin, the Marvin I know, has joined a gang and is selling dope?" Jermaine shook his head in disgust.

"I'll tell you what it is, Jermaine; the boy is just looking for love in all the wrong places. That's what drove him to being the way that he is. His mama isn't capable of showing him love because she doesn't even know how to love herself, and his daddy is too busy trying to be a player and don't give a fuck about him, so the boy feels that nobody loves him. His childhood was so fucked-up, you know, not having a positive role model or a normal childhood can drive a child to self-destruction. His mama's habits and choices have really fucked up his mind, that's the way I see it. The bad thing about it, Jermaine, is that she still hasn't learned yet. How in the hell can she explain to her children the fact of being married to another woman? Hell, they already think she's crazy, but wait until they find out about this. Anyway, Jermaine, I gotta run. Those kids are probably driving Bobby nuts right now. Nice meeting you, Sylvia, and I wish you both the best of luck in your marriage."

"Thanks, Jewell. Give my love to the kids, and tell Bobby I said hi. As a matter of fact, tell the kids I'll pick them this weekend and take them to Disneyland or somewhere."

"That'll be nice, Jermaine. I'm sure that they will love that," replied Jewell, smiling. She then left.

She could not wait to get home and tell Bobby about what she had just witnessed.

After telling Bobby about her encounter with Jermaine and his Mexican wife, Jewell then wrote a letter to Karen describing her conversation in detail with Jermaine. Of course, she exaggerated a lot like she often did, but excluded the derogatory things she had said about Karen.

As soon as Karen received the letter she wasted no time calling her sister collect.

"I got your letter today, sis. So that muthafucka married a Mexican bitch, huh?" Karen asked.

"Yep, and he told me that you are about to marry a woman too."

"If that's my prerogative, Jewell, then that's what I'm gonna do. I'm a grown-ass woman, and I'm capable of making my own decisions. No one has to live with the decisions I make but me," explained Karen.

"Yeah, you right about that, Karen, but the decisions that you've been making have led you to jail, and has caused me to be stuck with your kids," replied Jewell.

"Anyway, I don't have much time to talk, so how are the kids doing?"

"They're fine, all but Marvin. He jumped on Bobby a while back, and then ran away. We haven't seen him since then. I heard that he's out there selling crack and doing all kinds of illegal shit, but if he is, sooner or later it will catch up with him. Oh, and I also heard that he's gotten three different girls pregnant."

"Well, that's on him. I raised him to—"

"You didn't raise him, Karen. Me and Bobby raised him. The only thing you have done was give birth to him, that's all."

"Whatever, Jewell. You still have a sarcastic mouth, don't you?"

"Yep. And you still haven't learned how to be a responsible mother yet, have you? Anyway, girl, back to Jermaine, his new wife appears to be intelligent and she's pretty attractive too. He mentioned that she's in real estate or a loan officer or something like that. They look so happy and content that it makes me kind of jealous. To be honest with you, I think they make a good couple." Jewell figured that she'd struck a few of Karen's nerves by now, which were actually her intentions.

"Girl, I don't give a flying fuck about Jermaine or his bitch! I hope both of those muthafuckas burn and rot in hell."

"Don't be mad at them, Karen. Hell, they haven't done a

damn thing to you; you're the one who fucked up a good thing, but you're just too damn stubborn and stupid to realize it and admit to it. Jermaine was the best thing that ever happened to you and the kids—" Karen hung up in her face.

Jewell then began talking to Bobby.

"She hates to hear the truth, Bobby. She's been in denial and running from the truth for as long as I can remember."

"If you ask me, the heffa is just plain ol' brain-dead and dumb. The thing that really gets me is that she thinks she knows every fuckin' thing, and she doesn't know shit."

Jermaine had stumbled across Chad, from his previous job, while shopping one day at Home Depot. Chad was delighted to see Jermaine, but this was an encounter that Jermaine could have done without. Jermaine felt awkward conversing with him in public, but he still gave him a few minutes of his time only to get updated about his former coworkers. He knew that Chad had plenty of gossip to spread.

"You do know that Jennifer has changed professions, don't you?" Chad asked, smiling. He shamelessly shot occasional glances at Jermaine's crouch area.

"Nope, I haven't heard anything about it. You mean that she actually gave up all those years of and experience and commitment as an agent for something else? Has she elevated to being an investor or a developer or something?"

"Nothing like that, Jermaine. She has actually made a ninety-degree turn for the worse. Her career modification happened shortly after you and her met that night. My theory is that since you and her didn't hit it off the way she had anticipated, she decided to chase her fantasy of having sex with black men. She's now a porn star, and not only that; she stars in movies with black men only. And I mean humongous black men, if you know what I mean," replied Chad, smiling, then shot another quick glance at Jermaine's crotch area.

"Is that so?"

Jermaine thought back to how desperate Jennifer appeared to be that night.

"Yes, that's so. If you like, you can come by my apartment and watch a few movies she's in. And get this, her stage name is Jennifer Black."

"Thanks, but I'll pass on that, Chad. I've recently gotten married and believe me, I'm a very content and blessed man. Tell everyone I said hello, and you take care of yourself and have a great evening, Chad."

Life for Jermaine and Sylvia had been going blissfully well. They spent lots of quality time together. They were two lovebirds created especially for each other. To relatives and acquaintances they were the perfect couple. No flaws, no arguments, no cursing at one another or disrespect, and no pointing fingers blaming the other for anything. Neither of them made decisions without the other's approval.

Before going to work in the mornings they drank coffee and watched the news together. In the evenings they took walks in the park, then afterward would come home and watch talk shows, and then watch the evening news, and before bedtime they completed their day with some good lovemaking. Love, peace, and happiness was always in their midst.

Months later, while in the process of delivering Jermaine Jr., serious complications arose due to Sylvia's cancer. She had missed her last couple appointments with her personal doctor to be updated about her condition and things were not looking well.

A doctor came to the lounge and announced that

Sylvia's cancer was causing complications in delivering the baby. This news came as a shock to Jermaine, and now Mr. Siordia suddenly felt that he owed Jermaine an explanation.

"Jermaine, please take a walk with me. I am so sorry for not mentioning Sylvia's condition to you earlier, but she insisted on not bringing anything to your attention in fear of possibly losing you." Mr. Siordia was used to looking people in the eye when talking to them, but feeling that he had somewhat deceived Jermaine, he looked away when talking to him.

"Mr. Siordia, with all due respect, sir, I could have cared less if Sylvia had one leg, one arm, or was confined to a wheelchair, I would still love her the same. The fact of me not being informed about this really doesn't matter to me. I'm more so concerned about whether or not her and my son will pull out of this okay." Jermaine's voice was saddened and wounded. He felt like he had just lost his mother, or a major part of him that kept him going.

"My Sylvia is just like me in some ways, son; sometimes she can be so stubborn, and so—"

"It's all right, Mr. Siordia. I guess we're all set in our ways and stubborn to a certain extent," said Jermaine, in a distressed manner.

Suddenly a voice sounded through the intercom.

"Will the family of Sylvia Hopkins immediately report to room four-oh-nine on the fourth floor? Will the family of Sylvia Hopkins immediately report to room four-oh-nine on the fourth floor?"

Family members from both sides speedily responded to the page, but once inside the room they sensed that something was terribly wrong.

The doctors and nurses that staffed the fourth floor had done everything possible to save both Sylvia and her new-born, but unfortunately Sylvia had died and luckily, Jermaine Jr. had lived.

Because Sylvia had missed her doctor appointments, she had no knowledge of the cancer spreading to her uterus.

After hearing the devastating news from the head doctor, Jermaine went ballistic.

"Why! Oh, God, why did you take my Sylvia away from me! I had finally found my soul mate and you took her away! Why! Why Why!" yelled Jermaine, pacing the floor.

Mr. and Mrs. Siordia hugged one another tightly while mourning over the death of their daughter.

A relative of Jermaine's suggested that everyone join hands for a brief prayer, and after prayer a Filipina nurse approached the family.

"Would you like to see the baby?" asked the nurse, smiling. She hoped that seeing the baby would relieve some of the hurt and anguish from the family members.

Jermaine Jr. was a beautiful baby who shared the resemblance of both of his parents. He was a light-brown–complexioned, with had a head full of long, black hair, and a pair of pretty brown eyes. Jermaine was the first family member to hold the baby.

"Thank you, Lord, for seeing to it that my baby came out healthy and normal. But Lord, with all due respect, I'm still waiting on an answer as to why you took my Sylvia away from me. She was my world, Lord. You blessed me with her, Father. For you to just take—" He began crying.

Jermaine was mentally wounded behind the death of his wife, but like his father always told him, life goes on.

Even though he was blessed with a son, that just did not seem to substitute for his wife's absence.

He had taken a leave of absence from work, hoping to recover so that he could begin making arrangements for the well-being of his son. Not having any babysitting skills, Jermaine had asked Mrs. Siordia to tend to the baby while he began taking care of a few loose ends and pulling himself together mentally. But instead of taking care of business and pulling himself together, Jermaine spent his days and nights at home drinking hard liquor until he was totally drunk. The only time he left his home was when he had sobered up enough to go and purchase more liquor. His cell phone and home phone rang continuously, but he did not bother answering either of them. He kept the television and stereo on full blast during the entire day.

It had been a week and a half since anyone had heard from Jermaine. Mr. Siordia was awfully worried and decided to pay a visit to Jermaine's home.

"Who is it?" yelled Jermaine, from the sofa. There were empty beer cans and bottles of liquor scattered about. The house needed immediate attention, but that was the least of Jermaine's issues. Because he did not open any windows or doors, there was a foul smell, which came from the combination of dirty dishwater, fish, and chicken grease sitting on the stove, and the overfilled waste basket sitting in the kitchen.

"Jermaine, open up, it's your father-in-law."

Damn, thought Jermaine. *Oh well, whatever.*

Jermaine found no use to try to straighten up the house, nor did he try to pull himself together. He did not have time to do either. He trotted to the restroom and took a rapid appraisal of himself, and realizing how bad he looked, he quickly thought, *Damn. I look like a downtown bum.*

Entering Jermaine's home, Mr. Siordia glanced around, observing the empty liquor bottles and beer cans. He frowned to the foul odor and decided to stand instead of seating himself.

Unashamedly, Jermaine grabbed a liquor bottle that only contained a corner and turned it up, and then seated himself on the sofa.

"Everyone thought that you had dropped off the face of this earth, Jermaine," said Mr. Siordia, standing next to the big screen.

"I feel like I have, Mr. Siordia. I feel like I don't want to live anymore, but you wouldn't understand what I'm talking about. I apologize for not coming by to see my son, but I just don't want him in my presence at the time," Jermaine explained, and then walked to the fridge and grabbed another beer. He popped open the beer, took a long swallow, and then began pacing the floor while talking. Mr. Siordia silenced himself to let Jermaine vent.

"Now that we finally have a chance to have a one-on-one, I'd like to say a thing or two, that is if you don't mind, Mr. Siordia." Jermaine's voice raised a few notches. There were a few things he wanted to get off his chest.

"I know that you didn't like me when you first met me, because I was black. You only accepted me because your daughter loved me, and that you had no other choice but to accept me. You could not accept the fact of a black man sleeping with your daughter, but realizing that no matter how much you didn't approve of it, your daughter was not going to stop seeing me because we were in love. You see, Mr. Siordia, I had a precious daughter also. That's how I can relate to your feelings. It killed me when I found out that my daughter was having sex, and not just having sex, but having sex with an older guy. My first thought was to go and kill the muthafucka, but after giving it some deep, sound thought, hell, what was the use? The next day or maybe even the same night they were gonna find a way to be together. I couldn't play security guard over her body, so what I decided to do was to educate her on young men. Till this day, I can say that enlightening my daughter's mind paid off because I only have one grandchild and he's by the man that she married. My daughter rests in peace now, but at least I can say that I did my job in raising her well and respectful." Jermaine then took another long gulp and continued pacing. Mr. Siordia began talking.

"I sympathize with you, Jermaine, about your daughter and all, but actually that's irrelevant to this matter. It seems to me that you've given up on life, son, and that's a bad thing to do. Sylvia would not have wanted that, and I'm sure that you don't want your son growing up hearing that his father was a loser and a drunk. And you're right about my not approving of you in the beginning, but as time passed and hearing my daughter continually tell me how much she loved you, I grew to love you as if you were my own son. What you're doing, Jermaine, is destroying your mind and your body. This is definitely not the solution to your situation. Believe me, my Sylvia is in heaven watching you this very moment. Do you think she's pleased with the way you have chosen to carry on?"

Digesting Mr. Siordia's words, Jermaine calmly and thoughtfully seated himself.

"I'm sorry, Mr. Siordia." He began crying. "I'm so sorry. Please understand that Sylvia was all I had in this world. She was the only woman who ever understood me and respected me and truly loved me. She was the only woman that listened to me about everything. I miss her, I miss her so damn much it hurts. Why did God take away the one thing that I loved the most? Why? She was my life-support system, she was the queen of my soul, she was the only woman who ever said she loved me and actually meant it. She was my—" He began crying even louder.

Mr. Siordia approached him, then seated himself next to him.

"Son, I know you're hurt, because you loved Sylvia and so did I. After all, she was my daughter. But now you need to pull yourself together for the sake of your son, and more so to demonstrate to Sylvia and to yourself that you are strong enough to keep going forward in life regardless of what happened. When a tragedy occurs in one's life, son, it's time to be fervent and strong in order to deal wisely with situations and circumstances. You are family, Jermaine, and we all love you just as Sylvia loved you. Please, be strong, son, and get yourself back on the right track." Mr. Siordia then embraced Jermaine with a hug, and then afterward he shook his hand and left.

Immediately after Mr. Siordia had left, Jermaine took a long, hot bath and then decided to take a nice, long shower. After that he put on a Stevie Wonder CD and began thoroughly cleaning his house.

Later that evening he went to the Siordias' residence to spend some time with his son.

Apparently, Mr. Siordia's words had a great influence over Jermaine, because the following day he was back at work.

Chapter 22

Karen spent her days alone in her cell, reading fiction and spiritual books, writing letters to family and friends, contemplating life with Maria, and mostly masturbating while thinking about Maria's sensuous touch, and still fantasizing about Tyrone's huge penis. She was a nympho and a freak by nature and nothing would ever change that.

With her release date nearing, she felt it would be best to remain in her cell to avoid any form of trouble, and mainly to keep away from other envious inmates. Trouble had its way of finding inmates who were soon about to be released.

Before Maria's recent release she had paid a few trustees and also a corrupt prison official not to house anyone with Karen. Maria was an extremely jealous lesbian and her worse fear was someone diverting Karen's mind from her to them.

After hearing about the death of Jermaine's wife from Jewell, out of loneliness, boredom, and wanting to see what her ex-husband was up to, Karen decided to write Jermaine a letter.

The letter read:

Dear Jermaine; as I lay reminiscing about the good times, arguments, and sexual pleasures we've shared my afterthought was to write you mainly to see how you're holding up. I'm very sorry about the death of your wife because I know how much you really loved her. I heard through the grapevine that you two seemed so happy, and so much in love with one another. I have to admit that it made me sort of jealous, even though I played it off like it didn't bother me. I would like to apologize for all of the frustrations, anger, and deceit that I have caused you in the past. Today, I read my Bible daily, and I really feel that after doing this time I am a changed woman with an entirely different outlook on life, and a different way of thinking. I regret being here, but at the same time, I truly believe that God sent me here to experience Maria and also to renew my thinking.

As I told you when I last saw you, my plans are to marry Maria upon my release. I strongly feel that she is my soul mate and that we will have a good, peaceful, meaningful life together. I know you're not the kind of man who approves of a gay lifestyle, but I am basically just doing what makes me feel good, and sharing my life with someone who cares about me and who loves me unconditionally. Actually I still think I do need a dick in my life every now and then, and hopefully I can call on you when I get that urge.

Thanks for spending time with the kids and for showing them love. Maybe, if it's okay with you, we could go to dinner or watch a movie or something when I'm released. By the way, if you didn't know, I'll be out in two weeks. If you have the time please write me.

Sincerely, Karen

PS I'm playing with myself, and fantasizing riding the hell out of your dick. You know I used to have my way with your dick, don't you? Smile.

In reality, she lay naked with her legs spread open, eyes closed, playing with her pearl tongue, while easing three fingers in and out of her heated, wet pussy. She envisioned Tyrone's humongous dick in her hand, then imagined it inside her fucking her slow and deep.

Immediately after Jermaine received Karen's letter, he found himself fantasizing about having sex with her. He quickly pulled a picture from his wallet of Karen lying naked, holding her pussy open, showing all of its pinkness. He stared at it lustfully for a few moments, and then wasted no time stripping naked.

Looking at the picture, he thought about times that she had rode his dick slow and easy while looking him in the eyes. Then he thought about the nice, slow, head jobs she had given him, sucking him completely dry and swallowing every drop of his cum. His penis was now rock hard. Holding her picture, staring at it, Jermaine began stroking himself slowly then seconds later sped up his rhythm. He had not been this hard since last having sex with Sylvia. He stroked it faster, and then slow, and then faster still, gazing at Karen's pussy, then finally he released a thick load of cum that shot straight in the air, and then landed on his chest. Afterward he wrote her back.

Hi Karen. I hope this letter finds you in good health and in good spirits. I was surprised to receive a letter from you, but out of concern and love, and to wish you happiness and success upon your release I took time to reply.

My life is more boring now than it ever has been. My days consist of working at the office five to seven hours a day, then spending a few hours of quality time with Jermaine Jr. and then after that retiring on my sofa watching the news. I still manage to spend a little time with Stevie and Alexus. They really look forward to me picking them up. You're right about me not promoting or approving of a lesbian lifestyle, but it's life and you're gonna do what you want to do regardless of what anyone's opinions or suggestions are.

Anyway, congrats on your upcoming release date. Dinner and a movie sounds great. I'm looking forward to it. Here's my phone number, feel free to call me anytime.

Take care, Karen, and keep your head up, stay focused, and have a positive plan that will enable you to live a decent, civilized, stress-free life. Most importantly, stay prayed up.

PS You're absolutely right about the way you used to have your way with my dick. Believe me, the pleasures you gave me, I will never forget.

Sincerely, Jermaine

Karen was released from prison the following week, but she had not heard from Maria. She had made several attempts to place collect phone calls to Maria's mother's house, but her calls were never accepted.

After Maria was released, out of boredom and being in love, Karen wrote her two letters a day but she had not received any replies. *She's probably found another lover, or either went back to men*, thought Karen.

The bus ride to Maria's mother's house was both long and boring. Thanks to the three hundred dollars Maria had left on her books, Karen got off the bus at a mall and did some shopping. After all, it had been a long time since she had the opportunity to pick and purchase her own clothes. Afterward she went to a hair stylist.

Her fresh-out-of-prison appearance was astoundingly

gorgeous. She wanted to look impressively attractive for her wife-to-be.

Her sassy look and sexy walk made it obvious that she was responsible for the peachy odor that lingered distinctly throughout the entire bus. The bus ride lasted a little over two and half hours. Karen was now in the City of La Puente, California. Thank God Maria had left her with a telephone number, an address, and directions for her.

The address belonged to an attractive green-and-white house that was surrounded by a white picket fence. The lawn was well manicured, and the roses, tulips, and other beautiful flowers could not go unnoticed.

After waiting a few seconds, making sure there were no dogs in the yard, Karen then walked through the gate and then approached the front door. She rang the doorbell and waited impatiently for her lover to answer, but instead a Mexican woman, appearing to be in her late fifties, opened the door.

"Hi," greeted Karen. "Is Maria here?"

"She no here," replied the woman.

"Are you expecting her back soon?"

"I no see her since she get out prison. I think she's back on drugs," said the woman.

At that moment a little girl approached from inside and stood next to the woman.

"Are you looking for my sister, Maria?" asked the girl.

"Yes. Do you know where I can find her?"

"My Uncle Miguel said that she walks up and down the boulevard selling her body, and that she's—"

"Veronica, shut your mouth!" yelled the woman.

"Do me a favor," said Karen. "Please tell her that Karen came by if you happen to see or hear from her."

Karen then disappointedly walked away. Tears ran from eyes as she made her way back to the bus stop. She had no particular destination in mind so she began thinking. *How could I be so damn stupid? I should have known that bitch was just playing a fucking game with me while she was locked up. How stupid I was to believe that we were getting married. I feel like kicking myself in the ass. Fuck this stupid shit, I'm about to go get me some dick.*

Entertaining those thoughts, Karen exited the bus and then made her way to the nearest pay phone.

"Hi," she said excitedly, once Jermaine answered the phone.

"Hey, Karen. Are you out?" He sounded just as excited as she did.

"Yep. Fresh out, baby, and you know what I need."

"Is that right? Hell, based on our last conversation I thought that you had life all figured out and knew exactly what you wanted, and how you were going to get it."

"Well, that's a long story, babe, and it's a story that I don't care to discuss right now. Anyhow, are you busy?"

"Not really, just working on my book and playing with my son. Why, what's up?"

"Well, I was just thinking that maybe, if it's the Lord's will, that you can pick me up and we go see the kids together, that is if you don't mind?"

"I think that's a good idea, Karen. Where exactly are you?"

After giving him her whereabouts Jermaine's thoughts were, *What can it hurt? And besides, she's fresh meat. I'll bet she's tight as hell.* With that thought in mind, he hurriedly dressed Jermaine Jr. and rushed out of the house.

While sitting inside a McDonald's waiting Karen's thoughts were, *So far so good. His philosophy about the journey of a thousand miles begins with a single step is about to be initiated.*

Seeing Jermaine's black Beamer pull into the parking lot, Karen instantly jetted from her seat, ran outside, and approached the car. She greeted him with a long, wet, meaningful I-miss-you kiss. His kiss was in harmony with hers.

"It's been a long time, Karen," he said, while checking her out from head to toe.

"Yes, it has been quite a while, honey. You haven't lost your touch in kissing, that's for sure."

"Neither have you. Still those sloppy, wet kisses, huh?"

"I guess they were meaningful to you once upon a time, but I can't determine whether or not they're meaningful to you now, that's your call," she replied, smiling.

"So far, so good," he replied.

"Yeah, that's what I say." She shot a quick glance of hatred at Jermaine Jr., but played it off with a phony smile.

"Oh, look at the cute baby. He looks just like you, Jermaine. Look at those eyes and lips." She instantly hated the baby.

"What can I say?" replied Jermaine, and then asked. "Would you like to hold him?"

"I really feel like holding something else, if you know what I mean, but yeah, let me hold the baby."

"You're hot and ready, aren't you?" he asked, handing her the baby.

"What do you expect? It's been so long that I can't even remember the last time I had some dick."

"I think that I can accommodate you on that."

"I hope so, because my pussy is itching, wet, and hungry for some."

During the ride, Karen began telling Jermaine about incidents that had occurred during her incarceration, and he talked about his previous and present job, about life as a single parent, and what really pissed her off was when he began telling her about his relationship with Sylvia. She was in no mood to listen to his relations with another woman, but decided to be nice and hear what he had to say.

An hour later they had made it to Jewell's house.

Seeing their mother and Jermaine walk inside, Stevie ran full speed to his mother and embraced her with a long hug, while Alexus sped to Jermaine, yelling with excitement.

"Mommy, Mommy," shouted Stevie.

"Daddy, Daddy, Daddy!" yelled Alexus.

Afterward, Stevie embraced Jermaine, and Alexus jumped into her mother's arms. They both still referred to Jermaine as Daddy.

"Daddy, let me hold my brother," said Stevie, holding out his arms.

"Daddy, let me hold my brother, too," said Alexus, standing there looking jealous.

Karen held a pleasant look, but inwardly she did not like this Jermaine Jr. shit at all.

Bobby, who was sitting on a sofa drinking a can of beer, spoke to Jermaine, then shot a quick glance at Karen, and looked away.

Karen and Jewell had disappeared into the bedroom to have a brief sisterly talk.

"So, are you and Jermaine hooking back up, or what?" asked Jewell, curiously.

"I couldn't tell you right now, but I'm just going with the flow for right now. Girl, I hope this nigga can fuck me all night long, because I'm horny as hell, and can't deal with that minute–man bullshit."

"I heard that. Hell, Bobby stays so full of that goddamn liquor that he can't even last a half a minute."

They then began packing a few clothes of the kids and once finished they reappeared in the living room with the others. Karen was ready to get the hell out of Bobby's sight.

"I'll talk with you tomorrow, girl. We've got a lotta catching up to do," said Karen, smiling, while getting the baby from Stevie.

"I'll bet you do," said Bobby, sarcastically. He then said,, "As much as your ass get locked up, you ain't gonna never catch up. I don't understand how a muthafucka can stay gone away from their kids for long periods of time, and then show up thinking that they can patch things up over ice cream, a few new toys, and a muthafuckin' kiss and hug. I swear, y'all got life twisted."

"Whatever, Bobby. I can see that you haven't changed a damn bit."

"You ain't changed either, heffa! In a couple months you'll be doing the same bullshit all over again. Man, I wish I hit the lottery or somethin', so I can get the hell away from all y'all stupid muthafuckas."

"If you're a fool without money, you'll be an even bigger fool with money," said Karen, laughing while walking outside.

"Fuck you, ho!" Bobby yelled angrily, but she was already gone.

"Can we all just get along?" asked Jermaine, walking outside holding Alexus's hand.

"You didn't have to call her that, Bobby," said Jewell.

"Fuck you too, Jewell! You're always taking up for that no-good, crackhead, institutionalized bitch!"

After leaving Jewell's, Jermaine suggested dinner at Home-Town Buffet.

Karen was excited about being in Jermaine's and her kids' presence, but holding his baby irritated the hell out of her. She secretly hated Jermaine Jr. with a passion, but she was very careful not to show it.

Dinner had never been better for them. While they sipped wine and conversed about past and present issues, the kids were filling their bellies with soda, ice cream, and lemonade. Jermaine Jr. sat quietly in his stroller observing things.

After that, Jermaine headed to the Palmdale Mall and treated everyone to whatever they wanted. First they went to Babies "R" Us, where he bought Jermaine Jr. six outfits, all with matching shoes and hats, and also a basket full of additional baby items.

Then they went to Foot Locker where he purchased Stevie a pair of Nikes and a pair of Reeboks.

Their next stop was Victoria's Secret, where he spent almost six hundred dollars on perfumes and sexy lingerie for Karen.

Alexus was easy to satisfy, happy with a new doll, a new pair of tennis shoes, and a couple of outfits. Jermaine did not buy himself anything. Seeing that everyone else was happy made him content.

After that, Jermaine took his family to the fairgrounds, and then finally they retired at his home, watching movies. Stevie and Alexus were so exhausted that they both fell asleep ten minutes into the movie, and Jermaine Jr. had fallen asleep while inside the car.

After putting the kids to bed, Karen quickly suggested they take a shower together.

"Sounds good to me," replied Jermaine, trying to conceal his excitement.

He suddenly thought about the many past sexual encounters he had with Karen, which caused his penis to instantly get rock-hard.

After stepping into the shower together, Karen wasted no time getting on her knees doing what she did best. While massaging his balls, she licked up and down his shaft, and then began sucking and licking the head of his penis. It had been a long time since she'd last done this, but it took no time for her to get a rhythm going. She automatically began fingering herself. After three minutes of lips and tongue, Jermaine then picked her up and inserted himself inside her, and then mounted her against the wall and began fucking her at a nice, medium speed; not too fast or not too slow. A few minutes into ecstasy, Karen made a suggestion.

"Take me to the bed while it's still inside me. Your dick feels so good inside me that I never want you to pull it out. I want to ride the hell out of it, and then suck it, then ride it some more. I want your big dick to be a part of me forever."

The three things that Karen was really good at was sex, stroking egos, and influencing people into believing a lie.

Once in bed, Karen decided to suck it and lick it again, but this time she did it like the pro that she was. Minutes later he came, but she never stopped her groove. Momentarily, he had gone limp until she took the whole thing in her mouth, sucking it fast, then licking it up and down and all around. Then she climbed on top of it and mounted it and began riding, nice and slow. She enjoyed occasionally just the feel of the head of it inside her so she'd ease up and down with only the head inside her pussy, then she would sit on the whole thing and go round and round and up and down having her way with it. She rode it until she climaxed.

After the long, pleasurable ride Jermaine had immediately fallen asleep, but Karen was still hot and wanted more. She began licking and sucking it again, trying her best to get it back stiff, but it was no use, it was a dead soldier. She then put on an X-rated movie and began playing with herself while watching it.

The following morning, Jermaine asked her and her kids to move back in with him. Three days later they were in Las Vegas getting remarried.

Chapter 23

Not yet realizing Karen's hatred toward his son, Jermaine felt it was okay to let her tend to him while he was at work.

A few days later Karen suggested to Jermaine that his son live with the Siordias during the week and Jermaine pick him up on weekends, but Jermaine flatly rejected it, not knowing of Karen's abuse.

"I want to raise my son in my own household. I don't want him to be confused, you know. It's going to be complicated enough explaining why his mother isn't here, and the last thing I want to have to explain is why he was raised by his grandparents and not by me. Kids are always asking questions and curious about different things, you know. The bottom line is that I'm raising my own son, my own way, and in my own home. Besides, his grandparents are too old-fashioned and much too slow to raise a child in this day and age. Anyhow, I don't think that Stevie and Alexus would appreciate not being able to see or play with their little brother every day. They both adore him so much, don't you think so?"

"Yes, they have taken a liking to him." Her response was plain and impassive.

What she really wanted to say was, *Let the bastard live with them! I've had enough of changing Pampers and hearing a goddamn baby cry all night long. Give me a fuckin' break.*

The following morning after Jermaine went to work, Jermaine Jr. began continuously crying. Karen ignored the cries for as long as she possibly could and then finally, both angry and aggravated, she got out of the bed and approached the crib.

"Listen, you little bastard, I ain't your goddamn mama! It ain't my responsibility to tend to you! Take this damn bottle, and go your little ugly, half-breed ass to sleep! I ain't got time for this shit!" She shoved the bottle inside the baby's mouth, and then hatefully pinched him. The baby was quiet only for a few moments, and then he began screaming.

"Shut the fuck up!" yelled Karen.

The baby's cries combined with Karen's yells had awakened Alexus, who soon came into the room. Stevie had already left for school.

"Mommy, why you scream at the baby?" asked Alexus in baby talk, but Karen knew exactly what she was saying.

"Go back to your room and watch cartoons, Alexus! The last thing I need is you asking me a bunch of damn questions." Alexus sped out of the room instantly.

Jermaine Jr. began crying even louder.

"Shut the fuck up! I've told you, little boy, that I ain't your goddamn mama," yelled Karen, approaching the crib.

"Your mama fucked my goddamn husband, then came

you! Your mama violated me, you little muthafucka, and that's why the bitch is dead! I hate you! As long as you live, I'll hate you, you half-breed bastard! That's too good of a name for you; you're a mutt, that's what you are! A mixed mutt!" Then she grabbed one of his arms and roughly slung him around, and then pinched him again in several places. The baby cried even louder. His Pamper was soaked and had not been changed since Jermaine had changed it a few hours before he went to work. Karen had told herself that she was not, under any circumstances, going to change that bastard's diaper.

Thirty minutes later, Jermaine Jr. had finally cried his way to sleep.

Mr. Siordia's instincts had led him to believe that Jermaine was seeing another woman, and his intuition was confirmed the day when he placed a call to Jermaine's home and Karen answered the phone. He immediately brought this to his wife's attention.

"I don't want my grandbaby in the presence, or in the care of one of Jermaine's girlfriends. Regardless of him being a decent man, you never know how a child is being treated when they're in the care of a girlfriend. As far as we know this woman could hate the baby, or she might be on drugs or alcohol. Who knows, she may have even been a child abuser. I dare him to let another woman mother my grandbaby," said Mrs. Siordia, angrily.

"I agree with you a hundred percent," said Mr. Siordia. "There are too many crazies in this world today to let an unfamiliar person tend to a baby. The woman spoke with an attitude to me as if she didn't approve of my calling there."

"Why don't we pay an unexpected visit to Jermaine's house?" suggested Mrs. Siordia. "It's been almost two weeks since I've seen my grandson."

"That's a good idea, Cecelia. I'd like to see that discourteous woman face-to-face."

When the Siordias arrived, Karen was not impressive to them. After the Siordias introduced themselves, Karen turned up her nose and then pointed to the crib where the baby was, and then seated herself at the computer. The entire while the Siordias were there, Karen ignored them and acted as if they were invisible and displayed no hospitality whatsoever.

After picking up the baby, Mrs. Siordia realized that his Pamper was completely soaked and offered to change him. Karen tried defending herself.

"The Pampers are upstairs to the bedroom on the right. I just changed him a not too long ago, he must have just pissed again," lied Karen.

I wish these uppity bean-eating muthafuckas would hurry up and leave. The nerve of them to act like they're so goddamn important.

Since Karen was not courteous enough to offer him a glass of water, Mr. Siordia walked to the fridge to serve himself. Afterward, he seated himself at the dining room table.

Before the Siordias arrived, Karen had been sorting through some old papers and letters, and had not realized that she had left her prison ID lying on the table where Mr. Siordia was sitting. Being the inquisitive man that he was, he spotted it and stared at it a few moments, and then sneakily slipped it into his shirt pocket. Karen was still pretending to be busy on the computer.

At that moment Mrs. Siordia returned, smiling, holding the baby, but Mr. Siordia was furious and ready to leave.

"Let's go, Cecelia. We have a very busy day ahead of us," said Mr. Siordia. They then gave the baby a kiss and said good-bye to Karen and Alexus.

Karen slammed the door behind them.

* * *

After leaving the residence, Mr. Siordia pulled the prison ID out of his pocket and showed it to his wife.

"Oh, my God. My grandbaby is in the care of a prisoner."

"A prisoner is someone who's in prison, Cecilia. She wouldn't be considered a prisoner, but the fact of the matter is that she has been to prison, and this is our evidence. I'll notify our lawyer right away about this. As I see it, we shouldn't have a problem getting legal custody of our grandchild. I'm going to have our lawyer find out exactly what she went to prison for, and also have him dig up everything about her background. I bet this woman has enough dirt on her to open a cemetery," said Mr. Siordia.

The following day, Karen stumbled across her son, Marvin, while at a liquor store. She felt that now was as good of time as any to have a good, sensible, mother-to-son talk with him.

"Hi, baby," Karen said excitedly, and then embraced him with a long hug.

"What's up?" Marvin replied, emotionless.

Seeing her triggered sudden thoughts of him being placed in a foster home, then being raised by his aunt, and then not being allowed to talk to or see his father. He then abruptly thought about the times he'd seen his mother smoke cocaine and act violently toward him. He thought about the many times he had witnessed different men enter his mother's bedroom without speaking to him or even looking his way. Those thoughts generated Marvin's sudden attitude.

"You've gotten so tall, and so manly looking," Karen said, examining her son.

"Yeah, I guess," replied Marvin, dryly.

Then out of the blue Karen began lecturing him on right

and wrong and the things he should be trying to do with his life.

"Jewell told me that you've been selling dope and that you've joined a gang. I didn't raise you like that, Marvin, and I—"

"What the fuck are you talkin' about!" snapped Marvin. "You didn't raise me period, and I hope you don't expect me to call you Mama! You were never a mother to me! You were too damn busy smoking crack and fucking every Tom, Dick, and Harry that offered you a fuckin' hit! I hate you! I fucking hate you so much that I could beat your ass right this minute for sending me through the bullshit you sent me through!"

Standing face-to-face with the woman he blamed for his unfortunate upbringing made Marvin want to go ballistic on her that very moment. For so long he had wanted to voice how he really felt to her about things, and even though this was not planned, it was the perfect time.

The loud, harsh words coming from both of them had attracted a crowd of people that watched and listened, and even began giving their opinions about what was being said.

"You got a lot of goddamn nerves!" yelled Marvin, standing eye to eye with his mother.

"Boy, I'm still your mother regardless of what I did in the past, and you show me some respect and lower your damn voice, or I'm gonna—"

"You're gonna do what? You're gonna whip me with an extension cord again! Or are you gonna throw a toaster at me again! Oh, I know, you're gonna hit me with a baseball bat again, huh! I ain't that little boy anymore that you used to treat so badly! You can't make me stand in the corner with my nose touching the wall for hours and hours anymore! You can't tell me to go inside the closet while you take a hit of crack anymore! I hate you! I fuckin' hate you! You ain't my mama, and you never was my mama! Why didn't you let my father come and see me, and why didn't you give me his phone number so I could call him, or why didn't you tell me where he lived?" His fists were balled as he released tons of anger.

At that moment, Stevie and Alexus got out of the car and ran inside the store. Marvin gave them an evil look.

"And those bastards, I'll bet they don't even know who their real father is!"

"I can't believe that you have grown up to be so damn disrespectful, Marvin."

"You never taught me respect, so how in the hell do you expect me to respect you!"

She felt so embarrassed and humiliated that she regretted ever seeing him. The crowd felt like they were watching a drama television program.

Karen tried to switch conversations and to reason with Marvin. She attempted to explain what type of man his father really was, but Marvin did not believe her.

"Because of you and your bullshit, I don't have a fuckin' father! The closest thing I had to a father figure was Uncle Bobby, and everyone knows that he's a piece of shit. Now listen, bitch, don't knock what I'm doing, I'm just doing what I gotta do to survive, and besides, you didn't teach me any fuckin' better! You were a prostitute, a crackhead, and a sorry example for a mother! I hope you die! I fuckin' hate you, and hope you die!" he yelled furiously, not caring what people thought of him cursing his mother.

Karen responded by quoting Bible scriptures.

"A child is supposed to obey, love, and respect his parents. A child who disrespects his parents, days will be shortened."

"Every time you get out of jail you start reciting that Bible stuff, then a few weeks later you're either back on crack or back on the streets selling pussy! You can't tell me a goddamn thing, so don't even try it. God knows that you're a faker, and the whole family knows it too! You ain't foolin' nobody but your goddamn self! Now get the hell outta my face before I knock the shit outta you!" he yelled, pushing her aside. He then climbed into his car and sped off.

Chapter 24

After showering and changing clothes, Maria then placed an abrupt call to Jermaine's house, wanting to hear Karen's voice, but unluckily no one answered. She did not bother leaving a message simply because she was not sure that Karen was living with him. *There's one way to find out,* Maria thought, smiling, as she dug through a box for a letter with Jermaine's address on it.

At 5:00AM the following morning, Maria was parked a couple houses away from Jermaine's residence in her mother's car. She had stolen her mother's keys out her purse and hoped to be back before she awakened. She planned to call her father later and tell him that she needed another car.

She waited impatiently, hoping that within a couple hours or so Jermaine would leave for work, and then she could reunite with Karen. Thinking about Karen's touch, the way she licked her and kissed her, the way they made love to one another caused her to get wet between her legs. *I'll get her back if she's here,* Maria thought. *I still love her, and I know deep down inside she still loves me too. We're going to get married and live happily ever after just like we planned.*

At 7:30 Maria observed Jermaine getting into his car. "That's him," she said out loud, staring at his picture.

Sneakily, while in prison, Maria had intercepted several letters and pictures from the guard that were addressed to Karen while she was asleep so she knew exactly how he looked, and by her many conversations with Karen she knew what kind of vehicles he drove.

After warming his vehicle a few minutes, Jermaine then drove off.

"Yes!" whispered Maria.

It seemed like it had been a hundred years since she had last seen, kissed, or made love to Karen. She felt that even though there had been a large gap between her prison release, her promises, and the present, that she was still capable of winning Karen's confidence. All she needed was a few seconds, and then everything would fall back into place.

She glanced at the envelope and then proceeded to the address. Parked in the circular driveway to the address was a Beamer, a Lexus truck, a 5.0 Mustang, and a 1957 convertible Chevrolet Impala. *This has to be the right house,* Maria thought. *I remember her telling me that he has money, expensive taste, and that he doesn't mind spending on something he really wants. From the looks of these cars, this definitely has to be his house.*

She rang the doorbell and waited impatiently for her lover to appear. A few seconds later, she knocked again and rang the doorbell simultaneously.

"Who is it?" asked Karen, peeping through the peephole.

"It's me, Maria." She was smiling and waving her hand into the peephole. She felt like she had just won the lottery.

Karen opened the door with Stevie and Alexus at her side.

"Hi, stranger," greeted Karen, holding the door open.

"I can explain, baby, I—" Maria felt that she owed Karen an immediate explanation.

Stevie gave Maria a disapproving look, and then looked curiously at his mother. He was not accustomed to hearing another woman call his mother baby. Reading his expression, Karen quickly introduced them, and then suggested that Stevie go clean himself up and get ready for school, and that Alexus go upstairs and watch cartoons.

Suddenly Jermaine Jr. started crying, but like always Karen ignored him and pretended that he did not exist.

"That was pretty quick for you to be having a baby," said Maria sarcastically, hoping to get a rapid, acceptable answer for the baby's presence.

"You're in no position to be prying, Maria. You lied to me, misled me, made promises that you had no intentions of keeping. What really fucked me up was you swayed me away from my husband to deceive me, and like a fool I fell for it. Why? If all you wanted was a prison relationship, then that's all you had to say in the beginning. I wouldn't have had a problem with that at all, but you had to go and deceive me."

Maria touched Karen's lips with her index finger.

"Sheeeee," Maria whispered. Then she boldly drew Karen near her and began French kissing her while caressing her. Then she began fingering her pussy and playing with her clitoris. Karen was so heated and so deeply into the pleasure that she didn't care if Jermaine or her kids walked in on her. This was a feeling that no one else had ever given her but Maria.

The baby's cries suddenly got louder, irritating the hell out of Karen. Realizing she had to first deal with the baby in order to get some exceptional pleasure, Karen pulled away and suggested that Maria have a seat.

"Stevie," Karen yelled. "Give that brat his goddamn bottle before I strangle him!"

"I'm brushing my teeth, Mama."

"Alexus, bring that boy's bottle here so I can put some damn milk in it."

"Okay, Mommy," replied Alexus. She was always grateful to be of help, especially when it came to assisting with the baby.

An hour later Stevie had gone to school and Alexus had fallen asleep watching cartoons. The baby wasn't asleep, but the good thing was that he was not crying.

Karen and Maria had began kissing again and were both soon naked.

"Out of curiosity, how did you know where to find me?" asked Karen, as Maria's tongue began exploring her wet, hot pussy.

"I'll tell you later, not now, baby," whispered Maria, aiming to please.

Without getting out of rhythm, Karen eased up and grabbed a remote control and turned on the DVD player.

"We had made plans to watch pornos while doing it," said Karen, smiling.

"Yes, you're right, baby. Actually, we've made lots of plans," Maria whispered, and then suddenly climbed on top and began rubbing her pussy against Karen's. She prided herself on "what women want and exactly how they wanted it."

A few minutes into their sex session, Jermaine Jr. had began crying again.

"Shut the fuck up!" Karen yelled. She despised him even more for screwing up her and her lover's rhythm.

"Damn, I wish his fuckin' grandparents would keep him! He's not my son, and I'll never treat him like he is. I hate that crying brat," she said.

"Fuck him. I hope he cries till he dies," replied Maria. Then she thoughtfully said, "You know, there are ways of getting rid of him."

They looked at one another, smiling, and then continued their lovemaking.

The rendezvous between the secret lovers became quite frequent. Each day after Stevie left for school, Maria entered Jermaine's home welcomed by Karen's open arms.

The encounters with Karen were extremely pleasurable and meaningful to Maria, but her mind was still not quite diverted from drugs. She had tricked her father into believing that she was off drugs and that she had completely cut loose all the bad company that she associated with.

"I'm pleased by whatever makes you happy, Maria. All I really want is for you to leave the drugs alone so that you can excel in life. A mind is a terrible thing to waste, and no one can make it to the top without determination and a positive mind," is what her father had told her.

The following day he bought her a convertible Saab.

One weekend, Jermaine had suggested that he and Karen barbeque and invite over Jewell and her family.

While Karen and Jewell were in the kitchen seasoning and grilling the meats and the kids were outside playing, Jermaine and Bobby were watching a Lakers game. Jermaine was sipping a wine cooler and Bobby was already on his second bottle of Seagram's gin.

Observing Jermaine's home, Bobby began talking.

"Man, you got it going on, Jermaine. I mean, if I were you, man, I wouldn't even have a bitch living with me, especially a bitch like Karen. Man, you can have your choice of hoes, you know what I'm saying? I would have a different bitch over here every day, man. You've got a variety of nice cars, you got money, you're smart, you own real estate and shit, man, ain't no way in hell I would have a bitch living with me. To tell you the truth, homey, I don't even see how you sleep with the bitch."

Realizing that Bobby was already getting drunk and could not hold his liquor, Jermaine did not comment on his statements.

Karen and Jewell then suddenly appeared and seated themselves next to their husbands. The liquor caused Bobby to continue talking, and by now his speech was slurred.

"Somebody's gotta explain why I ain't got shit! Hell, I'm a man, I was born right here in the United muthafuckin' States, and I bleed and shit just like the next man, somebody gotta explain why I ain't got shit!"

"That's easy," Karen said. "It's because you don't want shit, and you are shit! I just don't understand why you even married this sorry, raggedy, worthless man, Jewell," replied Karen, after taking a sip of Martel.

"Just like I can't figure out what in the hell a man like Jermaine see in your stanky ass! The only thing I can figure out is that the nigga is hooked on the way you suck dick. Four of my homeboys told me that you suck a good dick, and I know that's the only reason this nigga is holding on to you. Yeah, bitch, you made me go there, so take it like a true ho."

"Bobby!" yelled Jewell, hoping he would shut up. "Stop it!"

"She started it. Me and Jermaine was just sittin' here chillin', and this slut just had to say somethin'."

"Fuck you, Bobby! You don't have shit, you won't ever have shit, and you'll always be a piece of shit," said Karen.

"That's all right. At least I don't suck dick and eat pussy for a living. I'd rather be without, than to do the shit that you've done. Bitch, you got a bad history behind you, and to tell you the truth, I think you're taking up space on earth and you'd be better off dead."

"Not again," said Jermaine. "Can we all just get along and have a good, peaceful time today?"

Karen would not be quiet.

"Your mama is a bitch and she'd be better off dead, you ugly, piece-of-shit muthafucka!"

"My mama, aw, you've fucked up now, bitch! I have told you about talking about my mama!" yelled Bobby. Then he stood and tried to grab Karen, but like a cowboy drawing his gun, Karen whipped out a box cutter from her pocket and cut Bobby twice across his chest before he even realized it.

Seeing blood pour from her husband's wounds, Jewell fearlessly grabbed Karen, causing her to drop the box cutter, and then began beating the hell out of her.

"You cut my husband, bitch! He might be nothing to you, but he's still the father of my kids, and he's my fuckin' husband!" said Jewell, while socking Karen in the eye and several times in the head. Then she put a choke hold on her.

Jermaine stood bewildered for a few moments before moving to help Karen.

"Nigga, if you touch my wife, I'm kickin' your ass," said Bobby, looking at his bloody shirt.

Suddenly, Stevie and the other kids walked inside.

"Let her go!" yelled Stevie. "Let my mama go, Auntie!"

"Let that heffa go, baby. Get the kids together and let's get the fuck outta here before I kill this bitch!" suggested Bobby. Seconds later, they were gone.

Jermaine condemned himself for buying Bobby the gin. He was careful not to get ignorant with Bobby or Jewell simply because that just wasn't his style, and he didn't want to get caught up in a bunch of family bullshit that had more than likely been going on for years.

After Karen had cleaned herself up, Jermaine and the kids took her to the local hospital to get treatment for her wounds. During the drive, Karen was continually cursing out Jermaine for allowing Bobby and her sister to physically and verbally abuse her.

"You're a coward, Jermaine," Karen had yelled. "What kinda man are you to let another man talk to your wife the way you let Bobby talk to me? And why did you just stand there and let Jewell kick my ass, and not try to pull her off me? You didn't try to help me at all! It was like you enjoyed seeing me get fucked-up! You just stood there acting like a scared, cowardly man! I'll bet anybody can kick your ass!"

"But you started it, Karen. Bobby was talking to me, and you just butted in. All you had to do was not comment on what he was saying, and none of this would have never happened," explained Jermaine.

"Regardless of if I were wrong or right, with you being my husband, you should've had my back."

"I'm sorry, Karen, but I don't defend or represent wrong. I apologize for not being that ghetto superstar with the Mike Tyson knockout punch, but I still say that you were wrong for butting in, when no was even talking to you."

"You're a wimp bitch! No, you're cotton-soft nigga, that's what you are! A muthafucka like you wouldn't make it in jail, and damn sure wouldn't make it in the ghetto. Hell, I'm only four foot two, and I could probably kick your ass if it came down to it."

"Whatever," Jermaine replied. He decided to be quiet, and not respond to her comments. That was the only way that she would stop talking.

* * *

After seven hours of sitting in the emergency room, Karen was finally called in for treatment. The doctor ministered to her black eye and then prescribed some medication for it. He also prescribed some medication for her headaches caused by Jewell's punches. In less than forty-five minutes they were done.

Later that night, Karen was horny and craved immediate sex. Her true desire was Tyrone or Maria, but what the hell, she thought, Jermaine would do fine for now.

Jermaine, not really anticipating sex, lay speechless next to Karen watching a *Law & Order* episode, and then out of the blue Karen rolled over and began massaging his penis until it was fully erect. He responded by kissing her and caressing her buttocks and rubbing her nipples. The foreplay lasted a good fifteen minutes, and then suddenly Jermaine felt the urge to go downtown on her. Using fingers from both hands, he held open her pussy lips and slowly licked her wet, pink insides. She had taught him well, therefore he knew exactly how she liked it. In the beginning she had labeled him a poor, inexperienced man who did not know how to eat pussy, but now, as far as eating pussy was concerned, he was the bomb.

Enjoying the pleasures of Jermaine's tongue and lips, Karen lay back with closed eyes, moaning and moving to his rhythm, but as she felt herself about to have an orgasm she made a sudden suggestion.

"Put on an X-rated movie, baby." Her pussy was so hot, wet, and ready.

After quickly fulfilling her request, Jermaine then went back downtown and began licking her pussy slowly and occasionally sucking her pearl tongue exactly the way she had trained him to. He then inserted his long snake tongue deep inside her and began twirling it around and around, touching all the right bases that caused her to moan.

"Uummee, yes daddy, right there. Yes daddy, ummee, yes." Then he switched bases and concentrated on slowly licking her clit and often sucking it.

"Ooh, yes, yes, uummee, yes daddy, damn." He could not compare to Maria, but as far as Karen was concerned he was doing a damn good job for the moment.

Instead of her eyes being closed, she was watching a scene where a beautiful black woman was giving a long-dick black man a head job. The man's penis was so long and humongous that the woman could not even get a fourth of it in her mouth. Seeing this, Karen instantly thought about Tyrone's dick.

"Suck the pearl tongue, suck it hard," Karen demanded.

"Ooh, yes, ummee, damn, yes baby, suck it harder, ump, damn," she moaned. This was her sixth orgasm.

Jermaine then turned over on his back. His erection was rock-hard and could hardly wait to receive Karen's first lick or suck. She had a technique that would make a dead man's penis stiff.

She stroked his hardness a few times, then began slowly caressing his balls, and then she eased her mouth onto the head of it, and began expertly licking and sucking.

"Ooh, yes mama, damn that feels good, yes mama, yes," moaned Jermaine, feeling like he was in heaven. This was a feeling that he needed and wanted every day, regardless of all the shit she talked to him. She could talk all the shit she wanted, and physically kick his ass each day of the week as long as he could often receive treatment like this.

She knew exactly how he liked it: slow licks up and down the back of his shaft, slow sucks on the head, and then a medium rhythm of up-and-down sucks while softly massaging his balls, along with occasionally deep-throating it.

With a continual seven-minute rhythm of non-stop sucking and licking, Karen's neck began hurting, which caused her to pause a moment. Thinking back to her past, she made a statement.

"I blame all those goddamn tricks who had me going up and down on their dicks for long periods of time for the pain in my neck today!" Karen said.

Jermaine was in no mood for conversation; he wanted her to keep doing what she was doing, but at the same time he did not want to upset her by not seeming sensitive, so he gently massaged her neck and shoulders, coaxing her to continue.

Karen then continued what she had started. She sucked, slurped, and licked with skill, efficiency, and precision. Moments later he came. She sucked him dry and then shamelessly swallowed it.

While watching three black men stand erect surrounding a white woman on the movie and seeing that Jermaine was going into limp mode, Karen began stroking him, and then sucking it and licking it until it was rock-hard again. She then mounted herself on top of it and slowly eased down on it, only inserting the head. Then she slid up and down, up and down, up and down on it satisfying herself, and then eased down an inch at a time until the whole thing was inside her.

"Yes, ump, yes, daddy, I can have my way with your dick," she said, smiling, while riding the hell out it.

She twirled her pussy round and round, then up and down, then round and round, swallowing his dick like a goldfish being eaten by a whale. They climaxed at the same time, and then rolled over and fell asleep.

The following morning, Jermaine felt that it was very necessary to discuss certain things with Karen since they were once again living inside of the same household. Even though Karen really did not want to hear what he had to say, to keep the peace, she listened.

Based on what Jewell, Jasmine, two of Karen's brothers, and a couple of her relatives had told Jermaine, and thinking back to some of the belligerent performances he had witnessed her do, he suggested that he immediately take her to Palmdale Mental Health for a refill on psych meds. Realizing that she had been diagnosed as a bipolar schizophrenic, and that the meds kept her mind balanced, he felt that was a necessity. To his surprise, without disagreeing with him, Karen went along with his request.

The following week, Jermaine had talked a friend of his, who was the human resources supervisor for Home Depot, into giving Karen a job. He was mainly trying to keep her busy, knowing that an unoccupied mind is the workshop of the devil.

Three months after she began working, Jermaine felt that he would give her the responsibility of paying two bills and contribute four hundred dollars toward the mortgage each month. Without dispute she agreed to. He was so used to her disagreeing with him or displaying ignorance toward his opinions it amazed him to see that she consented to his suggestions.

Karen's work schedule was 5:00PM. to 1:30AM. That meant that she was home with the kids while Jermaine was working, and he was home while she was at work.

Time did not change Karen's hatred toward Jermaine Jr. Recently she had mixed three types of liquid medicine, prescribed for her, in the baby's milk, and had even spit in his face one day when he would not stop crying. In addition to that, she had given him water from the fish aquarium that was filled with Oscars, Jack Dempseys, red devils, and feeder fish, in place of the regular bottled water he was supposed to drink. The bottom line was that she hated Jermaine Jr. with a passion, and there was nothing in this world that would change her feelings toward him.

One day during Karen's dinner break, she and Maria met in the parking lot behind a theater that was next to her job to have sex. Their date was brief, but very meaningful and pleasurable to the both of them, even though they were in the backseat of a car.

The thought of having sex with Jermaine when coming home from work, and having her pussy eaten by Maria during her break, was pretty cool to Karen, but Maria strongly disapproved of it. The fact of a man inserting himself inside of her lover turned her stomach. She had already cut two women over her ex-lover, and had beaten the hell out of another one with a tire iron, and she would not hesitate doing it again over Karen. Daily, she thought about ways to eliminate Jermaine and have Karen all to herself. Hopefully, that day would soon come.

Chapter 25

Hope for the Siordias came after their attorney's investigator had dug up Karen's past, and had also found out the name and background of her lover, Maria.

During two weeks of surveillance on Jermaine's home, Investigator Doss had found out all that he needed to know for a sure victory in this forthcoming child-custody case.

Fueled by the information he had received from Attorney Lago, Investigator Doss had simply done an outstanding analytical job. When it came to putting things together his instinct and gut feelings had never steered him wrong.

After receiving Karen's full name and prison number from the attorney, everything else fell into place for the investigator. A simple call to the Department of Motor Vehicles had led the investigator to finding out Karen's Social Security and driver's license numbers, and a call to the Department of Corrections allowed him to receive a copy of her prison record.

Karen's extensive record included convictions for possession of a controlled substance, a conviction for arson, forgery, possession of paraphernalia, for prostitution and petty theft, and what really put the icing on the cake was when he saw that she had been arrested and convicted for child endangerment. "Bingo," he said, examining the report, smiling.

The days that he had seen Karen escort Maria to her car each day, after being inside the home for hours each time, had raised suspicion in the detective's mind. He noticed that before driving off Maria had always put her arms around Karen and kissed her the way a man would kiss a woman; an aggressive French kiss. Instinct and common sense guaranteed the investigator that they were lovers.

After jotting down Maria's license plate number and then visiting the local DMV, Investigator Doss soon found out her identity. He then ran a background check and discovered that Maria and Karen had served time together in county jail, and also in prison. "Double bingo," he said to himself.

Maria's criminal background wasn't anywhere near as bad as Karen's was, but it was enough to secure a win, especially with the pictures he'd taken of them. He actually had enough evidence for the attorney to win, but this added more icing to the cake.

When the information reached the Siordias they were infuriated and irate.

"Oh my God," said Mrs. Siordia. "My grandchild has been in the company of career criminals. I sensed that it was something about that woman, I knew it."

"I had the feeling that evil was in the air, Cecelia," said Mr. Siordia. "But don't worry, soon our grandson will be in our custody where he belongs." He then hugged his wife and kissed her forehead.

Upon receiving and then checking out the information, Attorney Lago immediately passed the information on to the DA's office and on to the Department of Children Services, who wasted no time showing up at Jermaine's home to temporarily, until the court's decision was made, remove Jermaine Jr. from his custody. Karen was at work when they had arrived.

The social worker had no problem in displaying the evidence to Jermaine as to why his son was being taken away from him.

"What the hell!" Jermaine yelled, seeing Karen's record and reviewing the investigator's report.

"You mean to tell me that my home has been under surveillance and investigation? And you mean to tell me that Karen has been seen kissing and having sex with another woman, and this is her criminal record?" Jermaine was enraged.

"Yes, Mr. Hopkins, that's exactly what I'm telling you. Here are the pictures to substantiate the facts," replied the social worker, showing Jermaine pictures of Karen and Maria kissing outside of his home, and also showing him other pictures of Karen and Maria in a parking lot behind a theater in the backseat, kissing naked.

"Well, I'll be damn!" said Jermaine. "She told me that she had been to jail a couple times and that she was involved with another woman while incarcerated, but she told me that she had left all that shit behind her."

"All I can say, Mr. Hopkins, is that pictures and background reports do not lie. I feel for you, Mr. Hopkins, but this is not the kind of woman that you want tending to your child. You have a good day and I'll see you in court." Escorted by the police, the social worker then exited the home with Jermaine Jr. in hand.

Jermaine did not know whether to take Stevie and Alexus to Jewell's and then go to Karen's job and question her about this, or to just wait until she came home from work.

Either way, he knew that it was going to get real ugly when he saw her.

He sent the kids to their room and decided to wait for her to come home. He wanted to call his mother or his sisters to tell them what had happened, but quickly dismissed the thought, realizing they were all going to say the same thing to him.

"I don't know why in the hell that you started back messing around with her after all the shit she put you through! You're the biggest fool in the world, boy! The older you get, the dumber you get! That woman has put a mojo on your ass, boy. She's whipped her pussy on you and sucked your dick real good, and now she's got you hooked. Ain't no pussy in the world worth going through the shit that you go through!"

At this point he did not feel like hearing any of his people's shit. He had to calm himself in order to think straight. Now was the time to make wise decisions.

He sat at his dining room table and began thinking. I've let her back into my life and into my home, and this is the thanks I get? Every time I try to help someone I'm the one that gets fucked. I've lost custody of my son, and the cold thing about this is that I haven't personally done a goddamn thing wrong. I haven't done anything but try to be a good father and husband, a hard-working man, and a law-abiding citizen. She's gotta answer for this shit. Yep. She's definitely gotta explain about those pictures, her lesbian lover, and her criminal record. I know all she'll do is lie about everything anyway, but I just want to see the look on her face when I bring it to her. She has twenty minutes to walk through that door, and goddammit I want some answers. This time I won't accept pussy or head to make me forget about things.

Two hours later Karen entered the house.

"Where in the hell have you been?" Jermaine asked.

The truth of the matter was that she and Maria had a pleasurable meet in the backseat.

"I was at work, where do think I've been?" she lied like she normally did.

"I know that's another one of your lies, but anyway, children services showed up here, and guess what? Because of you, your fuckin' criminal record, and your affairs with your lesbian friend, they took my son away from me."

Good, she thought.

Jermaine was just getting started.

"You told me that your sucking pussy days were over! You also lied to me and told me that you've only been to jail a couple times, but they showed me your entire criminal record, and goddammit, Karen, you've been to jail and to prison umpteen million times!"

The more he talked, the louder he got.

"You're always believing every negative thing you hear about me, Jermaine. You never believe me, but you'll always believe a lie about me, especially when it's something bad," she replied, and then attempted to walk away.

"Sit down and talk to me, Karen, because we've definitely gotta talk. This is some serious shit, and—"

"I'm tired and I don't feel like talking about a goddamn thing right now! All I wanna do is take a shower, eat, and then go to bed."

"Is that right? My son has got taken away from me because of you, and all you wanna do is take a shower, eat, and go to sleep? You know what, you can get your shit, get your kids, and get the fuck outta my house right goddamn now!"

"Fuck you, Jermaine," she replied, giving him the finger. Then she walked away.

"No, Karen, it's fuck you!" he yelled, following her.

The kids were standing at their bedroom door listening and watching.

"You've been with that gay bitch tonight, haven't you?"

"Fuck you, Jermaine. If I have, that was my prerogative." She walked inside the restroom and turned on the shower, and then began taking off her clothes.

"I want you outta here, Karen, and I'm fuckin' serious! You don't appreciate a goddamn thing I do for you and your kids, and I just want you to get the fuck out of my life!"

"Fuck you, like I said. And as far as me and my kids leaving, we aren't goin' anywhere!" She then climbed into the shower and closed the curtain. He stood there angrily, yelling.

"I can get you out of here, that ain't a problem, but I'd rather you leave willingly than for me to have the police put you out."

"You're a bitch, a coward, and a muthafuckin' punk, Jermaine! You're always talkin' about callin' the fuckin' police to come handle your situations. You know why, because you're not a goddamn man, that's why. A real man would handle his own business, and a real man wouldn't get white folks or police involved in his business. Oh, but I forgot, you aren't a real man, you're a pussy!"

"I guess you would rather me beat the hell out of you than call the police, huh? I know that you're used to niggas beating the shit out of you, but I've got too much to lose, and you're not worth going to jail over."

"Fuck you, and double fuck you, you black, fat, punk muthafucka! I hate you, Jermaine. I wish you'd die tonight! Better yet, I wish you were dead already! Fuck you, fuck your mama, fuck your dead daddy and brother, and fuck your dead daughter! I hate all y'all muthafuckas."

"Why you gotta bring my family into this? This is between you and me, so leave my family out of it."

She then got out of the shower and began drying off. Suddenly, she decided to try reasoning with him.

"Okay, Jermaine, let's talk about this sensibly. First of all,

I'm sorry that your son got taken away from you because of me. You're right, I should have told you that I had been to prison many times, but I just didn't want to lose you, Jermaine. Losing you would be like committing suicide, and that's the way I felt." She then began crying. "I didn't want to lose you, Jermaine. I didn't want you to think of me as a bad person and not give me a chance. I know that I've done a lot of bad things in the past, but I don't do those things anymore, Jermaine. You've helped me change my life, baby. Because of you I no longer have the urge for crack, and because of you my self-esteem has been restored. You gave me a shot at a normal life and I don't wanna lose you, Jermaine. Please, don't make me go, please. I'm not ashamed to say that you're the best thing that has ever happened to me, and I just feel that there's no me without you. I can't go on without you, Jermaine. The kids love you and look up to you. I don't want to ever have to put another man over my kids. I've already lost one son, and I don't wanna lose the other, so please don't make me and the kids leave," she begged, and then continued.

He stared at the ceiling while listening.

"I admit to having a secret affair with Maria, but I didn't mean you any harm. She could never sway me away from you, Jermaine. Never. It's not like I'm having an affair with a man and having a dick inside me. She only fulfils the areas that you aren't capable of fulfilling. That's it. But if you want me to, I'll end my relationship with her right now. She's not worth me losing you over."

Standing naked in front of him, she had the sudden urge to hug him, which she did, and then she began kissing him. Being tempted once again by her nice round, smooth ass, and by the bush that covered her pleasure box, Jermaine responded in rhythm to her kisses. He then picked her up and carried her to the bed, and hurriedly got undressed.

After giving him some keen head and a good, long, pleasurable ride, he had forgotten about everything that had
taken place. Afterward they fell asleep in one another's
arms.

It had only taken one court date with the evidence that
was presented for the Siordias to be granted custody of
Jermaine Jr. Realizing that he was in a no-win situation, Jermaine accepted the verdict and also accepted the visita-
tion terms of being able to spend one weekend out of
month with his son.

Chapter 26

Three months later, instinct led Jermaine to believe that Karen had not been paying the two bills that he had given her to pay, simply because each time he asked her whether or not she had paid them she would always get angry and began cursing.

His instinct was confirmed one day after calling Southern California Edison and the gas company. After conversing with representatives from both companies, Jermaine discovered that Karen had not paid either bill in three months. In addition to that, final notices and disconnection dates had been mailed out from both agencies. Using his bank card, he paid both bills and apologized to the representatives for the delinquency.

Knowing that Karen made a little over eleven hundred a month from her job, Jermaine did not understand why Karen had not been paying those two bills. He had questioned her the last three months as to why she would only give him two hundred and fifty dollars, or basically whatever she wanted to give him toward the mortgage, when the agreement was for her to pay four hundred a month, but as usual she always had an excuse.

"The kids needed this, and the kids needed that. They didn't pay me for all the hours I worked. I didn't get my welfare check because I forgot to mail in my monthly form. My check got deposited into my checking account, but the goddamn bank hasn't made the funds available yet. Some company has been debiting my account that I don't even know." She was the master of excuses.

Later that day, Jermaine received a call while working that had caused him to take off early.

"This is Mr. Coleman from Page Financial. I'd like to speak with Mr. Hopkins, please."

"This is Mr. Hopkins, how can I help you?"

"This call is an attempt to collect a debt, Mr. Hopkins. You're three months behind on your monthly payment, and—"

"What the hell are you talking about, man? I pay all my bills on time, sir, and I'm not behind on a damn thing." Jermaine instantly got frustrated.

"Mr. Hopkins, I have a signed contract in front of me where you promised to pay a total of one hundred and forty-one dollars a month on the fourteen-hundred-dollar loan we financed for you. I—"

"Man, are you crazy! I haven't asked you or anyone else to finance a damn thing for me!"

After a lengthy conversation with the finance manager, Jermaine discovered that Karen had taken out a fourteen-hundred-dollar loan in his name. She had the finance company fax her an application, and using Jermaine's information she completed the app and then forged his signature and sent it back. She had also faxed a copy of his driver's license, Social Security card, and had sent recent copies of Jermaine's check stubs, reflecting his income as being a little over five grand a month. The finance company released a check the following day, payable to Jermaine and Karen Hopkins.

After the truth was revealed, Jermaine and Mr. Coleman continued talking.

"What I don't understand, Mr. Coleman, is how in the hell did you guys cut her a check without my presence? How can you just give someone fourteen-hundred dollars and never see them?"

"That's easy, it happens every day. She's your wife and as long as you and her are living together and she has pertinent information about you, your presence is not necessary. If you two were not living together, then that would be a total different thing."

"Well, you guys need to change that law, because that's stupid. She stole my identity and used it to get a loan without my knowledge, and you're telling me that there's nothing I can do about it?"

"If I were you, Mr. Hopkins, I'd press identity-theft charges on her, that's about the only thing I can tell you."

"If I decide to do that, since she committed a fraudulent act against your company as well as against me, will you press charges on her as well?"

"For now, Mr. Hopkins, like I told you in the beginning, this is an attempt to collect a debt."

"Has this shit gone on my credit report?"

"Nope, but if I haven't received payment within forty-eight hours then I have no other choice but to report this to collections."

"Damn! If it ain't one thing, it's another."

Wanting to get to the bottom of this right away, Jermaine left work early that day. While driving he began thinking. *What in the hell is wrong with that woman? She's trying to fuck up my credit because her credit is fucked-up. I gave her two small bills to pay and she can't even pay them. I asked her to give me four hundred dollars a month toward the mortgage, and she can't even do that. And now she's taken out a loan using my identity. I wonder, is she back on crack again? Or maybe she's giving money to another man, or maybe even another woman. I don't understand it, I really don't. I don't deserve this. She crossed the line fucking with my credit, and that's it. This is the last time she'll ever have a chance to fuck me. Now it's my turn to do the fucking.*

He continually called Karen from his cell phone, and even attempted several times to two-way her, but she did not answer the phone. *She should be home*, he thought, and then sped up a little.

Seeing her car parked in front raised an eyebrow. Why wasn't she answering the telephone?

He called for her upon entering his home, but still she did not answer. As he walked up the stairs he heard voices and the television set, but when making it to the top of the staircase he saw that his bedroom door and the door to Alexus's room was closed. Still hearing the voices, he eased open the door to his room and witnessed his wife lying naked with her legs wide open while Maria was downtown licking her pussy. An X-rated movie of two women making so-called love was on the television screen.

"What the fuck?" Jermaine yelled.

Karen and Maria turned and looked at him.

"What are you doing home?" asked Karen, in a state of shock. "You're supposed to be—"

"Ain't this about a bitch! Both of you, get the fuck out of my house!"

Jermaine's yells had awakened Alexus and seconds later she came out of her room and appeared next to him. She stared wide-eyed at her mother and Maria lying naked, and then she began staring at the movie.

"Alexus, go back to your room, okay. I'll be there in a few minutes," said Jermaine.

Stevie had left for school a couple hours earlier.

Maria was pissed off and decided to take it out on Jermaine.

"I told you before that she's mines and she'll always be mines. Whatever you do for her and to her, I can do better, you fuckin' asshole!"

"Get the fuck out of my house, you pussy-eatin' bitch!"

"Apparently I eat pussy better than you, because I've got your wife!" Maria shouted. She then climbed out of bed and began getting dressed.

"You just can't do right, can you, Karen?"

"Like I told you the other day; at least I'm not fuckin' another man."

"As a matter of fact, don't you go anywhere, Karen, because we've got a lot of shit to discuss."

"He just wants some pussy, that's all, and you better not give him any, Karen. I'm sick and tired of making love to you behind him," said Maria, then stormed out of the room, and then out the front door.

Karen had slipped on her panties and bra and sat at the edge of the bed holding her head down, thinking about how was she going to explain this one.

Jermaine took the stage.

"Lord knows that I did my best to trust you, to love you, and to believe in you, but once again you've let me down, Karen. You're cruel, deceitful, and you've proven to be an unappreciative bitch. Regardless of what I just busted you doing, you haven't paid the gas bill or the light bill in three months and you forged my name on a goddamn loan document and got fourteen-hundred dollars from Page Financial." He stood nodding and continued.

"I can't trust you anymore, Karen, and I want you out of my house and out of my life."

"I didn't forge your name on a damn thing, Jermaine. Don't you remember when I told you that I was applying for a loan and needed your information?"

"Don't even try it, Karen. Do you honestly think that I'd forget about something like that? As hard as I worked to get my credit A-one, do you think that I would forget giving you my information and forget you telling me that you're applying for a damn loan? I don't think so. You're a liar, and you're full of shit and deceit."

"You must have amnesia or you're suffering from CRS."

"What the fuck is CRS?"

"Can't remember shit!"

"Whatever, Karen. I'm filing for an immediate divorce, and this time I'm as serious as a heart attack."

"Fuck you, Jermaine. If you ever try to divorce me, I am not signing a goddamn thing. And as far as me leaving, I ain't goin' nowhere! Fuck you, you black-ass, out-of-shape, coward muthafucka! I wish you were dead, punk! Matter of fact, I'm going to have a few gangbanger friends of mines come and kick your ass! It's only gonna cost me a dime bag of weed and it will be my pleasure seeing them fuck you up. If you do happen to initiate a divorce, I'll make sure that you live a miserable, fucked-up life. You know what, I'm gonna have somebody kill you, yeah, that's what I'm gonna do! Watch your back, muthafucka, and watch your front too, 'cause you're definitely getting fucked up!" she threatened, and then began getting dressed.

Hearing enough of her foul mouth, Jermaine disappeared out of the room and went downstairs and began thinking. Minutes later he left.

His first stop was the courthouse in hopes to get an urgent, instant restraining order. It had practically taken him the entire day to get an emergency restraining order granted, but the good thing about it was that his patience had paid off.

Jermaine had revealed to the courts that Karen was extremely violent, that she was on psych meds and under the care of a psychiatrist at Palmdale Mental Health, and that she had an extensive criminal record that he had recently discovered. He also told the Judge that he feared for his life because of her threats. Without hesitation, the judge granted Jermaine's request for a restraining order against Karen.

His next stop was the police station where he asked to speak with a sergeant. After waiting a few hours, finally a Sergeant Brady appeared in the lobby. Jermaine felt that if he explained how Karen had used his identity and forged his name on loan documents that would be enough to have her arrested, but the sergeant told him different.

"Wives do this sort of thing everyday, Mr. Hopkins. If you two were separated then that would be a total different story, but that's not the case here."

"Regardless of whether or not we live together, Sergeant, I did not give her permission to use my identity or sign my name on any documents. I've been in court all day to get this restraining order on her, and I want her out of my house at once."

"As far as arresting her for identity theft, I can assure you that won't stick. However, hearing the urgency in your voice, we can exercise this restraining order and remove her from your home. Momentarily, we're dealing with a lot of nine-one-one calls, and the majority of them are domestic violence calls, so more than likely, we won't be able to accommodate your request anytime soon," explained the sergeant.

"Well, how soon can you send out an officer, sarge? I'm dealing with a violent career criminal on psych meds, and I know that some shit is gonna go down when I get home."

"The way things are going around here, Mr. Hopkins, I'd say anywhere between midnight and five in the morning."

"Damn. I thought that this emergency restraining order would have some type of bearing on this."

"Most times they do, but not on a day like today."

"Okay, but if I get home and she goes crazy on me and stabs me or maybe even kills me, that's an open window for a lawsuit, sarge. You guys can't say that I didn't warn you."

"If she goes berserk on you, Mr. Hopkins, then call nine-one-one and we'll immediately respond. That's the only thing I can tell you other than to not go home."

Jermaine then left the police station.

His next stop was at a place of business called the Divorce Clinic.

Since Jermaine and Karen did not have any community property or no kids together, initiating the divorce was simple, but costly.

"I don't believe that it only cost me forty dollars to marry her and it's costing me fourteen-hundred dollars to divorce her," Jermaine had said to the agent.

"Thank God you don't have any kids or property together. Believe me, Mr. Hopkins, it could have been a whole lot worse.

"Here, man," said Jermaine, handing the man his debit card. "I don't care how much it cost, I just want her out of my life."

"Do you think she'll sign and just keep this thing real simple?"

"She's already told me that she wasn't going to sign, and being the stubborn bitch that she is, no, she probably won't sign."

"There's always more than one way to skin a cat, Mr. Hopkins. After you complete this paperwork I'll take it to the court and file it, and we'll take things from there."

"Let's do it," Jermaine said, and then proceeded with the paperwork.

When Jermaine made it home Karen and the kids were asleep. He did not bother awakening them.

After eating some leftovers, he turned on the television and then made himself comfortable on the sofa, impatiently waiting for the police to arrive. Minutes later he fell asleep. It had been a long, tiresome day for him.

The sound of the hard rain and thunder awakened Jermaine. He had been asleep for close to three hours, and the police still had not came yet. He glanced at his watch and saw that it was a little after midnight. He tried holding his eyes open, but had soon fallen back to sleep.

At 2:30AM, hard, continual knocks on the front door instantly awakened Jermaine.

"Who is it?" Jermaine asked, nearing the door.

"Sheriff's department! Open up!" shouted an officer.

Jermaine sighed and then opened the door.

The sergeant that Jermaine had spoken to earlier had already briefed the officers about exactly what was going on at the Hopkins residence.

There were seven deputies, accompanied by a senior deputy, who entered his home. Some of them shined flashlights throughout the house, while some of the others began checking the closets and the restroom. Both of them were holding billy clubs.

"Do you have the copy of your restraining order, sir?" asked the senior officer.

"Yep, it's right here in my pocket. I've been waiting on you guys for almost eleven hours," said Jermaine, handing over the order.

"Better late than never, Mr. Hopkins. Where is she?"

"She's upstairs asleep," replied Jermaine.

At that moment four officers stormed up the stairs into the bedroom, while the senior continued to question Jermaine. Suddenly, Jermaine heard Karen screaming and cursing.

"Get your muthafuckin' hands off me, you white muthafuckas!"

She constantly yelled at the officers and had even hit one of them in the stomach. She called them harsh names like Bozo, KKKs, racist muthafuckas, and after they had cuffed her and bought her downstairs she called the senior officer a bitch. It had taken all four of them to manhandle her and cuff her. One of the officers remembered her from a past encounter.

"I remember her. She gave us hard times on a few occasions. I arrested her for prostitution a couple of times and if I recall, the last time I arrested her it was for possession of a crack pipe. Yeah, I remember her well because she gave us a hard time even then," said the officer.

Cuffed and now standing a few feet away from Jermaine, Karen began calling him names and even spit on him.

"You muthafucka! You ain't no fuckin' good! God gonna strike you down, Jermaine, cause you're wrong for putting me and kids out in the rain at two-thirty in the fuckin' morning. Fuck you, Jermaine, you're just mad because you saw Maria eating my pussy. You never were a good fuck, anyway, and you damn sure don't know how to eat pussy, that's why I got somebody else to do it," said Karen, shamelessly.

The kids had awakened when hearing Karen's yells, and now they were witnessing their mother in handcuffs and cursing Jermaine and the police. They both began crying.

"Take my kids to my sister's house, you fat, black, ugly muthafucka!"

"Okay, that's enough," said the senior officer. "Take her away."

Karen was escorted to the police car, but now she was facing a serious charge of battery of an officer.

The Sheriff's only intentions were to remove her from the household, but her lack of self–control and foolishness had earned her a ticket to jail. Once there, Karen's extensive criminal record placed the odds totally against her. In addition to being charged with battery of a police officer, Karen was also charged with identity theft and terrorist threats. The loan company had also pressed forgery charges on her.

The following morning Jermaine dropped off the kids at her sister's, then spent the rest of the morning researching counseling centers and programs, realizing that he needed to explore what made him endure his soon-to-be ex-wife's negative behavior, and even more importantly, why he continued to take her back. He needed to understand why he'd always been attracted to that type of woman in the first place. He also realized that he really had not grieved over the loss of his daughter, his wife Sylvia, and even his son, since he could only see him on weekends.

Before he could talk himself out of it, he dialed the number to Regional Health Center. The receptionist answered after two rings.

"Regional Health Center, how can I help you?"

"Yes, I would like to make an appointment for counseling."

Minutes later, after jotting down a soon-approaching date and time, Jermaine placed the receiver on the hook, and felt a sense of relief, knowing that he was making a step in the right direction.

Jermaine couldn't help by think about Stevie and Alexus, and could only shake his head imagining the life of chaos they were destined to be raised in. Although a part of him still wanted to reach out to the children, he knew that letting go of Karen meant cutting all ties.

He rose from his seat, and spent the afternoon thoroughly cleaning his home. At the end of the day, everything that would serve as a reminder of his marriage to Karen—letters, photos, clothing, shoes, books, tapes, toys—had been placed in large garbage bags and taken out to the curb. Right before Jermaine knotted the last bag, he twisted the thick band of gold and diamonds from the third finger of his left hand and dropped it inside.

"The mayhem is over," he affirmed out loud.

Jermaine, being fully committed to his own emotional healing and well-being, destroyed every letter Karen sent to him, not even bothering to open the envelopes, and kept every counseling session appointment for the next two years. Eventually, she stopped writing. There was no better reward for him than to hold his son in his arms again after regaining custody at the end of that two-year period.

Karen served three additional years in the state penitentiary, where she did all she could to continue to manipulate Jermaine. Not receiving any response from him, despite her written apologies and pleas for forgiveness, she concluded that Jermaine never loved her to begin with and began writing to Maria instead. A month after her release, Maria had persuaded her into taking a hit of crack while they were making love, but unfortunately, that very first hit that Karen took busted her heart and instantly killed her.

About the Author

Samuel was born in Indianola Mississippi, but raised in Compton CA. Samuel unexpectedly discovered his writing talent one day in the third grade while sitting in class visualizing charters making conversation and gestures while doing various things. Samuel immediately set aside his classwork and began putting his visions into words. Afterwards, while class was still in session, Samuel approached his teacher and handed her what he'd written. His teacher was so amazed by Samuel's creativity that she turned it into the principal. The principal was bewildered, but at the same time, proud to have a third-grade student at his school write something so attention-grabbing and worded so perfectly. The principal had his secretary run off over 500 copies of Samuel's short story, then proudly distributed the copies to students as well as staff members.

Samuel enjoys making the big bucks driving big rigs cross-country while dispatching 25 other company drivers. He plans to soon retire from truck driving and become a social worker. That will give him more opportunity to write more books and spend more time at home. Samuel is currently working on his third book.

NOW AVAILABLE FROM

Q-BORO
BOOKS

NYMPHO
$14.95
ISBN 1933967102

How will signing up to live a promiscuous double-life destroy everything that's at stake in the lives of two close couples? Take a journey into Leslie's secret world and prepare for a twisted, erotic experience.

FREAK IN THE SHEETS
$14.95
ISBN 1933967196

Ready to break out of the humdrum of their lives, Raquelle and Layla decide to put their knowledge of sexuality and business together and open up a freak school, teaching men and women how to please their lovers beyond belief while enjoying themselves in the process.

However, Raquelle and Layla must learn some important lessons when it comes to being a lady in the street and a freak in the sheets.

LIAR, LIAR
$14.95
ISBN 1933967110

Stormy calls off her wedding to Camden when she learns he's cheating with a male church member. However, after being convinced that Camden has been delivered from his demons, she proceeds with the wedding.

Will Stormy and Camden survive scandal, lies and deceit?

HEAVEN SENT
$14.95
ISBN 1933967188

Eve is a recovering drug addict who has no intentions of staying clean until she meets Reverend Washington, a newly widowed man with three children. Secrets are uncovered that threaten Eve's new life with her new family and has everyone asking if Eve was *Heaven Sent*.

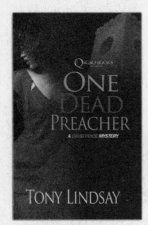

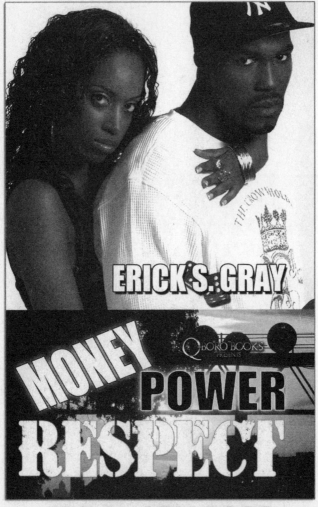